**STEVE N**[illegible] cian, born in Yorkshire b[illegible] the UK and Europe. A [illegible] shed writer, Steve is a r[illegible] Best Spoken Word Perf[illegible] *yth Gatherers* won the N[illegible] s most recent poetry publication *Nearly Man* has been described as 'brave, exhilarating, darkly comic, hilarious, dreamy, and dark'.

He teaches at Leeds Beckett University and *Remington Platypus* is his debut novel. Rumours persist of Steve's vampirism and his lack of a reflection has done little to allay those fears.

# REMINGTON PLATYPUS

## STEVE NASH

NORTHODOX PRESS

Northodox Press Ltd
Maiden Greve, Malton,
North Yorkshire, YO17 7BE

This edition 2025

1
First published in Great Britain by
Northodox Press Ltd 2025



ISBN: 978-1-917005-00-5
This book is set in Caslon Pro Std

Cover and Interior Design by T J Keane

This book is a work of fiction. References to real people, events, establishments, organizations, or locales are intended only to provide a sense of authenticity, and are used fictitiously. All other characters, and all incidents and dialogue, are drawn from the author's imagination and are not to be construed as real.



Printed and bound by CMP (UK) Limited,
G3 The Fulcrum, Vantage Way, Poole, Dorset, BH12 4NU

*For Winnie, Pixie, Deet, Sandy, Orphy, Raven, Bruce, Jaws the Revenge, and all the other animals who taught me something about being human.*

# Chapter One

Remington Platypus was not a platypus. What he was, he mused as he drew a paw over his broad, bruised snout, was a badger, and a hungover one at that. A persistent buzzing drilled away in his ears; someone was trying to call him. Remington sat on an upturned bucket pebbled with orange rust and holes, pushing tobacco-tasting breath from his leathery nostrils, willing the tingling resonance to stop. He eyed himself in the shard of mirror he'd perched against the wall. His bloodshot eyes were sunk deep in the greying fur of his head. Behind him, framed by his roughly carved window hole, the bleak belt of the city skyline unveiled itself through the morning fog.

Remington twitched his ears, chewed hard on his tobacco leaf, and tuned in to the humming harmonic frequency. He knew it wasn't going to be good news. It never was, but this was the last thing he or his hangover needed today. A body had been found just off Compton Street, and according to the overly caffeinated voice on the other end of the line:

'It looks like a murder.'

Remington's foreclaw fluttered on his forehead. He emitted a subtle series of harmonic signals, relaying his reply across the city's invisible network. 'You mean The Murder?'

Almost immediately, a response arrived through the same channel. 'Excuse me, Sir?'

The innocence of the voice put Remington slightly at ease. He didn't recognise it and whoever this new constable was, there clearly hadn't been time for the Superintendent or HR to go through all the usual warnings about keeping a close eye on Remington.

'I'll be there in twenty.' With a subtle shift in harmonic resonance, Remington harmonised and ceased the connection before the young constable could reply. He smashed the chewed leaf into the mouldering glass and dropped it into a small tumbler.

'Shit.' His shoulders slumped as heard the tell-tale splash of an unfinished drink.

Remington Platypus stretched his limbs and left the dwelling.

While Remington rarely wished to see morning this side of going to bed, there was an aura about the city before it had woken up that made him feel something close to content. The beep of street sweepers and the lazy din of delivery trucks would have seemed cacophonous back in the Burrow, but here in this monstrous chimaera of a city with its great stone, steel, and glass, it was as close to peaceful as you could get. It was also the only time you could wander the pavements without fear of being kicked or screeched at by some lunatic human. The morning people, lifting loads, cleaning gutters, or emptying bins into those enormous metal death machines were more likely to give you a smile or a nod, a mark of comradeship. Anyone out before the rush was just another one of the city's vermin, rodents running on a different wheel to the rest. A man in a dirty orange vest gave Remington a cheerful wink, and the badger duly blinked back.

As he rounded the corner into the relative shade of Compton Street, Remington pulled another tobacco leaf from a fold in the flesh of his foreleg and cast his eyes over the railings on both sides of the road, looking for the usual marker. Halfway down on the right-paw side he saw it, the macabre salute of a dismembered paw waving. One red glove sat perched on the railings in front of a signless shop, the windows soaped up, giving the impression of a blizzard on the inside.

Remington felt his fur prickle as he saw a young rodent standing at the foot of the railing nervously picking at the crumbling brickwork.

'Sorry, you can't come this way, Sir, police business,' the ferret just about managed to stutter. Remington arched an eyebrow. He recognised the voice from the call.

'Pretty sure you're expecting me,' he offered wearily, containing the urge to just push past. The darting eyes of the young champagne-coloured creature flicked over the looming figure of the badger. 'I'm the detective you phoned earlier… Remington?'

'But you're not a platypus,' the kit said, scratching his forelegs.

'You'll go far in the force with those skills of perception, lad.'

Remington wouldn't admit it of course, but he wasn't fond of ferrets when it came to police work. The fidgeting and shakiness, as though they had no stillness in them, didn't fit right. He liked the idea that the force were stoic figures, still in the swirl and chaos of the city. The jittery young stretch in front of him made a bubble of disappointment heave and burst deep inside him somewhere. Remington also shook, but there was a history to that. It was something he had nurtured through poor decisions and a thirst for blackness. This kit shook from his bones and Constable, Sergeant, Superintendent or whatever rank; he was always going to be a tremorous strip of fur and nerves.

'Pink socks in there, is he?' Remington asked, moving past the PC.

'What?'

'Little fella, squinty face, says he's a doctor?'

'Oh, the Doc? Yes, he's examining the…' Remington pushed past, disappearing into a hole in the building's decrepit brick.

Remington's sight had always been a problem. It wasn't the fidelity of his eyesight that was the issue, rather what lay within the frame of his field of vision. His snout, with its perpetually glossy nose, gave off a flare of light at the base of his sight which meant a constant need to adjust his neck and head. Stepping out of the morning glare into the gloom of the old building's foundations called for a moment of calibration. Slowly though, the scene emerged before him.

'Quills,' he said, and his foreclaw twitched against his forehead as the cause for his being out so early revealed itself. Amid brick dust and dirt, something lay spread across the floor. A grim mandala of feathers, fur and blood stretched from one corner of concrete to another, a square-foot cross-hatch of gore. It was impossible to work out what the constituent parts once were, but the splay of it gave Remington the sense of wings. Somewhere beyond the throb in his head, Remington heard the distant caw of a crow, and he felt his left eye tic.

Remington stepped carefully to a clear space in the bruise of ground and looked more closely at the sprawl in front of him. Between clumps of matted fur and severed feather, a dark fibre ran through the mire. Remington reached out a claw and crouched. He slowly moved the claw's tip toward the thread, careful to avoid anything stained red, and, just as it touched the dark thread, the remnants of flesh shifted.

'What the-?' Remington pulled his paw back but leaned closer as the blanket of gore began to pulse as though the wreck of the corpse had started breathing. The glistening surface seethed, and the fibres tightened sharply, too sharply. There was a tearing sound as a pair of sharp claws emerged through the rending flesh and Remington slipped backwards onto his behind with a squelch, finding his posterior nestling in the grotesque morass.

'Morning Doc,' said Remington with a sigh as a familiar dark head appeared in the fresh hole in the cadaver.

'What? What?' A high-pitched voice squeaked back as two squinting eyes whirled around the room and the pink nose of the mole fingered the air.

'Still living your best life then, I see?' Remington muttered as he stood and wiped clumps of death from his behind.

'Ah Rem, I didn't think they'd actually manage to get you up at this hour,' the mole said with his lower half still hidden in the quagmire. 'Quite the mess, eh?'

'What is this?' Remington asked as he tugged a clump of

gristle from his fur and flicked it to the opposite wall.

'Hard to say, hard to say, Remmy. We'll know more when we scoop this poor bugger up and take it back to the lab, but I think we can safely suspect foul play.'

'No teeth, or claw marks? Nothing to go on at all?'

'Not a worm I'm afraid my boy, but whatever did this has gone for full on evisceration. Can't even work out what species this is.' The mole hauled itself from the remnants of the body and shook sharply, sending spots of blood and flesh in all directions.

'Does it look like wings to you?' Remington asked absent-mindedly, his claws kneading circles in the fur of his chin.

'Now, now Rem,' the mole said as his nose caressed a particularly chunky lump of meat. 'That way madness lies.'

Remington watched with morbid fascination as the mole ran its dextrous pink nose over the gore, pausing only to let out a satisfied or confused grunt, mumbling to himself the entire time.

'That will always gross me out, Doc,' said Rem, his hungover stomach flipping in violent protest. 'Oh, I nearly forgot,' he added pulling a worm from under his arm. 'I got you some breakfast.'

'Careful, Rem,' said the mole as he scurried over. 'Folks might start thinking you care about something.'

Ignoring the comment, Remington pulled out his own breakfast, popped the tobacco leaf on his tongue and began to chew. 'What do you make of the kit out there?' he asked.

'Oscar? He's a good pup. Eager to please and has a keen eye.'

'What do you mean?'

'Well, he spotted that thread in the body before you did.' Doc squeaked and then cheerfully began gnawing on the worm, holding it tight with his sharp claws. 'Play nice, Rem.'

'It's just all that convulsing makes me nervous.'

'Ha! At least he's got an excuse for it!' Doc said, a piece of worm spilling from his mouth. 'It's in his DNA. I remember a certain badger losing his lunch in a cow carcass on his first day in the Big Smoke.' The mole let out a gleeful shriek.

'Shut up and eat your worm.'

After a further half hour of studying the scene, the din of the city began to clang like a call for last orders.

'Guess that's us then,' said Remington, raising himself up on his haunches.

'Barb's been asking after you, you know, Rem?' Doc said, his squeak becoming low and earnest. 'Why don't you come round tonight and see the brats? They'd love to see you.'

'Careful Doc,' Remington said over his shoulder. 'Folks'll think you care. Anyway, I'll see you back at base.'

'Be there for sunset. I'm telling her you're coming,' Doc called as the badger loped out of sight.

Outside, the pale flat glare of the city forced its way into Rem's eyes, and he saw the young ferret still twitching at his post.

'Smoke?' Rem asked holding out a limp tobacco leaf.

'Erm, oh I, well, I don't…' Oscar said, taking the offering anyway, and placing it gingerly in his mouth.

'Some mess for your first scene, this.'

Oscar would have replied had he not just turned a tinge of green from his first taste of tobacco and feared opening his mouth would lead to his own breakfast landing on the detective.

Remington chewed in silence pretending not to notice the PC subtly drop his leaf behind him, and then nodded as he turned to leave.

'Sir? Why do you call the Doc Pink Socks?' Oscar asked, the green ebbing from his cheeks.

'Because he's got a nose like a prolapsed bum,' Remington grinned back.

'That's not very nice, Sir.' The ferret's eyes paused their juddering movements for a moment.

'That's two for two,' Remington said. 'You'll make detective in no time, son.'

# Chapter Two

There was no point heading to the station yet. The crew wouldn't be able to collect the remains until dusk, and then he'd have to let Doc have a few hours with the mess before he could find out more. If Remington did make his way to the office now someone would no doubt find something to keep him busy, and he was still curious to find out why he'd woken up with a freshly bruised face.

*What's the last thing you remember?* He heard the ghost of his mother's voice in the back of his head. The mystery of the bruised snout could be today's puzzle. The mystery of the eviscerated corpse would have to wait until tomorrow. He suspected tomorrow's case would take more deduction than today's, and he set off in the direction of Squall's Bar.

Remington's hangover was lifting as he turned off the side street toward the square, prodding at his swollen face. Every inch of the city hummed with pulse and information. It had been almost maddening for Remington when he'd first arrived from the Burrow. There, information was slower, and less specific. It was a more general system passed through the ground. Using pawsentia, animals with the capacity could, through subtle shifts in texture, temperature, and vibration, detect rhythmic flows in the environment. It was less communication than feel, a keying into the essence of the habitat. The concrete of the metropolis had largely deadened Remington's pawsentia now, but he had been a natural when it came to communication via harmonic frequency. The emanations from power lines, radio waves, and other electromagnetic sources were a network of communicative frequencies that the animal world had repurposed, like so many other human artifacts, for their own usage. By tapping into the specific harmonic frequencies which flooded the urban habitat, animals skilled enough could attune, emit, or detect isolated signals allowing for near-instant communication with others on the same frequency. It wasn't fool proof, but it had been essential in the Met's efforts to hold order among the animal community who had chosen to opt in to the project of civility.

Squall's was unusual for a city drinking spot. Most of the settlers in the capital had their own haunts, each catering to a specific species, but Squall's was a place where folk mixed. Naturally this led to high tempers, but the prices were low, and the respect everyone had for Squall ensured things rarely got too out of hand.

A few feet from the gaping stone that marked the entrance to Squall's, Remington noticed a mound of newspaper and half-chewed polystyrene cups. Clusters of trash were hardly a notable feature in the city, but Squall prided herself on the cleanliness of the outer threshold of her establishment, which was ironic considering the state of the interior.

Remington stopped at the bundle and nudged it with his foot. There was a groan and then a small filthy paw appeared, pulling away a fold of trash to reveal a pair of round ears and two tiny black eyes.

'Got a drink, Mr?' It was a mouse, a young one, blinking up at him from within the bundle. He thought he detected a rural note in the accent.

'Sorry pup,' Remington said. 'Smoke?'

'Ew, gross,' she poked out a pink tongue and turned away, burying herself back in the paper and polystyrene.

Rem sighed and looked around at the street. He wasn't sure if it was true or if he'd been listening to too much bar griping at Squall's, but there seemed to be more and more youngsters finding their way into the city from the edgelands and beyond, most of them existing in the same way. He rubbed his head and made his way into the pub. That was the problem, he thought, humans think the city is a stationary thing. They build it. It stays put. But it's an ecosystem like any other burrow. It's never been arborescent. It's always been rhizomatic. Everything's keyed into everything else. It breathes, it seethes, its tendrils reach out and displace neighbouring tissues. Every green spot bordered by a thrumming pile of murder that won't stay in its lane. Like any habitat though, it can collapse. A sneeze could blow this monster down. All this Rem thought as the mother of all sneezes was fully inhaled, cocked, with both nostrils pointed toward his own. The great achoo was coming and none of these creatures had a clue.

As he made his way down the sloppily hewn dirt steps into the bar, he cast his eyes around for any signs that might stir his missing memory of the night before. It was always a bleak place at this hour. Solitary creatures nursing drinks and regret, eyes down.

'Ello gawjuss,' Rem said affecting an over-the-top cockney accent. Squall started and looked up from the scrap of newspaper she'd had her beak pointed toward.

'You can't be here, Rem,' she said, straightening her bluish black feathers. 'Not after last night.'

Rem took a seat at the bar and leaned on the makeshift counter, flashing his best attempt at a charming smile.

'When are you going to quit this place and just run away with me, Squall?' He reached for the drink she'd just poured for a particularly dour looking hedgehog.

She jabbed his paw away with the point of her beak and handed the thimble of fermented fruit to the sorry creature without looking.

'Bugger off, you tit, and don't give me any of that today.' She looked at him in a manner that recalled one of his old teachers from back in the Burrow. Squall was an old magpie and the years of city life had left a mark on her. Remington felt like a naughty child.

'You don't remember a bloody thing, do you?' She moved another container away from Rem's outstretched claws.

'Does it have something to do with this?' Remington pointed to his swollen face.

Squall gave a small shudder, raising her feathers, and placed her wing on Remington's face.

'Oh Rem, what are we going to do with you?' she sighed. 'I can't serve you in here anymore. You really Remmed this one up.'

Remington slumped. He'd messed up before. He'd broken the rules and had fights in there (only when someone really deserved it though), but a blanket of seriousness was starting to settle on his greying shoulders.

'Any chance you could jog my memory?'

'Okay, but then you've got to go.'

Rem nodded his assent and leaned in closer.

'Well, Rem,' she said in a whisper. 'It's the Rev.'

The name made Remington's stomach turn to stone. What had he done? Before Squall could continue, a loud sharp bark of his own name came blasting from the steps behind him.

'Remmy! Bloody hell son, what you doing back here?' He didn't need to turn around, and he felt the heft of a firm leathery paw beat him on the shoulder.

'Alright Nick?' Remington kept his eyes locked on Squall's. 'Our fearless landlady here was just filling me in.'

Nick was a badger much larger in girth and height than Remington. He rested his broad behind on the bar and leant back trying to catch Rem's eye. His fur was a dusty grey for the most part, a blending of black and white, unlike Remington's defined markings.

'Mind if I do the honours?' Nick asked Squall as she handed him a drink.

'Be my guest,' she said, still looking at Remington.

'Well,' Nick drained the drink in one go and he took a deep breath. 'Just another Monday down at Squall's, isn't it? We're all having a giraffe and old Rem's sat there making his way through the drinks menu when Mickey the Flip comes in with a couple of sorts.'

'Mickey?' Rem put a claw to his forehead and tapped as if trying to jostle a fragile machine back to life. This couldn't be good. Mickey the Flip was a crow, and not just any crow. Mickey was the nephew of the leader of a syndicate that called themselves The Murder.

'Yeah, old Rev's nephew himself,' Nick continued. 'Obviously he's all mouth and putting himself about to impress the cute little spurs he's with, right and naturally the gobshite spots you in your own little sett of misery and he can't resist. He's got to show the girls how untouchable he is, that he can beak off in front of a copper and still get away with it.'

Remington turned to face Nick as he grew more animated, the large badger's forelegs dynamically punctuating the story. Parts of this were starting to wake up in his memory.

'So, he's giving it all the feathers and brass, strutting about and you're there looking for all the sky like you couldn't give a toss, or you ain't hearing him.' Nick leaned into Rem. 'But of course, that just eggs him on, doesn't it? He comes over, right behind you and gets louder, making sure everyone in the pub can hear him. And then he came in close beside you and he says – *'Ow's the wife, Platypoos?* – and you…'

'I punched him-'

'You did more than that, mate. You dragged your claws down his face and nearly had his eye out.' Suddenly unclogged, the memory came spurting back. 'Well, then it all kicked off. He was shrieking out and trying to slash you up with his talons. You went full feral. It were a haze of wings, fur, claws and teeth, mate. Eventually you belted him with a plant pot, and he scarpered. That were the last we saw of either of you because you went off after him like a rat with rabies.'

Rem looked back up at Squall and mouthed the word *sorry*. His throat was dry and voiceless.

'Did you catch the little fleabit?' Nick asked. Rem shook his head slowly.

'Well at least that's something,' the large badger said with a nod. 'Right, I'm off for a widdle.' He slapped Remington on the back before bustling through the bar.

'And that Rem, is why you've really got to go,' Squall said. 'But I am sorry.'

'It's okay, I've got to be somewhere tonight anyway. At least give us a dram for the road, eh?' He hesitated. 'Best make it two. It's rude to turn up empty handed, right?'

'Where you off then?' She narrowed her eyes at him.

'Doc's. Apparently, Barb's cooking.'

'Well, you give him my best, won't you? Not seen the little man for an age.'

'Yeah, nothing like a couple of kids to swat a good barfly.'

Remington left the bar with his head spinning more wildly than it had when he'd woken up. He hadn't heard Squall tell him to *take care love*, and he hadn't got back to the street before he'd sipped from the first container. The bundle of paper and polystyrene was still gently ruffling in the breeze. He nudged the clump with his foot. The small eyes and ears reappeared.

'I told you I don't smoke, Mr,' she said.

'Here,' said Rem, offering her the second drink from Squall's. Using a claw, he scrawled a map on its side. 'It won't be safe out here soon, pup. Go here, there's folks who can help you.'

She took the drink in her small, filthy fingers without a word, and Remington headed back to his dwelling.

Remington sat on his upturned bucket. Sunset was a long way off and he knew it would be too risky to leave his dwelling before then. Word got around quick in the city. You were never out of range of something that could buzz your business across the metropolis in moments. If he wasn't yet being actively hunted, he would certainly be being watched. He stared at the open drink from Squall's, still trying to piece together last night's stupidity.

When Remington opened his eyes, it was morning. He could tell from the shade of the light streaming through the hole in his wall. His harmonic frequency was ringing again, and something felt like it was trying to escape from the inside of his skull. He pushed himself upright and the container from Squall's rolled from his chest, landing with a thunk on the floor. He peered around gingerly, looking for the drink, hoping it wasn't quite as empty as it sounded. What he spotted first, though, curdled his blood. There, on the floor of his flat, matted and broken, lay a single black feather. He pricked his ears and attuned to the hidden web of urban frequencies. He stared at the feather.

'Good morning, Sir,' came the same voice from yesterday. 'Is that DI Platypus? Hello? Hello?'

Remington tossed the feather on the bed.

'Yes! Quills, it's early, Oscar. What do you want?'

'Er, it's the Superintendent, Sir. She says you need to get down here, now.'

# Chapter Three

You're never more than six feet away from a rat, the humans like to say. It's hard to tell if they believe this, or if they ever stop to consider what it might mean. They give themselves narratives to try to insist on their own existence, narratives that veer from weird to batshit crazy. That *is* one phrase that works though. It's a truth widely acknowledged among the crawly, slithery, flappy community that bats produce the most toxic cocktails of weirdness from their less cute ends than anything else. Certain varieties of guano are so toxic that some of the more profit-minded (one of many traits scavenged and repurposed from the humans) among the beasts have used it as the basis for all manner of mind-altering substances. The current fad was a particularly addictive strain that had earned the name Heartbreak through a rapidly increasing roster of victims. Regardless of the chiropteran digression, the number is way less than six, and it's not just rats.

A curious side-effect of the years threaded around each other in this weird, however-many-feet-apart helix was how much various human narratives managed to impact upon the animal world. Remington stretched his legs and grimaced as he reached the thick hedgerow that marked the entrance to the Met station. A cluster of protesters blocked the entrance, squealing in a discordant monotony that sounded like an old Wurlitzer organ grinding too slowly.

The Take Back Eden movement had been around since Remington first moved to the city, but their numbers had increased suddenly over the past year or two. He was never clear what the group's end goal was. There had been various movements and agitators pushing for some form of unified fightback against the human world, but a general sense of acceptance and futility had long settled over the animal community at large. Life was hard and short enough as it was and so they focused on the things they could control. That was how the Met had been set up in the first place. It wasn't perfect, but there was a sense of control in the institutionalising of existence. If any creature wished to opt out, then they were welcome to stay feral and to survive in whatever wild comfort they could find. Take Back Eden was a harmless final refuge for those who couldn't quite admit the fight was lost, less a rage against the machine, and more a lip-service sigh against inevitability.

Remington watched three constables; a mouse, a rat, and young Oscar stand guard at the doorway. There wasn't likely to be any trouble, of course, but it was policy to make sure you had a visible presence. If nothing else, it helped to legitimise the protest and make the group feel heard. Oscar's midriff shifted to the left as if someone was trying to hook him off stage, and two looming shadows appeared behind him. Rem felt his lip twitch and he bared his teeth. Two crows parted the constables and paused, looking over the protesters; broad shoulders with sleek wings folded behind, long black beaks and eyes like oil, a walking eclipse. The bird on the right, Remington recognised as one of the Rev's regular bodyguards. There seemed to be a revolving door of overgrown corvus the Rev could call upon to act as feather shields. The bird on the left had a wiry gait. His movements seemed liquid, like a salamander, and the tips of his talons glimmered silver in the sunlight. This was Cull, the Rev's right talon. They stepped apart, and behind them stood the Rev.

Remington let out the whisper of a snarl and felt his claws dig into the pads of his paws. The Rev, a fearsome raven, was wider than either of his crow goons and bore a crack in the right side of his beak that gave the appearance of a fang. His eyes were fixed on Remington's. The badger tried not to blink, but the Rev's eyes could turn a squirrel's legs to treacle. If the Rev's goons' eyes were oil, then his were tar. Sure, there was something unsettling about seeing your own reflection in the glass marbles of a regular crow's eyes, but the Rev's weren't finished in gloss. They were matte black. To peer into those eyes was to peer into absolute nothing. Nothing could penetrate them, and nothing could escape.

'Eden must be returned!' Remington fell backwards as the weight of a brown shabby rat crushed into him. The creature's face was twisted and his hot breath assaulted Rem's nose as they landed. 'From below he rises,' it cried. Spittle peppered Remington's fur.

There was a screech, a flash of champagne-coloured fur, and the rat was flung from Remington. Oscar turned from the protester and helped Remington to his feet.

'You okay, Sir?' He seemed taller than he had the day before.

'I think you've got a collar to make son,' Rem said, gesturing to the dazed rodent on the floor. He looked back toward the station entrance. The crows were gone.

Remington sat in Superintendent Lennox's office on an upturned flowerpot. Her secretary, Cate, a toad as vacuous as she was venomous, had pointed for him to go in whilst giving him a withering glare, blinking each sticky eyelid in turn. He rifled through a few choice insults in his mind before thinking better of it. If Lennox was calling him in this early, then this was serious. The fact that she was pulling the 'wait alone in my office' ruse made Remington nervous. It was a trick she saved for being in full boss mode. They'd both been promoted to detective in the same class and, despite her star rising more swiftly than his, she only ever pulled rank on him when his behaviour forced her professional paw. He never said it of course, but he was grateful for that.

He picked up a round white pebble from her apple crate desk and ran a claw over its familiar surface, tracing the veins. The pebble, a scattering of papers, and a sketch of the Met's founders, the Three, were the only things populating Lennox's desk. She said she didn't like clutter, but Remington suspected it had more to do with her own lack of faith in herself. If you expect to be fired at any moment, you don't hoard enough to fill a further-endeavours box.

'See our visitors?' she said, making Rem drop the pebble with a thud as she hopped into the room. She threw herself onto the flowerpot opposite and fixed Remington with her gaze. She was a dark chocolate-coloured rabbit and, as she dragged her paws down her long silky ears, lopping them momentarily, Rem searched her eyes. They were wide and dark, and she always worked some kind of alchemy around their edges which made them hard not to find yourself falling into. What Remington was searching for though was the colour. She had brown eyes, but they were flecked with green, and the green seemed to shift within them depending on her mood.

'Rem?' she slapped the desk and twitched her black nose.

'Sorry?'

'Did you see the visitors when you came in?' She punctuated each syllable. He didn't need to study her eyes anymore. She was definitely angry with him.

'The Take Back Eden lot?' Remington shifted his eyes to the pebble.

'What? No, not the great unwashed, you dumb lump.' She waved her paw past Remington's eyeline to draw his eyes back to hers. 'Our friendly neighbourhood Don.'

'Ah, yeah, and the ugly sisters.' Rem tried a smile, but the look on Lennox's face made him dissolve it swiftly. 'So, what was that about?'

'Well,' she said, pulling another of her trademark boss moves by swivelling around to face away from him. The back of her head looked darker in full silhouette, one ear sticking straight up and the other folded from halfway, bowing to the morning light. 'You ever heard the phrase, you're never more than five feet away from a rat?'

'I thought it was six.'

'So help me,' she flashed him a look over her shoulder. 'I swear I will tear every whisker out of your face if you don't start taking this seriously.' She turned back again, rightly taking Remington's silence as assent. 'Well, who's the most well-known rat in the city, Rem?'

He knew where this was heading. She wasn't talking about an actual rat. She was talking about a crow. She was talking about Mickey the Flip. Mickey had gotten his nickname for being known to have turned on certain criminal colleagues and employees of his uncle. The only reason his beak was still attached to his face and his wings hadn't been clipped was on account of his family ties.

'You mean Mickey?' he asked. His throat felt dry.

'Yes, your recent dancing partner I hear?' Rem said nothing. What would be the point? 'That was really fucking stupid, Rem, even for you.'

'I held off, Len, honest, but the little prick…'

'That little prick is dead,' she said, and Rem nearly tumbled from the flowerpot.

'He's dead?'

'Found this morning.'

'How?' Remington blurted, 'I mean, do we know the cause of death?'

'Doc didn't get much chance to examine the body. No obvious signs pointing to murder, some nasty claw marks down his face, a day or two old.' She peered back at Rem. 'You know the crows and their funerals. They were here to claim the body. It's being picked up now.'

'Len, look we had a scuffle, but I didn't…' Rem said, and she cut him off, turning back around with a wave of her paw.

'I know, Rem. Look, it's Mickey, plenty of folk wanted him dead, and he may well have done it himself – some perverted sex game gone wrong, or maybe he overdid it on the Heartbreak. But it was still really bloody stupid. Think about everyone he's turned on, ratted out, just waiting for an excuse to do him in, and then they see a drunk, beaten down, over the hill copper giving him a hiding and then chasing him down the street.' Rem knew she was right, but Lennox was one of the few whose words contained the power to penetrate his thick old hide. 'You gave them the perfect chance to off him, and now…' She broke off.

'I'm sorry, Len, you're right. I don't know what to say.'

'The Rev wants you gone you know,' she said. 'If I don't get you out of the city, I'm not sure if it'll be safe.'

'We're letting them call everything now then, are we?'

'That's not fair, and you know it. I'm doing the best I can with what we've got here. I know you don't understand it, but everything here is about balance, and my bosses-' She gestured to the etching on the desk and narrowed her eyes at him. 'Just, please no more bar fights. No more surprises. Life's a thin thing, Rem. But, while I try to work out what to do with you, you should probably head down to see Doc. He's got some news about our other cadaver.'

Rem opened his mouth to speak, but found nothing useful to say. He stood up to leave.

'You used to be so full of words, Rem,' she said, making him pause in the doorway. 'I called last night by the way. Where were you?'

'I was at Doc's as it happens. You know Barb, no frequencies or shop talk at the table.' Lennox's face softened a little.

'That's good,' she said. 'Give her my best next time, won't you?' Rem nodded again and left the room.

In a warren below the main station, in his own special corner of murk and dirt, Doc was cheerfully muttering to himself, the constituent parts of flesh and liquid, of bone and feather spread out across a series of plastic bags. He looked up as Remington entered the room.

'Remmy, Rem, Rem, my boy!' he said, returning to his snuffling. He was holding a small piece of bone to a circle of glass in front of his eye. 'We missed you last night, Rem,' he said, and guilt seeped into Remington's stomach.

'Sorry, Doc, Len called. I meant to give you a head's up but time sort of got away from us. You know how it is.'

A smile slowly spread over the mole's face. 'Ah that's good, Remmy. Always good to have a pair of interested ears, eh?' He drew his attention away from the fragment of bone he'd been studying. 'She's not too mad about you and Flip the other night then?'

'Heard about that, did you?'

'Well, it's not every day the Rev willingly graces our humble little dwelling with his presence, is it?'

'Lennox said you had some news about this body anyway?' Rem gestured to the heaps of guts around the room.

'Oh, I do, I do.' Doc held up a flap of skin and turned it over to show Rem a mess of matted fur. 'See this?'

'Fur?'

'Bingo! Now have a peek at this.' Doc tossed the fragment of bone across the room. Remington caught it and rolled it between two claws. It was light and brittle. He held it up to the single spot of light Doc had excavated, looking through it like a telescope. 'See the calcification?'

'The what?' Remington said, admiring the strange crisscross of branches inside the tube.

'And this,' Doc ignored the question as he threw another bone to the badger. This one was heavier. Doc mimed a telescope gesture, and Remington held the second bone up to the light. It was solid and had rings like a chopped tree trunk.

'They're different,' Remington said.

'That the best the Capital's finest detective can do? Why

would something need light, hollow bones?'

'Bird bones?'

'Give that man a worm!' Doc said. 'We've got bird bones, and mammal bones. We've got fur and we've got feathers.'

'What are you saying, Doc?'

'I'm saying this isn't just one body.' He held up the cord Remington had spotted at the crime scene.

'Someone Frankensteined these poor bastards?'

'Either that or we've got some freaky new species strutting about the streets.'

# Chapter Four

Laying low didn't come naturally to Remington, but he had to concede that Squall's was off-limits until this Mickey the Flip business died down. He stretched his forelegs, ignoring the clicking from his bones, and arched his neck to let out a false yawn. It wasn't subtle, but it was the best he could be bothered to do. Remington peered through his lashes at the roofs of the buildings. He *was* being watched. Black smudges peppered the rooftops. Crows. Squall's being out of the question was a blessing. He suspected he might be grateful for a clearer than usual head today, but what really irked him was that his new feathery entourage forbade him from starting his investigation into the chimaera corpse.

Remington's first step in almost all investigations was to pay a visit to his regular coterie of criminal informants. They might be a bunch of junkies, thieves, and general wrong 'uns, but Remington couldn't risk their safety by outing them in front of the crows. It was one thing to be seen talking to the police if you had family ties like Mickey, but for anyone else, a rat was a rat was a rat. The foul breath of the protester from earlier came to his mind. What was it he said? *Eden must be returned?* Like there ever was such a thing.

A shadow passed overhead with a clatter of wings and the grating caw of a crow. They wanted him to know he was being watched. This was part of The Murder's M.O. – they functioned through intimidation for the most part. Keep everyone afraid and you rarely need to get your pointy bits messy. The fact that the Met had been so ineffective against them had stuck in Remington's canines even before his personal issues with the Rev began, but he understood Lennox was in a tough position. Intimidation was a shrewd tactic because there was so little the authorities could do about it. Not that this had ever stopped Remington trying though. His current surveillance gave him the urge to saunter straight to the pub and show just how unintimidated he was, but it wasn't just his safety in question. He growled softly to himself and dug his claws into his palms. *They go high, you go low*, he thought, and weaved his way toward the Underground stairs.

It was generally considered bad form to mingle into the throng of the city. You either kept to the undergrowth, the edgelands, or you made sure you were wherever you needed to be before the streets became a whirlpool of beige legs, stiletto heels, and pleated trousers. Still, if he couldn't do his job properly, he could at least make an overdue drop in and possibly shake loose some ideas. Two crows, one stone. The underground steps should have felt something close to home. After all, what were they if not a doorway into a sett, a series of subterranean tunnels, a network of incredible excavation and engineering, shielded from the sun? Humans had their faults for sure, but the underground was positively badger worthy. Still, there was something unsettling about the dark concrete maw. Each step was worn by the countless feet of weary commuters, layers of grime and dirt varnished into them. The metal railing that cleaved the stairs was alive with breeding germs, loving life in the sticky tarnish of their existence.

The smell was almost too much for Remington's bovine senses too. Decay mingled with stale urine, human sweat, a detritus of discarded food wrappers, and the ebbing residue of nocturnal creatures who sought out refuge in the shadow. The air throbbed with the aura of the city's discarded, a fresh blend of new coffee and yesterday's regret. Once down the stairs, mercifully unnoticed by the morning's first double-busy humans, he crept into the shadows and dropped down into the tunnel, savouring the cool breeze as it ruffled his fur beside the tracks.

The ghost stations of London's underground network were a sight to behold. Monuments to progress and absence. Luckily, the beast world knows how to recycle. That whole Womble thing was practically a documentary, although ironically the Wimbledon-based vermin are actually some of the most profligate in all the Boroughs. He clacked his claws louder than necessary as he neared the ghost station. This was politeness as much as anything. Humans had started to revisit these dead stations on historical tours and themed walks, and it was a massive pain in the hide to have to whip everything out of sight. The overly heavy steps were a hassle-free way of saying, *don't worry, just another furry thing passing through.*

'Fee-Fi-Fo-Fum, I smell the poop of a badger's bum!' Nick called over the platform as Remington emerged from the shadows. 'To what do we owe the pleasure Remmy?'

'Just thought I'd pop in, see what you'd done with the place.'

'As long as the world is cruel, we will be here to dish out the gruel,' Nick opened his forelegs in a ridiculous messiah pose.

'Jackass,' Remington said, but he had to admit the overgrown oaf was in his element here.

Remington looked around at the bundles of hay squeezed into spaces in the walls, and the tables of assorted foodstuffs. A menagerie of creatures, different breeds, sizes, and states of health or addiction were scattered across the cracked grey platform.

'Hell, Nick, I didn't realise it was this bad. Is this all Heartbreak?'

Nick dropped a heavy leg over Rem's shoulders. 'Not all of 'em. Some are the usual, lost homes or families and just need a bit of building up, maybe some lessons in how to handle the streets. But there's definitely more kids coming in than before though. We're doing okay, but if it keeps up, we won't be able to feed 'em all.'

'I'll send a couple of plods down with some parcels later, Nick.' Remington's eyes fell on the round ears and tiny black eyes of the mouse he'd met the day before. She was piling pellets and seeds onto milk bottle caps and handing them out to patiently queuing creatures, a smile fixed on her coffee-coloured face.

'One of our newest,' Nick said, following Rem's eyes. 'Came in half cut but she's made herself very popular. She's been doing the bedding, clearing shit, and a natural with the harmonics too. She's even helping out teaching the Breakers.' Nick nodded to the corner of the room where a cluster of rodents sat twitching and quaking, eyes vacant as they drooled over their own fur. Nick had always been keen to teach animals how to utilise the harmonic frequencies of the city. It could be a very lonely place, but if you knew how to ask for help, then there was always a chance someone might hear you.

Rem shuddered and shook his head. 'It's getting worse, isn't it?'

'Don't go all Take Back Eden on me Rem,' he said. 'There's always some new craze on the market. As long as we can keep offering a place to sweat it out and get the poor furballs back on their paws, then we'll be alright.'

Remington nodded, but he didn't share Nick's optimism. There had been a few fad narcotics during his time in the city, but Heartbreak was particularly insidious. It seemed to hold its victims in a kind of trance, and what made it even more difficult for the Met to deal with was that its creation was still an almost complete mystery. All they knew so far was that it came from bat guano, the faecal matter of the creatures that danced in the night. Bats had been a curious species who'd largely, like most nocturnal or subterranean creatures, opted to remain outside of the institutionalised animal world, so it was highly unlikely they had anything to do with the turning of their effluence into a recreational drug. Doc's best guess was that the guano was subjected to some kind of macabre alchemical process that transformed it into a sinister elixir that could open up the darkest feral recesses of the animal psyche. Whatever the process, the result was a fine black dust, a powder that possessed an otherworldly shimmer. When consumed, it was like you'd invited serpent venom directly into your heart. After that first hit, an explosive rush of euphoria flooded all sense and drowned out reality. Colours were more intense, senses were heightened and a feeling of blissful potential swaddled the user. But it was a deceptive nirvana, built on a broken promise.

After the initial high, Heartbreak showed its real face,

the face of a puppeteer pulling the threads of your heart. It squeezed the organ in an eagle grip and amplified pain and sorrow to unbearable levels. The user was trapped in a typhoon of emotional masochism. Animals became slaves to their own wretched despair. The only escape from those depths was to take another hit, but the high could only get you so high while the lows were limitless. It was an all-consuming, transformative drug. It changed personalities and warped faces. It wasn't considered civilised to say so, but Remington knew you could spot a Breaker just by looking at their face. A violent red rimmed their eyes, and eventually open sores appeared on their bodies.

There were also occasional clean up jobs required when some poor creature, new to the drug, decided to try to smoke it. No sooner was it lit than the user's head and most of their body would be completely eviscerated. Doc had excitedly explained this to Remington during his early days in the city. Bat guano consists largely of saltpetre, a substance utilised by those ever-inventive humans in gunpowder. While not quite the same chemical process as that used in extracting the relevant nitrates to make gunpowder, the refining process for Heartbreak amounted to a similar outcome. Remington couldn't be sure if you could get high from gunpowder, but he knew that if you rolled it in a leaf, lit the end and then took a drag, you'd be lucky if there was anything left of your head.

'Black gold my arse,' Remington muttered to himself.

Nick snapped a foreleg up in the air without looking and caught a tiddlywinks counter as it zipped toward his head. He turned and snarled jokingly at three voles who'd been playing frisbee with the disc before skimming it back to them. 'There is one thing though, Rem.' Nick pulled Remington in close. 'It's the Rev.'

'What now?' Remington felt his fur prickle.

'Well, he's been sniffing around. Not him obviously, but his minions, even Cull – hanging around the entrance, preying on the little ones.'

'Drugs?' Remington asked.

'No, that's just it,' Nick said. 'That was part of a cycle we could cope with. We clean 'em up. They leave, and of course they're easy targets for the pushers. They get messed up on Heartbreak again, and we do our best to clean them up again. It wasn't great, but I could deal with that.'

'What then?'

'You've heard the rumours about the Rev's, shall we say *tastes*?'

Remington's fur turned clammy. He had indeed heard the rumours about the Rev's proclivities for rodents. Young rodents. Male, female, it didn't matter to him. He just wanted creatures he could be certain of terrifying so much that they wouldn't fight back. That's what Rem had heard anyway, that the Rev got off on the power of being able to scare something so completely that it would be paralysed. He could imagine how it was possible too with those eyes of his.

Remington had hoped that Nick might be able to nudge some ideas loose about the corpse, but he was leaving with less of a clue than he had entered with, his head a washing machine of jostling nonsense and images wrung from nightmares.

'If you need a place, you know there's a cushion in the office that's still got your arse divots in it,' Nick said as Remington moved to leave.

'Thanks, but Doc's offered me a place to crash, and Barb does a way better breakfast.' Remington dipped his head and hurried off into the darkness of the tunnel.

As he made his way up to the noise of the active platforms, Remington clung to the shelter and shadow of the broken wall, casting his eyes up to the roof of the tunnel. On the crosshatching of metal that housed the cabling and lights, he saw exactly what he expected. A rustle of feathers and glittering eyes. The crows had followed him down and were awaiting his return. Say what you liked about the Rev, but his underlings were nothing if not committed to their task and eager to please the boss. They hadn't seen him yet, and he pondered staying put until dusk.

'Mr, Mr,' a small voice called, panting from the dark of the tunnel. Remington turned to see two little black eyes and a pair of round ears emerge from the darkness.

'I wanted to give you this,' the mouse said, offering a bright counter. 'I think I owe you a drink, Mr.'

Remington folded the mouse's tiny fingers back over the disc. 'You don't owe me anything,' he said. 'But you just keep an eye on Nick for me won't you, pup?' He used his claw to scratch his initials on it. 'Here, just come to the station and ask for me if you ever need any help, alright?'

She blinked back at him, taking the counter with a smile.

'You'd better head back sharpish anyway,' Remington said. 'It looked like you had a lot of work to do.'

He watched her scurry away, the darkness swallowing her up. He turned his attention back to the ceiling of the platform. Two crows were looking directly at him, circling their shoulders, and twitching their beaks. He waved, mouthed one of his favourite four letter words and made a beeline for the main street.

Remington tried to ignore the feeling of a thousand eyes watching him as he scooted home, darting from shadow to shadow in the midday city light. If they were coming for him, they were coming for him. There didn't seem much point in fighting it now. He wasn't hiding anymore. He might have blacked out, but he was fairly certain that someone else had placed the crow feather in his dwelling, and if that was the case then they already knew where he lived. Once he'd left the main thoroughfare, he made a point of staying in plain view. He wanted to make it clear that he wasn't hiding from them. He stopped at the entrance to the dilapidated warehouse that marked his residential block and popped a tobacco leaf in his mouth. He didn't look up. He rested his rump against the brickwork and chewed slowly making whirls of dust with the claws of his feet. He spat the used leaf into the dirt, cracked his knuckles and disappeared into the building.

A haphazard network of tunnels had been hastily hewn in the uncovered floor of the warehouse's backmost room. He slowly trotted past the doorways that marked the abodes of the neighbours he'd never bothered to meet. He'd seen and heard a diverse array of species, going about their dailies, having fights, parties, rampant sex, but he'd kept himself to himself. He told himself it was part of the job.

Remington sat on his bed, made from a scavenged cushion, and held the black feather, turning it over in his hands. Up close he was surprised to find that it wasn't just black. There were layers of colour between the fibres. If he could divorce the knowledge of what it represented from the object itself, he might have conceded that it was a beautiful thing. A crow feather was a calling card and a message. It meant you were marked and that you would soon be breathing your last. It was all part of the intimidation, and Rem dug a canine into his lip as he felt a shiver pass through him. He pulled a cylindrical length of metal about half his height from beneath the bed, faced the ill-fitting noggin of wood that he used as a door, and waited.

Hours passed, and Rem waited. The light that pushed through the sides of his door faded and Rem's back grew stiff as night deepened. He pushed open the door and leapt out with his metal cosh held aloft several times at the sound of paws or feathers. Twice, there was nothing there, and on three occasions he scared the worms out of his unfamiliar neighbours creeping to and from their dwellings. He almost admired the way the Rev was toying with him. Attacking him now would end all the fun. This was a much more effective torture. He was just about to give up and sacrifice himself to sleep when his harmonic frequency tweaked. It wasn't Oscar this time. It was Doc.

'Scuse the hour, my boy,' he said.

'I was up, Doc. What's the news?'

'We've got another one, Rem.'

# Chapter Five

Remington emerged from the dilapidated opening of his dwelling cautiously, his bovine senses on high alert. It was still dark, but a faint ghosting of dawn cast a fuzz of shadow over the thorns and weed clusters of the edgeland. A thin mist crawled through the air giving everything the whiff of a dream. His sharp old eyes scanned the area, searching for any lurking black feathers in the gloom. Satisfied, he stepped out of the thicket, his footsteps muffled by the damp asphalt.

The latest body had been found close to the Met station, called in anonymously. As he hastened to the scene, he absorbed the sounds and sights of the waking city. The façades of the buildings glittered with stories of their history. Graffiti bled over walls with their cryptic human symbols. The distant peal of traffic mingled with the steady chitter of rousing birds. Remington rolled his shoulders as he walked, trying to loosen his muscles and shake off the weight settling upon him. The animal world had its issues, but murders were rare in the civilised community, and the tug in his stomach told him something bigger lurked beneath the recent events. While he couldn't see any overhead, Remington smelled crow all over this.

He nodded to Oscar and beckoned for the young ferret to follow. There wouldn't be much call for him to stand guard at this hour, and he would just draw attention to them, shivering outside the hedgerow. Rem took a deep breath before pushing his way into the undergrowth. The scene was much less dramatic than the previous had been. No great mounds of gore, no puddles of blood. One body lay sprawled beneath a tangle of knotweed, legs intact with wings splayed out behind, like some fallen angel broken by the weight of the city.

'I'm not sure you need me for this one, Rem,' Doc said.

'Fancy taking this one, Ozzy?' Remington inquired.

'Erm, well, it looks like two creatures again,' he said. This was obvious but the constable still sounded unsure. 'Well, one is a badger, and it looks like someone has stitched it to the body of a, erm…' He paused looking over the great expanse of wings that sprouted from behind the torso. It was a small badger for sure from the neck down, except for the feathery appendages which stretched from beneath. The beaked head had been stitched to the neck with the same dark twine as the previous corpse. 'It's a bird.'

'It's a buzzard,' Remington said, and Doc squinted up at him. The air under the hedge suddenly felt heavy and close.

'And what does that mean?' said Oscar, sensing he'd missed something.

'It means,' said Remington, crouching down and running a claw over one of the wings, 'that someone is fucking with me.'

There wasn't time to go back to the dwelling, as a mandatory meeting had been called for dawn that morning. While not usually one to follow such orders, Remington knew he was on thin ice, and he had no desire to make Lennox's life any more difficult. It was a struggle to keep his snout shut while Lennox spoke. The superintendent had announced that the funeral of Mickey the Flip was to be held that day and, this being a crow funeral, that meant a day of police resources being dedicated to the safety and well-being of a bunch of criminals. Rem had to bite down on his black lip while she listed the constables who would be required to create a perimeter and ensure the day-long service of mourning and remembrance went ahead peacefully.

Assorted dignitaries from the Murder's extended families and business associates would be traveling into the city to pay their respects and show their duplicitous faces, all of them grovelling and simpering before the Rev. Remington was warned to stay away (although Lennox's words were less savoury than that), and he assured her that his mind was focused on the chimaera murder case anyway. She had caught Remington off-guard by opting to eschew her boss mode, and instead was relatively soft spoken and friendly with him, reminding him of the nights they'd used to spend at Squall's, drunkenly going over cases and laughing at the creatures who couldn't hold their drink. It was an interesting approach. And it almost worked. There was no way Remington wasn't going to witness the funeral, but as a compromise he resolved to at least keep a respectable distance, watching from the shade of a hedgerow whilst the ridiculous fiasco was set up. Mickey the Flip, silent, his beak finally shut, was laid on a mound of twigs and leaves, his lifeless eyes gazing blindly at the clouds, wings folded beneath him. An altar of stone and glass had been constructed at his head. Cull, the Rev's second in command, stalked the clearing, cawing orders at a seemingly endless procession of crows as they fluttered off and swooped back in carrying objects and messages. He was a clear head taller than the Rev though he didn't carry the same girth, and the ends of his pale talons glinted silver in the morning sun.

As the guests arrived it was obvious who carried the most importance and who was dispensable from how far from the body they were seated. A dark semicircle began to ink itself around Mickey the Flip as more black feathers filled the clearing. It was hard to make out each figure, and Remington couldn't risk creeping any closer, but he wasn't surprised to see that the guests weren't solely winged creatures. The Murder's insidious talons were steeped into every corner of the supposedly civilised animal community. Remington noted a couple of weasels, a hare, and one particularly large, brown toad, the boils on its broad back volatile and pulsing in the midday sun. The volume rose as the gathering thickened. The cawing of greeting, argument, and playful banter made the whole mess seem like a festival rather than a funeral.

Cull strode from the alter past the body, to the opposite side of the clearing and raised a metal-tipped talon. He snapped two of the metallic claws together. A spark shot from them, and silence fell like a bass drop. A shadow passed over the crowd, and the Rev, sentinelled by two large goons, landed behind the altar. The henchbirds stepped back, and the Rev cast his dull spectral eyes over the attendees. He lifted his head to the sky and let out a single caw like a thunderclap. The guests returned the caw and Remington winced. The volume of the off-key shrieks was almost enough to make him turn away and follow Lennox's instructions, but a second snap from Cull ensured silence reigned again.

The Rev shook his shoulders and spread his massive wings, a curtain of night against the green of the clearing. He twitched his head left and right. Remington saw that the Rev had a fresh scratch beneath his eye; small glistening lines ran down his cheek, somehow making him look even more sinister.

'Gentlemen,' the crow began. Even the wind seemed to have silenced itself. 'Ladies, divers, and dealers, sinners, light-stealers, peelers, and worse, we are here because time could not tell us. These lands would remain unchanged were it not for the storms shaping our lust for the darkness. We have arrived as all revenants do, to eat from their tables and pick the seeds of their labours from our beaks. The unguents of their fear will free our feral tongues, loosened with legacy, and salted with brick dust.'

Remington felt a growl crest his throat. It was gibberish, but they were hanging on every syllable. The Rev cocked his head in Remington's direction. Rem was sure he was hidden well enough that he couldn't be seen, but those vacant matte eyes were fixed on him.

'One of our number has fallen,' he continued still staring in Rem's direction. 'And this will not stand. We are family, and this is blood.' The Rev wheeled his eyes to Mickey's body.

A sharp pain pulsed through Remington's shoulder and a voice said, 'You shouldn't be here, copper.'

It was Cull, his silver tipped talons digging into Remington's shoulder. He tried to shuffle free, but there was no escaping Cull's grip.

'Just serving and protecting, Junior. Doing my job.'

'You know I could slit your throat right now and I wouldn't even get done for it, right?' He finally released his grip allowing Remington to face him. 'Maybe that's what you're after, eh?'

He raised a point of silver so it glinted between them. 'Just say the word, Badger. I'll put you out of your misery.'

'Nice nail varnish,' Remington said. 'Don't we look pretty for the party?' He was about to add a threat of his own, but his harmonic frequency tingled. It was Oscar.

'Oh dear,' Cull said, noticing Remington's distraction. 'That the wife, is it?' He made a snapping motion with his talon. 'Oops, no sorry. How silly of me to forget.'

'What is it Ozzy?' Remington held Cull's stare.

'They've found a body, sir.'

'Another chimaera?'

'No, sir…'

'Then call someone else. I'm on another case.'

'Sir, no, you really need to see this.' Oscar's voice was even more jittery than usual as he stated his location. Remington sighed and ended the connection.

'Hey, Badge,' Cull said as Remington turned to disappear through the hedgerow. 'What's black and white and red all over?'

Remington's shoulder throbbed as he trotted toward Oscar's location. It was too deep in the day to be travelling across the city so openly, but he did his best to remain unnoticed by the humans. Luckily the city offered plenty of cracks for the discerning mammal to slip through, even one who was leaking a thin trail of blood. More concerning was the location itself. The body had been discovered in the heart of Murder territory. It was well-known that the Murder's influence covered the entire city and much of the surrounding country, but there was also an unspoken rule that the meddling arm of the law stayed away from the sprawl of what the humans called Tower Hill, right across to Limehouse. Of course, Remington never paid deliberate attention to this rule, but even he didn't enter the zone without genuine reason. Even with the majority of the crow community being away at the funeral, the air was thick with their carrion musk. Remington could feel it soaking into his fur.

He never enjoyed encroaching on corvus turf, and the lack of crows somehow made it worse. Remington was relieved when he caught the familiar sight of the quaking ferret clinging to the shade of a dark shrub.

'This had better be good, Oswald,' he said as he drew up to the constable. 'Am I the only detective working today or something?'

'You'd better see for yourself, Sir.' Oscar led Remington off the street and into a wooded area shaded by a disused church.

'You know this is Murder territory, right?' Remington looked up at the cross-hatching of nests and webs that obscured the sun. Most of London's graveyards were Murder territory. It made sense. London had more graveyards than it did Starbucks. If you were looking to connect a network of thievery, smuggling, and worse, then graveyards were the real overground. The perpetual stench of death was an added bonus. The humans liked to call it a metropolis but any creature with half their senses intact could tell it was a necropolis. 'Everyone keeps telling me to stay away from trouble, and then you call me down here.'

'It's through there.' Oscar pulled back a bunch of hanging dark green leaves to reveal a hollow in the base of a long dead yew tree.

'Is Doc here yet?' Remington asked, stepping into the damp of the tree.

'He wasn't picking up,' Oscar said, but Remington wasn't listening. He was staring at the body on the ground in front of him.

Still as a rock, her neck at an unnatural angle, blood pooled by her open mouth, lay a young mouse.

'Oscar,' Remington said, his voice hollow and distant, a broken bell clanging in an empty church. 'Why did you call me?'

'Well, in her hand, Sir.'

Remington looked over at the tiny familiar fingers he'd seen gripping a container of fermented fruit not two days ago. They were bloody, the nails torn. He leant down and gently lifted the fingers to his face. Small black fibres were tufted in the caked blood of her nails.

'No, I mean in her other hand, Sir. I found this.' Oscar passed a small disc to Remington. He didn't need to look at it. 'That's your initials isn't it, Sir?'

# Chapter Six

Remington didn't hear Oscar call after him. In fact, Remington heard little over the thunder of blood in his ears. He was back out into the whirl and noise of the city afternoon before Oscar had time to contact the station. The badger strode carelessly among the cyclone of humanity as he took the most direct route back to the clearing, back to the funeral. It was one thing to be caught out in the daylight, and to have to scurry from hedge to verge, as covertly as possible, but Remington was in direct violation of one of the fundamental tenets of civilised animals. He wasn't just getting noticed, he was actively snapping at legs that interrupted his passage and snarling with hostility at anyone foolish enough to reach out toward him. Eyes and mobile phone cameras pointed in his direction, but he neither noticed, nor cared.

The shortest route back to the clearing was a direct line across the great river, and Remington marched toward the embankment without hesitation. He used to love water. His mother said it was strange for a badger to be so at home in the wet. She joked he must be half fish, big fat gills hidden under his fur. It wasn't so much swimming he had loved; it was the weightlessness of floating. He could lay on his back, buoyed by the rich meander of the ghylls in the Burrow, for hours watching the day candle into night, imagining the stars were the big city lights. He had been so desperate to escape to the metropolis and find out if the stories of what it had to offer were true.

And found out Remington had. He had tasted the kaleidoscope

synaesthesia of scent, sound, colour, the intoxicating overwhelm of sensory bombardment. He had felt the kinship of the determined creatures repurposing the detritus of the human world, its scraps of objects and the scraps of its structure, the institutions, the hierarchies, the tools to wrangle chaos into something with a mappable shape. He had bought into it all, and he had loved it. But Remington had also seen how control and shape were an illusion. He knew that chaos couldn't be quelled, and the hubris of thinking it could be set you up for catastrophe.

Remington had lived that lesson on this very embankment. Then, he had watched helpless as they had tried to breathe life back into his wife, limp and sodden with the murky water from the great river. It was easy to feel like you were sinking in the city, the prodigious stone labyrinth of countless voices and lives, but she made him feel afloat again. The fact it had been officially ruled an accident never made any sense. Though he had no proof, Remington knew who was behind it and now another innocent creature was dead at *his* talons. Then, Remington had done nothing, placated by Lennox's and others' assurance that he was grasping at straws, that his wife wouldn't have wanted him to get himself killed by going off half-cocked. Then, Remington had done nothing, except commit to being the biggest claw in the Murder's flank that he could while just about staying within the bounds afforded him by his position. Some days it almost felt like purpose. In reality, it was nothing. But that was then.

Remington stepped closer to the water. He willed himself to leap into the heaving brown of the river, but his body overruled him. He snarled, bit his lip, and tasted blood. He raked his claws into the embankment, churning up clumps of clay and mud. He gouged the earth, tore and tore sending brown flecks scattering violently in all directions. Remington turned and ran toward Tower Bridge.

The furious badger ignored the raging of his leg muscles, and the wheezing from his overclocked lungs as he pounded up the slope toward the bridge. Pedestrians shrieked as he scurried past them, a froth of saliva tinselling his snout. The sights and sounds of humanity merged with the swirl of fury in his mind. As the twin sentinels of Tower Bridge slid away behind him, Remington salamandered into a narrow passageway between two coffee shops.

The black sprawl of the funeral was still in session as Remington crested the rise toward the clearing. How he'd have loved to thrust his claws into each of the attendees; snivelling sycophants, happy to be minor pieces in the grand game the Rev played. Remington felt the switch in atmosphere as he was spotted by one, then two, then all of the funeralgoers. Cull landed suddenly in front of him, looming down like a promise of apocalypse.

'Found your invite did-' Cull began but was abruptly knocked silent by Remington's fist as it crunched into the side of his head. The sleek bird toppled, his silver-tipped talons flashing in the sun.

Remington pushed on through the dumbstruck crowd. They were either still under the spell of awe that the Rev had cast over them or they were stunned into inaction by the impossibility of the sacrilege displayed by the badger. He hopped directly up onto the burial mound that housed Mickey's body and stepped over him toward the Rev.

The Rev didn't move. He simply fixed those tar black eyes on Remington. The badger swept a thick stick from the pile and, as two of the Rev's goons moved to meet him, he aimed a fierce strike at the one on the left knocking him down, blood spurting from his beak. He swivelled, dodging the talon of the other and gripped his leg, unbalancing him. Remington drove his weight into the bird. It fell backwards with the force of the badger's ample frame pushing the air from him. Remington raised the stick and brought it down on the stunned creature's head. The stick split in two and he released it before launching himself into the Rev.

Remington punched him as hard as he could, and up close

could see the damage the mouse had done to the Rev's face.

'Finally picked on one who fought back, eh?' Remington roared as he brought his paws cascading down on the bird. The badger turned into a flurry of black and white as the guests looked on with gaping faces. A left fist. A right fist. A left. A right. A-

Remington's left fist remained above his head. He struggled to bring it down, but his wrist was bound by the sticky coil of a toad's tongue. He turned his head to see the bulbous, rippling toad he had spotted earlier, staring dead-eyed at him, its mouth a yawning, sick smile with the long, pink whip-like tongue spewing forth. The Rev kicked and pushed himself up with his powerful wings throwing Remington back into the altar. A piece of glass dug into the badger's back. The raven loomed up and over Remington, blotting out the sky.

Remington expected the Rev to attack, but he didn't need to. By this time, the funeralgoers had snapped out of their inaction and were swarming toward them both. Remington slashed at the toad's tongue with his claws and a torrent of blood sprang out. The toad groaned and released its grip.

It was too late though. The Rev's coterie was upon him. Remington heard Cull say, 'You really fucked up this time, Badge.' He felt talons. He felt slashes. He felt punches. He felt a curtain of blackness enveloping him, and then he felt nothing at all.

# Chapter Seven

*The badger sleeps, and without the soporific effect of alcohol, he dreams.*

*He dreams of four paws sinking into bracken.*
*He dreams of stars blurring for a blink.*
*He dreams of the moorland swooning like a tremor*
*through the cheekbone of a giant.*
*He dreams of a purple sky and air*
*that doesn't turn to coal on his tongue.*
*He dreams of breath on his neck*
*a snout nuzzling his own.*
*He dreams of two badgers in the shadow of a cairn*
*shimmering under a stutter of curlews.*
*He dreams of jade wings.*
*He wakes…*

Remington felt the cockroach legs of nausea crawl up his limbs. He willed his eyes open and moved to scratch the haze of dream from his eyes. He croaked out a bark as sharp pains jabbed at his wrists. Spider-webbing gauze bloomed with red across various parts of his body, and patches of bald fur glistened with cuts and slash marks. He felt like one broad violet sore. The first time Remington had woken up in the station's infirmary it had taken him a few moments in that borderland between sleep and waking to realise he wasn't in his dwelling. He may have been in worse shape than before, but he knew exactly where he was. The arch of soil above him and the jury-rigged equipment swam in his vision. The infirmary was deep below the station's main warren, north only of Doc's grim cavern of horror.

He shuffled, gingerly trying to escape the creeping nausea, and saw, to his right, curled on a tin bucket with her back crushed awkwardly against the mud wall, Lennox, one dark ear curtaining half of her gently snoring face. The visible half was contorted in exhaustion. Her mouth was agape, and her tongue lolled on the surface of the bucket. He raised a claw and traced the outline of her face in the space between them.

Lennox's black nose twitched twice and her eyes, each as wide as an ache, opened slowly. Remington's instinct was to close his eyes and feign still being unconscious, but instead he stared as her slumberous brown eyes, the green firing within them, found his.

'I was hoping you'd wake up,' she said, not bothering to wipe the drool from her face. 'So I could knock you back out again.' She slapped her paw down on his shoulder hard, making red hot pain bud beneath a patch of gauze. 'It would have been easier to pick a fight with a car or fill yourself with Heartbreak if that's what you wanted.' Her eyes glistened. 'Easier for me at least.'

'She was so young, Len,' Remington said, surprised by the words.

Lennox dragged her paws down her long black ears and crunched her eyes shut.

'Why am I alive?' he asked. A flurry of wings and talons thundered in his mind.

'Pretty bloody grateful for that police presence we wasted now, I suppose?' She circled her neck and stretched her forelegs.

'The Rev killed her, Len. He killed a young one.' A tear cleaved an itchy path down Remington's face.

'And that's procedure, is it?' she said, nostrils flaring. 'Best way to put the scumbags away, right? Attack them in broad daylight in front of a sea of witnesses – friends and fucking associates no less – assault five individuals, and desecrate a corpse like a feral?'

'He killed her, Len,' Rem repeated. He heard how pathetic

the words sounded but he had little else to offer. Why weren't those words enough?

'We know,' Lennox said.

'What?'

'We know. The only reason I am not here firing you is that you were right,' she slumped her chin into her paws. 'We found fibres under the kid's nails that matched the Rev's feathers. She was in their territory. We didn't need much more but seeing everything come down like that, you raving and wild, even got one of his own minions to turn on him and take a deal. Drugs and crime's one thing but preying on kids like that…' She folded her paw into Remington's. 'Even got them to own up to the chimaera killings. The badger, buzzard combo was a pop at you.'

Remington's head was whirling. 'I really got under his skin, didn't I?' he said.

'You've got a talent for that, Rem.'

'Who turned?'

'Look, none of that matters now, but there is one other thing.' She sat back and reached behind the bucket, bringing out a tobacco leaf.

'Thought you quit?'

'Doesn't count,' she said popping it into her mouth and chewing. 'These are yours.'

She leant over and put another between Rem's lips. Her eyes muted to dark brown.

'What is it, Len?'

'I've got to reassign you.' She watched her smoky breath drift to the ceiling and hang like a wraith on the warren's stale air. 'You can't be here anymore, and what you did…' She tossed the leaf onto the floor and thumped her foot onto it. 'The Murder won't let this go. There's a power vacuum now, and say what you want about that sicko, he kept things in check. The best way for any of them to make a play for the crown now would be to take down the copper who took down the boss. Cull is out for more than just your blood.' She looked over the sorry mess of badger. For once he wasn't arguing with her. Somehow that made it harder.

'Until everything realigns, we have to get you out of the spotlight,' she said. 'There's a position open in the Burrow.'

'Which Borough?'

'No Rem, *the* Burrow.'

He had heard her the first time but was hoping the blood pooled in his ears had caused him to misunderstand. 'You know I can't go back there.' His voice sounded small in the sparse room.

'Shh,' she said as she placed a paw on his head and brought her lips to his cheek. 'You know you can't stay in the city. But let's get you back on your paws first, eh?' She stood up to leave, adding, 'you stubborn old tit.'

'Len?' he asked, as she turned away. 'Is the Rev really going away this time?'

'He's upstairs in the holding cages as we speak. He's done, Rem. You got him.'

Remington watched her black tail as she hopped from the room.

Remington listened to the thump of Lennox's hops as they trailed off into the tunnel. She was right. He couldn't stay in the city, but he couldn't go back to the Burrow either and he also couldn't stay laid down, not while the Rev was directly above him in the station. He winced as he pulled some of the gauze from his wrists and inner forelegs. Blood spat from the sticky substance. He swung himself from the bed. Remington lowered himself to his paws, but his legs buckled. His eyes pulsed as though someone had tossed a pebble into the lake of his vision. He watched the world tear away with the ripples. He shook the sensation from his head and growled to himself.

Remington willed himself through the tunnel and up the warren's stairs, gauze flapping limply as he stumbled. He crept slowly, pausing in shadows to allow various officers, and assorted staff to pass by. If he was discovered, bleeding all over the warren, no doubt some helpful Samaritan would deliver him back to his bed, and this couldn't wait. If the Rev was being held, he had to see it for himself.

The main floor of the station was a chaos of activity. The power vacuum Lennox had warned about was clearly already having an impact. Creatures of all rank hurried about the place and the shrill call of criminals pleading their innocence clattered around the walls. To Rem though, everything sounded distant and hollow, as though the whole world was talking underwater. Remington pushed open the wood that blocked the opening to the holding cages and dragged a breeze block bench in front of the door behind him. His forelegs stung with pain as he heaved.

It seemed strange to Remington that the holding cages were empty. This was where they kept any creatures brought in on suspicion of wrongdoing. Like so many other human artefacts, bird cages had been found and repurposed by the Met. They hung from meticulously excavated sockets in the ceiling. He had half expected to find a sea of crows all beating at their bars and cawing for his head, but the room was clothed in silence. He lumbered past the empty cages hanging dark and dull like hellish Christmas decorations, until he found the one that wasn't empty.

He faced the cage, chest heaving. The dull voids of the Rev's eyes stared back unblinking. His massive frame filled the spacc. He did not move.

'I got you, you murdering son of a-' Rem's voice broke off. He felt weak, and his vision doubled. The Rev cocked his head slightly to one side, but he said nothing. The scratches beneath his eye were still raw.

'I'm not going anywhere, you know,' Rem said. The anger in his throat made his voice higher than usual. The Rev stared back, leaden eyes too steady.

A thud sounded from the other side of the room, and he heard muffled voices. Oscar and a couple of constables were fighting to open the door.

'Do you hear me? I got you, and I'm not going anywhere.' Rem slapped his paws on the bars of the cage. It rocked on its chain, but the Rev didn't move. He just stood and stared back at Remington, a caged void, a thing shaped from a fever dream.

Remington gripped the bars in his fists, pushing his snout between the metal poles as the young constables finally forced their way into the room and tried to pull Remington back from the cage.

'Get him back down to the infirmary now, and for fuck's sake keep an eye on him this time,' Lennox roared from the open doorway.

Remington didn't care. Nothing mattered, except that he'd finally done it. The Rev was off the streets, and he wouldn't be able to hurt anyone ever again.

# Chapter Eight

For the next two days, Remington was a model patient. He didn't argue with the nursing staff who tended to him. He didn't struggle against the spiders redressing his wounds. He stared at the ceiling and took the medication he was given. He diligently followed the daily exercises and stretches he was walked through by an overly excitable polecat called Tiberius (a name Remington was certain was as fake as any physio qualification he claimed to have). He laughed at Nick's repertoire of predictable gags when he came to visit: *You'll do anything to get out of work won't you, Rem? Lying down on the job, Rem? Case of the sleeping policeman, is it?* Neither of them mentioned the young mouse they didn't have a name for. He even managed to engage in some top-notch faux flirting with Squall when she smuggled in a bottle of something that smelt uncannily like the cleanser they used to clean out the holding cages.

Lennox didn't come. Instead, she sent Oscar as her proxy with updates on the various examples of chaos caused by his actions, and Rem nodded. Cull had taken control of the Murder but the city was still dramatically destabilised. He didn't care though.

'Superintendent Lennox also wanted me to brief you on your new assignment, Sir,' Oscar said during his obligatory daily drop-in on the third morning.

Rem rolled his eyes.

'She said,' the youngster continued undeterred, 'that I'm to make it clear that it's not a demotion. If anything, it's a promotion. You'll basically be acting chief while old Banks transitions into retirement.'

Remington couldn't quite believe Chief Banks was still going. He was a crooked grey thing when Remington got his posting to the big city, and even then, it was a running joke that the chief was losing more and more marbles daily. He had been a sweet old hedgehog though, sweeter than his wife who'd always been abrupt with Remington at the Burrow's meagre station hut. She ran the front desk but gave off the air of one who felt she was the most significant component of the little rural office.

'You won't be back to plodding or anything. There is a case that they need to send a DI up for and, well, considering everything here, and the fact you know the Burrow, well, it makes sense to be you.'

'Give it a rest Ozzy, will you?' Remington rubbed his head. 'There's no case, and the fact I knew the Burrow once upon a nightmare is exactly why I'm the last one who should go.' He looked at the young ferret, stood to attention as always, perhaps a little less jittery than he had been on the first morning they'd met.

'No Sir, there really is.'

'Someone lost a jam jar, have they? Or is it the mysterious case of a broken plant pot?'

'Details are classified, Sir,' Oscar said, drawing a raised eyebrow from Remington.

'Don't fuck about Osmund. Either talk to me or bugger off and stop skiving.'

'Well, I've heard a couple of things.' He lowered his voice and took a furtive look at the empty doorway.

'Let's have it then, lad.'

'I heard that there's some weird stuff going on, people going missing, and weird reports of something in the woods.'

Remington would have laughed if he hadn't already popped a stitch from overdoing the fake chuckling at Nick's bad jokes. It was sweet really that Lennox was so keen to protect him she'd give credence to the ravings of the yokels and turn it into a legitimate case.

'Tell your boss it's not happening.' Remington rolled over, presenting his broad patchy back to the ferret.

'She's your boss too, Sir,' Oscar said, and Remington growled back at him.

You can tell when you've convalesced sufficiently. It's when the joy of not having to drag your behind into work every day gets replaced by the seething desire to do exactly that, and Remington surprised himself by how motivated he was to book someone. Hell, he'd have happily spent an hour looking into flowerpot thefts, anything to not be laid in that bed for another day. He'd started to see faces in the roots and runnels in the ceiling. The knuckled arteries of rhizome twisted into myriad crows, all gnarled and desperate with crazy eyes. He saw buzzards and toads in there too. The whole arched ceiling became a living tapestry, themed by his fears. When they started to move before his eyes, he knew he'd rested long enough.

'What are you looking at, you big beaky-' Remington started to say to one particularly smug looking face in the mud.

'Oh no! We're too late. He's already gone and lost it,' Nick cried sarcastically from the doorway. He and Squall appraised him quizzically.

'The two of you together?' Remington said. 'Bloody hell, must be serious.'

'Serious as a scotch egg,' said Nick.

'Ignore the troll here,' Squall stepped into the room. 'How you feeling, Rem?'

'About ready to get out of here.' Remington pushed himself upright in the bed.

Nick gave an update about how things were going at the ghost station, and Squall gave a run-down of who'd been booted from the bar over the past week, giving a full account of their indiscretions and the odds on whether they'd ever return. They all would. It was a rite of passage, making a clown of oneself at Squall's.

An hour passed and the small talk grew thin, but Nick and Squall didn't give the usual pre-leaving signals. Remington noticed the pair glancing at each other, making eye contact and then quickly breaking away. If he didn't know them better, he'd have suspected something romantic had passed between them.

'What's going on?' he said. 'You two are acting like a couple of lovestruck teenagers.'

'What? Don't talk daft,' Nick said too loudly.

'You should be so bloody lucky, you fat flightless-'

'Alright, alright,' Remington said. 'So, what is it?'

'We got something in the post,' Squall tugged at her wing with the tip of her beak. 'This morning, the pair of us got one of these.'

From under her blue-black wing Squall pulled a long black feather. Remington felt the sickness return to his stomach.

'You too?' he said to Nick. The larger badger nodded but kept his eyes on the floor as if ashamed of the fact.

'It'll be one of the wannabes trying to scare you, that's all.' Remington turned the feather over in his paws.

'Maybe,' said Squall, 'or maybe Cull knows there's no point threatening you anymore because he knows it don't do no good. Maybe he knows there's only one way to hurt you, love.'

'You want me to give in to them?' Remington felt sweat begin to bead on his neck fur.

'It ain't just you, Remmy,' Nick patted Remington's arm. 'We just thought you'd want to know.'

Remington sank back down in the bed as they left. He stared back up at the faces in the ceiling. The beaks looked like they were opening and closing, laughing at him. 'I'm not going anywhere,' he said to them. They didn't stop laughing.

Remington stood on all fours and arched his back. Tiberius muttered to himself, appraising the badger's progress. As long as his old bones didn't suddenly fail him, Remington would be discharged and then he could show everyone just how unthreatened he was.

'What's the verdict, T?' Lennox smirked at Remington, who was looking back at her, upside down through his legs.

'Overweight, lung capacity of a fifteen-year-old pug, evidence of depression, and-'

'You letting me go or not?' Remington interrupted, straightening himself up.

'And serious attitude problem. But, sadly, yes,' Tiberius sighed. 'My license precludes me from keeping people in for living with all the sense of an unsupervised toddler.

'Result.' Remington winked at Lennox.

Lennox dismissed Tiberius with a wave and gestured for Remington to take a seat on the bed. She sat on the bucket opposite and gave him her serious boss face.

'What now?' Remington reached out for a tobacco leaf, but Lennox picked up the pile and held it behind her back.

'Now, we finish agreeing on where you're going.'

'Well, I know where it won't be.'

Lennox pulled her ears down over her face and let out a growl of frustration. 'You could do some real good up there now. I'm not just fobbing you off. There's a genuine missing person's case and the locals are saying some weird shit. They're completely ill-equipped to deal with it. You know what it's like up there, what they're like up there. Banks has been a good enough peacekeeper, but he barely knows what day it is. There are the young recruits to think about too. They could use a good copper to show them how we do things.'

'So, send them a good one then,' Remington sighed back. 'I just can't, Len.'

Lennox cast her eyes downward and shook her head. 'You heard about Nick and Squall?' she said.

'The feathers?'

Lennox nodded and looked up at Remington. 'I got one too,' she said.

'You?' Remington asked, and immediately wished he hadn't.

Lennox nodded. 'Yeah, this morning, and so did Doc. In fact, Doc got four, two for the kids and one for Barb for good measure.'

He looked back into her wide brown eyes. She was telling the truth, and he could tell how much this was hurting her. Barely any green moved in her eyes. They were dull and apologetic, robbed of their usual sparkle.

Remington wanted to howl at the ceiling with enough force to split it open, tear a fissure through to the overworld so every crow could hear. 'And if I say no?' He felt his shoulders slump.

'You won't. You're not that selfish. It's one of your few redeeming features.'

The urge to prove her wrong was almost overwhelming. 'Even locked up, he's still dictating everything,' Remington sighed.

'He's not dictating this. I am.'

'I still get access to Doc if I need?'

'You're being reassigned to the Burrow. You're not being exiled to the bloody tundra.'

'And you'll pop up and visit?'

'Mandatory, I'm afraid,' she smiled. 'I have to do performance evaluations on all reassignments for at least the first four seasons.'

'Four seasons?'

'Just focus on making some headway with the ongoings up there, and, as soon as we've got things back copacetic with the crows, and got Cull in line, we'll have you back in that gross Breaker house you call a dwelling before you know it.'

'And I need first class travel up there.'

'You'll get the finest the Met has to offer,' she said, as she hopped to the bed beside him and embraced him tightly. 'Thank you,' she whispered. 'And please have a bath before you go.'

# Chapter Nine

The trains that entered the city always looked like swans drifting in to land. They eased into the station with graceful relief. They slowed on approach and beamed the city's potential back at it from their gleaming flanks. The view from the train had seemed all wrong to Remington when he'd first arrived.

On that first trip he'd gotten passage on an intermodal container on the back of a juddering freight. He'd traded the lunch he'd packed with a bug-eyed vole in order to sit near a gap in the corrugated steel door. He hadn't missed the salad of bugs and nettles he'd meticulously assembled. He watched the skyline peel away behind, scarcely believing the world could be so big. The green sheets of the countryside flicked past, pocked with chains of gold crops, and spatters of white enslaved animals. In many ways he envied their simple existence. You didn't see them bolting for new horizons. Every blink felt like turning a new page.

The edgelands had taken him by surprise. In school he'd been taught about the city, its dangers and how different it was, that it blotted the stars and was never still or quiet, that its predators were more unpredictable and insidious. The spongy safety of the countryside mosses were where the clever children wanted to be when they grew up. The pupils were shown playgrounds in parks that the small humans swung around on, screaming whilst parents smoked and studied their phones. The city, so the metaphor seemed to be, was a climbing frame, all hard steel, violent promises, and neglect, but the Burrow was the cushion that surrounded it, always promising a soft landing.

He'd expected entering the city's arc to be like switching from winter to summer, leapfrogging spring, a sudden eruption into colour, but the gutter of edgeland between the country and the city gave him just enough time to question his decision to board the train. The border was a moat of tumbling brick, steel, and glass, mingled with vine and nettle. It was as though the city and countryside were locked in an arm wrestle neither could win; an unplanned ecology of disused buildings and unrealised dreams, the receding tide of industry leaving a moat of not-quite-anywhere; a desolate, sleepless void. It was then he felt his fur prickle for the first time. This land was filled with ghosts, and to Rem, its silence was a plea for him to turn back. When the train had moored up just shy of the station and a stout guinea pig hurried the travellers out of the steel box, down into the gully of the tracks, Remington had not felt relief.

As he watched the city's sprawl carpet away in the train's wake as they clattered toward the Burrow, he felt a tug in his chest as though a thread of him had been left tied to the platform. He fumbled with a bundle of tobacco leaves. He envied the younger him who'd travelled to the city without the urge to chew the smoke. He hadn't picked up the habit back then. Smoking (as the creatures called it), like most of his habits, had been nurtured in the shadows of the towering architecture of the city. As he peered at the towers shrinking into the distance, moving further away, he suspected one quick tab might briefly fill the hole that had opened within him. The violent buzz of the electromagnetic frequencies was ebbing away with the metropolis. Everything felt muffled and sparse. It was as though he was steadily being dragged deeper and deeper underwater. He considered seeing if he could send one last message to Lennox, but the frequencies were too jumbled and weak. His heart throbbed as if part of it had been left behind. Maybe it had been, a piece of him now forever entangled in the great electric web of a city that had opened its pocket and allowed him to nestle inside. He could sense something though, a hazy ringing, a signal too frail to tune in to, but unmistakably there. Even in the most rural of habitats, you couldn't escape the electric hum of human flow.

'Excuse me.'

Remington turned to see a field mouse and her child standing beside him. 'Would you mind if my son had a look through the gap?' The boy clung to his mother's leg, partly wrapped in her tail.

'Oh, please, be my guests.' Remington stood and moved to a dark corner of the container. He curled himself into the shadows and closed his eyes.

'Quick, quick,' a voice called, and Remington jerked awake. The container was still and the light from the gap at the end of the box had faded.

Remington and his fellow passengers were ushered from the container. As he dropped down into the yellow grass by the tracks, he could spy the human rail station glinting in the distance. From here he could see the valley laid out before him, spatchcocked and limp as it had always been. The long twin snakes of canals glittered like a scar, scratches of dykes and becks veining the hills and fields. From this distance it looked as though nothing had changed in all the seasons he'd been away. The horizon of the city seemed to change every morning, hell, every time you closed your eyes it felt like the bricks and steel were creeping toward you, freezing only when you looked directly at them. The valley though, was a time capsule, a land left to fend for, and feed on, itself. Remington's paws itched as they touched soil. Everything felt too alive. Everything sang and vibrated with messages and meaning.

The other passengers had fled quickly. The organisation of what the powers that be had called the 'civilised' domains and habitats were safe enough, but beyond their boundaries into the borders between and the wildness of the feral lands, the Met had no jurisdiction. They were outside of anyone's jurisdiction. The

Burrow gave way to the ghylls, a splay of marshy wet woodland he and his friends had termed the lava pits. There was no lava, but the danger was always present. It was territory claimed by those animals who'd refused to buy into the civilisation project. There was peace between the two groups, sure, but it was an unsteady one, and with the continual creep of the urban tide, the boundaries between the two were looking increasingly thin.

He and his friends would boast to each other that they'd strolled out to the lava pits often, but none of them would have dared to venture beyond the threshold into the ghylls. Out there you couldn't be sure of your safety. There were still areas of the animal world that resisted the rules and control that the civilised regime had tried to enforce. Wild was wild, but there was always something wilder. Even Remington, with his vast experience outside of the narrow realm of the Burrow, felt something stir within him when he heard tale, or caught a glimpse, of a creature adrift from the system. The freedom was intoxicating. You could smell it on the air nearby. But freedom came at a price.

The enclosure acts had first been tabled when the vanishing of habitats had reached crisis point. It became clear that the only chance of genuine survival rested in putting animosities, and a bloody swathe of history, to one side to work together. It hadn't been smooth, and still wasn't, but it had stemmed the bloodshed to a degree. Even those who rejected the idea of a civilised animal world, of what they saw as self-inflicted domestication, stayed in their own territories. They might not agree with the governing principles, but enough of the population did to make any attempt to disrupt the system futile.

'DI Platypus?' A broad faced bird with pale wings folded behind her clicked her beak at him.

'Unfortunately,' said Remington. He stretched his limbs and arched his back, shaking the remnants of sleep and train away.

'I'm Sergeant Vixx, the Burrow's eye in the sky.' The lenses of her eyes shifted like cameras. 'I'm under orders to take you to the station hut.'

Remington nodded his head in greeting. The word hut made him wince. 'Mind if we get started tomorrow?'

'Oh, I don't think anyone's expecting you to start any work today.' She trilled at a feather with her beak. Remington couldn't detect a rural accent, nor was he entirely sure to which family she belonged. Harrier was his best guess. Though her diminutive frame suggested otherwise, she had a cream-coloured head, which gave way to a deep brown feathering over her body.

'Great, so lead me to my digs then please.'

'That's just it, I'm afraid, Sir,' she said. The hope Remington had felt at her not sounding like a local started to fade. 'As the Chief you'll be staying in the quarters at the hut.'

'I'm not the Chief of anything.' Remington raised an eyebrow and scratched at his tingling paws.

'Well, we've been without one since Banks semi-retired and you're the highest-ranking officer, which makes you the de facto Chief.' She stared at him. 'It was all in the Superintendent's orders.'

This was another gift from Lennox, an attempt to keep him from going full hermit out here he supposed. It's hard to be a loner when you're forced to live at someone's place of work, but he resolved that he'd give it his best effort anyway.

'Well, lead me to my home office, no, wait, my home… work? Just lead on,' he said determining to come up with a better term for the setup later. Actually, 'setup' just about nailed it.

Vixx led them to a boarding point in the long reeds of a dyke and they clambered onto a free ply-board drift. They sat in silence as the current drew them eastward in the evening sun.

The Burrow was smaller than he remembered. The clusters of wild hedges and the smell of rampant berries was almost overpowering. Sparrows cascaded from tall oak to thin beech, and larger wings high above, beyond Remington's ability to see clearly, tilted through cloud, tracing geometric patterns.

The sparrows reminded him of the drunk humans in the city, clattering from one bar to the next barking, *Lads! Lads! Lads!*. He stumbled, not quite tripping, through a clump of vegetation and was dazed by the smell of wild mint he unsettled.

'Here we are,' Vixx said. Remington raised his eyes to the clearing and found only a cluster of stumps and a fallen chestnut tree, its trunk wrapped with thorns and vines, as though the space was trying to reclaim its dead. 'Just through here,' she said, leading Remington under the trunk to an opening behind the stump. Sure enough, a door had been chiselled from a notch in the tree. 'Deep breath,' Vixx smiled. 'Time to meet your intrepid team.'

The station hut was small but surprisingly well crafted in the hollowed-out relic of the old chestnut tree. Compared to the buzz and whirr of the city Met, the Burrow's station hut was a morgue. Two hedgehogs were the only occupants and neither of them looked in the direction of the door as Remington and the sergeant entered.

Vixx gave a single beat of her wings, scattering fragments of nuts, seeds, and shell across the hut. The hedgehogs looked up. Both were considerably old for working animals and their greying fur was thinning to the skin beneath.

'This is our former Chief, Banks.' Vixx hopped over to the male hedgehog. 'This is the new Chief, Sir,' she called into his left ear.

'Oh, the city boy, come to take my job?' he said, squinting in Remington's direction.

'Come on, Chief,' Vixx cooed to him. 'You're retiring, remember.' The old creature looked blankly at her and then back at Remington as the badger drew a tobacco leaf from under his armpit.

'Missing the exhaust pipes already, eh?' Banks said and wheezed. Remington thought he might be trying to laugh. He put the leaf away.

'And over here we have Maive.' Vixx sauntered to the female hedgehog and threw her wing behind the sour-faced creature, giving her a snowy backdrop.

'I remember Mr Platypus, thank you Vixx.' She narrowed her eyes at Remington. 'And that's Mrs Banks to you.' She offered the bird a grub from a jar. 'And don't be expecting me to do your cleaning or your cooking. I'm not your damn maid.'

'Wouldn't dream of it.' Remington offered what he hoped was a gregarious smile. 'So, is this everyone?'

'Well, we have a couple of boots,' Vixx said. 'Volunteers, doing some plod work part time to get experience. They're hoping to follow the Burrow's own legendary DI Platypus to the big city.'

'Really?' Remington said. A smile crept over his face.

'Quills, no!' Vixx clicked her beak. 'Well, I mean yes, we've got a couple of part-timers, but no I don't think you'll find any plaques or statues in your honour, Sir.' She watched Remington as he cast his eyes around the shabby little hut. 'Cuts, I guess,' she offered. 'Before they start stripping the force in the city, they give us the knicks first.'

'And label anything you bring in for lunch,' Mrs Banks added. Vixx rolled her eyes at Remington with a shrug of her wings. 'And don't touch anything that aren't yours. And we don't have any of those fancy cleaning staff you'll be used to, so we have a rota. The rota changes some weeks, but I update it so be sure to look it over. It's etched into the wall over there-'

'So, my digs?' Remington said to the Sergeant.

'And I have one afternoon off a week, and it aren't none of your business what that's for, but if you must know it's for my meditation classes.'

'Meditations on fermentation,' Chief Banks said.

'And if it's your turn to water the plants then remember-'

'Mrs Banks!' Vixx snapped suddenly. Even Remington jumped. 'I'm sure the detective will pick up how we do things in no time.'

'Did you tell him about the cleaning rota?' Chief Banks shouted.

Vixx leaned into Remington as she led him back out of the door. 'It's really good to have you here. Your quarters are round the back. Shall I set a briefing for tomorrow and leave you to it?' she asked. 'Or shall I get the file now and we can have a look.'

'First thing's fine,' said Remington, 'and thanks for...' Vixx was beaming at him. 'Thanks.'

He turned to leave. 'Oh, is there somewhere to get a drink around here?' he asked.

'We've just got the one bar, I'm afraid,' Vixx pointed with a wing. 'It's in the row where the old chapel used to be.'

'I know the one.' Remington thanked her again and left the hut.

# Chapter Ten

The Chief's quarters, a single sparse room, reeked of tremor-anguish, the sensation animals experienced when confined or immobilised against their will. It didn't look like anyone had ever lived there. There was a crooked plywood desk, a mouldering stick and moss bed, and some boxes piled atop each other in a broad speculation of kitchen cupboards. A note was etched into one of the cupboard doors. It read: *GET YOUR OWN DAMN FOOD. I AREN'T YOUR MAID! Kind regards, Mrs Banks.*

As the evening deepened, the light grew strange. There was no electricity in the Burrow, and his metropolitan eyes struggled to adjust to the pressure of natural light. The ceiling was pocked with holes, through which he could see the sky candle toward dusk. He wanted a drink, and he knew where the old chapel was. His mother had taken him there every weekend when he was young. He remembered bits of the sermonising that went on. Each week a different speaker would come and talk about life and what it might mean. Some lectured on the great swathe of the world, their place within it. Others focused on the local habitat, or those that they'd visited. Often the speakers were traveling creatures who roamed the country sampling the diverse ways that animals lived. If it was a bar now, he imagined half of the conversations would still be about the same things. He wasn't one to delve too deeply into the metaphysical, and the rise in various forms of spirituality in the animal world over the past seasons made his fur itchy. Remington found his claws digging into the pads of his paws as he listened to his team across the clearing getting ready to clear out for the day.

He considered staying put for the night but convinced himself that visiting the one drinking hole in his new jurisdiction would be the perfect way to meet some of the locals. He'd wait until the rest of the officers left for the day though. The visual of him arriving and then immediately flitting off to the bar wouldn't be great and no doubt word would get back to Lennox. He was grateful that Vixx seemed a solid copper but was certain she had been briefed to watch him with her harrier eyes and report back.

Once the Bankses and Vixx had left, Remington sat, listened to the serrated scrape of crickets, and waited for the stubborn evening to darken properly. When he did step out of his quarters, he gasped at the night sky. There were stars everywhere, a canvas drilled with millions of bullet holes illuminating the Burrow. He breathed a lungful of air that seemed to reach deeper into him than any breath he'd ever taken. He breathed it out and coughed, almost choking on the clean atmosphere. His paw pads prickled as they touched the earth again. His pawsentia, dulled from years plodding around on the harsh stone of the metropolis, was waking up. In the city, it was essential for any animal to survive that they attune themselves to the sounds, sights, and smells of the topography, but here in the Burrow the ground was alive with information. Subtle changes in texture, temperature, and the rhythm of vibrations were the language of the environment. He suddenly missed being called via harmonic frequency. With no human comms network to repurpose, there would be no sudden interruptions. He felt a wave of tremor-anguish as he realised just how far away from the city he was. Any messages from Lennox, Nick, Doc, even Squall, would have to be passed on via the old ways: the old roots, networks, and messenger creatures. *Looks like we're not in urbanea anymore.* Rem chewed on a tobacco leaf and snuffled into the night.

If he hadn't known where the bar was, he would have found

it by following his ears. Above the clicking of the crickets, the night creatures were stretching themselves into their day, a babble of voices and song drifted over the evening haze of the Burrow. He half expected the bar's punters to swivel in unison and eye him, chewing gnarled roots, but he barely raised a passing glance from anyone. Creatures of all sizes chattered together. It reminded him of Squall's, only it looked as though this place got at least a semi-regular wipe down.

Remington slid onto a flowerpot stool at the bar and watched the barmaid slink toward him. He was surprised to find a cat working behind the bar. Cats were a unique species who had somehow managed to straddle the divide between domestication and wildness, and it was rare to see them working in the service industries. Why would you serve others when you've somehow persuaded the world to serve you? Especially when, unlike canines, you've managed to convince people that part of your charm is your lazy aloofness? Still, something about their natural gait and predatory movements made Remington uncomfortable. He scratched his paw pads. She sauntered up to Rem and blinked slowly. Golden eyes disappeared beneath almond eyelids and dark lashes.

'For the guy with the gloomy face?' she purred. The glint of her sharp teeth flashed in the bar light. Around the edges of the bar's ceiling, a hodgepodge of reflective mirrors and glass had been fixed into place, reflecting the starlight all around the pub.

'What's special?' Remington said, trying to keep his voice level.

Her ears twitched and she raised an eyebrow, straightening herself up. 'Well, if you've gotta ask.'

Remington laughed and hoped the fur of his face was full enough to hide the hotness he felt come to his cheeks. She flicked a tumbler from beneath the bar into the air, caught it with her other paw and dropped it onto the stiff bark counter top. She filled it from a long bottle.

Remington sipped and felt his throat burn.

'Nailed it, right?' Her eyes darkened from green to black, or perhaps that was just the drink. Remington nodded and tapped the receptacle with a claw. She winked and refilled it before slinking to the other end of the bar.

A poster had been scratched into the wall: *Fight Night at Cat's*, it read. Two pairs of boxing gloves and some names that meant nothing to him screamed out in deep claw marks. Remington watched the cat as she served a particularly worse-for-wear otter. He was stumbling and eventually flopped his torso onto the bar. Remington watched in his periphery as the feline took advantage of the poor creature. She stroked his ear and purred something soothing to him. While she did this her free paw slid, with the dexterity of a practiced city pickpocket, to the otter's underarm. Barely touching a single strand of the otter's fur, she opened a space in the fold of his flesh and slid something from it. Remington doubted he would have noticed had he not cut his teeth in the city taking down organised units of pickpockets, youngsters who'd been sold on the promise of the big city only to be sold a more brutal lie about being the hunter or the prey.

'Feel better,' she called as she spun the dazed creature around and watched as he stumbled out of the bar. She poured herself a drink and knocked it back, looking over at Remington, and then started coming back toward him. He felt like he was being toyed with, a helpless furball in the path of a speeding car.

'Usual please, Cat,' a rat said, slapping the bar and making her pause on her route to Remington. 'Hey, you ever consider marrying out of species?' The customer leaned on the bar and flashed a toothy grin.

'Oh sure,' she said, and poured a drink. 'But I've only got nine lives and I'm not wasting one of those on you.' She smiled and drained the drink herself. She reached beneath the bar and slid a thick bundle to the rat.

'You're an angel. See you at the fight.' The rat raised the bundle to her forehead in a salute and left the bar without a drink.

'So, how come I've not seen you before then?' Cat said to Remington who was suddenly struck with an inability to form words, frozen in the golden beams of her eyes. He shrugged. 'Come on, you wanna pass the ball back here?'

Remington finished the drink, and she waved the bottle, cocking her head. He nodded and Cat stuck her lower lip out in a faux pout.

'You know this is my place,' she said. 'I could bar you just for being excessively quiet and making the place look untidy.'

Remington swallowed hard and cleared his throat. 'So, you're Cat? You're Cat the cat?' He grinned at her.

'Or I could bar you for being excessively sassy with the landlady.' She clinked a tumbler to Remington's and smiled.

'Well, I could always arrest you for pickpocketing drunks.' Cat's smile dropped. She looked confused. 'The wobbly otter,' he said.

She leant in close over the bar. 'So, you're the new chief? I thought they were sending a platypus.'

'I'm Remington. It's Rem Platypus.'

Cat's eye's brightened again and she laughed out loud. 'And you took the piss out of my name?'

'So, you want to tell me why I shouldn't arrest you?'

'Other than a free glass of my best fermented mix?' She purred at him again, and looked at him through her lashes, her face the picture of innocence. Rem stared back unmoved. 'Fine,' she said, giving him a 'rawr' noise. 'Poor Tim who's just gone stumbling out into the night is not in a good way. Wife's left him and taken the kids. He happened to have a small windfall tonight at the bones table though, and believe me when I tell you, you do not want to be wandering home drunk around here with fresh winnings.' She held a claw up to a waiting customer. 'He'll come in tomorrow retracing his steps like all good drunks do.' Remington looked down at the bar briefly. 'I can say, hey Timmy you dropped this last night. He can have his winnings back sober and nobody gets mugged.' She made another drink without taking her eyes from Remington's and slid it to the waiting customer. 'It's really not good business to go robbing your own punters.'

'So how about that free fermentation?' Remington asked.

'Tell you what,' she said, pouring another one. 'We'll compromise. You keep coming here, and maybe I'll decide whether or not I let you stay.'

'How's that a compromise?'

'Well, despite you being a copper who came into my place and accused me of thievery, I have decided that I'm not going to bar you, yet.' She slid her tongue over her paw and then ran it over her ear. 'Now, if you'll excuse me, something delicious just walked in.' Cat slunk away, rolling her shoulders as she moved.

Remington wasn't entirely sold on the fairness of the compromise, but also didn't want to push his luck. His chances of remaining sane in the Burrow seemed largely dependent on not being banned from its one drinking establishment. He dropped a fresh tobacco leaf on the counter as a tip and left. On his way back to the station hut, he heard quarrelling from a bush a few paces from the bar.

'If not tomorrow then when?' One voice said. 'Roadkill's not gonna wait much longer.' There was no second voice, just the sound of whimpering. Remington heard a crash then the scampering of tiny paws. He carried on his route but craned his neck to peer around the bush. He saw a glint of eyes in the starlight. It was the rat from Cat's bar. She looked up and saw Remington.

'You need anything, old timer?' The rat rubbed her nose. Her jaw was in perpetual motion and her eyes were red at the edges.

'No thanks,' Remington said. 'I'll catch you later.'

# Chapter Eleven

The Burrow had fully shrugged off the day by the time Remington found his way back to his new home and welcoming bed of old moss. He'd taken a long meandering route, pushing his paws deep into the earth as he walked, trying to reacclimate to the pawsentia that irritated his leathery pads. More than once he tried to attune his harmonic frequency to send out a call to Lennox. There were no signals strong enough to tune into though, and any electromagnetic field was too scarce to carry a message to her. There was definitely something in the atmosphere though, a distant juddering buzz, somehow out of reach. Like tinnitus, it lingered as an ever-presence, an aural injury in the atmosphere. The world was quieter here, and he supposed this was to be expected after so many seasons in the chronic calamity of noise that characterised the city. Still, he felt there was something missing in the Burrow's song.

Perhaps it was the clear air, or whatever Cat had been pouring him, but sleep came easily. He woke an hour or two before dawn. In the space between sleep and waking, the still-alien light flooded the room with strangeness. Remington thought he heard scrabbling on the roof of the hut, and he faltered to his paws. The starlight sliced through spaces in his wall painting bars across the dwelling. He cocked his head, angling his ear toward the sound. It came again, a skittering of claws above him. Something was scampering over the roof.

In his half-dreaming state, Remington reached under the bed for his cosh before realising the weapon hadn't made the journey with him. He peeled back the sheet of rag that was hung as a curtain over one of the openings in the wall. The sky still seemed impossibly bright. Stars glittered in the expanse. He cast his eyes out into the clearing. In the grey moonlight, shadows seemed to move before him revealing silver pathways through the grasses. He blinked the sleep from his eyes and listened.

The scampering had stopped and, having neither the ability nor desire to scale the hut to check the roof for himself at this hour, he shrugged and lay back down on the bed. He'd get used to the sounds and rhythms of the Burrow again, he was sure. For now, he was grateful for a few moments more rest before he had to go and convince his new colleagues that he was a professional with some idea of what he was doing. Sleep didn't come.

When Remington did go into the main station hut, he found Vixx, Mr and Mrs Banks, and a couple of young voles sat in a row in one corner facing the farthest wall.

'Call this first thing, do you?' Mrs Banks said, her forelegs folded, and her face drawn tightly.

'What's happening?' Remington dug his claws into his pawpads and smiled at the waiting team.

'The briefing, Sir,' Vixx said. 'Just awaiting your orders re the missing persons, Chief.'

'What's that?' Mr Banks said cupping his ear.

'Not you Chief, erm I mean Mr Banks,' Vixx gestured for Remington to come over to the group. There were some scratches of creatures carved into the wall.

'I tell you what,' Remington said. 'Why don't we keep calling Chief Banks here, Chief, and we'll just call me Remington, or Rem?'

Mrs Banks snorted. 'No sense of tradition or respect for protocol.'

'As you like, Sir.' Vixx shot a glare at Mrs Banks. 'So, shall we get started?'

'Certainly.' Remington cleared his throat and stood before

the team. He considered blagging his way through some general spiel about the Met's approach to missing persons cases but instead found himself saying, *keep up the good work*, as he raised his inner toes to them. Mrs Banks rolled her eyes and muttered to herself.

Remington turned to Vixx. 'Perhaps you could fill me in in the office?'

Remington's office consisted of a desk made of a flat stone, and a couple of buckets for chairs.

'Help me out here will you, Sergeant,' he said slumping onto one of the chairs. 'I haven't even looked at the file yet.'

'Sorry, Sir, I just thought you'd give them a quick pep talk about how well they were all doing and that we'd combine our efforts.' She looked away from him and clawed the floor. 'You know, something about how all your expertise from the big city could be used with their knowledge of the area and the locals and that we'd find the missing and bring swift justice to any wrongdoers.'

Remington looked up at her. 'Well, yes, that would have made sense.' He sighed heavily. 'You sure you don't want the gig?'

Vixx pushed a clay tablet across the desk to Remington with her beak. This was the file, and it was thin. A few markings denoting a handful of creatures, and little else.

'Is this everything?'

'I'm afraid so, Sir. We haven't really had a police presence to speak of, so all we have are a few statements. The rest is all rustling murmur and scent trails.'

Remington scanned the object. He knew it. There was no case here. Lennox was fobbing him off into early retirement in this hollow grove. He tossed the 'file' aside. 'Sergeant Vixx,' he said, gesturing for her to take the other seat, 'what do you want to do, force wise?'

'Well, it's silly I know, Sir, because birds don't usually make detective, but I'd like to be a DCI someday.'

'Do you want to do some real policework?'

'Well, of course, Sir.'

'Then tell me, does the name Roadkill mean anything to you?'

Vixx broke eye contact and rubbed at the corner of the desk with her wing. 'I don't think that's the case we're supposed to be focusing on, Sir.'

'You can tell the Superintendent that I'm working this nonsense.' He nodded to the file. 'But I'm going to scatter my acorns if I don't have anything to do, and that's not going to be good either, is it?' He leant forward on his bucket. 'Come on Sergeant, I can tell you're a good copper. Don't you want to spread those wings properly? I promise I'll teach you everything I know. We'll have you out of the Burrow before you know it.'

'Well,' she said and glanced back over her wing at the door. 'I've picked up some wind whispers. He runs *things* around here.'

'You mean drugs, right?'

'I think so, but we can never do much because people around here don't talk to coppers.'

'Detective rule number one,' he said, finally warming up to the chair he was in. 'Shake down your criminal informants.'

'But we don't have any, Sir. Like I said, folks around here won't talk.'

'There must be someone. Repeat offenders? You know the type, mischief mongers, harmless enough but always just on the wrong side of the line.' He leant back and popped a tobacco leaf in his mouth. 'Not shadow predators, just down on their luck or too stupid to be able to dig themselves out of their own hollows.'

'Well, there's Fingle and Glen,' she said. 'We end up confiscating drugs off the pair of them at least once a month. Small time though, just bogweed for the most part.'

'Hang on,' Remington bolted upright. 'Fingle and Glen are still here?'

'You know them, Sir?'

'I went to school with those two. Haven't thought about them in years. They always talked about going to the city to make their fortune in music.'

'Sir, I have tried you know,' Vixx said. 'They won't talk to the police.'

Rem smiled. 'Have some faith in the boss, won't you? Now, is there anything else you think I should know?'

'We've got a deal going with Cat about the fight nights.'

'So, it's state-sponsored violence then, is it?'

'Well, not quite. If anything, it works out better. We don't really get any aggro at the bar anymore. There used to be problems most nights, and, well,' she said gesturing toward the office door. 'You've seen our resources.'

'I'm still not sure I understand.' Remington touched his face. He felt the ghost bruises he'd earned at Squall's over the years.

'Now if people have a problem with each other, they get a chance to put their names down and settle their differences in the ring.'

'And it works?'

'I'm as surprised as you, but we always make sure we have a presence. Large crowds, bartering-'

'Gambling?'

'Don't go spoiling the fun or you're going to be very unpopular, Sir. We just make sure everything stays on the level you, know?' Vixx looked at Remington, waiting for him to voice another concern. He didn't though. Truth be told he liked the sound of this. Perhaps the Burrow wasn't quite as dull as he remembered.

He assigned the two young voles to talk to Cat about the weekend's fight and establish any security needs she might have. He then gave Mrs Banks the day off to pursue her 'meditation' classes in the hope that it might defrost her somewhat. Remington and Vixx headed for the wet woodland, leaving the chief snoring at his desk.

Part of Remington was genuinely glad to hear Fingle and Glen were still in the Burrow. Reunions were a dish best served with an air of superiority, and the power to arrest if possible. They'd been an odd but inseparable pair at school, Fingle an impossibly lanky ferret, and Glen a stout dumpy weasel, always staring at the clouds and dreaming of a world beyond the Burrow.

'Brambles!' Remington cursed, as his foot sank into the wet of the marsh. The ghylls didn't gradually move in to greet you unless you were able to read the signs. Remington had been away too long to notice the ground suddenly breaking red with cotton grass signalling the beginning of the bog. Vixx was keeping her distance, but he could sense she was up above him circling in the blue morning sky. The trees looked wind-gnarled here too, and Remington realised the landscape had changed. The broad canopies of the woodland trees had given way to the contorted shapes of ash and oak, cowering into the swampy ground, like the reeds of the ghylls were pulling them down.

Vixx let out a piercing note, her signal that Remington was approaching the target. Remington yanked his legs through the mud. Every step was like pulling his limbs from a vacuum. Perhaps he should have stayed at the office and enjoyed the quiet of the non-case he'd been assigned.

He smelled Fingle and Glen before he saw them. Despite the pungent aroma of the quagmire, the unmistakable sweet smell of bogweed filled his nostrils. He gripped the branch of an ash that had folded itself into a right angle and looked out over the murk. Two husks drifted on the sticky surface of the brown glaze. Thin tendrils of smoke rose from them.

'Hey guys,' Remington called. 'You got a spare for me?'

The longer of the two shapes curled upright slowly. Rem could just make out two blinking eyes through the haze.

'Is that?' The snake-like ferret blinked at the encroaching figure. 'Quills! Remo? Is that you?'

The smaller shape struggled up to a seated position, smoke

streaming from its nose. 'Remo?'

'The one and only,' Remington hollered to them. 'I'm back. Thought I might find you here.'

'We'll come to you, man,' Glen shouted, and the pair slowly paddled themselves with broad leaves over to Remington.

'You gotta come see our place.' Fingle gave Remington a tight hug that would need a week-long bath to wash off.

Fingle and Glen's 'place' consisted of a couple of broken pallets wedged unconvincingly into a corner of embankment at the bog's edge. Mounds of rubbish, and detritus covered every surface.

'Take a seat, man,' Glen said and threw herself into a pile of old newspaper as though it were a beanbag.

Fingle rolled some bogweed into a strip of dry leaf. He took a sharp flat rock and struck it against another. A small scatter of sparks hit the leaf. He blew on it, lighting the cheroot and passed the pungent stick to Remington. 'So, where you been, man? We heard you like moved to the city or something?'

Remington took a drag and fought back the bile that leapt into his throat. He nodded. 'That's right. Got a job and now that job's got me back here.'

'Right on,' Glen, said taking the joint. 'So, we heard about your wife, man.'

'That was some heavy shit,' Fingle nodded. 'But it's good to see you.'

Remington looked around at the pallets and the bog. 'So, what about you guys? You working?'

'Working's so full on. Who's got time for that?' Glen said.

Remington eyed the piles of filth all around them and took the joint back. 'Don't you?' He asked with a grin. Both of the creatures laughed.

'You gonna stay for dinner?' Fingle asked, pointing to a brown shape hanging from the corner of the pallet. Remington thought it might once have been a fish.

'I'm good guys, but thanks. Are you going to the fight at Cat's?'

'Hell yeah, we never miss fight night.' Fingle passed the bogweed to Glen. 'We're the house band.'

'Hey,' Remington said, 'do you know where I can get some, stuff?' He gestured to the joint.

Glen handed the joint to Remington. 'You're always welcome to our home-grown, Remo.'

'What about something a little stronger?' Remington asked. He took another drag and felt simultaneously sick and light-headed. 'I heard there's a guy called Roadkill?'

'Aren't you like a cop or some fuzz now, man?' Glen looked at Remington, her eyes narrowed. 'You trying to narc us out?'

'I'm just looking for some information.'

'Not cool, man,' Glen snatched the bogweed back from Remington and stared into the bog.

'I promise, I'm not looking to bust you guys or get you into trouble.' Remington held up his hands.

'We can't talk to you, man. You don't know who's listening or watching around here.' Fingle wheeled his head all around him, blinking into the mist of the bog.

The afternoon dwindled into evening, and the setting sun cast a purple glow across the ghylls. The starlight blinkers, and bog dancers began to lift from the surface soundtracking the change of day with their dreamy hum. They smoked and they talked. Remington felt like he'd stepped back in time. Fingle and Glen were exactly the same as he remembered; still talking of their dreams of making it big in the city.

A high-pitched trill from Vixx brought Remington back to the present.

'Well, I've got to get back to the station.' Remington stood and stretched his limbs. 'But if you think of anything-'

'We ain't talking to you, man.' Glen nudged a battered facsimile of a stringed instrument over to Fingle with her foot. Fingle nodded and began picking a sickly off-key tune. Glen leaned in close to Remington, her tone suddenly conspiratorial. 'Look, we can't say nuggets to you. There's ears everywhere.' She nodded to the miasmic layer of insects thrumming lazily over the wetland surface. 'But one of Roadkill's guys, Brigg, is in the fight. I got money on her. She's a rat, little but quick. She deals round Cat's a lot.'

'I think I might have met her last night,' Remington said, half to himself. 'So, who is Roadkill?'

Fingle's playing got louder at the mention of the name.

'Dunno. Never seen him. Just heard the name.'

'You're always welcome here, Remo,' said Fingle, lowering the volume of his string picking. 'Just leave the badge at home next time, man.'

Remington thanked them for the joint and fought his way back out of the bog. His mind was weighted down with the fug of the bogweed just as much as his feet were by the mire of the ghylls. Despite the downward pull of weed and filth, Remington felt a lightness in his shoulders. Lennox might have sent him to the Burrow to divert him from danger or mischief, but his nose was beginning to tingle with the unmistakeable scent of a genuine case to solve.

# Chapter Twelve

Twice over the next few days Remington woke to the scrabbling sound on his roof. He cursed his laziness and resolved to arrange some pallets at the side of the house so he could quickly ascend and apprehend the culprit. That or perhaps post one of the young voles up there for a stakeout. It would be good experience of real policing, especially the kinds of jobs they'd be forced to endure during their first season on the job. On the third occasion, Remington had already been awake. He sprang to the window, tweaking a muscle in the process. In the glitter of the starlight, he thought he caught the flash of a red bushy tail as it vanished into the shadow of the trees. Whatever, or whoever it was, they hadn't threatened him in any way. In fact, since his arrival, the most threatening thing that had happened to him, beyond Mrs Banks' daily withering looks and refusal to offer him a grub from her jar, was being caught in Cat's stare on the first night. He hadn't returned to the bar since but, of course, he'd be there for fight night.

'Good morning, Sir,' Mrs Banks said, skipping to the door to greet Remington as he entered the station house. 'Can I get you a drink, or perhaps some breakfast?'

Remington was convinced she was about to pull a blade from somewhere and drive it into his chest. He nearly turned and fled.

'What's happening?' he said, not daring to step fully into the room.

'Oh, Sir, you are a one,' she said and reached to squeeze his shoulder.

He batted her paw away twice. 'What are you doing?'

'Sir,' Mrs Banks said in a tone that sounded much more like her. 'Just let me fix you a drink.'

'Okay…' he reluctantly accepted and looked over to Vixx who was trying to stifle a laugh.

'Sir,' Vixx said. 'You've a visitor.' She then opened her beak to mime the word *Superintendent.*

'Thank you, Sergeant and thank you Mrs Banks. A beverage would be marvellous.'

As he wandered toward the office door, he raised his voice. 'You know the best thing about being up here with you lovely lot?' he said. 'It's not having to see that god awful pain-in-the-hide boss of ours.'

Lennox was sitting on Remington's bucket with her hefty black feet crossed on his stone desk, her eyebrow arched, and a half smile played on her lips.

'Oh, Superintendent Lennox, what a lovely surprise.' He shut the door behind him and plonked himself on the bucket opposite. 'That's my chair you know.'

'Not until the day you outrank me, you flabby cretin,' she said. 'So, that'll be never I should think.'

Rem smiled at her. 'Checking up on me already?'

'Well, obviously. Checking you haven't burned the place to the ground yet.'

'It's early days.' Remington searched the desk surface for a tobacco leaf. 'Seriously, what can I do you for?'

'I thought I'd tick off one of your performance reviews, and a not so little birdy in there told me there's something fun going on here tonight. So, I shall be staying. You don't mind sleeping on the floor while I nab your bed, do you?'

'Do I have a choice?'

'You have the illusion of it.' She picked up a container of liquid from the desk. 'Like you had a choice about coming here.' She took a drink and then let the fluid fall back into the cup from her open mouth. 'Oh, sweet worms that's vile.'

'Your drink, Sir,' Mrs Banks said, opening the door. She delivered the container with a ridiculous flourish, bowing to Lennox as she backed out of the room.

Remington immediately poured the drink into the flowerpot in the corner of the office. 'My turn to water the plants anyway.' Remington rolled his eyes. 'We have a rota.'

'Let's get some air, shall we?' Lennox said, and they took their leave of the station hut.

They didn't talk much as Remington led her on a tour of the Burrow. She gave him some updates; Oscar was becoming an exemplary officer; Doc was still enjoying his job far too much, and the Rev was officially locked up for good. The demon had apparently refused to utter a word in his own defence at the trial, giving them little alternative even if the evidence hadn't been so persuasive. Neither Remington nor Lennox mentioned the raven again. Cull had predictably taken the Rev's place in earnest, and Lennox hoped the city would start to return to its regular rhythms.

'I can come home soon then?' Remington asked.

Lennox put her paw on his shoulder. 'There's still a pretty big price on you down there, Rem, and anyway, you look like you're doing well here.' She gave his shoulder a squeeze and they continued in silence until they found their way back to the station hut. Remington didn't mention Roadkill or his intention to question one of the fighters that evening, and Lennox didn't mention the missing persons case either. If Vixx had reported back to Lennox, then the Superintendent clearly wasn't too bothered.

'Doesn't that buzzing drive you mad?' Lennox had stopped and was turning her head slowly, trying to pinpoint the frequency Remington had noticed when he arrived.

'I barely notice it now.' Remington tried to attune, but it was barely a whisper to him now. 'My paws were the worst thing. All that noise in the ground.'

'I quite like it. It tickles.' She thumped a paw on the earth, the white bracelet above her foot blurred in the light. 'But then I'm not a sensitive little primrose like you.'

Remington laughed.

'It's good to see you with a smile on your snout again, Rem.' Tears filled Lennox's eyes.

'Now who's the primrose?'

'Well,' Lennox, pulled on her ears and shook her head. 'I've got some paperwork to sort out, so we'll rendezvous back here this evening for the fight?'

'Wouldn't miss it, Boss,' he said and gave her a nod.

Remington was shocked by the number of animals who turned out for fight night. He'd had to muscle his way through all manner of species laughing and wittering to each other. The Burrow had seemed such a barren and empty place, but the clearing around Cat's teemed with the noisy menagerie. For a moment it filled him with a sense of pride and happiness, all of these creatures united in comradery, but then he remembered why he was there. Keeping order in this chaos would be difficult enough but catching a deeper scent of the mysterious Roadkill's trail was going to be an even greater challenge.

'I didn't realise you had so many souls to protect here, Chief.' Lennox nudged Remington in the ribs and handed him a thimble of sticky liquid. It smelled terrible.

'Best not, I'm on duty,' Remington said. 'And my boss is here.'

'I'm sure she won't mind. I hear she's a delight.'

'You must have the wrong rabbit. She's an absolute clawcrusher.'

Remington took the thimble. They clinked tumblers and knocked the fluid back.

'Seriously though,' Lennox said, as she looked out over the sea of creatures toward a ring of dusty earth at the centre of the clearing. 'All seems friendly enough, so far. It's nice to be away from the smog for a night.'

There were no time limits on the fights at Cat's and the night drew deep. Several undercard bouts occurred, all ending with knock-downs and the floored fighters raising their paws in acceptance of their defeat. As far as violence went, it really was peaceful, a pleasant hubbub of excitable sounds. The hoots and trills of the feathered creatures in the trees, the squeaks and grunts of those on land, merged with the repetitive, but not unpleasant, din of Fingle and Glen's rural twanging. Slowly though, silence seemed to spread through the clearing like a wave as two creatures stepped into the ring for the main event of the evening.

It was obvious from the moment the two fighters came together to touch legs that the rat Remington had spoken to on his first evening back in the Burrow was giving up a huge size and weight advantage to her opponent. Brigg, the rat, was younger though and the far more athletic of the two. Jackie was a boar, small for his species, but still he dwarfed Brigg and most of the gathered crowd. As soon as the bell rang for the first round the rat showed her speed and skill, darting beneath the cumbersome blows of the black-skinned boar, and landing myriad punches down the larger creature's flanks. One slip though and it would surely have been the end for Brigg. All Jackie needed was one swipe and he would devastate the rat's bones. They had agreed not to use claws or tusks in the fight, at least, not deliberately anyway. As long as Brigg could avoid Jackie's reach, eventually the boar would be downed from exhaustion.

Remington and Lennox surveyed the crowd. There must have been near a full hundred creatures there all told, and crowds like this made Remington's fur itch. Most of the onlookers seemed to be on Brigg's side, cheering when she slid between Jackie's legs and landed a series of rabbit punches on the snarling boar's hide. The diversity of the crowd extended beyond species too. Here the full spectrum of the Burrow's class system was evident. The well-fed and glossy-furred standing and cheering alongside the ragged and hungry. Thick guts and visible ribs nestled together in the throng.

Bookies roamed the crowd taking offerings and calling out odds. On a couple of occasions Remington and Lennox made eye contact with these pedlars, but a quick nod of ascent told them that the police weren't here to intervene. They were just here to keep the peace and ensure that all violence was kept in the ring.

A roar of displeasure erupted. Brigg had misjudged a head movement and caught a glancing blow from Jackie's right leg, blood spitting from the rat's mouth. Jackie had barely caught her, but it was enough of a warning. Brigg steadied herself and moved more cautiously, a dazed look in her eye.

Lennox nudged Remington and subtly pointed her paw toward the right side of the crowd. Remington had seen the same thing. The small figure of a dormouse, impossibly thin, slipped around the outskirts of the crowd. Remington gestured to the left-paw side of the crowd, and Lennox followed his pointing to see another dormouse, equally frail, eyes bulging and ravenous. They were picking their way through the preoccupied fight-fans lifting anything they could filch from the distracted crowd, sliding their prizes into reed bags tied tight around their shoulders.

In the ring, Brigg was finding her rhythm again and landed a series of punches on Jackie's snout. The frustrated boar stepped backwards to avoid the discombobulating effects of the strikes. The dormice, sensing the end of the bout, started to move away from the crowd. Remington turned to face Lennox without a word. This wasn't what they were here for. They were just here to watch creatures beat the hell out of each other and keep the peace. Lennox smiled at Remington and nodded.

'Think you've got the legs for this?' she said.

'You take the one on the right.'

The dormice split in two directions and moved slowly at first, not wanting to draw attention. Remington and Lennox moved to opposite sides of the clearing, each following their mark. Rem crept toward the crowd, keeping the small rodent in his eyeline. The volume of the throng was growing as Brigg pummelled her larger opponent down to his hind knees. Suddenly the dormouse broke into a run. Remington shot after it. The dormouse ducked behind trees, and scurried through bramble, but Rem felt like he had when he first joined the force, like he was able to guess the swift creature's next move before it was made. He dove over the bramble and threw his weight around trees, keeping his target in his sight. In his peripheral vision, he saw a flash of dark brown in the starlight. A shadow lost in the shadows. Lennox was also keeping up with her quarry. The dormouse ducked into a narrow burrow. Remington saw it go and gritted his teeth, hurling himself claws first after the tiny creature, tearing at the earth to drag himself through the meagre hollow. The tunnel opened up into a much broader warren. Whoever had made this tunnel, it wasn't a dormouse. This was the network of a larger creature and Remington could smell the panic peeling from the rodent as he charged after it.

Remington heard the clatter of another chase just beyond the warren wall to his right. If the creatures were drawing together once more, then perhaps they were heading toward a dead end. Remington breathed deeply and willed himself on, ignoring the pain that started to seethe in his muscles. The tunnels were leading to a cleared space in the earth. Rem could sense it in the air, and he could feel it through the pulse of his paws. He almost felt cohesion with his pawsentia for the first time since his return to the Burrow. The second dormouse came into view from the adjacent tunnel, followed by Lennox. They had them. He pushed himself forward to be in front of Lennox and the dormice slowed. A shadow blotted out the tunnel and Remington's head struck something hard. He dropped to the floor, his momentum carrying his rear end over his head, and Lennox skidded to a halt just behind him.

'What the..?' Remington said, shaking his head and pulling

himself upright.

'It's a door. Someone just slammed it behind those two,' Lennox said, her nose twitching over the rock that had just appeared.

Remington snarled. 'Police! Open up or we will smoke you out.'

Lennox looked at him and cocked her head. 'Smoke you out?' she whispered, stifling a laugh and panting heavily. Remington shrugged and wiped blood from his forehead with his paw.

'Leave or I'll kill them all.' A voice came from beyond the stone.

'Excuse me, Madam, we just want to talk to the dormice,' Lennox said in her most officious police voice.

'I'll kill them, I swear!' The voice was high and cracked as it strained out each monosyllable.

Remington rolled his forelegs over one another and mouthed *Keep her talking*. He quietly began to drag his claws down the tunnel wall that the rock was wedged against.

'Okay, Madam, we don't want anyone getting hurt.' Lennox nodded at Rem. 'My partner's taken a bad blow to the head from your rock here, so it's going to be a couple of minutes before we can get him out of the warren, but we'll go. There's no need to hurt anyone.'

'Don't mess with me,' the voice screeched. 'I'm not hopping around. If you mess with me, their funerals are on you.'

Remington pushed the claws of his forepaws into the gap he'd carved between the mud and the rock and looked over at Lennox. She nodded and mouthed, *One… two… three.*

Remington flung his weight backwards levering the rock away and Lennox pounced, pinning an old rat with cracked yellow teeth against the floor.

'Quills,' Remington said as he entered the room. A cluster of half-starved dormice clung to each other, pressed up against the wall, their eyes quaking. They were squeaking and crying out.

'My babies. Don't take my babies,' the haggard old rodent wailed.

'It's okay. It's okay. You're all safe now.' Remington held out his paws to the dormice to try to settle them down. The hollow was filled with piles of shiny objects, clumps of bogweed, and small mounds of fine black powder.

'Heartbreak.' Remington pointed out the bags to Lennox.

'Take her and send some help, Rem,' Lennox said, pulling the old rat up to her feet with her paws behind her back. She shoved her to the badger. Remington nodded and led the whimpering creature out of the warren back toward Cat's.

By the time Rem made it back to the crowd, the fight was over. Brigg had worn Jackie down and eventually finished him by unbalancing the boar, flipping him onto his back. By then, Jackie had been too exhausted to get back to his trotters. The rest of the evening entailed everything Remington hated most about police work. It was all logistics and admin, working out what to do with the dormice pups, and making sure the evidence was carefully documented. He was relieved Lennox had been there. She had a gift for organisation and by the early hours of the morning, she had most of the major issues squared away. She had even struck a deal with the Burrow's school, to take in the dormice until more permanent homes could be found. It was as dark as the Burrow's starlight could allow by the time Remington and Lennox had made their way back to his quarters.

'I can't stop thinking about those poor kids,' Lennox said. 'This was supposed to be a nice, quiet getaway.'

Remington nodded and poured them both a drink. 'You've still got some moves though.'

'Funny, I was going to say the same for you. Just like back when we started, right?'

'Yeah, I don't remember being this sore afterwards back then.' Remington stretched his limbs.

'It's not all bad though,' Lennox said. The green flamed up in her eyes.

'What did you do?' Remington narrowed his eyes and knocked back his drink.

'Well, amidst all the shiny bits, there was also, this.' Lennox pulled out a small lump of bogweed wrapped in a leaf. 'I might have forgotten to log this one into evidence.'

Remington picked up two sharp rocks from the corner of the dwelling and handed them to Lennox. She had always been better at creating sparks than him.

'There's just one tiny other thing, Rem,' Lennox said taking a pull on the rolled leaf before passing it to the badger.

Rem looked back at her. 'What now?'

'The deal I made with the school,' she said as she lay down on the dry moss of Remington's bed. 'You're going there in the morning to give the kids a talk on the dangers of drugs and other criminal activity.' She pulled an apologetic grimace. 'Community relations and all that.'

Remington wanted to be annoyed with her, and he knew he would be in the morning, but at that moment, he shrugged and lay down next to her. They lay in silence and passed the bogweed between them. They listened to the click and fizz of the night creatures and watched the smoke drift and spin lazily toward the ceiling.

# Chapter Thirteen

*The badger dreams...*

*of time made visible,*  
*of green tendrils spiralling*  
*from clocks carved into oak.*  
*He dreams of ancestors,*  
*of a cavern at the centre*  
*of a warren, air thick with mould.*  
*He dreams of tunnels winding*  
*through worm-eaten earth*  
*each lined with doors of rock.*  
*He dreams of culling.*  
*He dreams of eyes like tar.*  
*He dreams of falling into them.*

*He wakes.*

Remington opened his eyes to the familiar sound of scampering on the roof. He pounced from the bed, flung open the hut door and leapt down the front steps. He turned to face his quarters. Remington drew himself up, craned his neck, and stepped backwards over the cool, dew-slick grass. Then he saw something shift in the mist.

'Hey, who's up there?' Remington picked up a stone and tossed it onto the roof. There was a clang, and the shuffling stopped. Remington sniffed at the air. He never could detect much through his nose. His palate wasn't as refined as most of the other DIs, but that special extra sense that the old schoolers in the Met prized, his gut, had made up for it. The morning smelled of rain and grass.

Remington drummed his claws on his jaw and considered popping back inside to grab a tobacco leaf, but he didn't want to risk his new alarm clock disappearing into the mist and trees again. He rolled his shoulders, yawned loudly, and stomped up the two steps to the door. He gripped the slab of wood that formed his door and pushed himself flat against the wall. Remington flung the door back into the frame with a clatter. Tiny claws pattered over the roof toward him. He looked up to see the small, copper body of a young red squirrel fly over his head and land a cow's length in front of him.

'Stop,' said Remington. The creature jolted upright, its muscles tensed, ears pulled back. 'It's okay. You're safe. I just want a word.'

The creature did not move. Remington slowly moved around the squirrel, sidestepping through the damp grass. The squirrel's body remained still, but it followed Remington with its eyes as soon as the badger crested its peripheral vision.

'What's your name?' Remington kept his tone as light as he could. The squirrel stared. 'Do you live near here?' Nothing. 'Where's your mum?' Remington was now directly in front of the squirrel and could see she was a kit, barely past her first season.

'Can you speak?' Remington asked. The squirrel nodded. 'Will you speak to me?' The squirrel shook her head, still rigid from the neck down. 'Will you tell me why?'

The squirrel scratched one hand-like paw with the other. Her ears twitched.

'You know what this place is?' Remington gestured to his quarters and the larger station hut behind. She shook her head again, slowly, keeping her eyes on Remington's. 'This is the police station. I'm a policeman. That means it's safe.'

The squirrel opened her mouth, and in a high reedy voice

said, 'Stranger.'

Remington nodded. 'You're a smart girl. You shouldn't trust strangers but I'm a policeman and that means it's okay to talk to me.' The squirrel looked at Remington and scratched her legs.

'You've been waking me up running about on my roof every morning.' Remington said, offering his best simulation of the Met-issue reassuring smile. If the red squirrel knew the appropriate response for a civilian to give to the Met-issue greeting, she did not show it. She turned on her hind legs and sprinted, leaping into the mist. Remington thought about giving chase, but he was no match for a squirrel on his best day, and he could feel the stiffness in his legs from the previous night's chase. A tobacco leaf breakfast seemed a far more sensible option.

It wasn't until he re-entered the hut that Remington realised Lennox was gone. He sighed and ran a claw down his snout. She had left a note for him scratched onto the main box in his kitchen. It read: *Don't be late for school.*

The school, an assemblage of branch, bracken, and scavenged materials, was grander than Remington remembered. A legend passed from year to year when he was a cub, told of giant creatures who had built the school thousands of seasons before. Now though, despite its expansions, it seemed far less impressive than the repurposing and excavations that had gone into the creation of the Met. The sound of singing drew him like a current around the back of the school to its courtyard. He leant against the trunk of an oak that still housed the scar of his initials in its bark and watched. A pale rabbit was surrounded by the huddled figures of the dormice liberated from the old charlatan the day before. Their eyes still bulged unnaturally from their delicate skulls, and they shared the jittering quake of creatures who'd grown up in a fraternity of punishment, constantly on the lookout for where the next blow might come from. There were some smiles though, and all gripped morsels of food in their unfeasibly small fingers.

Some held the clumps close to their nostrils, savouring the tang, and others allowed themselves surreptitious licks, but for all the time Remington stood unnoticed, he didn't see a single tooth break into any lump of food.

'Would you like to join us?' the rabbit called, shielding her eyes from the sun with a paw. The dormice all jerked their faces toward Remington, eyes wide and glistening.

'Thank you,' Remington said. 'I'm the policeman.'

The dormice began to squeak. It was a rushed sound that seemed to vibrate on the air.

'Perhaps you should wait there,' the rabbit said, and ushered the dormice into the school building, leaving Remington in the courtyard.

Remington ran a claw over his initials, F.R.P. He remembered carving this on a day when his class teacher, Miss Plunkett, had sent him out of a history lesson. He couldn't recall what his offense had been, only that they had been learning about the history of animal councils and how they had worked, not worked, and been corrupted through the ages.

'I don't think you made a great first impression on them last night.' Remington turned to find the rabbit hopping toward him.

'I'm sorry?' he said.

'The greys,' she nodded toward the school entrance. 'It was you who found them last night wasn't it?'

'Yeah,' he held out his paw. 'It's DI Platypus, Rem.'

She touched her paw to his. 'You did a good thing.'

'I didn't mean to scare them.' Remington felt the rabbit's paw quake gently as it met his. She was a white-furred bunny with tall ears, and blue eyes.

'It's Miss Carrol,' she said, taking her paw back and smoothing down her fur. She seemed as nervous as the dormice. 'I wouldn't worry too much. They don't really understand what's happening. I'm not sure I do.' She twitched her nose. Her face carried black markings that reminded Remington of some human artefacts Doc had shown him once, inky splodges that mirrored each other on both sides.

'That makes all of us.' Remington took out a bundle of tobacco leaves from his underarm. He offered one to Miss Carrol. The teacher shook her head and crinkled her nose.

'It's going to take some time to get them back to being children again, if that's even possible.'

'How do you mean?'

'That awful fiend who had them. She's been filling their heads with all kinds of nonsense about the creatures and ghosts in the woods she was protecting them from.'

'Creatures and ghosts-'

'Francis!' a voice called. Remington froze. He knew that voice. 'Francis Platypus, we will have none of that here, thank you.'

'Miss Plunkett,' he said as he turned to face a formidable beaver. 'You're still…'

'Alive?' She snatched his leaf from him and tossed it over her shoulder.

'I was going to say *here*.'

'Well, I am both, young man.' She gripped Remington's chin and turned his head left and right, peering through her beady eyes at him. 'Let me look at you.' She sucked air over her teeth and tutted. 'Not been looking after yourself, I see. Given up on the P.E. as well. Are you drinking enough water?'

'Well, I, Miss Plunkett, I try-' he began but she cut him off, still holding his face.

'That's Head Plunkett to you, Francis,' the beaver snapped. Miss Carrol's eyes met his and she quickly turned away, biting her lip, the hint of a smile pulling at her cheeks. 'I am the leader of the institution now.' She finally let go of his face and straightened herself up. 'What have you got for us today?' She looked at him in the same manner that he remembered from the history lessons he'd had to prematurely vacate.

'Got?' he asked.

'Good grief, Francis. Still the same vacant expression and lack of preparation. What are you planning for the children today? How do you intend to use your expertise to engage and mould the minds of those impressionable and bright young things?'

'I thought I'd answer their questions.' He caught Miss Carrol's eye again and found himself having to stifle a laugh.

'Always the chuckler weren't you, Francis? Those children don't know what they ought to or want to ask. It's your job to answer the questions they didn't know they should be asking.' Head Plunkett rolled her eyes and sighed. 'Well, this won't do. You'll have them joining gangs and dropping out of school within the month.' She placed her digits on the sides of her own head and circled them as though Rem had somehow triggered a migraine. 'Perhaps Miss Carrol here can help you to plan something more edifying.'

Miss Carrol opened her mouth to voice an objection, but the Head hushed her with a wave.

'We know where you are,' Plunkett said. 'We'll organise something with the station, and we'll try again tomorrow. Right…' She turned to Miss Carrol, 'I believe you have a lesson to teach.'

'Yes, Ma'am,' the teacher said and, with a subtle dip to Plunkett and a brief glance at Remington, she hopped back into the school.

'She's a good one, that doe is, Francis. Now, be off with you and do something useful with your day. There's a good lad.' Plunkett pulled a speck from Remington's whiskers with a tut and nudged him on his way. 'Oh, and Francis,' she said as she placed a paw on his back. 'Thank you for getting those pups out of that fiend's clutches. They'll be alright with us.'

Remington took the long way to the station hut, his mind swirling like the morning mist at his feet.

# Chapter Fourteen

Remington felt like a cub again as he loped away from the school. The power Head Plunkett was still able to wield with that strained voice and withering stare was enough to make him want to confess to every piece of graffiti he'd ever carved into a desk and each spitball he'd bullseyed onto a teacher's back – never hers of course, the adulation of one's peers was only worth so much. He considered heading back to ask if she fancied joining him for the interrogation of the rat he and Lennox had apprehended the previous night. The plan had been to question the old swindler in the afternoon, but he supposed his shortened school day offered the opportunity to regain some of the authority he'd just had zapped from him.

The rat had been stewing (not literally, although one of the Take Back Eden movements' complaints was that the Met was a barbaric institution) in the cells beneath the station hut all night and that was usually enough for any detainee to make their way through the typical stages of the recently arrested. First there was the anger, all claws and writhing; then came the begging: *please let me go. I'll give you a bigger prey, someone really savage.* He would find out from the voles how she'd responded so far when he got there. While he was at it, he'd also find out their names.

'Weren't expecting you until the afternoon,' Mrs Banks said as Remington entered the hut. 'You could've let us know if there'd been a change of plans.'

'Good to have you back to normal, Mrs Banks,' Remington said. She scowled. Remington dropped a worm onto Chief

Banks' desk with a wink.

'Oh no you don't.' Mrs Banks stomped across the room and picked up the wriggling creature. 'He's watching his bloods.' She opened the door and flung the worm out into the day. The chief rolled his eyes at Remington.

'A thousand apologies, Mrs Banks,' Remington said. 'So, how's the prisoner?'

'You'd have to ask Chris and Claire, wouldn't you? I've got quite enough on my plate, thank you very much, what with all the admin that comes with taking on an army of bloody dormice.'

'You're an angel, Mrs Banks. The Met is truly lucky to have you.'

Mrs Banks stopped scowling briefly. It made her face look odd. 'Yes, well, Chris is on watch now. He relieved Claire just after the sun came up.'

'Thank you very much,' he said, and for the first time he was actually grateful to her as she'd saved him an awkward conversation regarding the names of the trainees.

A gust of wind rattled through the hut as Vixx appeared in the doorway.

'Perfect timing, Sergeant,' said Remington. 'You up for an interrogation?'

A hollow in the corner of the hut led to the crypt which housed the holding cells. There were only two.

'What do you do if you have more than two suspects in here?' Remington asked.

'I think that'll be a puzzle for you to solve if it ever happens,' said Vixx. 'Mind you, more than one and we'd have to find a new archive room.'

Remington peered into the first cell. It was crammed with boxes and general detritus. 'We really are far from the city,' he said to himself. Vixx gave him a cock of the head but said nothing. 'How's our guest, Chris?' he called down to the end cell. The vole jolted upright.

'I'm Claire, Sir,' she replied, standing to attention.

Remington made a mental note to find an extra juicy worm for Chief Banks tomorrow. 'Of course,' Remington said. 'Dark down here, isn't it?'

'She said anything?' Vixx asked. Remington gave her a glance. He was surprised by the bird's forthrightness but if she wished to take the lead then he had no objections. It was some distance from the tentative young officers he was used to working with.

'She hasn't shut up all night,' the vole replied, stretching her spindly limbs. 'But she's not said a word to me or Chris. It's like we aren't even here.'

'Thanks, Claire. Feel free to take five.' Remington accepted an awkward dip of respect, and she hurried out of the tunnel.

Remington and Vixx looked into the cell. Beyond the cage bars, the repurposed remnants of some sort of human railing, the old rat sat on a hump of hay. She could have been mistaken for a heap of dirty rags were it not for the words falling breathlessly through her broken, yellow teeth.

'They think they're alive,' she muttered. 'They don't know it's over. They don't know this tunnel, this Burrow, this world will outlive them. They don't know they are already ghosts.' She stopped and craned her neck. 'The wisp is here, the wisp has come, come for you when the day is done.' Her ears flicked back and forth. 'Yes... no... I didn't,' she said, her jaundiced eyes raw and glistening.

Vixx rapped on the bars. Remington flinched and cleared his throat.

'Excuse us, Madam,' he said. The rat continued craning her neck as if listening for a frequency.

'Her name's Malin,' said Vixx. 'Old crone was a teacher for a while at the school, and a few years back she just upped and left. That's what Plunkett told us anyway but seemed to me there was more to it.'

'You've been busy, Sergeant.'

'Oh, I didn't mean to be presumptuous, Sir.'

He waved away her comment. 'No, no, you keep it up. You're doing a fine job of covering up my rust.'

Vixx nodded and turned back to the cage. 'Malin, cut the snake whispers and talk to us.'

'The wisp is here.' The ragged rat ignored her and continued. 'The wisp has come, come for you when the day is done. From below he rises.'

Vixx wrapped her talons around the bars and opened her beak, but Remington held up a claw to stop her from speaking.

'Sir?'

'I know that song. My mum used to sing it to us when we were cubs.' He dragged a claw across his snout. 'The wisp is here, the wisp has come, come for you when the day is done. Sleep now little one, don't say a word. The wisp's in the wind and the wisp's in the herd…' He paused as he tried to recover the rest of the words.

'How bloody sweet,' said Vixx. 'Stuff of feather plucking nightmares.'

'I never really thought about it but, yeah, you've got a point.'

'Everybody's dead anyway,' Malin said. Something close to a laugh escaped her mouth.

'I've had enough of this.' Vixx gripped the railing and pulled it open. She grabbed Malin by the shoulders and shook her. 'Enough, you old bat.'

'Bats? Yes, always the bats.' The rat's eyes rolled to the root that crossed like a beam on the ceiling of the cell.

'You want to see your babies again?'

The hag stopped raving and her eyes dropped back down to meet Vixx's. 'Lies?'

'Maybe, maybe not but talking to us is the only hope you've got of ever seeing them again, and I *can* promise you that.'

'It's the wisp, and the bats. Always the bats.' She turned her head to look at Remington. 'And him, the badger. He knows. He hears it.'

Remington stepped into the cell and gestured for Vixx to move back. He crouched and looked at the prisoner. 'So?'

'You have very low friends in some very high places,' she said. A wheezing laugh bubbled in her throat. 'They know you're here.'

'Who does?'

'Everyone. The messages get sung through the trees, drawn through roots like burrowers from tunnels in subtle shifts. The whole wood is rustling now. Things are awake. Things are growing.'

'What can you tell me about Roadkill?'

'What? Silly boy Toady? Roadie Roadie, king of the toadies? He's not what's hunting you. Pay him no mind.'

'So, who should I be looking out for?'

'From below he rises.'

'Enough of the nursery rhymes,' Vixx said. Remington had almost forgotten she was there.

'Oh no, not a rhyme, no songs from the wisp. The wisp just is.' She raised a finger and pointed at Remington. 'He's seen. He knows.'

Remington furrowed his brow and scratched his head. 'I have no bloody clue what you're on about. But you're saying Roadkill's a toad?'

The hag cackled. Vixx looked at Remington and cocked her head. Remington shrugged and popped a tobacco leaf on his tongue. The rat's cackling stopped. She eyed the tip of the leaf as it poked from Remington's lips.

Vixx snatched another from Remington's paw. 'Right, you want a smoke? Cut the whispering willows crap and tell us something about Roadkill.'

'Toady's of no consequence.'

'We might be the police but we're not completely clueless.'

Vixx took a corner of leaf and chewed it in her beak. 'In amongst all your filth and shiny stuff we found enough bags of batshit-based fun to keep a drove of donkeys dancing until December. So, spill.'

Vixx pointed the rest of the leaf toward Malin's mouth. The crone nodded and gratefully accepted. She chewed hard for a few moments.

'I maybe got some stuff off one of his lackeys. Little rat lady, pretty devil for a flea circus, but I never…' Vixx tore the leaf from the rat's open mouth and tossed it. It bounced off the cell wall leaving a gleam of saliva.

'Steady on, Sergeant,' said Rem.

Vixx gripped Malin's shoulder, letting her talon pierce the skin.

'You were running that pickpocketing scam for Roadkill, weren't you?'

'Not my babies,' the rat cried out.

'Roadkill gave you drugs. You gave him whatever those poor little things could pilfer.'

Malin howled in pain as Vixx's talons sunk deeper. She tugged at the flesh.

'I can't. He'll kill me.'

'Maybe I'll fly you out of here right now and make sure that pretty little rat you're so fond of sees us getting all cosy. Roadkill fond of all types of rat, is he?'

'Sergeant, enough.' Remington put his paw on the top of Vixx's wing. Vixx let her talons sink a little deeper. The rat screamed.

'I don't know where he is. He has a place, a secret place, a cave-'

Vixx finally released the pathetic creature. 'What's at this secret place?'

'It's where he makes his stuff,' the rat moaned and curled up on the hay sobbing. She buried herself in the dry yellow fibres. 'Please let me see my babies,' she whimpered.

'Not a chance,' Vixx spat at her.

'We'll see what we can do,' Remington said and tossed a

couple of tobacco leaves beside her.

'Quills, Sergeant,' Remington said as they made their way out of the tunnel. The rat's sobs faded into the darkness. 'We need to have a chat.'

'Sorry, Boss,' she said. 'Was that a bit much? I figured we were going for a good cop, bad cop thing on her.'

'Well, I wasn't unimpressed, but there's bad cop and then there's psychotic cop. Let's just take it steady, eh? And maybe no more physical violence.'

Vixx looked devastated. She hung her head low.

'Unless they're really asking for it,' Remington added.

'Oi! This isn't a bloody creche, you know!' Mrs Banks greeted them as they emerged into the light of the main room. 'Visitor in your office.'

Remington looked over to the open doorway. The young red squirrel was sat nervously hugging her own tail, hunched up on a bucket.

'Says she'll only talk to the badger policeman.'

# Chapter Fifteen

The sun had fully broken the morning and the squirrel's fur bloomed a fierce red in the light. It looked like the bucket was cradling and stoking its own fire.

'Hello again, kit,' Remington said as he walked into the office.

The squirrel started and flipped around to face him. 'Can the door shut?' she asked.

'Sure.' Remington pulled the thin strip of wood over the opening and sat behind his desk. 'Do you want to tell me your name?'

She shook her head. Her eyes were focused on Remington's but the rest of her was a continual flux and judder of movement. Her ears flicked. Her tail twisted and rolled. Her claws scratched at her fur.

'Okay, well, I'm Remington.'

'Policeman?'

'Yes, detective actually.'

'Not policeman?' She paused in her movements.

'Yes, it's a special kind of policeman.' He gave her a reassuring smile, but she eyed him doubtfully. 'I solve mysteries.'

'Like if people disappear?'

'That's right. Is that what you want to talk to me about?'

The squirrel shuffled on the bucket and looked around the room. She pulled her tail in front of her and squeezed it tight as though cuddling a teddy. A scarlet feather was wound into her tail fur. She rubbed her nose on its edge.

'Do you know someone who's disappeared?' Remington asked.

She started to shake and was soon juddering again as though

someone had started a motor deep within her heart. She nodded.

'Okay, Red, who's gone missing?'

'You can help?'

'It's my job.'

'Mum,' she said so quietly Rem barely caught the word.

Remington scratched his cheek. He'd guessed this might be where the conversation was heading. The truth was that missing people weren't something the organised forces focused on. Sure, the policing network had been put in place as part of the grand overarching move toward instilling some form of control and governance over the population, but wild was still wild, and dangers were everywhere. A missing mother was as likely to be found again as a crow was to give up its wings.

Remington pulled the tablet with the missing persons etchings in front of him and placed a claw on its surface. 'Okay, Red, when did you last see her?'

'You'll help?'

'It's a mystery, isn't it? I told you, that's what I do. I solve mysteries.'

The squirrel wriggled in her seat. The hint of a smile appeared on her face. 'It's been a long time.'

'How long?'

'I was smaller.'

'How small?'

The squirrel jumped from the bucket and stood upright. She held her hand-like paw at neck height.

'So, quite a while then,' Remington said. He rested his head in his paw and looked at the kit. 'Do you have any clues?' He felt a twinge of guilt as he said this, but surely the truth would be crueller.

'I followed tracks.'

'Tracks?'

The squirrel nodded and bounced back onto the bucket. 'Yuh huh. I got her scent, and I followed her claw marks on trees, and I got really far, but…' she stopped bouncing. 'I keep getting stuck.'

'Stuck?'

'I lose the tracks.'

Remington raised his head from his paw. 'Would that be on my roof by any chance? The hut you were on top of when I saw you?'

The squirrel nodded and tears welled in her eyes. 'I keep following them, but the smell is gone, and there's no more tracks.'

'Can you tell me where you live?'

'It's safe?'

'Policeman, remember.'

'It's the tall tree next to your hut. We have a place up real high.'

'Is anyone else at home?'

The squirrel shook her head slowly. Tears were running from her eyes now. 'Just me and Mum.'

'Do you have food?'

She nodded. 'We were real good at collecting… before.'

'Okay, we'll get to the bottom of this,' Remington said.

'I can help?' The squirrel hopped onto her feet on the bucket. The tears stopped.

'I'll need you to,' said Remington. 'You will be my deputy detective. It'll take both of us to solve this one.'

The squirrel nodded and jigged up and down. 'What should I do?'

'I need you to get yourself home safe, and quickly. And then, come to see me first thing tomorrow at my hut, okay?'

The squirrel nodded.

'Okay, Deputy,' he said. 'Now what shall I call you?'

'Red's good.' She beamed at him.

Remington sighed deeply as he watched the small red bundle of fur flash out of the hut, scattering papers and making Mrs Banks spill her drink.

'I'm clocking off early,' Remington announced.

'Afraid not,' Mrs Banks said with a smirk. 'You've got one more appointment today, Sir.'

Remington's shoulders dropped. He looked at her and raised an eyebrow.

'Yes, Sir, Headmistress Plunkett sent a messenger. You've got a lunch with one of her teachers, to rectify the pig's ear you made of it this morning.'

'I've got a lunch? What am I, a bloody beaver?'

'Do beavers have lunch meetings?' Mrs Banks said. 'And a thank you wouldn't go amiss.'

'Mrs Banks,' Remington said bowing deeply as he backed out of the station hut. 'A thousand thank yous for your dedicated service. This place would surely crumble were it not for your gracious and diligent presence.'

Under the warmth of the afternoon sun, Remington felt a chill that seeped through his fur to the roots. Autumn in the Burrow felt like more of an animal than a season. You had to tread with care, or it might wake and flinch suddenly. It was a dreamless, shifting thing. The breeze had the bite of Winter, but the Summer was not long smothered and the leaves still crackled with warmth. Despite his reluctance to attend any meeting set up by his old teacher, Remington was relieved to cross the threshold of Cat's and shut out the Burrow behind him.

Miss Carrol was already seated by one of the holes in the wall that served as windows, her paws tightly gripping a large thimble of steaming something. She was staring out beyond the auburn camouflage of shrub and hedge that clung in tight groupings around Cat's. This place, the Burrow, felt as far away from Rem's old life in the metropolis as the rabbit's mind seemed to be. She turned and waved, offering a smile as she saw Remington hovering in the doorway. Remington stumbled on the uneven floor and gave an embarrassed grin as he sat opposite her.

'Miss Carrol,' he said and held out his paw.

She shook his paw. Remington felt the heat from the pads pulsing with residual warmth from the thimble.

'Someone's been a naughty boy then?' Cat purred as she appeared at the table, a gleam in her eye, her bright white fangs showing as she smiled.

'What?' Remington looked up startled.

'Been sent to see teacher, I see,' Cat laughed. 'Now what can I get my favourite plod? Same as the other night?'

'Best not,' said Remington. 'I'm on duty.'

Cat nodded with a look of mock wisdom on her face. 'Perfectly understood, nothing fermented for the working boar.' She stalked away as silently as she'd appeared.

'She's something, isn't she?' Miss Carrol watched Cat as she slunk back to the bar. Every movement looked practiced and predatory.

Remington studied the markings on the rabbit's face. The black shapes seemed to move of their own accord as she twitched her nose, and her fur caught the light.

'Terrifying,' said Remington. 'So, I gather I failed my first day back at school today? The old battle-axe not too angry, is she?'

'Oh, Headmistress? No, she's very formidable, but she does mean well.' Miss Carrol lifted her thimble and sipped.

'How are the little ones doing?'

Miss Carrol looked at Rem over the rim of the vessel. 'They seem okay, considering. Keep asking after Mamma though.'

'And by "Mamma" they mean..?'

'The old rat that had them all stealing.' She put down the thimble and huffed sharply.

'Think it would be good for them to see her?'

'Is that a possibility?'

'Well, it's probably not protocol but whatever's best for them.'

'I don't know,' Carrol looked down into her drink. 'Probably not, but it's a challenge just to get them to stop staring out the windows. I think they feel like prisoners in the school.'

A tumbler was thrust under Remington's nose and he

flinched as Cat appeared next to him again.

'Quills!' He shook his head and looked up at her. 'I wish you wouldn't do that.'

'Naw, come on Detective.' She pinched his chin between a couple of claws gently. 'You know it's bad business to prey on my customers.' She mouthed the word *enjoy* and slid to another table where a hedgehog was nursing a large receptacle of something fermented and volatile.

Remington took a drink from the cup and coughed. Whatever it was, it was definitely fermented. Cat was looking over at Rem. She smiled, tilted her head, and raised an enquiring paw. Remington gave her a smile and returned the gesture with a claw of approval.

'Yep,' said Remington, half to himself. 'She is something else.'

'Did Malin say anything?' Miss Carrol asked, and the smile dropped from Remington's face.

'You know her?'

'It's a small Burrow, Detective.' She rubbed her paws on her cup. 'Just about everyone knows everyone, and it's all anyone's been talking about today. She was my mentor at the school when I started.'

Remington felt an itch in his gut. 'I'm told she just left one day.'

Miss Carrol nodded.

'No warning at all? Even looking back, nothing comes to mind?'

'Not really. I mean, she was stressed out like we all are. It's not as easy a job as everyone thinks.'

'I'm sure,' said Remington. 'Long holidays must be nice though.'

Miss Carrol's grip tightened on the mug and she let out a grunt of frustration. 'If you weren't the police chief, I'd slap you for that. Do you have any idea what it's like to take responsibility for all of those tiny souls and try to either not mess them up, or try to tidy up the mess that's been done to them? All of that while not being sure if today you'll be covered in puke, wee, or snot?'

'I'm kidding,' Remington said, holding his paws up in

surrender. 'The puke and urine sounds familiar though. You thought about becoming a police officer?'

Miss Carrol's pursed face softened. 'No, I'd rather try to get to them before they turn into criminals.'

Remington raised his drink and Miss Carrol clinked it with hers. 'So, tell me, what was Malin like before she disappeared?'

'Am I being interrogated, Detective?'

'No, quills no. Sorry, I'm just interested. I spent the morning chatting to her, and she seemed... well... I don't know. I just felt a bit sorry for her.'

Miss Carrol blinked at him. 'She kidnapped kids and turned them into criminals.'

'Yeah, true, but it didn't look like anyone else was looking out for them.'

'Those pups are half bloody starved and riddled with mites. Whatever she was doing, it was not looking out for them.'

Remington took another drink and let the sensation of whatever Cat had served burn its way down his throat. 'Yes, you're right. Sorry, maybe it's the city making me soft.'

'That doesn't sound right.' Miss Carrol relaxed into her seat again. 'I thought the big scary city was supposed to toughen everyone up and beat the soft country life out of you.'

'Ha, true, but someone like Malin offering shelter in return for lifting a few easy marks would be seen as a philanthropist down there.' Remington looked over at Cat who was mixing drinks and putting on a show, dextrously flipping containers over her head and catching them. 'You'd be astonished how many youngsters just vanish into the brickwork and smog.'

They sat in silence for a while as they watched the landlady perform her dizzying cocktail pyrotechnics. Remington drained his cup and looked back at Miss Carrol, surprised to find she was looking at him.

'So, anyway,' he said. 'I suppose we'd best keep that boss of yours happy and get down to work.'

'Absolutely!' The teacher's eyes grew wide, and her face was suddenly more animated. 'Let's plan your first lesson.'

A gust of wind lopped one of Miss Carrol's ears and a shadow was thrown over the bar as Vixx landed outside the window next to them. Remington tried not to let the relief show on his face.

'Yes, Sergeant?'

'I've found something out in the ghylls, Sir.' Vixx said under her breath.

'And what kind of something is it?'

'A trail, Sir. Red squirrel fur's my guess, but I couldn't get close enough through the alder canopies to be sure.' She cast a sideways glance at Miss Carrol and raised her wing through the window, screening herself and Remington from the rabbit.

'Okay, Sergeant, I suppose I'd better take a look. Give us two secs.'

Vixx withdrew her wing back through the window and stepped a few paces away.

'I'm afraid I'm going to have to go,' Remington said.

Miss Carrol's mouth tightened. 'But we haven't started-'

'I'm sorry. Maybe we could pick this up again later?'

'Oh, you just assume that I don't have any plans?'

Remington shuffled in his seat. 'Okay, perhaps we can just say that we-'

'I'll see you here at sunset,' the rabbit said. 'You're buying.'

Remington nodded. 'Sounds fair to me. Oh, and one other tiny thing,' he said as he stood up. 'Any chance you've got room for another little one at the school?'

# Chapter Sixteen

After a brief detour via his dwelling to pick up the leftover bogweed, Remington followed Vixx as she led him toward the wet woodlands. His plan had been to offer the contraband to Fingle and Glen as a peace offering, but he needn't have bothered. Vixx's route to the ghylls had looped around to the opposite side of the boggy edge. He wouldn't have time to trek back around if he were to make it back to Cat's for his meeting with Miss Carrol.

'Where are you taking me?' Remington muttered under his breath as he watched Vixx circle overhead, leading him steadily into the thick fug of the ghylls. He spotted the bleed of cottongrass this time as he picked his way through brambles and into the darkly knotted canopy of tangled willow and alder. Vixx had been right. There was no way she'd have been able to risk swooping too low here for fear of tearing a wing, and if she'd walked in on the ground, she'd soon have her talons stuck in the thick suck of the boggy mud. Still, her eyesight amazed him. That she'd been able to pick out even the hint of potential red squirrel fur seemed a minor miracle considering his own visual impairments.

He stumbled as his paw caught on a root, and cursed as his nose met the thick, sodden floor. He lifted his head and groaned. The trees looked drunk, wilted things that cowered into the brown, treacly mire choked with ragwort. He felt the blister of a thousand eyes watching him. He wheeled his own around the macabre woodland graveyard. Save for the buzzing of mosquitoes and the occasional flash of dragonfly wing, he was alone. The gnawing at the back of his mind would not cease though. He was sure someone was watching him, and it wasn't just Vixx.

It didn't seem to matter what the time of day was, the ghylls held their own climate and they were militant in always keeping it in an uneven state of humid gloom. Murk and mist clung to the half thickets, and shadows of branches. Everything hung with grey. Rem pushed himself onto his haunches, wrenching his forepaws from the powerful suck of the bog. He looked up to the crosshatch web of branches. If Vixx was still there, he had no way of knowing. The young sergeant had impressed him so far though. She was eager to please, ambitious, and seemed to have a mean streak that could serve her well if she were reposted to the city. Remington was keen to take her back with him when he made his return. She'd be a good addition to the team, and he was lacking in feathered allies. A dark shadow shifted through a clump of yellow flag iris. *Crow*, Remington thought immediately, but a subsequent splash brought him back to his senses.

Remington kept still and twitched his ears. Something had slipped into the deeper water ahead of him. It would be tricky enough to feel a route through the mire where he could keep his body largely above the surface without having to worry about something else joining him. The uneven ground of the ghylls required a slow pace of tentatively feeling for dips and holes. It was probably a harmless feral frog. Dotted around the wetland were pools and ponds which provided an ideal refuge for small amphibious creatures. Remington sniffed the air but couldn't catch the scent of anything animal over the stench of rot. The wealth of partially submerged trees caused an olfactive soup of decomposing wood. Puny amphibians were of no concern, but where there are small harmless animals, one usually finds their predators.

Remington shook the thought from his head and tried to refocus on looking for strands of red fur. He walked steadily forward, feeling the water gradually rise over his belly. His paws had found a runway of sedge in the water that stretched from one side of the bog to the other. As long as he kept to his narrow pathway, he knew he should be spared a battle with the grasping mud of the deeper marsh.

The glistening surface trembled and Remington stopped. He scanned the murky water. A small flutter of ripples fanned out to his left. He considered turning back. The twitching face of the young squirrel, Red, swam into his mind. He wouldn't turn back. How could he? As Remington stood motionless, his keen senses honed in on the subtle movements in the water. The ripples had a peculiar rhythm, not the typical pattern of a frog or a fish. His heart quickened. The ghylls, with its tangled wetlands and secretive inhabitants, had always been an enigma, and Remington prayed it would keep its secrets to itself.

He strained his eyes and tried to pierce the gloom. The oppressive humidity made him feel as if he was wading through fog. His fur stuck to his skin. Through the gaps in the knotted canopy, tall birch trees arched into the sky. He couldn't see Vixx. The stutter of sunlight cast a dappled hue on the water's surface, creating eerie patterns that seemed to dance and taunt him.

A sudden splash erupted from the water to his left. Remington was definitely not alone. His mind jangled with thoughts of the potential dangers that might lay hidden beneath the surface. As if sensing his fear, the water trembled again, and this time, he caught a glimpse of movement. A dark shape slithered through the shallows. Remington's breath caught in his throat. He watched the slow, purposeful slide of reptilian skin as it crested the surface and then disappeared. He peered into the dark water. He had been a powerful swimmer once, but that was before. He saw a flash of his wife's lifeless face next to the Thames. He would be no match for the lithe athleticism of a snake unless he was on dry land.

He studied the surface and took a gentle step forward, trying to cause as little disturbance in the water as possible. He was perhaps fifty paces from the dry haven on the other side. The water was still. He took another pace forward. Wild or not, and regardless of Remington's current state of fitness, it would be a brave serpent that openly tried to take on a badger. This was the snake's habitat, its home, Remington told himself. It was probably just keeping an eye on the intruder. No need to panic. He took another step forward.

With barely a break in the water's surface, the snake's tail shot from the murk and coiled around Remington's hind leg. Panic surged through him. He tried to shake the snake loose, but its grip tightened with each desperate twist of his leg. The snake's scales were cold and alien against his fur, and he felt a rush of primal fear deep in his bones. Remington fought to free his leg. He clawed at the snake, making deep gashes appear in its side. The powerful coils only tightened further, pulling the badger off balance, and dragging him toward the deeper boggy water. Mud and liquid splashed around Remington as he struggled for his life.

Remington clawed at the sedge, but it melted away in the mire. He could find no purchase to cling to, and soon he was under the water. His free legs scrambled for a surface to stand on but there was none. The snake coiled around him, and Remington saw its face through the dirt of the water. Round red eyes with black pupils shone like headlights through the grim pool. Remington kicked out but the snake tightened its hold. It seemed to grin at him as it squeezed. It had two rows of small needle teeth with no fangs. Remington had never heard of grass snakes being this aggressive, but he had little time to be thankful for the creature's lack of canines or venom.

The snake leered in close and bit down on Remington's shoulder. The badger seized his opportunity. He allowed the reptile its bite and slashed a claw down its right eye. Black blood plumed from the wound and the snake released its hold. Remington kicked to the surface and forced his body through the water toward its edge. Pain throbbed at his shoulder as he swam, but he refused to slow until he met the bank.

Remington struggled through the thick mire. Every stroke was an arduous battle against the grimy water. Just as his claws met the more substantial mud signalling the end of the bog, he felt a sharp sting in his hindleg. The snake struck again, sinking its teeth as deep as they would go into the badger's thick flesh. Remington kicked back with his long rear claws, but the one-eyed reptile swerved and caught the paw in a tight coil. It hissed wildly and threw itself backwards, dragging Remington into the water once more.

Remington floundered, gasped for air but only drew filthy water into his lungs. He spluttered and fought back against the serpent's embrace. The snake coiled itself around the badger's neck. Its cold scales constricted as it drew Remington down below the surface, pushing his face into the suffocating mud below. Remington tried to cry out, but he swallowed a cocktail of putrid water and muck. He struggled and tried to kick but he couldn't move. He felt the coils tighten around his neck once more. He churned up mud with his claws. He saw his wife, sodden with the filthy water of the Thames, her tongue drooping from her mouth, no breath left in her. He dug. He kicked. He grasped clods of mud in his paws. And then, he let go.

# Chapter Seventeen

Remington's throat filled with the cruddy detritus of dead plant and sphagnum moss. The faint murk of his vision bled to near black as the snake's muscular body rolled him onto his back. The world above the surface, out of reach, shimmered in a hazy orange glow. He knew the life was leaving his body as he felt the serpent's grip less and less. The orange light bloomed through the water and Remington felt teeth clamp firmly onto his neck fur. He was pulled upwards and broke into the dank humidity of the air. His back pulsed with pain as he landed in a splatter of dirt and sediment slush.

Remington tried to lift his head, but his throat was still clogged, and his muscles failed him. Through his fading vision he saw a blur of reddish orange clattering down into the bog. The meagre light glinted off scales as the snake reared back and twisted wildly. The red-orange figure rose and let out a high-pitched shriek, a mixture of cry and scream that reverberated through the ghylls. It was a fox. Remington wished he had the energy to drag himself away and leave these wild creatures to their battle, or at least the strength to cover his ears. He tried to cough, to push the effluence from his lungs and throat. He heard a splash, and then the shrieking stopped.

The fox loomed back into Remington's field of vision. It was larger than he. A fierce look burned in its yellow-green eyes. It pulled itself up on taut hind legs over the badger's useless body. Its fur shimmered like fire. Remington willed himself to roll away, but his lack of breath forbade him. The fox brought the full force of its weight down, paws first onto Remington's stomach. The badger lurched as sludge erupted from his open jaw spilling into the night and back onto his face. Remington coughed and gulped at the air. He took deep draughts of oxygen that burned as he choked it back. He lay there, still, tears streaming from his mud-filled eyes as the air slowly returned to his blood. Finally, he wiped the grime from his eyes. The fox stared down at him. That's when Remington smelled it, the stench of nostalgia, the scent of a thousand years of kinship.

Remington tried to speak, but his dirt-ridden larynx wouldn't allow it. The creature had blood dripping from its face. It bared its teeth and spittle dropped from between them. Even if he could speak, what could Remington say? He knew the land beyond the ghylls was fox territory. His status as a police officer meant nothing here. A crack sounded through the trees. The fox swivelled and began fidgeting. It pawed the ground and let out a reedy cry. Remington followed the fox's gaze. His eyes were still clouded, but as he peered through the murk, he was sure he saw a dark figure sweep through the treeline.

Remington pulled himself upright, and the fox spun back to him, its eyes still aflame with agitation. It hissed, and Remington raised his paws slowly in submission. He didn't have near the strength to fight the wild fox off. It sniffed at Remington, first his face, and then the wound on his shoulder which quickened with pain as the fox drew the badger's attention to it. Remington groaned and looked back to the treeline. Nothing moved.

The fox dipped its head and nudged Remington's front leg.

'I don't understand,' Remington managed to croak out.

The fox nudged his leg again and let out a low whine. Slowly Remington raised his foreleg and placed it over the fox's lowered neck. The fox stood carefully, lifting the ailing badger to his paws. Tentatively, without a word shared between them, the fox walked Remington around the edge of the bog. They paused occasionally for Remington to regain his breath and some strength. The fox's lithe movement outpaced the badger's feeble steps, but the bristling creature stayed with him. The path through the wet woodland wound through a diverse array of habitat. The ground, softened by fallen willow and waterlogged soil, continually provoked Remington's pawsentia but there was too much wildness in it for him to untangle its perplexity. Trailing creepers and slithering vines snagged at his limbs as though the topography was trying to prevent his escape.

Further into the deep afternoon, the sounds of the woods enveloped them. The vague chitter of birds blended with the croaking of frogs and the perpetual rustle of beings in the underbrush. The fox's ears snapped toward each sound, its senses tightly attuned to the resonances of its habitat. More than once Remington thought he saw a large figure keeping pace with them through the treeline, but he could do little more than cling to his saviour and keep his paws moving.

Time felt distorted in the ghylls. The light faded further into twilight and then seemed to slide back, hours blurring as they stepped through a miasma unhitched from the laws of Remington's usual life. The fox communicated through silent gestures, with occasional points of its nose or gentle nudges. Remington felt water rise up about a paw's depth and he worried he had been led in a circle, but the fox urged him along through the mire. As they struggled through a heart knot of bracken, he saw a wild expanse of bog break free before him. Two lumps drifted lazily through the fug of the murky ghyll air and Remington slumped to the floor with relief and recognition. It was Fingle and Glen.

The fox barked in a rapid succession of even beats. It looked at Remington. The fox said nothing, but with a final touch of its nose to the badger's, it turned away and disappeared into the darker woodland. Remington waved his paw in the air and then slumped to his back. He heard the faint splash of water as

Fingle and Glen paddled across the bog toward him.

'So, Remo, what the bogweed happened to you, man?' Glen was pressing some moss into Remington's wounded shoulder.

Fingle stretched out his long body as he dragged the plywood husks they'd used to row Remington back across the bog onto the semi-dry embankment. 'Yeah, you look like you've been through some twisted times.'

Remington grimaced as Glen bound the moss dressing. 'Long story, guys. I was following a lead and found a snake. He was not happy to see me.'

Fingle passed him a rolled bogweed, and he took a drag. He ignored the pain of the smoke in his ragged throat and waited for the first hit to dull his jangling nerves. 'Thought my number was up but that fox saved me. They're okay with you being so close to their territory?'

Fingle leaned back. His lanky frame almost blended into the boggy surroundings. 'Yeah, man, it's a bit of a dance, you know? We play our music, and they kinda just let us be. We never step on their turf, and they don't mess with us.'

Remington took another drag. He felt the soothing effect take hold, at least momentarily easing his pain. He looked at Fingle and Glen, their eyes curious but guarded.

'Listen, guys, I know you don't want to get involved but-'

'Badger can't put down the badge.' Glen's eyes darkened, and the stout weasel grabbed the bogweed back from Remington.

'If you could see what Heartbreak is doing to kids in the city…' Remington pressed his paw to his wound dressing.

Glen and Fingle exchanged a look. Glen passed the bogweed to the ferret. 'Roadkill is not someone you want to mess with,' she said.

Fingle nodded in agreement. 'He's dangerous, Remo. If you're poking around in his business, you gotta be careful. He's *connected*, and we stay out of it, man.'

Remington took a deep breath. 'I don't want to get you involved, but I got a lead about a cave somewhere in the Burrow.'

Fingle and Glen eyed each other. Remington felt like they had a telepathic connection. Fingle passed the bogweed back to Remington.

'Make you a deal,' Glen said, as she let smoke drift from her nostrils. 'If we point you in the right direction-'

'Don't-' Fingle lurched upright.

'Come on, man.' Glen raised her paws. 'We both know he's gonna find it anyway.'

Fingle slunk back into the gloom with a sigh.

'If we point you in the right direction,' she continued. 'You promise not to do anything on your own, and you've got to stay the night here. You're in no state to go dragging yourself back to the station tonight.'

'Badger's honour.' Remington held the bogweed out to Fingle, but he shook his head slowly. His eyes quivered in the ebbing light.

'Alright, Remo,' Glen leaned close to Remington and lowered her voice to a whisper. 'You remember where the thick is, the ancient wood, out beyond the northern edge of the ghylls?'

Fingle was twitching his ears and staring hard out over the bog.

Remington nodded. 'The dead wood, we used to call it.'

'Through the first chapters of the undergrowth,' Glen continued. 'The willow trees get taller and more tangled. There's one massive alder, probably the oldest in the whole place, with a trunk that's all gnarled and twisted-'

She paused, her gaze fixed on an imaginary spot in the distance. Fingle was staring at the same place. Remington peered out into the haze of buzzing insects.

Glen turned back to Remington. 'When you find that tree, look to the left of it. There's an overgrown thicket of ferns and mosses, and just beyond that, you'll see a cluster of large stones. That's the entrance, but you'll have to crawl through a gap in them. Just through them you'll find the cave. Watch your head, mind. It's pretty cramped in there.'

'How do you know all this?' Remington asked before he could stop himself.

'Come on, man. Seriously?' Fingle was shaking his head at Remington.

'Sorry, I just mean, are you sure?'

'Chill, Fingle, will you?' Glen snapped and Fingle sighed in submission. 'We supplied a bit of bogweed to Brigg. You know, small time, nothing serious. She wanted us to come work with her.'

'You worked for Roadkill?' Remington felt his gut twinge.

'No, quills no. We turned Brigg down. Too busy finding our sound to work for anyone else.'

'So, how do you know about the cave?'

'I followed Brigg one night to check out her stash. Figured I could try a different strain.'

'Sure enough, there she was squeezing through the rocks.'

A crack sounded through the trees. All three creatures bolted upright.

'Seriously,' Fingle said. 'That's enough, right?'

Remington nodded and mouthed a thank you. They spoke no more of Roadkill, Brigg, or the cave and instead reminisced about Miss Plunkett, compared their chequered histories at school, and Remington let Fingle and Glen's meandering lectures on music and sound wash away his encounter with the snake. As the dark settled on them, the bog came alive with night sounds. In the orchestra of creatures, Remington felt there was an instrument missing, though he couldn't put a claw on what it was. He watched the moon as it slid beneath clouds then beamed out again like a city street light. Then he counted all the stars he hadn't realised he'd missed in the metropolis.

# Chapter Eighteen

When sleep came, it came heavily. Remington dreamed of rising water, and he woke to rain pattering over him like tiny fingers. He pulled the rough hessian sheet that Fingle or Glen must have laid over him up over his head. He dreamed of stabbing cold and woke shivering in the deep night. The bog had a green hue under the moon's stark eye. He curled himself tight under his makeshift duvet and pulled it close around him. Despite the music of the night-dancing insects across the murk, Remington still couldn't shake the feeling that something was missing from the harmony of the dark; one crucial element he hadn't noticed until it was gone.

Then he dreamed of the city, *his* city, the great wen that had opened its smoggy forelegs to him and given him purpose. Except it wasn't his city, not quite anyway. It was the space of his city. He knew this from the smell, harmonic frequencies, electromagnetic pulls, and its shape. This was his city alright, but the buildings were gone. The people were gone. It was a desolate blueprint, a map, or speculation of a city, a flat, sparse topography skied with a dome of grey. The air was heavy with dread. As he gazed around the absence that should have held the metropolis, Remington saw a single tree in the distance, dead and weathered, its black skeleton jutting up toward the spectral sky. A dark shape sat abreast its upper branches.

Closer, Remington could see the tapestry of scars and crevices that decorated the ghostly tree's bark. From each line whispered ancient voices. They told of stories long forgotten, of histories of the woodland, of legacies left behind. The shape in the upper branches was a broad oval, like a giant ostrich egg, somehow a deeper black than the tree. It convulsed sharply, and then began to grow taller. As the base of the shape rose, talons appeared beneath it, gripping the gnarled branch. The front of the shape began to split in two, like automatic doors parting. A sound like the scuff of a match broke the silence as it began to reveal its true form. Wings, parting wings. Remington tried to snarl but found himself incapable. The wings separated, and the bird's head revealed itself from behind them. Two tar-black eyes met Remington's. The raven spread the huge wings, blotting the grey sky behind. Its long, hooked beak bore a crack in one side, and a claw mark ran down the side of its face.

The Rev stared at Remington, and the badger's legs almost buckled. Suddenly, the raven took flight, pulsing its span across the dead air. Remington was flattened by the force of it. He dragged himself back up and found himself giving chase. He stumbled over uneven ground. The flat abstraction of his city became alien and hostile. Obstacles emerged; walls, holes, sharp undulations in the abruptly twisting realm. Shadows loomed in the periphery of his awkward vision, strange grotesque figures, fragments from the corners of his mind. He was losing sight of the Rev, but he could hear more wings beating overhead. A cacophony of caws and shrieks echoed all around.

Remington slammed into a wall, tasted blood and brick. He turned and found another wall. He was trapped. His city had betrayed him. He tore at the walls with his claws. The bricks spat dust and dry mortar back at him, but the walls stood firm. One claw caught and he winced in pain. Blood spurted from his paw as the claw tore loose from his flesh. He looked up to find a platoon of crows perched on the tops of the walls, cawing and laughing down at him. He tried to jump, to scale the wall, but he couldn't find purchase. He fell back down, and the caws grew louder, more mocking.

A shadow slid over Remington's cell and the crows fell silent. The Rev hung in the sky like a black star. He paused for a moment and tilted, as if on an axis. The Rev dropped, beak first, toward Remington. The badger fell onto his back and watched as the soundless thing of fire and darkness plummeted toward him. He tried to cry out, but no sound would come. Still, the raven came, closer and closer, gathering velocity, the tar-black eyes growing with each moment. Remington heard his name being called. He couldn't move. He couldn't take his eyes from the enveloping black meteor. He heard his name again. He raised legs in front of his face. He heard his name. He felt a beak in his paws. The touch of the beak tore him from sleep.

'Remington. Remington. Sir, are you okay?' Vixx's voice was frantic and shrill.

Remington swatted the beak away and choked on his own panicked breath. His chest was heaving, and he could feel his heart drilling too fast within him.

'I was looking everywhere for you, Sir. You vanished in the ghylls. I couldn't get to you.'

'I'm... I'm okay,' Remington stammered. He tried to slow his breathing.

Vixx was twitching her cream-coloured head and blinking close to Remington's face. Her eyes focused and refocused, irises sliding large and small as she studied the badger. 'You're wounded, Sir. It's my fault. I should have insisted we bring Chris and Claire, or scope the area out properly-'

Remington put his paw on Vixx's brown wing feathers. 'It's okay, Sergeant. My fault. I should have reported back to let you know I was okay. These two fixed me up and I... I was exhausted.' Remington gestured over to Fingle and Glen. Both were oblivious to the current commotion in their home. Glen lay on her back, all four little legs pointing straight up into the air, and Fingle's long body was curled around her. Both were snoring loudly with their pink tongues hanging from the corners of their mouths.

Vixx had brought her eye close to Remington's shoulder and was staring intently at the bindings. 'This is a mess, Sir. We should get this redressed properly. Can you stand?' She looked down at the wound on Remington's hind leg.

'Only one way to find out.' He laboured to his paws and tested the wound. Pain surged up his leg and across his shoulder, but he could walk.

Vixx insisted he use her as a crutch, and the two animals walked steadily, as the sun rose behind them, toward the station hut.

'Five years since I've had to use this first aid kit,' Mrs Banks complained as she forced open the mouldering box where she kept the station hut's medical supplies. 'Five years and you're not even here five weeks…'

Despite her wittering, Remington was surprised how adept Mrs Banks was at her duties. She cleaned the wounds, while complaining about Glen's use of moss as gauze, and checked the bruising around Remington's neck.

'What was it, anyway?' Mrs Banks asked, as she tightened the binding.

'Grass snake,' Vixx answered for Remington.

'How did you know that?' he asked her.

'The teeth marks, Sir.' Vixx gestured toward his now covered wounds. 'No fangs, so not an adder.'

'No venom to worry about, at least,' Mrs Banks said absent-mindedly as she surveyed her work.

'And unless we've got something new in the Burrow, safe bet's a grass.' Vixx was watching Mrs Banks as the hedgehog adjusted the binding on Remington's shoulder.

'Right, that's you.' Mrs Banks patted Remington's arm firmly. 'Probably best take the day to rest up.'

Remington waited for a final snide comment, but it didn't arrive. 'I will. Thanks, Mrs Banks.' He stood and stretched gently, testing his movement. Mrs Banks had certainly done a much better job than Glen. 'I've just a couple of errands to run first.'

'Sir, I don't think-' Vixx began but Remington waved her objection away.

'Nothing serious, I promise. I've an apology and a delivery to make.' He placed a paw on Vixx's wing. 'Thank you, Sergeant. Keep up the good work.'

Vixx refused to take the rest of the day off and, seeing the guilt on the poor bird's pale face, Remington knew the kindest thing was to give her the chance to feel useful. The young harrier suggested continuing the search for the red squirrel and Remington gave his blessing. He knew it was a futile task though. If the fur Vixx had spotted the day before had belonged to Red's mother, she had likely stumbled upon the same angry serpent Remington had. Sure, she might be able to outrun a grass snake but if it had tugged her into the thick soup as it had Remington, then she didn't stand a chance. If the snake had spooked her and she'd bolted into fox territory, he didn't think much for her chances either. While there was some spit of hope though, and while Vixx was in need of something to occupy her anxious mind, it did no harm to allow the search to continue. He also knew from experience that a young recruit on a mission to assuage unwarranted guilt was liable to get themselves in serious trouble. However he sliced it, it was better to have Vixx distracted today.

Remington slouched to his dwelling and sat on the front step. He rested his broad frame against the door. His eyes ached pleasantly with tiredness as he surveyed the clearing, and he didn't mind the stinging from his wounds either. The air was crisp and sharp, but it soothed his ragged larynx, while the scent of decaying leaves and damp earth seemed to glitter around his nostrils. Bees hummed and threw their awkward shapes, and an occasional chirp signalled a cricket in the underbrush. A white-faced darter dragonfly hovered gracefully in the air, its wings shimmering, iridescent in the sunlight. It darted back and forth, dipped to hoover up a drop of dew clinging to a blade of grass and then spiralled up into the sky. He placed his hind paws directly onto the forest floor and closed his eyes. Remington felt the faintest ghost tapping on the back left corner of his paw pad. He opened his eyes and saw a family of ants marching in rhythm to the subtle tap on his paw, each carrying a leaf or twig or morsel of food. He closed his eyes again and, through the myriad undulations on his paws, he focused on a tickle in the centre of his left-most pad. He opened his eyes again and looked over to the left. A ladybird was crawling up a tuft of rough meadow-grass. The flowering leaves wafted the air as the tiny creature tenaciously climbed for the tip.

Remington closed his eyes again and twitched his ears. Behind the symphony of woodland noise, he could still make out that one discordant frequency. He tried to reach out for it, to attune his senses to its particular levels, but it was agonisingly out of reach. His ears picked up something else though, something much closer, an interference in the trees behind him, just above his dwelling. He listened again and tried to build a picture of his surroundings. He started close. He could hear his breathing, his heart, the heavy throb of his wounds. He could hear the insects around him, the steady creak of grass and weeds. Slowly he moved his circle of attention outwards, allowing his pawsentia to aid in the process. He could feel the life around him, and it was cacophonous.

A clang snapped him out of his reverie. Something had landed on the roof of his dwelling. Remington leaned back and looked up. A tuft of red fur appeared first, and then two tiny black eyes met his.

'Good morning, Deputy.' Remington said. The squirrel giggled. 'Are you ready for your first assignment?'

Red jumped from the roof and landed at Remington's feet. She stood up straight and nodded.

'Excellent.' Remington rose and stretched his back. 'Right, we've got work to do.'

# Chapter Nineteen

The light flooded the burrow with a golden tint as Remington picked his way through the dense woodland toward the school. Red scampered up tree trunks and flung herself from branch to branch clumsily. Occasionally she clattered down to his side and reported back information about other creatures harmlessly going about their daily lives, before zipping off into the branches again, the scarlet feather still wound in her tail, waving in the air as she went. Remington rotated his ears and pressed his paws firmly into the woodland floor. He found he was able to roughly track a vague approximation of Red's progress, and whenever she told him about a particular animal scavenging in the underbrush, or nesting quietly, he reached out with his senses and found he could almost pinpoint them too. He still missed the way he could map the electromagnetic frequencies of the city using just his ears. It had a precision to it, a meticulous pragmatism that this sensory amalgamation did not. But the ambiguous miasma of the Burrow's organic communication was starting to make a kind of half sense to him.

The previous night's rain had left behind a stillness that hung in the air like a promise. Remington sensed the hubbub of youthful life as they neared the edge of the wood, and the threshold of the school grounds. On seeing the school through the treeline, Red had grown anxious and slowed her movements. Remington sensed this too. He remembered feeling something similar when he was a pupil there. The school had a sensory aura of its own, and as a cub Remington had interpreted that aura as one of foreboding and imprisonment. Every school day felt like a lifetime to him. The building was a chimaera of scavenged materials, a patchwork testament to animal ingenuity. As they reached the treeline, Remington felt Red grip his paw. He smiled at her and pulled her into the clearing.

Out of the woodland cover, the school revealed itself in all its bewildering shape and puzzlement. He could feel the cocktail of Red's trepidation and wonder through their entwined paws. Remington felt like he was seeing the school for the first time through her eyes. The amalgamation of discarded stone and wood were woven together with vine and weed, held upright by the jut of stumps and roots. The central structure of the school resembled an enormous bird's nest. Dried clay and mud had been mortared between twigs to create a rough-hewn exterior that blended into the surrounding earth. The main entrance was framed with delicate tendrils. It reminded Remington of the elegant archways in the heart of the metropolis, except that these ones were alive. Everything thrummed with organic energy. Branches stretched from the main hub nest, becoming bridges and pathways leading to smaller satellite nests. He couldn't be sure if this had all been here when he was young, or if the school had expanded. Tiny etchings peppered the surfaces. Each generation and class of students had continued to leave their imprints, just as he had.

Beneath the structure, gaps in the earth betrayed the network of burrows and tunnels that salamandered away under the school. It was a labyrinth that purred with life, a complicated ecosystem where exploration and education met. As he looked over the main entranceway, he saw a figure hop purposefully out into the clearing. The rabbit folded her front legs and glared at Remington. He felt Red's paw pulse with sudden fear. The expression was so stern on the rabbit's face that Remington thought for a moment it was Head Plunkett, but it wasn't. It was Miss Carrol, and she did not look pleased to see him.

As Remington and Red drew closer, Miss Carrol narrowed her eyes at the badger.

'Well, well, if it isn't my missing date from last night. Get a better offer, did we?'

Remington cleared his throat and accentuated his limp. Miss Carrol saw his bound shoulder and leg. Her face softened a little.

'I'm so sorry,' he said with affected tiredness. 'Something came up, but I promise it wasn't nearly as appealing as an evening with you.'

Miss Carrol almost smiled but she caught it and maintained her demeanour. 'Police business? Are you alright?'

'Just a scrape or two, while searching for a lost soul.' He gestured toward the animal cowering at his side. 'Red, meet Miss Carrol, the finest teacher in all the Burrow.'

The rabbit rolled her eyes at Remington and crouched down. 'Hello Red. I've heard lots of wonderful things about you.'

Red blushed and leaned into Remington's fur. 'Really?' she said.

'Of course.' Remington gently levered Red from him and placed his paw on her back. 'I've told Miss Carrol all about your special mission as my deputy.'

'Mission?' The squirrel gaped up at him. Her eyes quivered.

'Yes, that I need you to investigate the school for me and keep an eye on some dormice about your age. I also need you to make sure Miss Carrol is safe.' Remington gave Miss Carrol a wink.

'It's a very important mission.' The rabbit took Red's paws in her own. 'I'm ever so grateful to have you here to protect us.'

A ball flew from the open doorway behind Miss Carrol, thunked Remington on the head and looped into the air. Remington caught it as it came back down. It was made from tightly bound leaves. Two dormice scuttled from the dark, laughing as they emerged into the daylight. They saw Remington and froze, eyes wide and glistening. Remington smiled, tossed the ball into the air, and then juggled it from limb to limb. He ignored the pain in his shoulder as the ball landed there and he let it roll across his neck and down his other leg before flicking it into the air and balancing it on his nose. The dormice burst out into fits of laughter. Red joined in. The reedy noise sounded thoroughly musical to Remington. He jerked his head, sending the ball flying back into the entranceway. The two dormice took off after it, clambering over one another, giggling as they went. Red looked up at Remington and took his paw again. He could feel the excitement vibrating through her.

'Why don't you go and play with them?' Miss Carrol urged.

Red looked from her to Remington. 'No time like the present, Deputy,' he said.

Red bounced on her hind legs and scuttled into the school.

'Well, aren't you a dark horse?' Miss Carrol's face had lost all similarity to Head Plunkett's. 'Any other hidden talents I should know about?'

'I guess you'll have to find out,' Remington said and almost blushed at the line. He half expected her to laugh in his foolish old face.

'I guess so. How about you make last night up to me tonight?'

Remington shuffled on his paws. 'I'm afraid tonight's not great-'

'Of course. Don't worry.' Miss Carrol waved her paws in front of her face and shook her head.

'It's just a lead I need to follow, a police thing-'

'You don't have to explain.'

'How about tomorrow night? Dinner on me?'

Miss Carrol lowered her paws. 'That would be acceptable,' she said, suddenly sounding very teacherly. 'But this is your last chance, Inspector.'

Remington nodded and fiddled with his claws. 'So, erm, how are the little ones getting on?'

'Much better. Still some way to go yet mind, but they're almost behaving like children.' She ran her paws over her ears and twitched her nose. 'I should probably get back to them before total chaos breaks out.'

'Of course. Don't let me take up more of your time. Thanks for taking in Red too.'

'She seems a sweetie. What's her story?'

Remington sighed. 'Lost her mum. That's where I was last night but ended up having a run in with a snake.'

Miss Carrol put her paw on Remington's wounded shoulder. 'Do you think she's out there?'

Before Remington could reply, Red came running from the doorway, a huge smile across her face.

'I wanted to give you this.' Red was untangling the scarlet feather from her tail. 'Mum gave it to me for good luck.' She scrambled up onto Remington's back and tied the feather into a few strands of his back fur. 'It will protect you while you find her.'

Red gave Remington a tight squeeze and then scurried back into the school before he could say anything.

'A bit of colour rather suits you,' Miss Carrol said, and she turned away to follow Red into the entranceway. 'Tomorrow night. Cat's. No excuses,' she called as she slipped into the darkness.

He didn't know if it was the lack of sleep, the adjustment to the rural miasma, or the after-effects of his fight with the grass snake, but Remington felt lightheaded as he lumbered back through the woodland away from the school and Miss Carrol. Part of him wanted to rush back and tell her that tonight would be ideal. But, despite the awakening of his old pastoral senses, Remington's gut was still his guiding force, and his gut was telling him that he had to find Roadkill's cave.

Remington reached out with his senses as he walked, testing the limits of his sensitivity. It wasn't that any one of his senses had become keener, but that the communications between them all was more fluid. The translation of information between each was smoother and more alive. It was close to synaesthesia, a blending of sense into the borderland between feeling and meaning. It was a tuning into the pitch of the world around him and finding that the notes of the scale were infinite. Beneath the strange beauty of the sensory dance, a darker melody played in his mind; one that made him think about the shadow he thought he'd seen through the treeline the night before; one that infected his other senses with the musty aroma of crow. Remington tried to close his mind to the darker melody, but it only grew louder and drowned out the lazy hum of the rest of the woodland. His shoulder and leg wounds started to call out to him. He needed to rest. For now, there was nothing to do but let the day dwindle into night. Once it was dark, he could seek out the cave and find out exactly what, and who, he was dealing with.

# Chapter Twenty

Remington allowed himself a few hours of rest. He eschewed his bed for the cool embrace of his mossy floor, letting the organic carpet soothe his bruised and aching body. Sleep would not come. The woven bark of his ceiling was alive with images of his encounter with the snake and the fox. Now and then Miss Carrol's face would reveal itself in the knotted wood, before sliding into the darker leporidae form of Lennox. As the sun dipped below the horizon, shadows spread from the woodland into his dwelling, blotting out the images. Remington tested the resolve of his body. His wounds still simmered with freshness, but they didn't impinge on his movement. A well-targeted blow to his shoulder or leg would be enough to drop him, but he didn't intend to get into any brawls tonight. This was surveillance. He would be silent and keep to the shadows. He just needed to know what was happening in that cave, and perhaps put a face to the name, Roadkill.

He half expected to find Vixx waiting for him as he opened his door, but there was no sign of the eager-to-please sergeant. The station hut was silent too. Remington closed his eyes and let his senses drink in the Burrow's evening air. If any of his colleagues were still at work, he couldn't detect them, only the slowly waking rhythms of the Burrow's nocturnal life. The woodland whispered secrets to him as he picked his way toward the ghylls. Leaves rustled conversations and tiny creatures drummed out their beats with wings and limbs. The tingle in the badger's paws no longer irritated him. Instead it felt like they were reading the notes of a symphony that played throughout his whole being.

Remington found that his step was lighter and more graceful too. Grace wasn't something he'd ever been blessed with, but he found the thump of his paws easier, and his gait less cumbersome. He let Fingle and Glen's instructions repeat over and over in his mind as he pushed toward the ancient wood where the trees loomed taller and more twisted. Fortunately, his destination lay at the northernmost tip of the ghylls which meant he could skirt around and avoid any potential reunion with his dancing partner from the previous night. He took a longer route than he normally would to ensure he didn't meet anyone along the way with the same destination. The last thing Remington wanted was to spook Roadkill into suspicion.

As he approached the ancient woodland, the air grew heavy. It clung to every breath he took. The damp scent of earth mingled with an acrid tang. It was like the aftertaste of a lightning storm. The further he ventured into the labyrinth of alder, the thicker the air became. Remington's head swam, but he shook the sensation away and regained his senses. The strange half frequency that had plagued his arrival in the Burrow became more defined too. It was still too vague or incomplete for Remington to attune to, but it persisted in his ear like tinnitus.

Just as Remington was starting to wonder if he would be able to pick out the specific alder he was looking for amidst the endlessly unspooling maze of them, the ancient tree revealed itself. The size of it took Remington's limited breath away. The gnarled trunk screwed wildly, with long serpentine branches that jutted in all directions. The ancient woodland's great sentinel. In its presence, Remington felt the abstraction of the word ancient melt away. He pushed his paws into the root-riddled earth at the tree's foot. There was a steady pulse, a deep pressure humming beneath the surface. It was so strong that it drowned out any other signs of life. Remington twitched his ears and listened. Beyond the low irritation of the strange frequency, he heard movement, but it was muted, as though he was listening under water. To the left of the tree, exactly as had been described, an overgrown thicket of fern and moss beckoned to Remington like a threatening invitation.

Remington pushed through and found the large stones that Fingle and Glen had told him about. He squeezed himself through a gap at their base, each movement a pained struggle, guided by the moonlight steadily filtering through the thicket. He bit his lip as the stone grazed his wounds, careful to maintain silence. Once through, the cave's entrance gaped before him like open jaws.

Inside the mouth of the cave, shadows pulsed with lives of their own. Remington felt his paws rumble with the movement and echo of animals deeper down. He could hear the distant resonance of voices, and the clink of activity. The cave was cold and damp, but the air was hot and dry. The thick, acrid aroma was almost unbearable inside. Remington could feel the tendrils of the toxic atmosphere wrapping around his brain. His eyes began to sting. The badger slunk deeper into the cave, melding into the shadows as best as he could.

The cave mouth narrowed to a slope that looped down into darkness. Remington followed the path. With each step, the air thickened further. Remington's head was reeling by the time he saw a small ember of light bud in the passageway below him. He crept closer and heard voices, two in particular that he could make out, though their words were distant and muffled. Remington clung to the wall and slid silently closer, using the cave's morass of rock and stalag to shield him.

The voices sounded so remote and muted that Remington didn't realise how close he was to their source. He crept from the shelter of a jagged rock and saw two creatures in spitting distance on the pathway below him. Remington darted back behind cover, his claw causing the faintest scuff on the path. He placed his paws over his jaw to silence his breath. The voices had stopped.

It could only have been a few moments before the creatures continued their muffled conversation, but to Remington, it seemed he held his breath for an age.

'-ahead of schedule, Boss. Three more days, I reckon.'

The voice was assertive and high-pitched. It peaked a tingle of recognition somewhere at the back of Remington's mind.

'Then the schedule is three days.' The second voice was deep and watery. There was a thickness to it that turned Remington's stomach.

He peered slowly around the rock. A rat and a toad faced each other. It was difficult to gauge their expressions as both wore rough moss masks over their faces from below the jaw to just under the eyes. Despite this, Remington recognised them both. The rat was Brigg, the victorious combatant from fight night. Her wiry frame juddered in the shadows of the cave. The broad toad was the same one he had tangled with at Mickey's funeral. The toad's back convulsed with volatile warts. Each one was on the verge of erupting.

'I've made promises, and you'd best see that they're kept, aye?' The toad's words seemed to bubble in unison with its back. So, this was Roadkill, Remington thought, and he didn't need his detective skills to work out whom the toad had been making promises to. Remington would have staked his reputation on it being the same raven whose face he had been pummelling when he first met this vile creature. Remington allowed himself a momentary smirk as he recalled the feel of his claw slicing through the grotesque toad's tongue, even as his gut churned at the notion of the Rev still somehow malevolently puppeteering from his cage.

Remington's head throbbed and his vision blurred again. The fumes were too much. He was about to retrace his path, but Roadkill continued.

'Shall we check on the children?'

Brigg nodded and the two moved deeper into the cave.

Remington squeezed his eyelids tight and regained his composure. He dug his claws into his paw pads, and slunk after the creatures, deeper into the molasses of air and darkness.

The cave seemed to unspool endlessly. The ember of light grew larger, making the badger's attempts to remain in shadow more difficult. Eventually the long passageway narrowed to a final opening in the limestone wall from which the light bloomed. Remington made his body as flat as possible and crawled through the opening. The air was so thick with the putrid fug that he almost passed out on the spot. He pushed his paw over his nose and mouth and allowed his eyes to adjust to the light.

The cave opened out into a large circular chamber. A fire plumed at the centre. Moss-masked creatures of various species scurried back and forth, feeding the fire with twigs and sticks.

'Quicker!' Brigg barked. 'That fire dies, we all die, right?'

Remington slunk behind a stalagmite and surveyed the area. A whip cracked to his left and he heard a mouse cry out. Roadkill was using his tongue as a weapon, lashing at the animals as they worked. Beyond the flames at the centre of the chamber, rows of creatures busied themselves at individual stations. Remington couldn't tell through the thickly shimmering air what it was they were doing, but each of them looked thin and ragged. Their red eyes bulged in the sockets, and their slumped frames were skeletal and wretched.

He watched as a hedgehog gathered something from the stations, sweeping a substance into a large box. The starved looking creature carried the container on its head and heaved it toward an enormous mound of glistening black powder. Heartbreak. It faltered and tripped, spilling powder across the cavern floor. Many of the animals swivelled to look on in terror. It wouldn't take more than a handful of the black evil to touch the fire in the centre of the cave to cause an explosion, and if that explosion led to sparks reaching the larger mass of Heartbreak, this whole cavern would be gone in moments. Roadkill turned and sprung to the prone hedgehog. Remington let out a gasp of surprise at how agile the toad was. It loomed over the terrified animal. The hedgehog was shaking its head. Its mouth guppied the air. Roadkill reared back, his tongue spat forth and invaded the helpless hedgehog's mouth. The toad's warts coursed across its back, undulating like waves. The hedgehog couldn't breathe. It writhed and convulsed. The other creatures watched motionless as Roadkill asphyxiated the defenceless beast. Its face began to turn blue beneath its filthy fur.

Remington couldn't stand by and watch. He jumped to his paws and sped around the walls of the chamber. Still, Roadkill choked the small mammal. The other inhabitants looked on. Remington was almost within pouncing distance when his legs were taken from beneath him. His chin met the floor hard. The taste of dirt filled his mouth. Strong limbs coiled around his own. He was about to cry out when his assailant grabbed his snout, holding it closed. A red squirrel, grey flecked across her fur, was staring into his eyes. Silently she shook her head and raised a digit to her masked mouth. Someone else was holding Remington down, gripping his legs firmly. He couldn't see them, but he could feel their heft upon his back.

The squirrel removed her finger from her mouth and then pointed up toward the far end of the cave, drawing Remington's gaze to the dark mass that covered the ceiling. Remington looked up at the huge patch of shadow, confused at first by what the squirrel was trying to show him. As his eyes adjusted though, his stomach lurched with a deep sickness. The patch of shadow was moving. It wasn't shadow at all, but rather a cramped mass of bats. They were crushed together in tight rows, bound at the feet to the rocks, helplessly hanging and trapped. They were alive but limp, and no sound came from them. Remington blinked and tried to refocus his vision. Their heads were bound with something denying the creatures the ability to cry out.

The realisation hit Remington like a punch in the snout. The missing element from the night's music in the Burrow; it was the bats. He hadn't heard a single bat since he'd arrived. The loss of their echolocation was more dissonant than any flat note.

The hedgehog had stopped struggling. Remington tried to shrug the other creature off his back. The red squirrel nodded to her accomplice and the badger was released. A thick-set weasel came into view. Remington stood, but his head swam again, and his legs buckled. The squirrel took off her mask and placed it over Remington's face. She mouthed, *follow me*. He was too weak to argue and knew in this state he would be no match for the toad and Brigg together. He clawed his way along the path. They moved deeper into the cavern, and the squirrel led Remington through a tight gash in the main chamber's wall. She led him purposefully through a meandering keyhole passage. The air became crisper as he clawed his way through. He could hear the trickle of water. Eventually the passage sloped, and Remington slid, his wounds grazing along the rock, and he tumbled onto his back into the mercy of the open air.

Remington blinked up at the stars with relief. He tried to sit up, but the red squirrel leapt onto his chest, pinning him down.

'Who are you?' she said. 'And where did you get this?'

Her bloodshot eyes were huge and watery in her gaunt skull. In her hands, she was holding a red feather.

# Chapter Twenty-One

Remington's first reaction was embarrassment. He'd forgotten about the feather Red had coiled into his fur. There he'd been, trying to become one with the shadows as stealthily as possible, a bright red feather jutting from the broad flat of his hide.

'Where?' The squirrel tugged a handful of Remington's chest fur. He saw a flicker of familiarity in her wild eyes.

'It's okay, she's safe.' Remington gently raised himself and the squirrel slid from him. 'She's been looking for you. Actually, we both have.'

The bony creature clutched the feather to her face and sobbed.

'I'm with the police,' Remington said, shaking the effects of the Heartbreak fumes from his aching head. 'Come with me, and I'll take you to her.'

She recoiled slightly. Her eyes darted around her. 'I can't,' she whispered. 'If I leave, Roadkill will come for her.'

'I won't let that happen-'

'You don't understand. He's cunning and cruel. He does unspeakable things to anyone who escapes or betrays him.' Her voice quaked with anger. 'I have to protect my daughter.'

'I need to put an end to this.' Remington gripped her shoulder. 'Whatever *this* even is.'

'Heartbreak,' she said. 'They force feed the bats day and night to keep them producing guano and he has us make the powder.'

Remington swayed and screwed his eyes tight.

'That's the fumes.' The squirrel took the mask from Remington and held it up. 'They have us keep that fire stoked to burn off the worst of it, but it's not enough. It makes you see things, feel things.'

A faint splash sounded from the beck babbling mildly beside them and the squirrel shot to her paws, arching her back. Her spine was visible through her skin, her ribs pronounced in the starlight.

'I need to get back before they notice I'm gone.' She handed the feather back to Remington.

'I'm coming back with the full force of the Met, and I'm giving this back to you.'

'Please keep her safe,' she said, and then she scurried back up into the opening they'd fallen from.

The stars seemed to dance and shimmer in the stark canvas of the night. Remington couldn't shake the image of the poor hedgehog, its eyes wild with terror as Roadkill's tongue blocked its airways. He knew he owed Red's mother his life for stopping him, but by the time he reached the station hut the guilt had worn him thin. Remington knew he had to get a message to Lennox. He clattered into his office and smashed his paws onto the desk. He'd been so focused on getting a message sent to Lennox that he hadn't realised he didn't know how communications from the Burrow to the city worked. He also hadn't noticed the bird crouched in the corner of the main station room as he entered.

He heard the clack of talons and the rustle of feathers. He looked up to office doorway. The silhouetted shadow of the bird moved toward him. Remington snarled.

'Sir, it's just me.' Vixx stepped into the faint light of the office. 'Is everything okay?'

'Quills, Sergeant.' Remington expelled a deep breath. 'Why are you creeping about in the dark?'

'Sorry Sir,' she said and tugged a feather with her beak. 'I was just plotting my next search perimeter for the missing squirrel.'

Remington sank onto his chair and rubbed his pounding head. 'No need. I've found her.'

Vixx cocked her head left and then right. 'Where is she?'

Remington relayed the night's events to Vixx. The young bird was by turns perplexed and astonished by the details. Remington watched her carefully. An operation as big as Roadkill's to continue unnoticed and unchecked didn't make any sense to him. The bird's shock seemed genuine enough, and her guilt certainly did. She admonished herself for not having caught the whiff of the scale of the narcotics operation that was right beneath her beak. She knew that there was a minor drugs issue in the Burrow, but they had always thought it small time. With the limited resources available, the meagre police unit had turned a blind eye, focusing instead on any immediate threats to life and keeping the boundaries between the feral and civilised creatures as robust as possible.

'We have to shut it down, Sir,' Vixx insisted.

'Oh, we will.' Remington drummed a claw on his forehead. 'Now, tell me, how do we get a secure message to the city?'

'We've got a network of regular flyers, Sir.'

'Can they be trusted?'

Vixx trilled at her wing. 'I could go myself.'

'It's too dangerous.' Remington said. 'You've been seen with me, and I've got a feeling I'm being watched.'

'Watched, Sir?'

'I've seen-' Remington broke off. He reached for a sliver of clay and started to scribble something on it with his claw.

'Sir?'

'Is there anyone you trust absolutely, not connected to the force, with the wings to get this to Lennox today?' He tossed the tablet to Vixx.

'Sir, I don't understand,' she said catching it between her talons. 'Why don't we just tell the messenger what you want to say?'

'We can't risk Roadkill or *anyone* else knowing we're on to him. Is there someone?'

'Well, yes, but this doesn't make sense.' Vixx was shifting her eye lenses over Remington's scrawl. It read: *Surprise birthday party for RP tomorrow night. Closest friends only.*

'Will this really work?' Vixx said and clamped it in her beak.

'Just tell them to get that to Lennox asap.'

The bird nodded and flustered out of the station hut. Remington heard the rattle of leaves as she took wing.

Remington dozed in the office until the day's first light, and Mrs Banks' hollering into the half-deaf Chief's ear roused him. His paws were too itchy for him to stay at the station and there was little for him to do. He signed off on some perfunctory orders Mrs Banks placed in front of him, mostly requisitions for equipment. He also had to sign off on the release of Malin. They didn't have the resources to keep her fed and watered much longer and the old rat didn't seem that much of a danger to herself or others. The crone was freed under caution with a clear warning that any further suspicion of criminal activity or attempted contact with the dormice would result in an indefinite stay somewhere even grimmer than the station hut cells. The ordinariness of the daily work irritated him. Here he was, engaged in utterly menial nonsense when deep in the earth so many souls were enslaved and in peril.

He took his leave of the hut and made a tour of the Burrow, hoping to see the inevitable signs he must have missed. Surely there was evidence everywhere, great glowing beacons screaming of the danger that lurked amongst the creatures here. He spoke to civilians he passed, not raising any suspicions but just trying to get a greater feel for the place and its kin. Nothing but civility and friendliness greeted him. He heard the occasional story of missed family members but there was no suspicion of foul play. Animals had left for the city in the hopes of making a different life for themselves, but messages had been returned saying all was well. Most families seemed to have a similar, perhaps eerily similar, tale to tell.

He found himself in the treeline of the schoolgrounds and

watched as various teachers led their charges in classes. Some seemed far more educational than others, but he admired the kindness and patience that the teachers showed the children. It was a far cry from the lessons he recalled with Head Plunkett. Miss Carrol emerged with the dormice trailing in a neat line, Red along with them. Remington kept to the shadow of a tree to avoid Red spotting him. She seemed full of joy, raising her paw politely and playing with the dormice. Miss Carrol did see him, though. She shielded her eyes and waved. Remington waved back. She mouthed, *still on for tonight?* Remington nodded and allowed himself a smile. He thought about going over to talk to her and reintroduce himself to the class, but he caught sight of Head Plunkett bustling from the main entrance and slunk away before she could accost him again.

Waiting did not come naturally to Remington, but there was little else for him to do. Even if Vixx's contact made good progress and the message to Lennox had the desired effect, she wouldn't get to the Burrow until the next day, and even he wasn't foolhardy enough to take on Roadkill and Brigg solo. Too many souls were at risk. And so, the badger waited.

Remington and Miss Carrol arrived at Cat's at the same time. Technically Remington had arrived early, waited out of sight until he spotted the rabbit hopping toward the bar, and then he made himself known. He reached out for a pawshake as Miss Carrol leant in for a hug and they bumped heads awkwardly. She laughed at his clumsiness as he gestured for her to enter first.

'Welcome to the finest bar in all the Burrow.' Glen greeted them with a wide grin and a deep bow. 'Well, well, if it ain't our fearless police chief and the ever-enchanting Miss Carrol. Welcome to Cat's.' She winked at Remington.

'And where is Cat?' Miss Carrol was looking around the busy bar. The intimidating feline was nowhere to be seen.

'Not under new management, are we?' Remington asked as Glen led them to a table by one of the roughly gouged windows.

'No, no.' Glen shook her head and dusted at Miss Carrol's lap with a rag. 'Tell you the truth, not sure where she is. We turned up to thrill the masses as usual, and she wasn't here, so we figured we'd do a good deed and keep things ticking over for her.'

'Has this happened before?' Remington asked, swatting Glen and her rag away from him.

'Bloody hell, Remo, take a day off will you,' Fingle called from the bar where he was pouring fermented fruit and spilling most of the liquid all over the floor. 'Probably just a furball or she's taking some Cat time.' He tossed a receptacle in the air and tried to catch it behind him. The sound of it breaking told him he'd missed. 'Knackers.'

'Anyway,' Glen smiled. 'Our food is almost as legendary as our music, so allow us to shred your tastebuds.'

'Legendary, you say?' Miss Carrol twitched her nose at Glen and widened her eyes. 'That's a lot to live up to. What do you recommend?'

'Ah, well, it's legendary but limited.' Glen scratched at her behind. 'For my favourite couple, the lovers' special, coming up.'

'We're not-' Remington began but Glen had already scuttled off to greet two new customers.

'We're not what?' Miss Carrol glared at Remington.

'I… erm… we're-'

'I'm messing with you.' The rabbit laughed. She seemed more relaxed than she had during their previous meetings. Even Remington's awkwardness eased as the night drew on. As they settled in and ignored the revolting excuses for food that Glen brought out, the conversation flowed as easily as the noxious liquids Fingle was mixing. Remington watched the splodges of black on Miss Carrol's face as they shifted in the light. Her blue eyes were bright and animated when she talked about the school, and the children. They darkened briefly when the alcohol allowed the conversation to drift into some of the more melancholy experiences they had in common. Miss Carrol too had been married, and she'd had a family. Her tragedy had been caused by an ill-judged road crossing, but being on her own had made her more resilient, she insisted. Whenever the conversation flowed into dark waters though, Fingle was on cue with a well-timed shattering of a drink container causing the entire room to erupt into derisive cheers. If Remington hadn't known the ferret so well, he might have suspected he was doing it on purpose.

The night was drawing on and the bar began to thin out. Creatures in various stages of drunkenness stumbled out into the starlit Burrow. Neither Remington nor Miss Carrol were keen to leave and they moved on to Fingle's pitiful excuse for a digestif.

'I dreaded coming back here, to the Burrow I mean, but I guess it's not that bad, Miss Carrol.' Remington put his paw on top of the rabbit's.

'It's Daisy,' she said.

'I guess you could say that.'

'No, my name. It's Daisy.'

Remington looked doubtfully at her for a moment. 'Oh, I see.'

'You didn't think my name was Miss, did you?'

'What do you think is in this?' Remington deflected and lifted the liquid to his nose.

'You know, Inspector,' Daisy said. 'Life can be really unpredictable, but sometimes it throws you what you're looking for when you least expect it.'

Remington nodded. 'Sometimes it feels like the shadows of the past will envelop us completely, but then along comes a spark of light. And sometimes that's all you need.' He felt blood rush to his cheeks. 'Sorry, must be the drink.'

She clinked her tumbler to Remington's. 'You have a way with words, Remington.'

'I think that's the first time you've called me by *my* name.'

'Well,' she said, a mischievous glint in her eye. 'I could always call you Francis.'

'I've locked people up for less than that.'

She raised her paws to Remington, wrists facing upwards. 'Then take me away, Detective.'

Remington began to laugh. Daisy leant forward and kissed him softly. A spark fluttered through the badger. He wasn't sure if it was the drink, or the kiss but he suddenly felt very hot.

'Well, I don't know about you,' the rabbit said as she pulled away. 'But I can't drink this.' She tilted the tumbler. The thick liquid oozed toward the edge but didn't spill. 'I don't suppose you've got anything better at yours, do you?'

They left the bar like giddy adolescents, Daisy huddling into Remington for warmth. They stumbled occasionally with the effects of Fingle's cocktails still filtering through them. As they reached the station clearing, they stopped and shared a second kiss in the moonlight. Remington felt dizzy as he closed his eyes to the world around him.

Daisy pulled back suddenly.

'Do you always leave your door open?'

Remington turned. Sure enough, the door to his dwelling was ajar.

'Stay behind me,' he said. Soberness descended on him.

Remington edged up the steps and peered into the gap. Moonlight cleaved like a blade across the room.

'Hello?' he called, but there was no answer.

He pushed the door fully open, allowing moonlight to flood the room. Daisy gasped behind him.

On the floor of his dwelling, sparkling black in the moonlight, lay a body. Remington stepped around the blood that had pooled about the figure.

'What is that?' Daisy was staring at the mess.

Remington understood the rabbit's confusion. It wasn't a species anyone had ever seen before. The old, withered, lifeless head belonged to Malin the rat, but her body was altogether different. It was younger, more sinuous, but painfully thin. From its rear protruded a large, bushy red tail.

# Chapter Twenty-Two

Remington crouched by the chimaera body. Malin's jaw was open in a silent cry, her rotten teeth glaring and yellow even in the gloom of his dwelling. Last time he'd seen her, she'd been wailing in her cell under the station house. Now she looked like an ancient relic. He could see her skull through patches of balding fur. It was veined with scars, testaments to a life hard lived. Beneath the gently curved cranium, her eye sockets looked empty in the dark, her deep-set eyes barely catching a glint as Remington examined. Her narrow snout and blunt nose were similarly weathered but bore no sign of recent violence. Grim as it was, Malin's head was in no worse shape than it had been when she'd been raving in her cell. It had only been that morning he had signed her release.

The body was similarly unblemished. A patina of dried blood ringed the neck just before one creature awkwardly transitioned into the next. He couldn't see any thread stitching the constituent parts together this time. The body looked whole, like one cohesive entity. The squirrel's paws, with their delicate fingers, and sharp claws were pushed together as if in prayer. The body was thin, ragged, ribs visible through the rich red fur tinged with grey. Patches of white blotted through the red creating an odd visual discord. Remington was sure it was Red's mother.

He reached out to where the dried blood curled like a necklace to see what had been used to fuse the animals together.

'What are you doing?' Daisy was slumped against the wall behind him. Remington had forgotten she was there.

'You shouldn't have to see this,' he said and stood up. He led Daisy, shaking gently, from his hut.

'Give me two minutes and we'll get you home.'

Remington secured the door of his dwelling, sealing the horror inside from the clearing. He left a note for Vixx detailing the discovery and warning her not to let anyone inside until Doc had been able to examine the scene. He would still report the incident, but if his message to Lennox had been successful, Doc should have been arriving with Lennox in the morning anyway. For now, he had to get Daisy home and he couldn't risk leaving her alone. Malin was one thing; anyone could have known she'd been arrested and talked to the police, but Red's mother confirmed it: Remington was being watched, and probably had been since he first laid his paws back in the Burrow.

After securing the scene as best he could, Remington sat down next to the rabbit.

'I'm sorry you had to see that.'

Daisy stared into the grass, cartoonish and grey in the moonlight.

'Let's get you home.'

Remington helped the silent rabbit to her feet. Her blue eyes had dulled. Shock had vastly different impacts on individuals, but in the eyes, it was always the same. It was like a small piece of the individual left, taking some spark with them. Usually that spark returned, but not always. Remington bit his lip and hoped that he would see the blue of Daisy's eyes fully restored.

'Can you show me the way?' Remington asked, raising her chin.

Daisy looked confused.

'I don't know where you live.'

The rabbit blinked at him, nodded slowly, and turned away from the station hut.

They walked in silence. The night air felt unseasonably cold, as though the autumn had turned its back on the scene of the crime.

Twice Remington attempted to put a foreleg around Daisy, for warmth, for comfort (hers and his own), but both times she shrugged him off without a word. The moonlight made long creatures of shadows, and the absence of the bats' night song was deafening. Remington blinked into the dark, the image of Red's mother scrabbling up trees with Malin's withered old head played in his periphery. As did the ghost-hint of black feathers.

As they approached the small round mouth of a burrow, Daisy's shoulders suddenly tensed, and she stopped.

'You okay?' Remington put a paw on her back. She was rigid, but she didn't shrug him off this time.

'It's just... yes... sorry, I didn't realise we were nearly here.'

'It's the shock. A drink and a night's rest-'

'You can't come in.' Daisy turned to face him. The dull in her eyes was already beginning to ebb away.

Remington raised his paws. 'That's fine. Just wanted to see you home safe.'

'No... I mean... I want you to come in... but... I... just, give me a minute, will you? It's such a mess.'

She disappeared into her burrow. Remington rested his rump against the stiff mud of the threshold and looked out into the surrounding trees. The scant light made shadows of space, and the gentle breeze ensured continual motion to snatch at Remington's attention. He pushed his paws into the soil and reached out. Beyond a few subtle tickles, there was nothing to alarm him. It was a quiet night, and they were as alone as it was possible to be in the Burrow.

He could hear Daisy hastily shuffling around deep in the tunnel behind him. Now and then he caught the hint of her harshly whispering to herself. He thought about slipping down into the burrow and reminding her about the state she'd seen his place in this evening, but he thought better of it. It was strange how trivial everyday concerns could help dispel the fissures that occur in the psyche after an onslaught of trauma.

Having a quick, panicked tidy of her dwelling might be just the thing to stymie the rabbit's impending spiral, and knowing that the always immaculately turned-out teacher might secretly be a bit of a slob at heart cheered Remington greatly.

'You can come in now.' The rabbit's ink-splotched face appeared through the darkness of the hollow. Her facial markings seemed more defined in the darkness. She gripped Remington's paw and led him down into her abode.

'I'm so sorry about the state of the place,' she said.

'What state?' Remington looked around the small but flawlessly ordered burrow.

They drank water and huddled together. Eventually Daisy spoke.

'Have you ever seen anything like that before?'

Remington nodded.

'What kind of monster could do something like that?' she asked. 'A feral?'

'Not all monsters are wild.'

'You know who did it?' Daisy turned to face him. Her whiskers brushed his own.

'I have a good idea.'

'Are we safe?'

'I'll make sure of it.'

Daisy rested her head on Remington's shoulder, and he pulled her close, wrapping his limbs around her. She breathed deeply into him, and he felt her heart beating in time with his. She pushed him onto his back and cuddled into his broad body, finding a nook to rest her head. She was asleep and snoring softly in moments. He felt her body soften as she loosened into unconsciousness. The detective in him wanted to stay awake, to keep watch, but the night's excitement, the lilt of the rabbit's snoring, coupled with the lingering effects of Fingle's drinks, was too heady a cocktail to resist. Remington closed his reddening eyes.

Remington found himself on the platform of Nick's underground ghost station. The platform, dark and slick seemed somehow insubstantial under his paws. Fog quilted the floor, and he stumbled over the greasy platform. The fog didn't stir. There was no sound. By the thin gloom of a spectral light, he saw a figure, human, legs drawn deep inside a long, wet coat. Its arms were clenched tight around a hunched torso. The face wasn't visible, swaddled in a sodden woollen scarf. Remington reached out a paw and began to unwrap it, but the unspooling was endless. He was like a solemn magician interminably drawing handkerchiefs from a sleeve. Finally, it fell. The grey hood lolled open, empty. The rest of the coat followed. It swooned and tumbled open, vacant on the concrete.

A scurrying across the floor snapped the badger to attention – mouse, rat, or something else? Remington groped against moss-scabbed brick, following the sound. His paw met a doorhandle. It was stiff but not locked. He pushed the door open, and a blade of light leaked through, cleaving an old ticket office. Wet lettering spidered across the fissured wall. Remington stepped carefully into the room and raised his eyes. The glistening words read: *Do you meet with phantoms in your sleep?*

The door slammed behind him. Remington spun on his hind legs. A huge black bird loomed over him. It spread its wings then slammed them together in a beat like a thunderclap. The light went out.

Remington opened his eyes and blinked into his strange surroundings, the odd space between waking and sleep leaving him disorientated in the alien burrow. Morning light was leaking into the chamber, revealing just how spotless the teacher kept her home. Remington bolted upright.

'Miss Carrol?' he called out. 'Daisy?' There was no response.

# Chapter Twenty-Three

Remington levered himself up and surveyed the burrow. It was daytime and the sunlight funnelled into the immaculately hewn hollow in the earth. As he'd suspected the night before, Miss Carrol kept a tidy boat. He felt as though his presence was enough to spoil the neat aesthetic. Two openings, smaller than the entrance tunnel, curled away from the central room, their contents half covered by dangling strips of cloth. The rabbit didn't appear to have any kind of ornamentation or memory-triggering artifacts in her home. Lennox's sparse office popped into his mind, and with it the grim images of what he'd discovered in his dwelling.

Remington's tongue felt thick in his jaw. A dull ache throbbed at the edge of his skull. The air felt sullen and stale. Something about the clinical tidiness of the space quarrelled with the memory of his own shambolic quarters and the new chimaera body that decorated his floor. He listened hard for signs of life beyond Daisy's home, but the entrance tunnel had been expertly excavated with enough turns and ribbage in the walls to ensure any sound was swallowed up before it reached the main burrow. Miss Carrol clearly sought a peaceful existence. He could understand that, and he felt a twinge in his stomach as he considered the impact he'd had on her simple life in such a short time.

'You're awake,' she said, as she hopped through one of the entranceways curtained with cloth strips.

'What time is it?' Remington stretched out his broad back.

'Nearly midday. Here.' She held a small container of fluid in her paws.

'Thanks, but I should probably get back to the station. I expect the boss might be here by now.'

The rabbit nodded and nuzzled lightly into Remington.

'What should I tell Red?'

'For now, let's just keep this quiet. We can't be sure that it's her mother yet.'

Miss Carrol looked into Remington's eyes. 'It is though, isn't it?'

Remington nodded. 'I suspect so. We can decide what to tell her tomorrow.' Remington squeezed her shoulders.

'Why tomorrow?'

'Because I'm going to put an end to this tonight.'

'Is there any point in me asking you to be careful?'

'Don't worry,' Remington said. 'I won't be on my own.'

Remington felt a tug somewhere deep within him at the sight of his dwelling cordoned off. The feeling surprised him as it welled like seasickness, his legs momentarily not under his command. The place was hardly a home, or so he'd thought, but the presence of Chris and Claire standing guard, and the vines roping off the clearing, made him feel violated. It was a hovel, sure, but it was his hovel and it had been breached. The door was open, and Remington could see movement inside. He sniffed the air. Over the notes of decaying flesh and the young voles, he caught two scents he knew well. Lennox and Doc were already at work.

He was about to request a status report from the very alert recruits, but Lennox's voice stopped him.

'Remington, in here, now,' she called.

Remington nodded to Chris and Claire and stepped up into the dimly lit hut, where Doc was meticulously fawning over the heaped mass staining his floor.

'Make yourself at home, Doc,' Remington said. He offered Lennox a smile. Concern was etched into her dark chocolate face.

'Do you know how many reported murders there's been in

the Burrow in the past five years?' She tugged on her ears.

'Including this one?' Remington asked.

'Including these two, you mean,' Doc added helpfully.

'There's been none, Rem, literally zero reported murders and then you set up camp and-'

'Reported,' Remington interrupted.

'What?' Lennox let go of her ears and let them roll back up.

'Zero *reported* murders.'

'Don't start with me, Rem.' She looked from the badger to the chimaera carcass on the floor. 'What's going on?'

'I'm getting something else,' Doc said, running his nose over the body. His claws were already full of flesh and gristle.

'Something else?' Remington crouched next to the corpse. Malin's lifeless eyes gazed up at him. The manic shimmer he'd seen when he interrogated her still seemed to crowd the edges of them.

'There's rat,' the mole said and wheeled his nose around the room. 'There's red squirrel, and there's another animal, but it's not part of the body, Rem. Rabbit if I'm not mistaken.' He gestured to Lennox. 'And it's not you, ma'am.'

'Ah,' said Remington. He dug his claws into his paw pads awkwardly. 'That's just a…a friend. She was with me when I found this.' He could feel Lennox looking at him.

'You've been busy, Remmy, my boy.' Doc nudged at the base of Malin's head where the fur suddenly broke into the red of squirrel. 'That solves that at least.'

'Look, Len,' Remington began, keeping his eyes on Doc's interfering with the body, but she cut him off with a raise of her paw.

'We got your message. Not the most subtle of codes by the way. But Sergeant Vixx said this must've happened later. What was so urgent you needed us to drop everything and drag ourselves up here?'

'Hear me out,' Remington said. 'It's the Rev.'

'Oh, for the love of-'

'Hear me out-'

'He's locked up, Rem.' Lennox punctuated each monosyllable.

'I know how it sounds, but he's behind it.'

Lennox let out a sound somewhere between a growl and a sigh. 'I need some air. You good, Doc?'

'I'd be grateful for the peace and quiet, ma'am.' Doc didn't look up. He continued his excited snuffling over the wretched abomination.

Lennox jutted her head toward the door. Remington acquiesced to the gesture and plodded out into the clearing, telling Claire and Chris to take a well-earned break. Lennox followed with two of Remington's tobacco leaves in hand.

'Right, you've got precisely however long it takes me to get sick of this,' she said, and popped the leaf onto her tongue. 'But I'm warning you, this is going to go much better if you avoid any Rev talk, because you sound like a raving Take Back Edener.'

Remington filled Lennox in on Roadkill and the guano cave, the bats, the enslaved animals. He told her about young Red, and her mother who he now suspected lay so pathetically incomplete in his own dwelling. He avoided any mention of thinking he'd seen the Rev watching him in the ghylls but did point out that he'd made Roadkill's acquaintance once before, at Mickey's funeral. Lennox chewed and listened. Her brown face glistened in the dappled daylight. He expected one of two reactions. She would either react angrily at his seemingly endless ability to discover trouble in the most mundane of places, or she would be horrified and want to leap to action. He half-expected to have to hold her back from demanding an immediate unplanned assault on the cave. Neither happened. Instead, she remained placid. She listened, she chewed, and when he was finished, she spat the remnants into the soil.

'So?' he asked.

'So, what exactly would you like me to do?' Lennox's voice was distant and thin.

'I'd like us to raid the cave and free the poor fuckers.'

Lennox sighed deeply. 'It's not that simple.'

'What do you mean? I saw it with my own eyes.'

'From an unsanctioned search that had absolutely nothing to do with the case to which you'd been assigned.'

'Oh, come off it-'

'You come off it.' Lennox started to beat her foot on the earth. 'I'm so sick of having to tidy up after you. Do you have any idea how delicate the balance is with everything we're trying to do?'

'What? I-'

'There are higher pressures I have to deal with, and every movement my force makes must be accounted for. You were given a case, and that's what you were supposed to be focusing on.'

'Len, this is so much more important than-'

'Do you have any clue the mess you left in the city? With the Rev gone, that power scramble has caused chaos. He was a dark wrong 'un for sure, but we knew who he was, and he kept his side in check. Cull is a whole different beast. He's unpredictable and things are happening that we... Without the Rev, it's all we've been able to do to hold everything from the brink of anarchy.' Dust ploomed up between them as Lennox's foot slammed harder.

'What about Red's mother?' Remington shouted over Lennox's thumping.

'Oh, I'm sorry, doctor. You get proof back from the lab proving that's her, did you?'

'Come on-'

'No,' Lennox stopped suddenly. Her chest heaved. 'You had one job, and this was not it. Those animals are dead because of you. It's time you considered consequences.'

Lennox hopped away to the main station hut. Remington heard her shout, *Not now, Mrs Banks*, and then the wood of his office door slammed into place.

Back in his dwelling, head still ringing with Lennox's words, Remington slumped against the wall. Doc popped up from the body, sending gristle and blood across the room. He scurried over and sat next to Remington.

'Give her a minute, Rem,' the mole said. 'She's under a lot of strain and she's just worried about you.'

'Yeah, I could hear the love loud and clear, Doc.'

'She sent you here because she thought you'd be safe. She's just blaming herself.'

Remington huffed deeply and gestured to the body. 'So, what's the verdict? Any light to shed?'

'Well, not much I'm afraid, my boy. Not so much as a cause of death for either of them.'

Remington narrowed his eyes at the mole.

'The fatal wounds must have been to the parts of the body we don't have. Both looked like they were close to the end though. The teeth on that rat are rancid, infected gums like you wouldn't believe, and the squirrel's half starved.'

'So, is it?'

'Is it what?'

'The Rev?'

'Quills, Rem. No, he's caged up.'

'It's the same MO.'

'Not quite, my boy.' Doc crawled back over to the corpse and put his claw on the neck of the chimaera.

'How so?' Remington moved in close to the body.

Doc slipped his claw beneath the fur and pulled. The head slid away from the body.

'No thread,' Remington said and scratched his chin.

'Not a stitch. Now do an old mole a favour.'

'What's that?'

'Go make nice with the boss, will you? I do not want to share a journey back with her like this.'

'Fine.' Remington dragged his paw down his snout. 'Oscar

not with you?'

'He is, as it happens. Couldn't keep him away. He's off with your young sergeant. She's got a bright future that one.'

'Too good for this place,' Remington nodded.

'Now,' Doc pointed to the door. 'I know it's hard, but go and make nice with the one person who's always had your back, always stuck up for you, kept you in a job, fought off calls for your demotion, firing, death-'

'Alright, alright.' Remington rolled his eyes and left the dwelling.

'Not now, Mrs Banks.' Remington swotted away the small mammal's attention as he entered the station hut. He knocked three times softly on his own office door before entering. Lennox had her back to him.

'I'm sorry, Rem,' she said. 'That was uncalled for.'

'No, you're right. Don't think I don't know the trouble I cause you. I figured we both thought it was worth it in the end though. Greater good and all that stuff.'

'It is. It is, but it's getting harder. I don't know what I'm doing down there. It's not the same without you either.' She peered back over her shoulder. 'Massive pain in my arse that you are.'

'I know I don't understand how all of this works, but I can't just leave those creatures in that cave. This isn't about the Rev or Red's mother. It's about saving them.'

'I hear you, but there's procedures. I'm under strict instructions to make sure any case and any operation is sanctioned. This will need to get reported first and then a decision will be made above my station about what resources, if any, get assigned to it.'

'How do you do it, Len? How do you just sit by and not do anything?'

Lennox slumped her chin onto her paws. 'I focus on the things we do get to do. It's not nothing.'

'Wait,' Remington jumped up and started digging around in the mess on his desk. 'What we do get to do…'

'What are you doing?' Lennox shoved her bucket back as Remington squeezed between her and the desk, scattering things across the room.

'Where is it?'

'Where's what?'

'The file. The file.' Remington was frantic.

'Rem, calm down, man.'

'Aha,' Remington held a small clay tablet. 'Here.'

Remington threw the file down in front of Lennox.

'What's this?' She looked at the object and the markings on it.

'This is what we can do.'

Lennox sighed and lowered her head.

'Well?' Remington asked.

When Lennox raised her head, a hint of a smile was playing on her lips.

'Yes,' she said. '*This* is something we can do.'

# Chapter Twenty-Four

Remington had often playfully mocked Lennox for the way she would wind herself up before having to give a team briefing or some galvanising speech. He'd laugh at the way she paced her office muttering to herself, punctuating the air with her paws as she rehearsed her lines. It had always seemed so silly to him. *Just get out there, tell people the facts, and let them get on with it,* he would tell her. Now though, Remington paced. He paced back and forth in his own office. His brow was knotted tight, and he clenched and unclenched his paws as he walked. Lennox had agreed to sanction a raid on Roadkill's cave under the guise of the missing persons investigation Remington had been assigned to. There was one clear proviso though – this was to be Remington's show. Lennox's involvement needed to be minimal, and she had to be able to deny any knowledge of Roadkill's narcotics operation prior to the raid. If there was to be any blowback as a result of their actions from up on high, Remington would take responsibility for it.

This was what filled his mind most as he paced; not concern for taking the fall, but the further trouble that could be laid at Lennox's burrow. He'd never given much thought to the broader connotations of his actions on the force, or what they might cost his superiors. There was right and there was wrong. You could drive yourself mad chasing your own tail through the grey warrens in-between, but he wondered now about the excess manure his naivety had piled on Lennox's shoulders. Still, if this went squiffy, he would offer himself up as a sacrificial lamb and leave the force, one final good, worthwhile deed done.

There was a rap at the door and Vixx's blinking head poked into the room.

'We're ready for you, Sir,' she said.

Remington slapped himself lightly on the sides of the jaw with his paws and huffed. 'Thank you, Sergeant.'

The station's main room was dim. The windows had been covered, and the doorway securely sealed. Remington waited a moment for his eyes to adjust to the gloom. The team awaited him. The Chief and Mrs Banks, along with the young voles Chris and Claire, had been excused for the rest of the day. It was important to keep the circle tight for this one. Oscar, Vixx, and Doc sat before a wall upon which had been scrawled a map, along with various images and names. To the right of it stood Lennox.

'Detective,' she said. 'We're all ears.'

'Ma'am.' Remington gave her a nod. 'Right, team…' Remington's throat felt dry. 'You all know I was sceptical about the missing persons case.' He gestured to the names and sketches of the missing creatures from the thin file. 'But I have reason to believe that they are being held against their will, here.' Rem circled the cave on the map with his claw.

Vixx raised her wing.

'Yes, Sergeant?'

'Did you see them for yourself, Sir?' Her eyes shifted their focus, narrowing sharply.

'I did not, but I did witness many others, and I'm confident they're likely there somewhere too.'

Vixx nodded, but her expression remained sceptical.

'Problem, Sergeant?' Lennox stepped in.

'Well… I… can I speak freely?' Vixx twitched her gaze from Lennox to Remington and back again.

'Always.' Lennox gave a reassuring nod.

'This just feels a bit suspect, boss,' she said tentatively. 'If this is all above board, why are we pretending it's a missing persons?'

Remington looked at Lennox. The air in the room felt heavy and stifling with the windows covered.

'We're going after Roadkill, aren't we?' Vixx shifted her eye lenses once again.

Remington opened his jaw to speak, but Lennox stepped forward.

'Thing is, Vixx, I don't have the authority to sanction a new investigation, and now that there's a chance Roadkill's on to us…' She gestured toward an etching of the chimaera corpse found in Remington's room. 'By the time I get the official say so for an operation this scale, it might be too late.'

'So, this isn't legal?' Vixx tugged at a feather with her beak.

'Strictly speaking, no, but if Rem's right about what's going on in that cave, then I can't just leave those poor creatures like that.' Lennox lightly thumped her foot as she spoke. Vixx looked at Doc and Oscar, checking for a sense of shock at the flagrant disregard for rules.

'If any of you would rather not join us, then that's okay. I understand and this is going to be dangerous. We've seen what Roadkill's capable of.'

'You proved it was him?' Vixx asked, looking across at Doc.

'Not yet,' Remington said. 'But I told you what I saw him do in the cave.'

'What about procedure though, Sir?' The bird was wide-eyed now, and she started to scratch at the floor with her talons. 'We could all be struck off.'

'I'm taking full responsibility for this. Nobody outside of this room needs to know anything more than we were following a lead. Lennox, Doc, and Ozzy were here because of the body. That's standard procedure, and they decided to join me when I told them about a lead I had on the missing persons. If things go sour, I'll take the hit.' Remington stood in front of Vixx. 'You don't have to join us, but I think we'll stand a much better chance if you're with us, Sergeant.'

Vixx nodded. Oscar raised his paw. Remington was surprised at the steadiness of Oscar's limbs. He was a long way from the juddering streak of champagne Remington remembered.

'Ozzy?' Remington gestured to the ferret.

'Well, sir, how do we know this isn't an elaborate trap?'

'How so?' Lennox stepped across to join Remington at the front of the group.

'I'm just trying to get it straight in my head. The detective inspector infiltrated Roadkill's base of operations. He was then aided by a creature whose decapitated body we suspect has been left in the detective inspector's home?' Oscar opened his forelegs wide and raised his paws. 'Doesn't it scream trap to anyone else?'

'Valid concern,' Remington said. 'But I've dealt with his kind before. If it was him, he's just trying to scare me… us, off.'

'We will need to be cautious though,' Lennox added. 'He's clearly not to be underestimated and we know Roadkill's associate, Brigg…' She pointed to a sketch of the rat. '…is an exceptional pugilist.'

'If they are still there,' Vixx said. 'Are we concerned about any resistance from the ones we're there to rescue? If they haven't tried to escape yet, how do we know they even want to?'

'From what I saw, they want out. Roadkill's made examples of anyone trying to get out, and he keeps the rest of them in line with threats to their families.' Remington felt a tug deep inside him as Red swam into his mind.

'We need to stop this,' Vixx said.

'We will,' Remington stated. 'Now, any questions?'

'What's the plan?' asked Oscar. A slight tremor passed through the ferret from his tail up to his shoulders.

The plan was fairly straightforward. Lennox and Doc would approach the cave from the beck, using the entrance Red's mother had to get Remington out of there. If she was right in her assertion that 'they' didn't know about that passageway, then there was no concern about Roadkill or Brigg escaping through there. Remington, Oscar, and Vixx would enter through the front. Remington knew his way in and from the higher vantage point they would be able to watch for Lennox and Doc entering. Vixx would stand sentinel at the front entrance of the cave ready to accost Brigg or Roadkill should they be spooked into running. The priority was to free the bats and the other creatures, but it was essential they brought Roadkill in too. Failure to do so could mean putting the families of the other creatures in peril. Once all four officers were in the main chamber, they would positively identify Roadkill and work their way toward him as covertly as possible. If all went according to plan, they could accost him in unison and restrain him before he could fight back. Brigg could be a complication, but one they would have to work around on the fly.

'One more question, Sir,' Vixx asked after they'd gone through the admittedly vague plan a third time. 'How do we pull this off without keeling over from the guano fumes?'

'Glad you asked,' squeaked Doc as he scurried to the corner of the room. He came back holding a strip of tightly packed moss. 'There's one for each of us.' He strapped the device around his face. 'We might still feel some effects, but these should filter out the worst of it.' His voice was slightly dampened but still clear.

Night was steadily quilting the Burrow by the time the team crested the northernmost tip of the ghylls. The day's warmth still crackled under Remington's paws as he reached out, trying to sense any other creatures who might be abroad. Though he sensed very little, he couldn't shake the feeling that they were being tracked. Something uneasy trickled through his blood, but his skin tingled with excitement too. The ancient wood was steeped in shadow and a frozen mist was already descending, threading itself between the gnarled old branches.

'Anyone else getting that?' Doc had stopped and was craning his neck.

'The frequency?' Remington asked. 'Like an incomplete tone? I sensed it last time too.'

Doc let his nose caress the air. 'It's coming from beneath us.'

'Could be the cave. Roadkill?' Lennox was surveying the trees.

'Let's stay focused,' Remington said. 'We need to split here. Just follow the beck around to the left. We'll wait for you up top.'

'Don't engage the toad until you've got eyes on us,' Lennox ordered.

'Yes, ma'am.'

'I'm serious.'

'Badger's honour.'

Lennox gave Remington a squeeze on the foreleg and she and Doc disappeared into the night, swallowed by the shadowy mist between the trees.

As they descended beyond the rocks into the mouth of the cave, the moon's silver glow made a vague approximation of light. Eerie shadows danced around them. Remington and Oscar left Vixx stationed just inside the cave's mouth, and they slunk deeper into the earth. Remington led the way, light on his paws, navigating the rough path of rock and mud. The walls glistened with moisture and the air still tasted thick with guano despite Doc's masks. The drip of water seemed to match the thump of his heart in his ears. A dim light filtered through the cracks in the ceiling and the glow of the main chamber fire was just visible at the edge of the tunnel beneath the path.

'I can hear them,' Oscar whispered. 'There must be over a hundred of them trapped in there.'

'Not for long, Ozzy.' Remington raised a claw to his lips and slipped onward toward the tunnel and the light.

Remington led the way, slinking from one obstacle to the next. The pathway seemed clear, but he enjoyed demonstrating the ideal practice to Oscar. The young ferret was much better suited to slinking in the shadows though. He flattened himself against the floor, and then walls. He seemed almost liquid in the meagre light. They crouched on opposite sides of the main chamber entrance. Remington nodded to Oscar and slunk into the chamber, hunkering down behind a broken stalagmite. Oscar followed and gaped at the scene. The huge fire burned grander than it had before. It cracked loudly and the sound careened back and forth against the cave walls. Equipment was sprawled across makeshift tables. Containers seethed with guano. Creatures moved all around, their ribs visible, their eyes bulbous and shining in the firelight. On the ceiling, the black bruise that shuddered horribly caught Oscar's eye. *Bats*, Remington mouthed to the youngster. Oscar gasped beneath his mask as he realised what he was looking at. His eyes filled and he blinked hard.

Remington peered down into the main chamber and surveyed the cave. Cages lined the desolate scene, with bodies lying like heaps of rags inside – dead or near death, Remington couldn't tell. It was a wretched sight. And there, rippling in the gleam, steam rising from his shuddering warts, was Roadkill, dark eyes filled with malice.

Remington signalled for Oscar to follow and look for Brigg. They slipped closer to the cave floor, slinking along the circular sloping pathway ringing the chamber. If any of the enslaved animals noticed them, they did not register it. All continued to work, glassy eyes steady and unwelcoming. Remington peeked out over the edge. Lennox and Doc should have made it to the chamber by now. Where were they?

Oscar continued to slip forward. His movements were serpentine and measured. Just as he was about to signal to Oscar to halt, Remington saw the dark brown of Lennox's ear poke out from a rock behind Roadkill. She carefully raised her head and looked up toward the upper edge of the cave. Remington waved a claw. She nodded. Remington and Oscar crept down toward Roadkill; silent, invisible.

Roadkill was lashing his tongue toward two creatures in front of him, pulling it back just before it reached their flesh through their ragged excuses for fur. Remington and Oscar were just a few paces from Roadkill. Lennox and Doc were ready on the other side. Just as Remington began the charge, a sound echoed around the chamber walls.

'Boss!' Brigg howled and jumped toward them from an alcove in the far wall.

'Mine,' called Oscar and changed course.

Remington dove onto Roadkill's left hind leg and squeezed with all his strength. Lennox did the same with the right. Roadkill flipped onto his forelegs and kicked out hard trying to throw them both off. His tongue lashed out wildly in all directions. Doc scurried beneath its movements and gripped one of the toad's forelegs around the wrist. He pulled hard and Roadkill, unbalanced, crashed into the floor face first. Blood spattered from above his eye.

Oscar leapt toward Brigg, met nothing but air, and felt a deep sting in his stomach. Brigg had ducked around the ferret and delivered a stiff blow to his gut. Oscar dropped to the floor gasping for air. Brigg turned around in time to see Remington yank her prone boss's hindlegs behind him and tie them. Lennox was sealing the toad's mouth, binding it tightly shut. Roadkill's eyes were wide and pleading. Brigg turned and ran for the main entrance.

'Oscar,' Remington called, struggling with Roadkill's thick muscular legs. 'When you're finished lying about, Vixx might need some help with that.'

Oscar pushed himself spluttering to his feet. 'On it, boss,' he said and took off after the rat.

With Roadkill secured, Remington, Doc, and Lennox began freeing the creatures. Most of them were too wired on

Heartbreak fumes to be able to understand what was happening, but a few had the lucidity to assist. A steady line of desperate creatures made their exodus toward the beck.

Oscar hollered from the upper entranceway. He was supporting Vixx, her wing slung over his shoulder. Blood matted her feathers.

'Sergeant,' Remington called, rushing to Oscar's aid, and taking Vixx's other wing.

'I'm sorry, Sir,' she said. 'She was so fast. She was too fast for me. She got away.'

'Don't worry, kid. We got the one that matters.'

The bats were a more substantial problem than the other creatures had been. Only Vixx had the capacity to reach the cave ceiling and it took her a few moments to regain enough strength to do so. Once freed though, the bats stayed where they were, seemingly entranced by something. Their leathery wings pulled tight around them, their black eyes glassy and unmoving.

'The frequency,' Doc said. 'It's that sound, it's messing with their echolocation.'

Doc scurried around the chamber floor, kicking up dust in his wake. He stopped now and then to raise his head. Finally, he found what he was looking for. In the alcove where Brigg had emerged, a strange human device, all metal and hard edges with a long thin antenna was sending a note into the air so high-pitched it was just on the edge of Remington's register.

Doc dragged it over to where Roadkill writhed against his bindings on the dusty floor.

'We need to turn this off,' said Doc. 'But we don't know how long they've been like that. It could free them, or it could be catastrophic.'

'We can't leave them like that,' Remington said, looking up at the pitiful silent creatures.

They both looked at Lennox.

'Do it,' she said.

Doc flipped a large red switch and the sound peeled away. It didn't stop immediately, rather it seemed to drop like a scream backwards through the blood. There was a crackle at first above them, and then the sound grew. The mass clattering of serrated wings shook and echoed around the chamber. Roadkill moaned through his bindings as if in agony. And then the air bloomed with bat song. It swam through Remington's head like a dream. The thing that had been missing from the Burrow's natural soundtrack returned with an almost demonic force and it felt right. He couldn't understand their sounds, but it felt like it had meaning, somewhere between logic and dream, between life and death. A frequency with the palpable rhythm of death, reminding the world what life is. It squeezed through the cracks of his being and filled him up. Remington's mind suddenly flashed with images, images of soaring shapes, of breaking vines, of doors flying off hinges, and strange creatures scattering like dust out into an infinite sky of stars and colour.

The bats, one by one, began to take wing, slipping around the fire in loops. More and more joined, and soon the fire was engulfed in a whirlpool of black, a vortex of shadow thundering, clattering around the flames, their song skittering out into the night beyond the cave. Remington felt Lennox slip her paw into his as they watched the dance, until almost as swiftly as it had begun, they streamed out of the entrance way, careening, screeching down the tunnel into the freedom of the Burrow and the ancient wood. Remington imagined them rattling over the fields, scattering over the spray of breaking waves, their sound somehow a joyful cry and sorrowful laugh all at once. Their frequency, with its rhythm of death beating out its pulse through a mournful breeze. He thought of them joining the bats in the city, flashing their black promise over the neon scree of the urban facades. He squeezed Lennox's paw and drank in the night's energy, its soundtrack now complete.

# Chapter Twenty-Five

The night was long, and the elation of the return of the bats' song to the Burrow was soon replaced with the logistical reality of what had to come next. Over a hundred creatures, in various states of starvation and drug-dependence, were now strewn along the bank of the beck.

'Looks like a bloody battlefield,' said Rem as he joined Lennox and Doc in the moonlight outside the cave. The strange helter skelter of images echoed in his head, but they were beginning to fade.

'We're going to need some help on this one.' Lennox surveyed the sorry scene.

'We need to find out who we can trust first.' Remington kept his voice low.

'I'm not sure we've got that luxury, Rem. It's not just these sorry folk. It's the Heartbreak. We can't leave that lying around.' Lennox shuddered. 'That fire. I can't believe they haven't already blown themselves off into the fucking sky.'

He knew she was right. It was going to be a big enough task just getting these creatures back to the station clearing. Some of them couldn't stand and others had the wild-eyed stare that only came with serious Heartbreak addiction. The Burrow didn't have the staff, the infrastructure, or the know-how to return them to physical health, let alone to dry them out properly, and there was the matter of recovering and securing the Heartbreak still lying unattended in the cave.

'Look out!' Oscar yelled. The bound, gelatinous figure of

Roadkill slid helplessly from the tunnel, and skidded to a stop next to Remington. The toad's eyes burned with anger.

'Careful, Oscar,' said Lennox. 'We don't want any complaints about police brutality, do we?'

Roadkill groaned through his tight gag. Lennox gave him a swift kick, making his warts ripple horribly.

'Sorry, Ma'am. He slipped.' Oscar clambered down, dragging a large sheet behind him. 'He rolled off. I'm not sure I'm going to be able to drag him all the way back. He weighs a bloody ton.'

'We'll manage, Ozzy.' Remington pointed to the creatures lining the beck. 'Getting him back's the least of our worries.'

Vixx was the last to emerge from the cave. She was cradling one wing in the other. Blood clung to her feathers.

'What are we waiting for?' she asked.

'Just trying to work out how to get this lot back to the clearing,' Lennox said, thumping her foot.

Vixx nodded and stepped down toward the beck. 'Listen up,' she called out. 'Who here is strong enough to walk?'

The creatures who were conscious blinked back at her.

'Wakey wakey! Who here is able to walk?' She tried again with a sudden bite in her voice.

Slowly, animals began to stand up. Paws were raised. 'Right then, you lot, we need you to spread yourselves out evenly. We need everyone in a line. Start helping everyone to their paws. If anyone is unable to walk, we'll carry them, or we'll drag them, but we will get everyone back to safety tonight.'

Some of the creatures nodded but nobody moved.

Vixx snapped her talons together three times. 'Well, move!'

And move they did.

'Thank you, Sergeant,' said Lennox and looked at Remington.

The badger grinned back and gave her a wink. 'She's wasted in this place.'

Remington, Lennox, and Doc, started to patrol the line, helping creatures to their feet and to support each other. About halfway down he saw the weasel who had restrained him when he first entered the tunnel. He was struggling to lift another creature, whose too-thin red forelegs were limp and dangling.

'She's alive,' Remington said as he hurried to help the weasel. He pushed his shoulder under Red's mother's dangling limb. Together they supported her.

'It's you,' the weasel said. His eyes were saucers and the little white that was visible was horribly bloodshot. 'She said you'd be back.'

'How long has she been like this?' The squirrel's mouth was slack, and her tongue lolled from it. The tongue was dry and covered in tiny lacerations. Her neck fur was worn away in patches, dark bruising visible beneath.

'It was Roadkill, this morning. He strangled her with his tongue.'

Remington opened one of her eyelids. The pupils were vacant but there was a hint of movement. Her breaths were shallow and ragged. The badger felt rage swell in his chest. 'Why?'

'No reason. He just picks on us now and then. Sometimes he goes too far.'

Remington noticed the weasel's skin was also visible on his forelegs and shoulders. Deep gouges and welts marked his flesh.

'This way.' Remington and the weasel dragged Red's mother to the edge of the beck. Remington cupped his paws in the beck and brought the water to the squirrel's mouth, dropping a small amount onto her tongue.

'She needs more,' said the weasel.

Remington shook his head. 'She could go into shock. We need to get her back safe.'

They re-joined the line and slowly, oh so slowly, the sorry parade of animals made their way from the ancient wood back toward the centre of the Burrow, to the clearing. Oscar and Vixx shared the burden of dragging Roadkill along. Despite being bound tightly, he still made an awkward passenger and repeatedly managed to squirm free of the sheet. That combined with repeated pauses to pick up fallen creatures, breaks to allow the weak animals to rest, and the need to gather some rogue individuals who suddenly fled in Heartbreak-induced frenzies, the journey took most of the night.

Back at the clearing, Mrs Banks, the chief, Claire, and Chris were roused and, after an initial round of complaints about not being kept abreast of goings on, Mrs Banks proved a surprising asset. She directed the voles to where she had maintained stores of hay and straw beneath the station hut and set the chief to preparing food. Eventually the rescued creatures were separated into three classes: those in need of urgent medical care; those dangerously strung out on the effects of Heartbreak; and the rest, most of whom were severely malnourished and suffering from the inhalation of narcotics. Those of the third class, Mrs Banks set to work aiding the other two. It wasn't something Remington would have thought of, but it was a masterstroke. The shared experience of the creatures had led to a clear bond between them. Lennox had been right though. They would still need help. A recovery centre would have to be set up and they desperately needed the medical expertise of the city Met.

The toad had been thrown in the station's cell. Lennox and Rem restrained him while Doc ungagged him. Remington expected Roadkill to struggle, to have his tongue shoot forth and attack, but he didn't. Roadkill refused to even open his mouth. There was a brief attempt at interrogation, but the night had drawn deep, and every paw was needed up in the clearing.

'Let him stew until tomorrow,' Lennox said. 'We'll station someone at the top of the stairs. He's not going anywhere.'

Remington reluctantly agreed. He was exhausted and was keen to check on Red's mother.

'Len?' he asked as he turned to leave.

'What is it?'

'Did you, erm, see anything in there when we set the bats free?'

'Other than bats?' She gave him a puzzled look.

'Never mind.'

When Remington found Red's mother, she was alone, still unconscious. An old rag blanket had been placed over her frail body, and Remington was relieved to see movement beneath the material, the gentle rise and fall betraying her shallow breaths. Remington untied the feather from his fur and placed it on the blanket beside her. He held her paw and placed his forehead upon it.

'Sir, Sir.' The voice felt like it was swimming through a dream at first. 'Detective.' Remington was jostled awake. He awoke to see the still sleeping face of the red squirrel. 'Sir?'

Remington looked up to find Vixx standing over him. Her eyes were wild and frantic.

'What is it?' He blinked up into the sky. The night was beginning to bleed into morning. A subtle shiver of grey ghosted the horizon.

'You've got to come, Sir. It's the toad.'

Remington would have blinked to check his eyes weren't deceiving him, would have dug his claws into his flesh to prove he was awake, would have screamed. He would have done all of these things had he not been frozen from tail to nose by the scene before him. Roadkill slowly rotated, his powerful legs hanging almost straight, the tips of his webbed toes grazing the floor, his round belly sagging and bulbous. The warts of his back no longer rippled and were no longer slick with slime. His skin seemed dry and hard. He was hanging from the course root beam of the cell top, the noose his own tongue; the same tongue Remington had slashed with his claws at Mickey's funeral; the same tongue that had been used as a lashing whip on creatures in the cave; the same tongue Remington had witnessed the toad asphyxiate a defenceless hedgehog with; the same tongue. Roadkill's black eyes shone Remington's gawping face back at him.

'Sergeant,' Remington eventually croaked from his dry throat. 'Who was on shift?'

Vixx hung her head. 'It was me, Sir. I was standing guard up top, but I checked on him at regular intervals like you instructed.'

'Nobody could have got past you?'

'No, Sir.'

Remington looked around the corridor and felt at the walls. 'There's definitely no other way in or out?'

'It's completely sealed, Sir.'

Roadkill's gently swaying revolutions were hypnotic. The tongue was looped up and over the beam and then back down and around the vile creature's thick throat.

Remington pressed his face to the cool metal of the cell bars. 'He did this to himself.'

'But why?'

'You want to be a detective?' Remington asked, keeping his eyes on the lifeless amphibian pirouetting on air. 'You tell me. Why would an arrested criminal take his own life?'

Vixx twitched her head to one side then the other. 'Fear of incarceration?'

Remington pulled away from the bars and looked at her doubtfully. 'Or?'

'Or… I'm sorry, Sir, I don't know.'

'Or it might be a preferable fate to what was waiting for you when your boss found out you'd cocked up and been caught.'

'But we could have protected him.'

'Come on, Vixx. I know you're not that naïve.'

Vixx nodded. 'Shall I untangle him and get him down?'

'No, we'd best get Doc first. He's going to love this one.'

# Chapter Twenty-Six

Doc went about his duties inspecting Roadkill's body with an enthusiasm Remington thought bordered on disturbing. He and Lennox watched as the mole snuffled around the cell, checking every tiny slither of floor and wall before turning the nodules of his nose to the lifeless mound of toad that seemed to hover like a hideous angel. He nuzzled over the dull grey-green skin. He nudged at the now still warts on his back, and then slid down the limply hanging legs. Doc squeaked and chittered to himself all the while, punctuating each new mark of interest with an appropriate sound effect.

'All signs point to suicide,' he said, the burst of his pink nose having finished its macabre business.

'And it would be possible for him to have done this alone?' Remington was looking up at the root beam, decorated as it was with the grim tinsel of Roadkill's thick leathery tongue.

'Yes, Remmy. That thing is more than strong and dextrous enough to do the job. All he needed was the determination to do it.'

'Nothing else you can enlighten us with?' Lennox asked. She nudged Roadkill's body with her paw and watched as he swayed like a revolting punchbag.

'Smells like a bellyful of narcotics and bile, but that's hardly surprising considering what he's been up to. I'll have to get him down to the city to find out anything else.'

'There'll be transport tomorrow,' Lennox said. Remington shot her a look. 'We've got people coming for the recovery centre, and we need to secure the Heartbreak. You don't have the resources here, Rem.'

Remington drew a paw down his snout. 'I know, I know. Head's up would have been nice.'

'Consider this your head's up.'

'Yes, Ma'am.' Remington stretched his limbs and then gripped one of Roadkill's legs, pushing his shoulder under the toad's posterior. 'Now, you wanna grab the other leg so Doc can untie this thing?'

Lennox rolled her eyes but shouldered the other leg. Together they lifted and Doc was able to climb up Roadkill's bulbous body to where the tongue had been awkwardly tied behind what little neck the toad had.

Remington watched Doc from beneath the toad. 'Imagine tying your own-'

'I'd rather not, thank you,' said Lennox as she grunted under the heft of the combination of toad and mole. 'Take your time, Doc.'

'Nearly there, nearly there.'

'Seriously Doc, this fucker smells awful.' Remington shuffled his weight slightly and dug his heels into the cell floor.

'Nearly… nearly… and… there.'

There was a coarse scraping sound, and the massive toad flopped forward like a sleeping bag full of bowling balls. He landed with a not unsatisfying thud.

'Quills,' Remington said through the dust that plumed around them. 'I'll get Chris and Claire to package him up for you.'

'No need, Rem,' the mole said, returning his attention to the corpse. 'I've got him from here. I imagine you'll all be needed up top.'

'Alright, well, give us a shout if you need anything,' Lennox added as they left. Doc waved them away with a nod, already back to running his nose over the body.

'Must be nice to love your work that much,' Remington muttered as they walked back to the surface.

'Be nice to love anything *that* much.' Lennox stopped

suddenly. She was staring out of the window of the main station hut. 'Quills.'

They must have lost track of time down in the cells because the sun was up and the day was candling toward afternoon. They'd tasked Sergeant Vixx with gathering some volunteers to help with a makeshift recovery centre until the city staff arrived. The clearing buzzed with energy as creatures hurriedly moved about carrying liquids, food and hay, their footsteps a percussion of purpose in the morning air. Beneath the pale glow of the late morning sun, various materials had been stretched and secured like tarps, creating rudimentary shelters that huddled against each other in the clearing.

Remington and Lennox stepped into one of the long tents. The wounded, eyes still crowded with the shadow of Heartbreak, were nestled in beds of hay and straw. Just outside the first tent, a spider with a glistening trail of silver had spun a gossamer tapestry capturing drew drops. The threads, sparkling like starlight, were being swept by an old vole Remington didn't recognise. The dewdrops were cradled onto leaves and brought into the tent. The vole smiled and nodded to Lennox and Remington. They dutifully nodded back.

The scent of freshly prepared food wafted on the air. Remington's stomach snarled.

'Francis!' A familiar voice called.

Lennox turned to the source of the sound. 'Is she talking to you?'

Remington groaned, hung his head, and turned slowly.

'Francis!' A large beaver was bustling toward them with food piled high on broad flat leaves.

'Good of you to volunteer, Miss Plunkett,' he said.

'Head Plunkett if you don't mind, Francis.'

'You going to introduce us, Francis?' Lennox was barely containing her glee.

'Apologies for him, my dear. Take this, you poor thing.' Head

Plunkett handed them a leaf each. 'You look absolutely exhausted.'

'It's Lennox, Superintendent Lennox. So, how do you know Francis here?' Lennox asked and began to pick at the food.

'He was one of my pupils way back when he was just a pup. Always thought he had it in him to make something of himself.' She dusted at Remington's dirty fur with her paws. 'Who knows, maybe he will someday.' Plunkett laughed and Lennox joined in enthusiastically.

'This is wonderful,' Lennox said. 'And he's right. It is good of you to give up your time.'

'Not at all, not at all. As soon as your young Vixx flapped by and told us, we knew we had to help. Most of the teachers are here doing what they can.'

'Is Miss Carrol here?' Remington asked through a mouthful of grub. Lennox gave him a brief glance.

'Good grief, Francis, don't talk with your mouth full. No, we needed at least a few to stay behind for the children. Your sergeant insisted we keep things as normal as possible for the children and parents. I think that's why she came to us – a decent number of able paws all under one roof.'

Lennox glanced at Remington. 'Wasted in this place,' she said. Remington nodded.

'Anyway, I'd best crack on,' she squeezed Lennox's shoulder warmly. 'And apologies we weren't able to do a better job with this one.' She gestured toward Remington.

'What?' he said, and food fell from his jaw.

The beaver bustled off and continued preparing food with startling efficiency.

'Well,' said Lennox, beaming at Remington. 'Francis, she is an absolute delight.'

'Shut up,' he said.

Lennox cocked her head at him.

'Shut up, Ma'am,' he offered.

'Better. Now, come on.'

They continued their tour of the tents. In these simple, improvised shelters creatures, foreign and familiar lay next to each other, united in the journey they had shared. The whole clearing had become a mosaic of life stories, all of them decorated with threads of survival and resilience. The mosaic was far from a perfect tableau though. There was still so much uncertainty, with many creatures fighting for each breath, and others still steeped in the nightmares Heartbreak could project in their minds.

When they found Vixx, she was aiding an orb-weaver spider as it bound the wounds across a quaking grey squirrel's back. They watched as the sergeant spoke softly into the creature's ear with a soothing trill and gently rolled it into position for the spider to do its work. Once finished, she smoothed the feathers of her good wing over its head as it drifted off to sleep.

She looked up and started, surprised to see her superior officers standing there.

'Ma'am, Sir, I was-'

Lennox raised her paw and shook her head. 'You've done exemplary work, Vixx. Great thinking with the school and the teachers.

'Least I could do after I messed up with the toad.' Vixx scuffed at the floor with her talons.

'Not your fault, Sergeant,' Remington said. 'I stationed you up top. We make sure they're unarmed, and we stand guard. We don't stare into their cells all night.'

'But still I-'

'Nobody could have guessed he'd do that,' Lennox assured her. 'Now, you need to get that wing seen to, and see Head Plunkett about some food.'

'But Ma'am-'

'I think that's an order, Sergeant,' Remington said.

'Yes Sir.' Vixx reluctantly left the tent.

Lennox and Remington completed their rounds of the tents. Vixx had done a remarkable job, and each of the volunteers had a clear role and purpose. They helped as best they could, and Remington checked on Red's mother. Her breathing was still shallow but there was a renewed purpose in the beat of her pulse. A rest tent had been assembled for the volunteers to sleep in between shifts and, not without protest, Remington, Lennox, and Vixx, were all convinced by Head Plunkett to get some sleep. With the situation in hand, no toad to interrogate, no clues as to Brigg's whereabouts, and the urge to be sharp and alert for the arrival of reinforcements the next day, there wasn't much reason to fight sleep any further. Remington and Lennox settled down in adjacent bundles of straw. Lennox was asleep and snoring within moments. Remington took a little longer. Roadkill revolved in his mind over and over, as did Daisy's ink-splodged face. Eventually though, to the soundtrack of the volunteers' steps, and the occasional cry of a patient, Remington let sleep take him.

# Chapter Twenty-Seven

*The badger dreams*
*of a sett in the hollow of the Earth's heartbeat.*
*He dreams of shaking off the city's smoke,*
*scattering it like sawdust across the floor.*
*He dreams of pushing the metropolis*
*from his lungs, of pressing his ear to the soil*
*and hearing a song of stone.*
*He wakes…*

Remington always felt moments of transitions acutely. As he lay on his back listening to the general hubbub of creatures moving through the tents, helping, feeding, comforting, he could feel the rhythm of the Burrow beginning to shift. It wasn't a sudden change of time signature, more that nature's drummer was just starting to lag behind the beat. This was how it always began, this subtle shift in rhythm which led to a feeling in his gut, worming away like a termite through a beam. It was this dissonance in the Burrow's song that had made him leave his family sett, his ancestral home, in the first place, and flee to the city. He wasn't tempted by the allure of the metropolis' many neon promises like so many others had been. He just needed a change of track because the Burrow's no longer made any sense to him. There had been other transitional discords in his life, but even when it was a sudden event that caused everything to change, Remington would look back and feel as though he had heard the tell-tale tempo shift on the wind beforehand. He could feel it again as he stared up at the tent's inner surface, watching droplets of the morning's faint rain drift into each other before running down the sides. He didn't want to be at the mercy of the transitions, not this time. He felt like balling himself up tight, to shield his thick old hide from the undulations of fate, but that would never work. Instead, he had to focus on what he could change.

The movement of the drops brought Daisy's face to mind, the tears that had bloomed in her clear blue eyes. He rolled onto his side and pulled his forelegs close to his chest. He remembered her laughter in the fading light of the bar, the touch of her fur on his as they walked the Burrow in the night. It all felt so silly and naïve now, some holiday romance, as though the rules of the real world didn't apply just because he was far from the city. The real world hadn't just burst his bubble. It had crashed into his home, grabbed him by the fur, and forced him to acknowledge its presence. The real world didn't involve dates with schoolteachers, or drunken meetings with old friends getting high on questionable bogweed. The real world demanded constant vigilance and respect. Turn your back for a second and it will find a way to punish you. Only yesterday Remington had suspected poor little Red's mother had been murdered after being in his presence for the briefest of moments. That had been a warning shot, one he couldn't risk repeating, not with Daisy, not with anyone.

Remington admired the work of the volunteers, their selflessness, and the sense of community that spread throughout the clearing. The comradeship of the creatures, many of whom he had never met nor spoken to, was clear. The Burrow looked after their own, and while he was met with welcome as he patrolled the tents and checked on recovering animals, offered his strength, his problem-solving nous, his experience, Remington felt ill-at-ease. He didn't belong here, and he began to long for solitude.

Over the course of the next few days, more police arrived from the city, and this did little to ease Remington's anxiety. They were perfectly acceptable officers, seemingly keen to do their duty, but Remington's gut twisted tighter and tighter as the week drew on. The tents were upgraded to impressively well-equipped recovery centres, and there was a growing sense of good feeling from the creatures in the clearing, the volunteers, the officers, the medical spiders, everyone in fact, apart from Remington. He watched the newcomers closely, suspicion nibbling at the corners of his mind. The Met was a positive institution. He believed that, but it had its share of shadows, and the Rev and Cull's feathered web could easily have ensnared more than a few of them. Every offered paw of assistance, every concerned look, made him question motives. The new phase of assistance, with this labyrinthine compound of aid, was a many-thorned rose.

At first Remington had checked off in his mind every new officer who arrived, their physical bearing, classification, rank, and his gut sense about them, but eventually it was futile. Due to the volume of Heartbreak in the cave that needed to be recovered, the transports were eventually being used multiple times in a single day. It was risky, of course, to have so much animal activity occurring on human train lines, but they couldn't leave so much volatile substance where it was. It wasn't so much the potential for theft, although with the street value of the black gold being so high, it was a concern; the real issue was how dangerous it was. One spark of flint a little too close and there would be a crater where the cave used to be and an influx of concerned and excitable humans. This also meant the powder could only be transported in modest quantities too. It needed to be taken back to the city where it could be stored safely or disposed of, but they couldn't risk a blast on a human transport. They might have kept themselves to the relative safety of intermodal rail containers, but any accident on board would mean human enquiries, investigations and possibly more heavily policed or watched containers, never mind the potential risk to animal and human life. Remington shuddered as he thought back to the enormous fire Roadkill had kept his slaves stoking to burn off the fumes. The upshot was a continual coming and going of animals, a tide of creatures as constantly flowing as the city's great river. As for keeping track of the creatures from the metropolis, it was impossible. So, Remington gave up, but that didn't make him any less anxious.

He saw less and less of Lennox as the recovery effort continued, busy as she was with the marshalling of such a large team and operation. Oscar had accompanied Doc back to the city with Roadkill's corpse soon after the initial examination. Better equipped though the Burrow was in terms of the influx of staff and equipment, Doc needed to get the toad back to his lab under the Met to complete a full investigation. Vixx, still reeling from having let Brigg slip through her wings, dedicated herself to finding the rat. Remington didn't hold out much hope of the sergeant tracking her down, but he couldn't help but admire her efforts. Now and then she would report back with a lead – tracks, scent, fur, and Remington accompanied her to the site, more to get away from the commotion of the clearing than anything else.

Remington took to sitting by Red's mother's bedside. He held her paw and talked to her about nothing much; Red mostly and how she'd bravely started her own investigation, determined to find her mum. She regained consciousness and some strength. At first, the scale of her malnutrition was so abject she was unable to keep any food down, but eventually she managed a morsel, and then one morsel became two, and finally she was able to raise herself upright in her straw and hay. She was still unable to speak, and the deep bruising around her neck was visible through her fur. There was a sparkle in her eyes when Remington talked about little Red though, and he assured her, she'd see her again soon.

One morning, once Remington had delivered her breakfast and was chatting away about the weather or something equally inane, a welcome voice belted through the tent.

'Excuse me Madam, is this overactive sporran bothering you?'

Remington didn't need to turn around. 'What cretin let you out of the city, Nick?'

The two badgers embraced. Nick pushed Remington away, still holding his shoulders and appraised him.

'Well, they're clearly not starving you up here in the backend of beyond, are they?' Nick poked Remington's belly.

'Look who's talking.'

'I do not believe we have had the pleasure,' Nick said, turning his attention to Red's mother. He bowed low and shook the squirrel's paw. She beamed back at him.

'I'll come by later on, okay?' Remington said. Red's mother smiled and nodded. He shoved Nick toward the exit.

'And maybe I will too,' he said. Red's mother gave a silent laugh.

'Come on, you goon.' Remington led Nick outside into the clearing. 'What are you doing all the way up here?'

'Well, Doc told us what happened and said you had an army of folk strung out on Heartbreak. Seemed the least I could do. Been dealing with this stuff down in the city for years now.'

'We could definitely use the help.'

Remington escorted Nick to the Heartbreak recovery tent and showed him the scale of the problems they were facing.

'Quills,' Nick breathed as he looked at the rows of straw and hay. 'How long have they been using?'

'Months, some of them. They've been forced to make it, inhaling the fumes.'

Nick nodded as he surveyed the area. Some of the animals had already started showing signs of recovery; they were awake and alert, slowly eating their food while still needing help with basic grooming tasks. Others were in more serious states of addiction and withdrawal, trembling, unresponsive or staring into space. Nick nodded in understanding and walked around the tent, inspecting each of the critters in turn. The squirrels, rabbits, mice, and more; some lying still in their sleep, some twitching and mumbling. Nick made a low humming sound as he went from animal to animal, offering encouraging words as he passed by each one. He rubbed his snout thoughtfully as he observed them before finally turning back to Remington with a determined expression on his face.

'Right,' he said, and rubbed his wrists. 'I'd best get started.'

Remington introduced Nick to the scattering of volunteers currently on Heartbreak duty. Remington assisted as best he could but before long found himself surplus to requirements. The larger badger soon had the recovery tent reorganised and was sharing his experience with the small team. Nick always did have a way with people. When Remington gave instructions, he got the distinct impression he caused aggravation, but Nick's gregarious nature made people want to support him, something about his open curiosity. The badger shone with good intentions despite his intimidating stature. Remington slipped out of the tent, leaving Nick in his element.

As soon as he emerged into the clearing, a high reedy voice called to him. Little Red was walking steadily toward him, fur like deep fire in the sun. Daisy was at her side.

'You found her,' Red beamed, and then she leapt up to embrace him with her skinny limbs. 'I knew you would.'

'I had a lot of help,' Remington said as he safely plopped her back onto the ground. 'She's still very poorly, so you'll have to be gentle, okay?'.

Red nodded. She was shivering with excitement and twiddling with her digits.

'You okay?' Daisy mouthed at him. Concern was written across her brow.

Remington tried to give a reassuring smile. He looked down at Red. 'Well, let's not keep her waiting, eh?'

Remington pushed open the tent. Red's eyes widened at the sight of her mother sitting upright in her cot of hay. The moment their eyes met, Red bounced on her hind legs and then shot toward her mother. She leapt onto her, paws reaching out to touch the frail face, and bruised throat. The older squirrel's eyes filled with tears as she pulled her daughter tightly to her. She looked over at Remington through the shuddering plume of Red's tail. Every strand of worry and anxiety melted away from the badger as he smiled back at her.

Daisy cleared her throat. 'Rem, can we talk?'

He nodded and followed the rabbit out of the tent. The clearing felt suddenly close and quiet, despite the sound of Nick directing volunteers.

'I know you're busy with all this, but I was worried. I've not heard from you since…' Her eyes were searching his own.

'Sorry, yeah, with all of these newcomers it's been a lot to organise and keep on top of.'

Daisy nodded, but she looked doubtful. 'You know I'm here too, if you need any help, anything.' She reached for Remington's paw, but he raised it and scratched his forehead with a claw.

'I'm just not sure it's safe right now.'

'What are you doing?'

'Nothing, I just think it might be better, safer, for you if you kept a little distance-'

Daisy silenced him with a kiss. His instinct told him to pull away, but he found himself unable to. When she did release him, she gripped his jaw in her paw.

'Your heart's in the right place,' she said. 'But that's not your choice to make.'

Remington was about to protest, but she turned away and hopped back into the tent. The badger followed, more than a little dazed. Red was excitedly telling her mother all about her investigation, clutching the red feather. She rambled about the school, Miss Carrol, her new dormice friends, and the brave badger who'd helped her. Her mother smiled and mouthed silent replies, her facial fur wet with tears.

'Come on, you,' said Daisy. 'Your mum needs to rest.' She looked back at Remington. 'But we can come back tomorrow.'

Red kissed her mother and then scurried to Remington and gave him another hug. Remington hugged her back tightly. The young squirrel's mum was glowing as she watched them.

Without a word to Remington, Miss Carrol led Red out of the tent. Remington followed and watched as the two figures disappeared out of view at the edge of the clearing into the surrounding trees.

'Now then,' Nick boomed as he slammed a heavy paw onto Remington's shoulder. 'Tell me there's a bar around here, mate. Because you look like I need a drink.'

# Chapter Twenty-Eight

The sun was just ticking over to its highest point, casting a sickly yellow veil over the Burrow as Nick and Remington ambled toward Cat's. Nick was explaining the steps he'd found most beneficial when dealing with Heartbreak addiction. He mentioned some of the volunteers by name and rambled on about their families, jobs, preferences in terms of their duties in the recovery operation. Nick's affinity with others was remarkable to Remington who felt more than a little guilty at barely being able to recall the names of his colleagues, but it did his mood no harm to have his friend's wittering back in his life. As they reached the fork in the woodland that broke off toward Cat's, Nick fell silent.

The path leading toward the feline's establishment was framed by nettles and ferns, and while this was always the case, something in the air felt off. By now, even on a slow day, they would have been able to hear creatures enjoying the suspicious drinks Cat liberally poured, but the breeze carried only the thin warble of a mournful note.

'What is that?' Nick asked, cocking his head.

Remington pressed his paws into the earth, reaching out for a semblance of activity. There was none.

'Come on,' Remington said and quickened his pace.

The towering nettles had felt like a threshold between the everyday sleepiness of the Burrow and the livelier realm of questionable decisions offered by Cat's bar, but now Remington was acutely aware of the shadows they cast, the ugly jag of their edges. At the crest of the sloping path the bar came into view, nestled in its crook between two gnarled old oaks. The usually welcoming building looked somehow unfinished with the lack of animal activity visible through its windows or spilling out into the surrounding area. An uneasy stillness hung about it like a tinsel of mist. The usual hum of chatter, laughter, the clinking of receptacles, was gone. Even the familiar smell of fermented fruits was stifled and stale.

'Bloody hell, Rem,' said Nick. 'You really do know all the best places, don't you? I don't think they're open.'

'Shhh.' Remington was turning his ears toward the strange whining. 'What is that?'

Nick listened. It was a slightly discordant sombre tone, the kind a breeze could make when it passed through damp reeds at just the right angle. 'It's coming from inside.'

The usually busy entrance was vacant. The sign hanging above the door creaked softly in the wind, harmonising with the peculiar sound emanating from within. Both badgers stopped and traded a look.

'After you, chief,' said Nick. 'You're the copper, after all.'

Remington slowly pushed the door open.

Inside, the bar was a catastrophe. Chairs were scattered, drinks sat half-filled on tables, and a noxious odour made the air thick. Fingle lay on his back on the bar top staring at the ceiling, scratching at his stomach. At the far end of the room, Glen was drawing a reed across an odd-looking instrument. Her eyes were closed and sadness was etched on her round weasel face. The strange sound was coming from the instrument, its haunting resonance seeming to make the air throb. She moved the reed slowly back and forth over taut fibres, creating a curious doleful song.

Remington cleared his throat. 'How's business?'

Glen's eyes sprung open, and she stopped playing with a final jarring scrape of the reed. Fingle started and toppled off the bar.

'Remo?' The ferret barked as he clambered upright. 'You're our first customers of the day.'

'*Your* customers?' Remington picked up a fallen bucket and turned it upright. 'Where's Cat?'

'Still not seen her since the other night when you and Miss Carrol came in.' Glen dusted off another stool and placed it in front of Nick.

'You've been running the place since then?' Remington asked.

Fingle poured two drinks and delivered them to the badgers. 'We've been trying, but we don't know how she did it on her own. We were trying to keep things ticking over until she came back, but...' He gestured around the room.

'She's never disappeared like this before?' Remington's gut was starting to turn.

Fingle shook his head, his fur as greasy and matted as ever. 'She's gone off a few times, but always left word before she went. It's never been for this long.'

'You wouldn't know anything about Cat being involved with Brigg-' Remington began but was cut off by Nick spitting his drink across the bar.

'Quills, that's grim,' he said and put down the tumbler.

'Oh, Fingle, Glen, this is Nick,' Remington gestured back and forth absentmindedly.

'Brigg?' said Glen, offering Nick a quick wave and smile. 'Why d'you ask?'

'My first time here, Cat gave her something. Couldn't quite make out what.'

'Wouldn't know anything about that,' said Fingle.

Remington frowned at them both. 'Guys, come on; you heard about what happened with Roadkill, I assume?'

'Small burrow, man.' Glen let her claws scrape lightly over her instrument.

'Then, seriously, if you know something-'

'Rem,' Fingle looked at him earnestly. 'This is Cat we're

talking about. We'd tell you if there was anything.'

Remington narrowed his eyes. 'Mind if we take a look around then? Maybe there's something that could point us in the right direction?'

Glen nodded and set her instrument aside. 'Of course, Remo. Anything for Cat.'

Fingle pointed toward the back of the bar. 'You should probably start with her office. We didn't want to make a mess.'

Nick's eyes widened and he looked around the shambolic room.

'Didn't want to make a mess in there,' Fingle corrected himself.

Cat's office was a dramatic contrast to the rest of the bar. Everything was immaculate and ordered. Papers were stacked neatly on her old crate desk, and every item seemed to have a precise place.

'Wow,' said Nick. 'Does a psychopath live here?'

'No,' Rem began. 'Well, actually, maybe.'

'Sounds like my kind of animal.'

'She would eat you alive, my friend.'

'What are we looking for?' Nick asked as he pawed through some of the items on the desk.

'Anything that might seem out of place or tell us something about where she could have gone. I'm not sure-'

'Ooh shiny,' said Nick. From beneath a bundle of dead, wild catnip he pulled a strip of cloth with a silver medallion hanging from it.

Nick held it up to Remington. The cloth was red and the small silver disc at its centre had letters engraved into it. *Winifred.*

'Thought you said she's called Cat.'

Remington was puzzled. 'What do you mean? What is this?'

'You've never seen one of these?' Nick rolled his eyes. 'It's a recognition collar. Human thing, they put them on animals as a way to stake a claim on them or something.'

'I've seen them on some of the cats in the city. I just thought it was a fashion thing. What's Winifred mean?'

Nick laughed at him. 'Usually it's the animal's name.'

'Which means Cat's not who she says she is.'

'Alright, steady on, *Francis.*'

'Who told you-' Remington began, before answering his own question. 'I'm going to kill Len.'

'As if you could take her.'

'Fair point.'

After what seemed an age of rifling through the contents of the room, they realised there was little more of use in the office. The collar was their one lead, and it was difficult to imagine how that could direct them anywhere. Just as Remington was about to give up and suggest they both go back to the bar, he heard the muffled sound of conversation beyond the office door. He strained his ears and recognised the distinctive tone of overly authoritative animals.

Remington pushed the office door open slightly and peeked out. Two of the city police officers were in discussion with Fingle and Glen. One, a stocky marten with piercing eyes, had snatched the bogweed Glen had been smoking from her mouth and was waving it threateningly in front of her. Remington pushed open the door and stepped out.

The other of the two animals, a tall well-muscled otter noticed him immediately. 'Detective Inspector Platypus, Sir.' He didn't salute, because that's not what the Met do, but there was an air of pomp in the way he addressed his superior. 'The superintendent sent us to bring yourself and Nick back to the clearing immediately.'

Remington felt his pulse quicken. 'Why? What's happened?'

The marten stepped forward, still holding the joint. 'It's classified, Sir,' he said giving a look of disgust to Fingle and Glen.

'Spit it out,' Remington ordered.

'There's been an attack at the Met,' the otter said gravely. 'We don't know all the details yet, but there was an explosion.'

'Explosion?' Nick's jaw hung open.

'Yes, localised in the tunnels below the station.'

'Doc?' Remington whispered. He felt as though a chasm had just opened beneath his legs.

# Chapter Twenty-Nine

The two officers either knew no further details or they refused to say. Remington, Nick, and their escorts hurried back toward the clearing. The day tasted wrong, like a forest fire had filled the air with ash and soot. The nettles seemed to close in, and whenever Remington reached out in the hope of gaining some sense of connection to the Burrow's rhythms, the beat felt off. It wasn't a beat at all, but a random, distorted thumping. His fur itched and his gut churned. He was acutely aware of the marten and the otter behind them. It felt like being stalked.

'I don't know how you cope with the prickling in your paws out here,' Nick said.

'What?'

'You know, all the noise from the ground, mate.' Nick shook each paw as he lifted it. 'It's like a dull sting, like an itch I can't scratch.'

'Oh,' said Remington. 'You get used to it.'

'Bet you miss the frequencies though?' Nick turned his head one way then the other as if trying to pick up a signal.

'Not as much as you'd think.' Remington was barely listening. He was too focused on getting back to the clearing.

'Never could get the hang of it meself, but I miss the music, you know?'

'Mmhmm, the Burrow has its own kind of music-'

'I would recommend we travel in silence now, sirs,' the marten interrupted.

Remington glared at him over his shoulder. The ghost of a snarl welled from his chest.

'The trees have ears and all that, Sir.' The marten grinned at him.

If it weren't for Remington's thundering need to get to Lennox and find out if Doc was okay, he'd have slapped the grin off the smug creature's face there and then.

'How very fucking dutiful,' Nick whispered.

The trek back to the clearing felt slow despite Rem's hurried steps. Everything was hushed, like a quilt of spelt had been pulled tightly over the woodland canopy. The trees that once chattered like drunken storytellers stood silent, sentinels waving their dark limbs, bark crinkling like forgotten paper. It was as though the entire Burrow had collectively inhaled. The murmuring of the coppice, the whispers in the crowns, the patter of small critters in the fallen leaves, all of it was gone. The world was holding its breath, waiting for the spell of silence to break.

Even Nick's usually gregarious spirit was compressed by the darkening funk that pervaded their path. Now and then Remington caught him casting sudden glances toward the underbrush. The otter and the marten's shadows lengthened and merged into the badgers', spawning a black chimaera ahead of them. Any snap of twig or crackle of dry leaf was amplified in the oppressive quiet. Was the woodland already in mourning? Could the land care about a single creature who'd long-since abandoned the pastoral for the electric resonances and numb ground of the big city?

When they reached the clearing, the station hut was so full of officers that Remington and Nick had to force their way in. Nick's ample frame came in handy as he parted the crush of animal life muttering in the main room. Conversations were hushed but intent. Remington felt every eye linger on him. Nick dug his way to the front of the group and Remington followed, keeping his eyes low. Lennox stepped out of the office, her face composed and still. Remington made a movement toward her, but she gave him a look and motioned with her paw for him to stay. She pulled her ears down and sucked air through her front teeth.

'Team,' she began. Her voice stern and authoritative. 'Following a Code-11 alert, officers were dispatched to LM1, aka the Met, at approximately half sun this morning. The Code was localised in the tunnels below the main station.'

Remington felt a pain in his chest. It wasn't that he'd doubted what the officers had reported at Cat's. It was the cold procedural language coming from Lennox. It made everything feel like a distant event, something to be taught by Plunkett in school. He dug his claws into his paws and bit his lip.

Lennox continued. 'The responding officers secured the scene, and the above-ground station was successfully evacuated. The tunnel network was rendered structurally unsound due to the blast, delaying an official assessment of the cause of the explosion. However, initial indications from the CBR suggest the use of a high-impact explosive.'

Nick leant toward Remington and whispered under his breath, 'CBR? What's that?'

'Chemical, Biological, Radiological, response unit. It's bad.'

'While we are confident the damage is minimal,' Lennox's voice cracked faintly. Remington doubted anyone else would have noticed. 'It is believed that Doc was conducting an examination of a cadaver at the time of detonation. Rescue efforts are in progress, and specialists have been carefully excavating the collapsed tunnel, however, we have been unable to establish any form of contact with Doc post-incident.'

Remington's legs failed him, and he almost crumpled to the floor, but Nick gripped him by the shoulder and steadied him. For a moment Remington's vision blurred as the cold matter-of-fact words and the reality of the event tangled with each other in his mind.

'Check the call wall for your officer number,' Lennox said. 'If your number is on there then you'll be joining me on the next transport back to the city.' She rolled her head as if loosening her neck muscles and set her face. Remington thought she looked formidable, and were his head not filled with the buzzing visions of Doc trapped beneath the Met, unconscious, unable to dig, he might have ventured to tell her so. 'We work hard, and we know the risks.' Her foot began to thump on the station hut floor. 'We know how delicate the balance is, and we accept an avalanche of shit on a daily basis, but today we have been attacked. Today, someone tried to take us down. Today, someone thought messing with one of our own was a good idea.' Her foot was beating harder and faster as she spoke, the white bands around her ankles blurred as she quickened her pace. 'Recently, things have been chaotic in our city. We all know it. I'm not blind to it. But we will not let our city descend into anarchy. We will show them what happens when they fuck with us.' She stopped her pounding and appraised the officers before her. There was a steady murmuring of agreement. Some animals were nodding, some wrung their paws, others snorted wafts of dusty air from their nostrils. 'Transport leaves as soon as I'm on it. If you're not there, don't come back tomorrow. Dismissed.'

She turned around and hopped into the office, while the station's main room clattered with the purposeful fluster of puffed-up police. Remington followed her in and gestured for Nick to join him.

'What are Doc's chances?' Remington asked.

Lennox was watching the steady parade of officers through the large hole in the wall. 'Honestly, I'm not sure,' she said without turning. 'It's frustrating being up here. Everything's so slow. That's why I'm heading back down there now. I'll send word as soon as I know anything-'

'Sod that,' Remington snapped. 'I'm coming with you.'

Lennox turned with a flash of anger in her eyes. 'I'm sorry, did I miss your promotion to Superintendent?'

'Len, it's Doc,' Nick said.

'You stay out of this. You shouldn't be in here anyway.'

Lennox gripped her ears tightly and pulled on them. 'Sorry, Nick, do you mind giving me and Rem a minute?'

Nick raised his paws in submission and backed out of the office.

'I have to help.' It was Remington's voice that cracked this time.

'The way you can help is by staying here. If we are being targeted now, then you being down there will only make that target more glaring.'

Remington knew it was pointless arguing with her, but he still would have had it not been for the anxious face of a ferret surreptitiously peering into the hole that served as a window. It was Oscar, and he was trying to mouth something to Remington. The badger squinted. Lennox turned to see what he was looking at and Oscar ducked out of sight.

Lennox clapped her paws together. 'You listening to me?'

'Yes… I… erm… yeah… I get it.'

Oscar reappeared, the champagne fur on the top of his head glowed in the sunlight. He was pointing toward Lennox and then shaking his head.

'You're still the chief here, remember, and look at everything we've got going on. This was your gig, right? Roadkill? The cave? The bats? The-'

'I get it. I get it, Len, but promise me you'll update me on everything with Doc, no matter how small.'

Oscar pointed to his right, toward the rear of the station hut, and then he vanished.

Lennox reached out and touched Remington's cheek. 'I promise, if so much as a spec of dirt falls, I'll send word.'

Nick requested a spot on the transport back to the city and Lennox agreed. His organisation of the Heartbreak recovery tent had been invaluable, but now the volunteers were armed with his experience, Nick's priority was to help in any way he could with Doc. Things looked bleak but the badgers joked that if anyone could survive a tunnel collapse, it was a mole, and if any mole had the savvy to escape a bombing with his paddle-like front feet intact, it was Doc. They could see in each other's eyes that neither was convinced though.

As soon as they were out of sight, disappearing into the treeline at the far edge of the clearing, Remington slipped around the side of the station, checking to see he wasn't being watched or followed. Oscar was waiting a short distance from the station hut. His fur shivered in the sun. The young constable had looked so confident and calm during the raid that it was a surprise to see him return to the more common gait of his species.

'Detective Platypus,' he said almost in a whisper. His eyes were darting back and forth. 'Thanks. I didn't know what to do.'

'Alright, Ozzy, take a breath. What's going on?'

'I don't know what's the right thing here.'

A bird chirped and Oscar flinched hard, nearly throwing himself into the station wall.

'Quills, Oscar,' said Remington. 'Why don't we get you inside?'

'No,' the ferret jerked away. 'I haven't been cleared to leave the city. I shouldn't be here.'

'Okay.' Remington put his paw on the ferret's shoulder. 'Ozzy, why are you here?'

'I didn't know who else to tell, Sir. It's the Rev.'

Remington's fur began to rise as a growl tunnelled from the base of his stomach up through his throat. 'Oscar, spill, now.'

'I was down there when it happened this morning.'

'No wonder you're such a mess. You're probably in shock.'

'No, I'm fine. I'm fine.'

'Why don't you sit down?'

'Listen to me,' Oscar snapped suddenly. Remington took a step back and nodded.

'When it happened,' the ferret continued, his eyes still in constant motion checking the treeline. 'I was up on first, with the cells and the cages.'

'Go on.' Remington could feel a tight coil begin to wrap

around his insides.

'We got the shout to evacuate, and obviously that meant emptying the cells. I asked about the Rev in the cages and got told not to worry about it. I know I shouldn't have but, I doubled back to check on the cages, and...' Oscar paused, and sniffed at the air.

'And?'

'He wasn't there. He wasn't in his cage anymore.'

'You're sure?'

'I'm telling you he's gone.'

'Maybe they got him out separately, Oscar. It would make sense. For all we know, this was an attempt to break him out. You don't want him mixing with any of his Murder goons.'

'I thought about that too, but something about the way she said not to worry about it, just bugged me.'

'Who told you not to worry about it?'

'It was Lennox, Sir.'

For a brief moment the air seemed to thicken around them, but Remington shook the sensation away. 'Lennox knows what she's doing, Ozzy. I appreciate you coming to me, but she's always got her reasons-'

'There's something else.' Oscar shook his head. His eyes were wide and wild.

'Go on.'

'I checked the logs.'

'You don't have clearance.'

'I have my talents, Sir.'

'Alright, and?'

'The Rev was released *before* the attack.'

'What?'

'Clear as day, I swear. He was released before the attack. So, I'm thinking maybe it was the Murder, somehow got in with an inside man. They get the big raven out and then use the bomb as some kind of distraction, so we don't even notice.'

'Not the worst plan.' Remington's skin felt itchy and hot. If the Rev had escaped, then he knew he wouldn't be safe. Nobody would be.

'But the logs show who it was, and it wasn't the Murder.' Oscar stopped and looked around him again. His agitation was infectious.

'Oscar, who let the Rev out?'

'Sir, it was Lennox.'

# Chapter Thirty

Over the trees that walled the clearing, the horizon was purpling into late afternoon. Remington watched the jitter of champagne fur slink from rock to tall grass, before finally disappearing into the treeline. Oscar had to be fast and stealthy if he was to make it onto the transport and back to the city before anyone noticed he was absent. The chaos of the day's events would ensure plenty of distraction, but eventually the young ferret would be missed, and questions would be asked. For now, it was essential Remington had someone he could trust in the city. Trust, though, was a luxury in short supply. The badger leant against the station hut and surveyed the clearing, the recovery tents now filling most of the space, and a swirl of animals continually hurrying around. Rodents mixed with small mammals, and Vixx's 'regular flyers' swept in and out with resources. The trees that ringed the clearing seemed dark and close, as though they were growing too thickly together now, a fierce ancient blockade. He considered treating himself to a tobacco leaf, but his chest felt tight, and each breath seemed to lack sufficient oxygen.

Beyond the trees, the great splayed expanse of the valley bled on toward the city, but without being able to see it, Remington started to wonder if it was really there at all. How long had he been cloistered in the Burrow now? He considered rushing after Oscar, ensconcing himself on the transport to get back to the metropolis, to confront Lennox, to claw through the remains of the subterranean network of the Met, to find Doc. He'd be stopped immediately though, and what would Lennox do then? Lennox. The name curdled in his mind and sounded wrong, the consonants suddenly brittle and threatening. She seemed so far away now, and not just because she would soon be shuttled over the border into the city. That transport was a bridge between two worlds, an oscillation between the clatter and hum of the electric capital, and the slow organic pulse of the Burrow. Two worlds, so disparate, but intimately connected, just as Lennox and he were, or so he had always thought.

A shape shifted just beyond the treeline; large, dark. Remington squinted and angled his head.

'Cuppa?' A soft voice pulled Remington from his thoughts.

'Sorry?' Remington turned, surprised to find it was Mrs Banks, her face slightly unsettling in its warmth.

'They've pretty much all gone, love,' she said. 'Why don't you come and sit down?'

Remington looked back toward the trees. All was still, save the faint sway of branches. He smiled and allowed himself to be led into the station hut. It was disorienting to find the main room so quiet and empty. Chief Banks was grumpily nibbling at a leaf, while Chris and Claire were straightening the station up. Sergeant Vixx was deep in thought, staring out of a window.

'Here we are,' Mrs Banks said gesturing to five tumblers on her desk. 'I think we could all do with one, don't you?'

'I think you're right,' Remington said and sat down. 'Thank you, Mrs Banks.'

'My mother always said, there's nowt that can't be cured with a cuppa.'

Remington tried his best at another smile and drank. They all did, and slowly the oppressive silence of the room began to lift. Mrs Banks asked Chris and Claire how they were doing with the recent chaos, and Remington felt a twinge as he realised this was a question he really should have asked before now. It was difficult to focus on anything but Lennox. The conversation around him just about filtered through his twisting thoughts of her. Chris and Claire had been a pair of capable and willing rookies to Remington, but that was all he had known. A few moments listening to them in conversation with Mrs Banks, though, and Remington felt like he knew their life stories. He made a mental note to make use of her in any future interrogations. The voles were siblings and their grandmother had schooled with both the elderly hedgehogs. Remington did his best to chip in with the small talk, but he contributed about as usefully as the old chief did. Still, the warmth between the odd bunch quelled the churning in his gut somewhat. Whenever there was a lull in the conversation, the insistent shadows of his mind crept back in.

'I feel like I've gone half deaf now they've all shipped off,' said Vixx, twitching her head one way then the other.

'Wish it was all of them,' Mrs Banks muttered and blew on her drink.

'Really not a fan of the city dwellers, are you?' Remington scratched his jaw.

'Well, they come marching in here with their heavy claws, messing up the place without so much as a word to us-'

'I was thinking more about my arrival.'

'Oh, well,' Mrs Banks was almost blushing. 'Yes, perhaps I judged you a bit early. It all just came as a bit of a shock. We only got the message the morning you arrived, and I was told to clear out the old dwelling, and you looked like you'd rather be anywhere else, and-'

Remington raised his paw with a grin.

'Anyway, I am sorry,' the hedgehog said.

'Mrs Banks,' Remington stood up and put down his tumbler. 'You'll never need to apologise to me.' He squeezed her paw. 'And, besides, I know I'm not the easiest to warm up to.'

Remington stretched out his creaking bones and headed to the door.

'Actually,' he turned to face the small team. The two hedgehogs, the vole siblings, and the harrier looked at him. 'I know it's been a bizarre time for you all since I got here. You didn't ask for any of this, and Mrs Banks is right. I didn't want to be here. But you're an exemplary team and you've done the Burrow proud.' He felt the blood rise in his face as he spoke. 'It's been a pleasure.'

The animals sat in stunned silence for a minute, apart from Chief Banks who continued nodding and smiling in his way, pretending to have heard every word.

'You going somewhere, Sir?' Vixx asked.

'No,' Remington said. 'Well, nowhere in particular.'

'Mind if I join?'

'Be my guest, Sergeant.' Remington and the young harrier ambled out into the fading afternoon.

'How's the wing?' Remington asked as they toured the clearing.

'It's a bit stiff, but just about repaired.' Vixx stretched out the flag of her wing, a lump, like a heartknot of roots bulged from the meeting of quills at the upper alula.

Remington nodded but his attention had been drawn to a sudden movement in the sky. Vixx followed his gaze. A pair of sparrows were playing in the growing blush above them.

'About Brigg,' Vixx said. 'I should have-'

Remington interrupted her gently. 'My fault, Sergeant. I saw her batter that boar at Cat's. I shouldn't have left you up there on your own.'

'Still, it's like she disappeared. I can't seem to find any hint of her anywhere.'

'I don't think you will, I'm afraid.'

'How do you mean, Sir?'

'Well, this wasn't just Brigg and the toad,' he said absentmindedly. He was staring out toward the dark trees. Either the fading light was playing tricks on him, or something was shifting just beyond the treeline. 'An operation that size, they were working for someone else.'

'You're talking about the Murder?' She was looking out to

what had caught Remington's attention. The lenses of her eyes shifted as she focused.

'And she's either gone to earth, or she's already been picked up by one of them.'

The shadow was close to the ground, barely noticeable beyond the thick grass that edged the clearing. It seemed to slide through the underbrush.

'You see that, Sergeant?' Remington asked.

'Can't see anything, Sir.'

'Must be my old eyes.'

'You're not *that* old, Sir.'

Remington cocked his head at her. 'Oh, thanks very much.'

'Oh, I didn't mean… I…' She lowered her beak to the ground. 'Is there anything I can be doing, Sir? I feel like a spare part.'

'Just keep your eyes open.'

'Always, Sir.'

Remington pulled his gaze from the treeline. Still, he was sure something slithered through the grassy edge, but Vixx's young avian eyes were more trustworthy than his own exhausted ones. After they parted, Remington peeked into the tent where Red's mother was recovering. She'd been making good progress, but he had stayed at a distance. It had pained him not to catch up with Red when she came to visit, but she was always accompanied by Daisy. It was important for her own safety that they weren't seen together, or so he told himself. It was for her own good.

He peered into the tent and, sure enough, there was little Red, eyes wild and full of excitement, bouncing on the bed, her little digits fumbling with her red feather. Her mother, still unable to speak, listened and smiled. The love in her eyes struck Remington hard in his chest. He wanted to stride in and wrap the young squirrel in his forelegs, but he didn't. Head Plunkett sat beside the bed, her eyes as distant as the stars. She twitched her nose and looked up, the flat shovels of her beaver teeth glinting. Remington jumped away from the tent and let the flap fall. His eyes felt heavy, and his back ached.

His stomach was flipping viciously. He needed rest.

Remington took one final lap of the clearing, traversing the treeline, seeking out any sign of movement through the pressing of his paws into the soil. Nothing but creepers, and the tiniest of buzzers disturbed the dying afternoon. More than once, he thought he caught sight of a looming shadow in his periphery but each time he turned he found only trees and the dense underbrush. The sensation of being watched wouldn't leave him though. It clung to the back of his fur like a cleaver.

He loped up the steps to the chief's quarters and pulled the vines that had cordoned off the crime scene away. The floor had been cleaned well. Barely any evidence of the chimaera corpse remained, save the faintest darkening on the floor, the ghost shadow of the macabre grimness that had been there. He stared at the patch and let his mind drift to Doc. He cursed the Burrow's lack of electrical frequencies. If Doc was found, safe or otherwise, how long would it be before he found out? He fluttered a claw over his head, sat down, sighed and closed his eyes. Behind his eyelids, images of Lennox, Doc, and Daisy swam. A twig snapped with a fizz. He jumped to his paws and shot to the window. The light was fading, but the only movement was the occasional hustle of a volunteer creature, and the tents gently rippling in the breeze. Everywhere he focused there was nothing to cause alarm, but in his periphery he would see a looming black shadow. When he turned his gaze toward it though, it would slip away only to appear in the corner of his vision again.

He lay down and tried to sleep, but at every creak, every whisper of wind through a gap in the dwelling, he was at the window again, searching in vain for an elusive shape to materialise. Something he could give chase to, something he could arrest, something. Slowly though, as the futility of his rising merged with the deepening of the evening, the badger fell into a shallow and uneasy sleep.

# Chapter Thirty-One

Remington's rest was so shallow and agitated he didn't think he had slept at all, but, when a soft scratching noise roused him, the darkness confirmed that time had passed. It was night and the thick void around him felt airless. The scratching came again. Remington tried to keep his body still as he slowly turned his head toward the sound. A pale light from the crooked smile of the moon slanted in through his open doorway.

He remained still as he listened for the noise again. It sounded like a claw, or a talon, being dragged over wood. It seemed to drift closer and then ever so slightly further away. He instinctively reached for the cosh he kept beneath his bed in the city and cursed himself for not getting round to arming himself in the Burrow. Every strand of his fur was screaming danger at him. He rolled, as slowly and silently as his hefty frame would allow, onto his paws and blinked into the dark of his dwelling. He willed his ageing eyes to adjust. Too many years of being awake in the daytime had eroded his nocturnal senses but, through the crinkly haze of his sight, the room began to solidify.

The scraping came again, and Remington started, before taking in a deep draught of air. He hadn't realised he'd been holding his breath. The scraping was coming from the bottom of his door as it lazily waved to and fro in the night's cold wind. Remington gripped the slip of wood and studied his dwelling. Nothing seemed to be out of place, and he was alone. A gust of wind blew in through the gaping doorway. The thick scent of rot and earth swam up into his leathery nostrils. The body that had so recently lay where he stood came back to his mind, and he almost retched.

He looked out into the clearing, his fur still tingling with alarm. The tents seemed to hang like looming ghosts, and the trees beyond added shadows to the shadows. He felt eyes upon him. The night Burrow rustled in every direction. He dug his claws into his paws. He couldn't stay here. Whether Lennox had her reasons or not, the Rev was no longer in a cage, and his dwelling had already been breached. Remington bit down on his lip and snarled softly to himself. It was one thing to have stayed in his dwelling in the city while being tracked by crows every ticking moment of the day, but here he was a beacon for them to descend on the clearing, and that meant putting the other officers, the volunteers, and the recovering creatures in danger.

The badger took a final look around his dwelling, sniffing at the floor for any sign of another creature's presence. He knew he had closed his door. Someone, or something had been in here. But what for? There was no message, no black feather. Had they watched him sleep? Had they put a blade-like talon to his throat and savoured a moment of knowing that his life was theirs to take if they wished? Had something slithered in to squeeze the breath from him, only to be scared off by a different creature looking to claim him as a prize? All he could sense was the pungent remnants of death that clung to the fabric of the dwelling now.

He couldn't stay there, and so, making his decision, Remington took a deep, agitated breath and stepped out into the clearing, pulling the swaying door tightly closed behind him. He gazed into the grey night. Moonlight tilted with the wind, and the muted nightsong scraped like one of Fingle and Glen's badly tuned instruments. He sensed no sign of movement from anything larger than insects. He pushed his paws against the earth and set off to somewhere nobody who might be seeking to do him harm knew about; somewhere he promised himself he would never set foot ever again.

Under the dense veil of night, Remington's pawfalls were muted by the Burrow's floor. Each step felt like a struggle through an invisible barrier. He twitched his ears, searching for sound, but the blood raging in his head drowned out everything but the pounding of his heart. The woodland seethed around him; each breath of wind echoed like a ticking clock. At the edge of the clearing, the woodland transformed before his eyes. The gnarled trees twisted and reached out with untidy limbs, the underbrush a labyrinth of archways and tunnels. Branches groaned wistful laments, and the wind struggling through leaves and grass wheezed out screeching warnings for him to turn back. The faint light of the spit of moon filtering through the puzzle of canopy and brush intensified the shadows, casting strange hieroglyphs on the floor, unreadable cyphers from some other world. The undergrowth felt denser in the dark, more tangled. It was like wading through a stream of whispers. Shivering voices seemed to rise from the earth beneath his paws, begging him to remember something he'd locked away somewhere deep beyond his reach. He resisted an overwhelming urge to look behind him again and again, focusing on the path ahead.

But then, a shudder of movement at the edge of his range made him stop. A dark shape slithered through the brush to his right. He thought about his encounter with the grass snake, its body coiled around him as he inhaled the filthy ghyll water. He thought about its scales, its cold evil eye rearing back, ready to strike. But, just as the image took shape in his mind, it disappeared. Nothing was there. The woodland floor breathed below him. Every step kicked up the scent of wet earth and decaying leaves. He struggled through a tight thicket where a mess of shrubs reached out, clawing at his fur and flesh like tiny blades. He pictured Cull's silver-tipped talons and allowed himself the whiff of a smile as he remembered knocking the vile crow on his smug backside at Mickey's funeral. But the clawing at his skin, like skeletal fingers, quickly tore the smile away. It was like the prickling of tiny eyes all over him, watching, waiting. The underbrush kept rustling. Each time he swivelled to find the source he found nothing, just the still, decaying foliage of the night's floor.

As he pushed on, deeper into the woods, he was sure he caught the caw of a distant crow, ghosting on the wind. He tilted his head, pivoted his ears. It sounded distorted, as though the trees were reconfiguring the noise before they let it reach him. A clatter of wings echoed overhead. He looked up to the treetops. Again, there was nothing. Remington quickened his pace, slinking in and out of vague pools of moonlight like spotlights. Shapes shifted around him. Light slackened between crooked tree trunks. His imagination started to fill in the gaps in his senses, creating nightmares out of the mist and shade. The temperature had steadily dropped, and Remington's breath clouded the space before him. The further he drew himself away from the clearing, the stronger the sensation of being watched grew. His gut churned within him and urged him to retrace his steps. He knew he was doing the right thing, the sensible thing, but his instinct that had always served him so well told him he was running from safety into something else, something dangerous; a nest of vipers.

By the time he reached a thinly trickling stream, his fur was clammy with cold sweat. A vague hint of the moon's glow reflected off the shallow surface, lighting the path with a sickly pallor. He thought he heard a faint splash. A ripple swooned toward him. He looked toward its origin, but nothing was there, just the mud lying still beneath the veneer of the eerily glowing stream. He crossed through to the other side and settled himself in the undergrowth, listening. Remington sat in the prickly discomfort of his cold damp fur and waited. It had been a long time since he had set paw here and, while he wanted anyone who wished him harm to know he was no longer in his dwelling in the clearing, it was equally important that nobody knew his intended destination.

While the feeling of being watched wouldn't abate, only when

Remington was as satisfied as he could be that he was truly alone, did he stand and finish his journey. Through a network of briar and bramble, more knotted and overgrown than it had been when he had left for the city so long ago, Remington found what he was looking for. The entrance was obscured with a thick clumping of creeping buttercups, their wilting yellow flowers white in the moonlight, but it was still there – marked by a spoil heap slowly trodden down over time: his family sett, his ancestral home.

Instinctively, Remington reached out to tear the creeping weeds away, but drew back, deciding instead that this natural veil was a valuable disguise. He pushed through the curtain of wilting buttercups and the entrance to his family sett opened its throat to him. He paused on the threshold and inhaled. The history of countless generations flooded through him. The sett was no simple hole in the earth. It was a meticulously excavated subterranean world that had housed his bloodline for hundreds of seasons.

He stepped further into the tunnel and the world outside faded as the musty scent of the familiar channels wrapped around him. Memories of scampering through these same passages drifted into his mind, his mother's playfully stern words echoing through the walls. He touched the powdery soil of the sides with his paws, feeling the cool earth, the scratches and marks, the whole living tapestry of his family's past. He let the rhythms of the sett, the internal music of its roots and breath, lead him onwards. Each chamber, every tunnel, bore the markings of generations past. He let his claws brush the walls, letting fine dustings of dry soil trail in their wake. These were spaces where his forebears had expanded their homes, had dug, and excavated, shaped and hollowed, driven by a primal sense of duty and family.

As he ventured deeper, he felt the air grow cooler on his damp fur. He remembered retreating to these deeper areas in the sweltering summers, while the winter would see his mother, father, and himself dozing in the safety and warmth of the upper chambers. There had been carefully selected entrances in multiple places before his time, but most of these had been sealed off or collapsed when just the three of them had populated the sett. Some had remained, purely to allow the wind to flow through and keep the tunnels filled with the fresh Burrow air.

He paused at a junction where the tunnel split off into three paths. Each one of them, like every other, held a story and history of its own. One led to a chamber that had caved in when he was young, and this brought Doc back to his mind. The central path led to a storage hollow they would fill during the autumn, and slowly graze their way through during the harsher winter months. The final one led to the chamber that had been used as a sick room. It was where his mother had given birth to him and his two siblings. There they had stayed for weeks after they were born, staying, as is customary for badgers, until they were strong enough to venture into the outside world. Only Remington had made it that far. A tear fell from his cheek, and he shook his head.

On the wall of the tunnel, he could just make out the crudely carved outline of a badger. It was his own work, and it had almost eroded away, unmistakeably a badger, and unmistakeably his. He pushed his paw onto it and closed his eyes. A wave of dread passed through him. A sudden vibration, a tremor through his paw made him hold his breath. He placed his other forepaw onto the wall. A skittering, frenetic energy was pulsing through it. Remington closed his eyes again and listened. Something was there. It was faint, barely audible, but nevertheless, it was there. Remington took a deep slow breath in, focused his mind, and let the oxygen gently leave his lungs. Somewhere in the twisting tangle of the sett, a sharp dissonance was lilting through the air. It was foreign, entirely out of place, and every cell in the badger's body told him to run. Remington strained his ears again, hoping it was another trick of his weary senses. But the sound came again, pained, and angry. With a chilling lucidity, Remington realised he wasn't alone.

# Chapter Thirty-Two

Remington's breath became stuttered and shallow. The walls of the tunnel felt like they were closing against him. Every scrape of his claw on the earth sent tremors through his legs. The sett and whatever else was in it seemed to wrap around him like a tight skin, one that pulsed with its own blood. Through the darkness, the dirt walls swam with echoes of his past, mingling with nightmarish flashes of his present. Images, vague and fragmented, shivered before him. He saw the ghosts of his siblings who never came to be, faux memories of playfighting and curling up together. He saw his mother's eyes, those warm, loving, generous orbs that had once meant home, now cold, milky, unseeing. He saw the first time he brought a girlfriend back to these same tunnels, her whiskers tickling his cheek, but her fur began to singe and fall, her body twisted, her bones snapping back on themselves.

He slapped his head with his paw, trying to batter the pictures from his mind. With each step further, the visions persisted and became stronger. Remington huffed sharply and tried to push down the protests from his gut telling him to turn and run. He pressed on toward the pained, angry sound. It was a faint wail, coming from somewhere deep in the belly of the sett. At tunnel forks, Remington was forced to pause and wait. The sound wasn't constant, but instead came in waves, bubbling up and bursting. He considered that it might be the natural sounds of the underworld. It often did carry its own confusing quirks of rhythm and tone. This had become more and more the case with the increasing spread of the human element. Profligate poisons from mechanical inventions had long been seeping into the ground, causing all kinds of volatility. There'd been talk of spectres haunting the woodlands, will-o-the-wisps the humans called them; nothing more than the accumulation of noxious gasses in the earth gathering and finding a way up through the surface.

This was no belching of the suffering soil though. It was a wail, and each time it crested the tunnel, it sounded louder, more insistent, angrier. Whether it was calling out to him, or warning in its rage, Remington couldn't tell, but something pushed him forward. Another image clattered into his mind: a bird with a shimmering black eye, its long smooth beak dripping with an inky substance. Remington felt the viscous goop pool around his paws. The image was so clear, so lucid, that he found himself looking down. The tunnels felt much smaller than he remembered. His head grazed the rough ceiling, and he felt the walls scrape at his flanks. If not for the terror that squeezed at his heart, he might have allowed himself a joke at his own expense about the shape he was in. He was short of breath though, and the once-familiar sett was now an unrecognisable labyrinth. Still, the wail drew him onward, deeper into the dark.

A piercing shriek bounced through the tunnel with such force that Remington almost felt his fur ruffle. Whatever it was that awaited him, it was enraged, but there was also so much pain in the cry that the terror it evoked in him was matched by his empathy. The shriek ended abruptly, but its resonance lingered. He could feel it vibrate in his bones, tingling at the marrow. Was it real? Or was it too, like the images in his mind, a falsity; a trick of his tortured psyche, mingling with the sett? The sett was alive after all, like all habitats. Perhaps this was the sett's way of reminding him of the pain that had once echoed through its chambers and still lingered, imbued in its roughly hewn walls and arteries.

More than once he reached what seemed to be an impasse, but

something in the back of his mind triggered a memory of the sett's mapping, and he dug his claws in and revealed a partially closed off tunnel. The images were growing more intense, but the wailing had become thinner since the scream. Quieter, the sound was somehow more unsettling. With a final digging of his claws, he uncovered a chamber he knew well. It was a larger cavernous hollow where they would gather as a family. It was illuminated by a strange, soft, green luminescence. Remington peered around the room to see where the light was coming from. Clumps of fungus dotted the edges of the room, and from their sickly-looking tendrils a green glow ebbed dreamily. It lit the room dimly, writhing like living shadow.

The cry came again, softly but within the same room. Remington edged toward it. At first, he couldn't make anything out through the vague green light, but as he moved steadily closer, a crooked shape distinguished itself from the wall. It was an oily black, shaped like a thin pinecone. Remington stepped forward and reached out a claw. It shuddered and wailed again. A strange sawing sound emitted from the object as it moved, as though it was serrating the air. Remington reached out again and touched it. It let out a long, mournful wheeze, and slowly began to unfurl. Remington noticed the hands first. Two hands at the tip of the object seemed to be holding smooth black sheets, and as they moved away from each other, Remington realised what it was. It was a bat, and as it opened its leathery wings, another pained cry creaked out from it. It was feeble and struggled to part its wings. Remington could see that it was wounded. One of its wings was twisted horribly at an unnatural angle and its aged eyes were quaking with fear and pain.

Remington hesitated. He had never been so close to a bat before. Sure, they would occasionally swoop low on their looping paths, hunting down buzzing creatures, close enough to touch, but then they'd be off; a flash of serrated wing and shadow, and they were gone. They were an anomaly, something alien in their manner. They were one of the few species who seemed unaffected by the enclosure acts or the struggle toward civility. Bats just continued about their strange otherworldly business. Standing before the wounded creature now, Remington couldn't turn away.

The bat whined long and slow. It looked deep into Remington's eyes. Suddenly, a flood of images poured into the badger's mind. They were quick and scattered, each one an ephemeral thing, like a dream immediately half-forgotten upon waking. At first, Remington was dazed by the scattergun visions, but something about the glimmering black of the bat's eyes drew him in. The creature closed its eyes in a slow and deliberate manner. He wasn't sure why, but Remington closed his too. He breathed deeply and tried to quiet his mind as he did when using his pawsentia.

A blaze of night sky peppered with glittering stars came into view. He saw the bat soaring over treetops, wind gusting past its ears as the full moon cast a glow over the Burrow. Remington felt giddy with freedom. His skin tingled, tickled by the cool night air. Remington opened his eyes and gasped. He looked up at the bat again. The withered old creature continued to stare back, placid. It closed its eyes again. The badger did the same. Insects, though it was difficult to discern the type, danced under a lamp. Their wings shimmered as they fluttered crazily in random patterns. Remington felt hungry, and helpless suddenly. He wanted to hunt but felt trapped and confined.

Remington opened his eyes and looked at the bat. For a second, staring into the dark shimmer of its eyes, he felt overwhelmed, but the bat let out a thin chirp, and without closing his eyes, Remington saw an image of the bats in Roadkill's cave. He saw Doc flipping the switch on the odd machine transmitting the discordant signal. He saw Lennox, and he saw himself. While still looking at the bat, Remington watched as the memory of his team freeing the bats morphed into a rose, opening slowly in the moonlight, its red petals black in the eerie glow of the night.

Remington was beginning to understand. He'd seen images like this before. When they freed the bats in Roadkill's cave, strange pictures had clouded his mind. He had assumed it was the fumes from the Heartbreak, but it was the bats. They had been trying to communicate with him. The bat wheezed. The process was clearly exhausting for the old animal.

With caution, Remington focused his mind and tried to build a picture. He thought about how he might offer help to the bat. He pictured himself recuperating after Mickey's funeral, spiders tending to his wounds. The bat closed its eyes and Remington's vision dissolved into an ocean, then a lake, then a river, then a drop of water falling and falling endlessly. It wasn't just the image though, there was a feeling with it. Remington couldn't quite grasp the sense of the feeling, it was something close to freedom, but there was a fluidity to it. Perhaps there was too much information in his message, or it was too rigid, too specific.

He focused his mind on a memory of himself as a cub, bathing in the warmth of the sun. He remembered how he felt on that day, content and happy. He closed his eyes and tried to will it to the bat. The bat gave a brief flutter of its good wing. It sent an image of a dense, lush forest, trees threading together, roots reaching far into the earth, connecting everything. Remington felt a spark rush through him. His second message worked because, despite their differences, there was a shared understanding and experience contained within it. The bat's message back was a reminder that while they may seem alien to each other, they were still bound together in the same web, network, and rhythms of life.

Remington saw two trees intertwined and he nodded at the bat. The bat nodded back slowly. Remington did his best to communicate awkwardly through image and meaning as he tended to the bat's twisted wing. He gathered moss and worked it into a spongey gauze which he packed into the tear in the black sheet. The bat continued to pass images into Remington's mind as he worked. He didn't always understand the meaning, if there was meaning, but he always got a sense, a feeling about the bat's intention. When the bat felt pain, it was almost as though Remington felt it too. He tenderly untwisted the mangled wing and fixed a splint of sticks to it. It pointed out awkwardly, but it was stable.

Once he finished, Remington and the bat sat together in the soft glow of the luminescent fungi and passed messages back and forth. It wasn't quite conversation, but it was connection, a shared sense of not quite understanding, but sensing, feeling each other, and the world beyond. It was like a translation of emotion somewhere between essence and meaning. Now and then the light faded but the bat closed its eyes and Remington sensed it was communicating, but not with him. The fungi would thrum back into life, and they would be enveloped in the strange glow once again.

They 'talked' long into the night, sharing feelings and memories, bridging the gap between the nocturnal and the diurnal, each of the creatures lost in the tapestry of the other's existence. The bat shivered and Remington saw snow falling through the sett in his mind's eye. Remington nestled close to the bat and put his foreleg around him. The glow of the fungi dimmed finally, and in the dark clinch of the sett, Remington felt the bat relax into sleep.

# Chapter Thirty-Three

When the apricot haze of dawn breathed the morning into the sett, Remington couldn't tell if he had slept or not. He'd continued to witness a stream of images throughout the night, and whether they were dreams or more attempts at communication from the bat, he wasn't sure. In the stillness, he felt a shudder of movement as the wounded old creature quivered its delicate wings. Tender flurries of images emanated from him like ripples over a calm pool. Cerulean expanses touched wisps of clouds; the sensation of weightlessness cradled Remington. It was gratitude, profound, raw, distilled into a singular sense.

Remington nudged the bat with the bridge of his snout and rumbled a soft promise that the creature was safe here and welcome as long as he needed. As he spoke, he tried to will companion images to come to his mind: an embrace between parent and pup, a full table. It was difficult to keep the focus upon one image at a time, as memories of Lennox, of Red, of his wife kept digging their way into his thoughts. When this happened the bat would blink, and it seemed to Remington that it was an act of reassurance, that it was okay. The bat knew this was difficult, and still, he understood.

In a secluded alcove, Remington dug away the dry, hard shell of soil, allowing the pungent scent of earth and dew to plume into the space. He lined it with soft moss and helped the bat into the more comfortable spot. The bat wrapped its good wing around the badger and held him tightly. For a moment,

Remington saw the night sky and a thousand bats arcing and looping. As they parted, the wing stiffened suddenly. An urgent flicker crossed its glassy eyes. Once again, Remington felt the tingle of transmitted imagery: a labyrinth of shadowy, serpentine tunnels, spiralling endlessly onward. The narrow pathways throbbed like a heartbeat, shifting and pulsing. He saw claws rending the earth. Remington pulled away. A bubble of foreboding was rising inside him. The bat blinked slowly. Remington saw a bat and a badger, standing side by side. A third figure emerged between them. The interloper was obscured though, and impossible to identify.

'Someone else is here?' Remington asked. The bat stared back blankly and then it curled its slick black wing around itself, the dark orbs of its eyes disappearing from view. Remington stepped back and pushed his paws into the sett's brittle earth. The bat was right, something was moving through the dirt beneath them, and it was getting closer. A faint vibration tickled Remington's paws. Dust slid and cascaded from the walls, slowly at first, but then more aggressively as the trembling became more intense. It was erratic, frenzied even, imbued with an urgency that made the fine hairs of his fur tingle.

A chunk of dirt broke free from the ceiling of the chamber, crashed to the floor, and shattered. Remington felt the ground beneath him quake and shift. Suddenly, with a burst of earth a black creature tore into the space, throwing itself spent and exhausted at Remington's feet. It was Doc. His fur was caked with mud, matted with blood, and his eyes were wide and red. A cut, jagged and angry, ran along the mole's side. Freshly-turned earth had been smoothed awkwardly over the wound as a makeshift bandage.

Remington dove to his friend's side.

'Doc… I thought…' His voice shook. 'Quills, are you okay?'

The mole nodded, panting heavily. After a moment, he spoke.

'Took a bit of a battering, Remmy, my boy.' He took a deep

drink of the air. 'I'm still just about ticking though.'

'But… I… how?'

Doc smirked and tapped his nose. 'Your scent. When I couldn't find you at the station hut, I knew you couldn't have gone far, and I hate to be the one to break this to you, but in case you didn't know, you carry quite the scent in that hide of yours, old friend.'

Remington rolled his eyes and gently helped the mole to a seated position against the wall.

'Don't suppose you could snuffle out a worm for me, could you?' Doc clutched the wound in his side.

'Really? You've been tunnelling since London, and you didn't find any worms on your way?'

'London?' Doc spluttered. 'Good grief, no, I couldn't have done the trip from the city even if I wasn't leaking everywhere. Managed to sneak onto a transport and hopped off just before we came into the Burrow.'

'But, the bomb-'

'Please, Rem,' Doc raised his paw. 'Get us a worm and I'll tell you everything.'

It was almost unbearable waiting while Doc made his way through his breakfast. The mole was clearly in a great deal of pain, and even the subtlest movement of his jaw made him flinch. The frantic journey he'd made to find Remington must have been agony. Once he finally finished, Doc leant back against the wall and closed his eyes. If Remington were a better badger, he would have let the poor mole sleep. Remington was not a better badger though.

'Why didn't you let them treat your wound at the Met, rather than dragging your sorry little backside all the way out here?'

'Because Rem, I don't know who to trust.'

'You think someone targeted you?'

'Me or,' Doc shuffled and pushed himself upright. 'My lab.'

'I don't follow.'

'What are they saying happened?'

'Botched attack on the Met.'

Doc chuckled and shook his head. 'Figured as much.'

'You're saying they were just after you?'

'Or the lab.'

'Why? What makes you so sure? And how *did* you get out?'

'Well,' Doc began, but he caught sight of the bat huddled under its own wing and stopped.

'Don't worry, he's okay.'

Doc looked sceptical but he shrugged and continued. 'I was down in the lab. They'd finally unpacked our friend Roadkill, so I was starting the final autopsy, but I got this little tickle in my nose.'

'Tickle?'

'Tickle. A little tingle of Heartbreak.'

'I'm not surprised,' Remington said. 'The toad had been bathing in the fumes for quills knows how long.'

'That's what I thought, at first, but it was just a little sharper, a little more metallic than Roadkill's musk. So, I followed the scent, and sure enough, guess what I found?'

'Heartbreak?'

'Heartbreak. That's what they used to bring down the tunnel.'

'What makes you think it wasn't a botched attempt to bring down the Met?'

'There was nowhere near enough of the stuff for that, Remmy. It was targeted to be local. Whoever did it knew what they were doing, and it was an inside job. No way anyone's getting Heartbreak that far into the Met if they haven't got clearance. I'd bet my burrow on the Heartbreak being from the stash we recovered from Roadkill's cave too... the stuff that was already there.'

'Fine, say you're right.' Remington fluttered a claw over his forehead. 'Why would someone be trying to take out you or your lab?'

'Maybe it wasn't me, or the lab per se, but what was in it.'

'You mean the toad?'

'See, there is still a detective in there.'

'But why would anyone want to get rid of someone who's already dead?'

'Did I speak too soon on the detective thing?' Doc asked.

'Ugh,' Remington huffed. 'Why wouldn't someone want a body hanging around?' Remington drummed his claws on his snout. 'Either you're worried about hygiene, but then you wouldn't use an explosive to bring a tunnel down on it.'

'Which leaves?'

'You're scared of someone finding something.'

'Bingo! Life in the old badge yet, eh?'

'Even half dead you're a pain in the rump.' Remington groaned. 'So, we've got insiders trying to blow us up, and our potential lead is buried under half a ton of dirt?'

'Oh yea of little faith. You hurt my feelings, Remmy.' Doc pulled his face into a pout.

'You found something?'

'Isn't that why they pay me the big worms?'

'To think I was so happy you weren't dead.'

'Alright, alright,' Doc chuckled and coughed. 'Lucky for us, I'd already examined our slimy friend.'

'And?'

'Somebody pinned him. One tiny little puncture wound in the neck. Could've been poison, or just a blade of some sort. I didn't have time to cut him open, but someone definitely offed him and then strung him up in his cell. Which means…'

'It wasn't suicide.'

'Well, yes, Captain Obvious, but it also means that unless you know something I don't, one of your Burrow team did the deed.'

Remington's jaw fell open. 'What?'

'Wasn't it your people on watch all night?' How does anyone get past them to toad face if they're not in on it?'

Remington stretched. 'Right, you wait here. I'll be back as soon as I can.'

'Where are you off to?'

'I'm going to check the cell again. We're missing something, Doc. I know it. While I'm at it, I'll get some stuff to sort out that mess too,' he said, gesturing to the mole's wound.

'Be careful, Rem. Trust nothing but your gut.'

Remington nodded and turned to leave. As he reached the exit of the chamber, he stopped.

'Doc,' he said over his shoulder.

'What is it, my boy?'

'Where's the Rev?'

'Still in his cage. Small mercies and all that.'

Remington nodded and disappeared into the tunnel.

# Chapter Thirty-Four

To the west, the sky bled amber as the sun's ascent latticed gold across the Burrow. Remington crunched over the woodland floor, his four paws unsettling the first frost of the season. This place that had never felt like home when he was young, no matter how hard he tried, had started to welcome him into its pastoral embrace. Now every scuffle of leaves, every tweet from the treetops, every scent, and seed, seemed to threaten him with hostility. He kept his eyes low, and his pace quick, Doc's words repeating in his head.

The way Remington saw it, there were three options: number one – Doc knew about the Rev and Lennox's releasing of him, and he was helping her to cover it up; number two – Doc was being honest and he had no idea about the Rev or Lennox's part in his newfound freedom; or option three – Oscar was wrong. The more he thought about each possibility, the more questions spooled forth. He growled to himself and pushed on.

The station hut loomed like the broken old relic it was, its rotten wood and peeling façade stripped of the charm Remington had once seen. It was a not fit for purpose effigy. Fitting, Remington thought, for the institution it represented. Remington nudged open the door, disturbing the aroma of must and stale wood. The gloomy interior swallowed up the daylight. A draught slipped through one of the many gaps in the hut. Remington twitched his nose, catching a familiar scent.

'Sergeant,' he called. 'That you?'

'Yes, Sir.' Vixx's face suddenly appeared in the window.

'A word, please.'

A fluster of feathers, another gust of wind, and Vixx was in the doorway, her silhouette framed by the morning's glow. She looked completely black. For a moment, Remington thought he was looking at a crow.

'Sergeant,' Remington began. 'I need to know about the night Roadkill… well… you know. Anything strange?'

The harrier fidgeted with one of her feathers, tugging at it like the hem of a skirt. 'It was quiet, considering everything, Sir.'

Remington kept his face as neutral as he could and said nothing. It was a trick he'd learned early on in his detective career; one of the most effective tools in the interrogator's tool bag was silence.

'I kept my post at the top of the stairs.' She hesitated, her eyes darting to Remington's and then quickly away. 'I checked on the prisoner on the reg.'

'Nothing suspicious at all?'

'Suspicious, like what, Sir?'

'Anything at all; sounds, smells, anything look amiss?'

'Quiet like I said, Sir. I heard some rustling from the back of the hut at one point-'

'And you didn't think to check?'

Vixx's eyes shifted. 'I did, Sir. A few times, but each time, it was just night creatures and shadows.'

'Shadows can be deceiving, Sergeant.'

Vixx clicked her beak and her eyes flashed. 'I did my job, Sir. I always do.'

Remington nodded. 'Yes, you've certainly impressed.'

'Do you think I had something to do with it?'

'With what?'

'With the toad stringing himself up.' She scratched at the floor. 'You're suggesting I had something to do with it?'

'Not suggesting anything.' Remington rubbed his jaw. 'Just trying to piece a puzzle together. Every detail, every memory, counts.'

Vixx took a deep breath, her breast heaving. 'I did my best. I kept to my post, Sir. He must have done it so quickly.'

Remington searched her eyes. They were nervous, but he couldn't read a liar in them. Despite the fact he had every reason to doubt his ability to sniff a liar out, he released a long, defeated sigh. 'What if I were to tell you it wasn't suicide?'

Vixx's beak guppied the air. 'Sir?'

Remington cocked his head and shrugged.

'Impossible, Sir. That would mean someone snuck past me, got to Roadkill, overpowered him, set that whole tableau up, and then somehow got back past me.'

Remington narrowed his eyes.

'I swear, Sir. There's no way.'

'Alright,' Remington studied her for a moment. She looked horrified. 'Then we need to have another look at those cells.'

Vixx nodded. 'Of course, Sir. Follow me.'

As they made their way down the mud steps into the corridor that housed the station's two cells, Remington felt a twinge in his gut. It was the nagging feeling that the answers were right under his snout, but somehow, he couldn't quite catch their scent. The narrow passageway smelled like a stagnant pond. The door to the empty cell groaned as Remington nudged it open. He stood in the centre of the space, raising himself up onto his hind legs. He spread his forelegs and could almost touch both sides at once.

Remington ran a paw along the bars. He noted the rusted railings and the way they wobbled on their worn hinges. It wouldn't take much to force the cell open, even it was supposedly sealed.

Vixx watched him from the freedom side of

eerie, Sir,' she muttered. 'Sort of feels like he's sti

Remington looked up to the beam from wh

body had hung. 'Door doesn't seal properly,' he s

Vixx scraped a talon on the mud floor. 'We've always known that, but we've never…I mean, as long as someone's on watch-'

'How did I miss this?' Remington seemed to be talking to himself.

Vixx twitched her head. 'What are you thinking, Sir? What makes you think he didn't do himself in?'

Remington hesitated and drew a paw along his snout. 'Let's just say I've got my sources, but I can't share them just yet.'

Vixx nodded. 'Okay, Sir. So how did the culprit get past me?'

'Quills,' Remington muttered, and slapped his head with his paw. 'No, no, no.'

'Sir?' Vixx stepped aside as Remington pushed past her into the corridor.

Remington stood in front of the other cell and huffed. He had made a mental note to do something about the 'archive room' when Vixx had first showed him it. Still, it was cluttered with stacks of old files, discarded equipment, and other detritus. Mould and the acrid tang of decay made his nose twitch. Remington sifted through the piles and pushed the old apparatus toward the edges of the room. A particular stack caught his eye. It seemed a little too…deliberate. It spoke of intent rather than carelessness.

Remington's gut growled as he kicked the pile away. A patch of the floor looked as though it had been recently disturbed. He pushed a claw into it. The soil was loose, and as he grabbed pawfulls of dirt, shovelling them to the side, the truth clanked down on both animals.

'Is that a tunnel?' Vixx asked, her beak gaped.

Remington nodded but did not reply. His snout hovered just over the opening. He drew in the smells that wafted up into the station hut. The cool underground air tickled at his whiskers, carrying damp earth and the ghost of something more elusive. He pointed his ear to the space and closed his eyes. There was ·rely the faintest shuffle or muted echo. Only the earth was whispering its secrets in the tunnel now.

'Shall I call in Chris or Claire?' asked Vixx. 'They'd be small enough to get through there.'

Remington looked at her and cocked his head. 'What are you trying to say?'

'Oh… I… sorry, Sir. I didn't mean-'

'I think I can manage, Sergeant.' Remington lowered himself into the tunnel. 'Besides, we need to keep the circle tight now. Understand?'

'Loud and clear, Sir.'

'I need to find out where this goes. Cover it up behind me, okay?'

By the time Vixx had voiced her affirmation, Remington had already been swallowed up by the earth.

# Chapter Thirty-Five

The tunnel was tight but well-hewn. In the unending shadow its walls, slick with moisture, were difficult to examine reliably. As he dragged himself through the passage, Remington took deep drinks of the earthy air. The coolness of the soil seeped through his paws and pushed into his flanks like an embrace. The excavation wasn't deep. Very quickly, Remington found himself levelling out and moving horizontally toward the front of the station hut. Whoever had dug this tunnel had done so swiftly but well. From the inconsistency of its shape, Remington suspected it was not made by a natural digger. The way the soil had been moved spoke of someone with the wrong tools for the job.

He propelled himself onward and the tunnel expanded slightly, the walls receding like boundaries of a growing world. The air changed too. Faint sounds began to drift into Remington's ears. There was a hushed conversation, the shuffle of fabric over fur. The darkness became punctuated with occasional flickers of light casting flashes of shadow in the space before him. The tunnel swung upward abruptly, and Remington groaned as he engaged rarely used muscles to drag himself higher. More than once, he coughed as he inhaled crumbling soil. *Some badger*, he thought. Remington's claws touched something soft. With an open paw, he pushed aside some sort of fabric sheet. He was blinded by a sudden flood of light.

The air thrummed with herbs and medicine. Remington blinked, trying to will his vision back into focus. For a moment he was confused as his eyes refused to distinguish anything beyond a block of pale colour. He blinked again.

'Detective Platypus?' The voice came from behind him; weak, crackling with insecurity.

Remington swivelled, all but his head and shoulders still hidden in the hole. As he did, the pale colour receded, and Remington realised where he was. The colour was the sheeting of one of the recovery tents. The tunnel had deposited Remington into the corner of one. He hauled himself out, trying to stifle the groan as he did so.

'It is you, Detective?'

The cots in the tent were empty except for one. Upon it lay Red's mother. Her fur still dull, but the ghost of its former lustre glittered her flanks. Her eyes were clouded, but wide with surprise as she looked at the Remington.

'It's me.' He stepped closer to the bed.

A smile broke across her face, her features transformed, and her eyes sparkled. 'I thought you'd stopped coming to see me.'

'Sorry, it's all been a bit crazy-'

'Thank you,' she said. 'Pixie won't stop talking about you.' A tear rolled from the corner of her eye.

Remington knelt by the side of the bed and squeezed her paw. 'Pixie? Suits her.'

'She's been trying to get me to call her Red.'

Remington let out the hint of a laugh. 'So, you got your voice back?'

'They tell me I'll be climbing trees in no time.' She squeezed his paw back. 'Will you come and see her when she visits later? She'd love to see you.'

'It's best if I keep my head down for now, for all of your safety…erm…Ma'am.'

'It's Anne.' She placed her paw on the side of the badger's snout. 'Trying to do everything on my own is what got me in this mess,' she said indicating the bed of hay she lay in.

Remington nodded and lowered his snout. Anne stroked the top of his head, and before he could stop himself, the badger began to weep. His shoulders shook and tears streamed from his tired old eyes. The squirrel continued to stroke his head. He was mortified and willed himself to stop, to get up and leave the tent, but he was lost in the wave of whatever was happening to him. The world beyond the tent seemed to drift away, and Remington felt his body slump as the squirrel traced gentle patterns in his fur.

'I'm so sorry,' he murmured eventually, wiping away tears with the back of his paw.

'Don't be silly, you daft old thing.' She squeezed his paw firmly and then pushed herself more upright in the bedding.

Remington huffed and shook his head. 'I don't suppose you remember your first couple of nights here, do you?'

'I was pretty out of it.'

'Do you remember seeing anyone coming or going that you've not seen since?'

She shook her head.

'Nothing strange at all?'

'Strange is all there is when you've got Heartbreak in your system.'

Remington nodded and sighed. 'Not to worry.'

'I did have a weird dream back at the beginning.'

Remington's ears twitched. 'A dream?'

'I think so. Like I said, I was pretty out of it, but I remember thinking it felt so real at the time.'

'Go on.'

'I thought I'd woken up, and I panicked because I didn't know where I was. It was dark and I couldn't move. I tried to shout out but couldn't make a noise. I heard something rustle in the darkness, and then I thought I saw someone.'

'Someone?'

'You'll think it's silly.'

'Try me.'

'I thought I saw a big black bird.'

Remington felt the fur on his back begin to rise. 'A crow?'

'It was so dark,' Anne shrugged.

'Did it… do anything?'

The squirrel shook her head. 'No, it just looked back at me, and then vanished.'

'This was the first night?'

'I'm not sure. I think so. It was early on, but it's all a blur.'

Remington scratched his jaw with his claws.

'It probably was just a dream,' Red's mother said.

'Mmhmm, yes, you're probably right.' Remington gave her paw another squeeze and stood up.

'Will you come by later and see Pixie?'

Remington shuffled and ran a claw along his forehead.

'There's no point in avoiding her, you know.'

'It's not Red… Pixie I'm avoiding,' Remington said and bit his lip.

'The teacher? Daisy?'

'That obvious?'

Anne chuckled and winced. She would not be climbing trees anytime soon. 'She hasn't dropped her off for a while,' she said, swallowing back the pain.

'Really?'

The squirrel nodded. 'It's been that mad old headteacher for the past week or so.'

'Then maybe.'

Anne beamed at him.

'I said *maybe*.'

'I'll see you later on, Detective,' she said and closed her eyes, a smile still playing on her face. Remington patted her paw and left her to rest.

Hushed, concerned tones greeted Remington as he stepped

back into the station hut. Mrs Banks and Sergeant Vixx were hunched over a desk. Vixx's eyes were scanning a slither of clay. Chief Banks was staring vacantly out of a window. Mrs Banks looked up. Her face was drawn and gaunt. Remington stepped closer and peered at what they had been reading. The thin clay tablet bore the emblem of the city Met upon it.

'What's the news?' he asked.

Vixx cleared her throat. 'It's Take Back Eden, Sir.'

'What is?'

'They've claimed responsibility for the explosion at the Met.'

'Still no news of Doc either I'm afraid, love,' added Mrs Banks.

Remington bit his lip as he swallowed down a minor hiccup of guilt. 'And the Met thinks it's a reliable claim?'

'Says here they've been recruiting heavily across the city in all the recent chaos.' Vixx passed the report to Remington with her beak.

'But why the terrorism all of a sudden?' Mrs Banks' voice cracked as she spoke. 'They've been around for ages and never been violent.'

'Desperation,' Chief Banks said, still staring out of the window. Remington nearly dropped the clay. 'Desperation breeds recklessness. The city's been on the brink for years, and they've just given it the final nudge.'

'But what do they want?' Vixx asked. 'All the protests were always about returning to nature or recreating a world without the influence of the city. But this… what can it achieve?'

'There's more to this than we're seeing,' Remington said. He tossed the report back on the desk.

'Speaking of,' said Vixx, straightening her feathers. She ushered Remington over to a corner of the room. 'The tunnel?'

'Oh… yes… follow me, Sergeant. I could use your eyes on this.'

# Chapter Thirty-Six

The flap of the recovery tent rustled as Vixx and Remington slipped inside, their breath visible in the brisk air. Anne was snoring gently, and Remington gestured with a claw to the snout, for quiet. He led the sergeant over to the dark maw in the corner of the tent.

'All yours, Sergeant,' Remington whispered, pointing to the still uncovered tunnel entrance.

With a professional glint in her shifting eyes, Vixx peered down at the hole. Her talons delicately sifted through the soil. Remington watched as she examined the width of the tunnel, the unevenness of the walls, the haphazard way the earth had been displaced.

'Not the work of a natural digger,' she muttered. 'See this?' She pointed to a flurry of inconsistent and shallow scrapes along the tunnel's edge. 'These marks are irregular, too frantic, and it's too narrow to be a creature of substantial size.'

Remington crouched down and scratched his jaw. 'So, that means?'

Vixx straightened up and shook the dirt from her feathers. 'Based on what little we've got, I reckon our tunneller was a small one, most likely a rat. Claws aren't designed for digging, but with enough pace and the desire to do it, a rat could have pulled this off.'

Remington ran a claw along one of the small scrapes and watched the dry dirt flake away in a fine powder. 'Fair enough, Sergeant. So, you want to give us a working theory?'

'We don't have enough, Sir. It would just be speculation.'

'That's why we call it a theory, Vixx.' Remington was still looking at the scrapes that decorated the tunnel entrance's inner rim. 'Humour me.'

'Okay... well... we arrest Roadkill and bring him here. Brigg escapes...' Her voice wavered slightly. 'But she knows whoever their boss is will likely take them both out if there's a risk of one of them talking to the police. So, she sneaks into the clearing during the chaos and, in the darkness, she tunnels her way in, strings up the toad and then flees.'

'Brigg's tough for sure, but strong enough to overpower Roadkill and then truss him up like that?'

'So, she had help? Or drugged him?'

Remington's ears pricked up. 'Follow that through, Sergeant.'

'She tunnels down. Roadkill sees her and thinks he's being rescued, so his guard's down. Brigg's quick, she could easily slip him something before he realises it's a murder not a jailbreak.'

'It tracks... except...' Remington hesitated and narrowed his eyes.

'Sir?'

'Well, our patient over there thinks she might have seen a large black bird here that night.'

Vixx's eyes flashed. 'Thinks she *might* have?'

'Could have been the effects of Heartbreak, and... well... she was barely alive when we brought her in.'

'But you think she did.'

Remington shrugged.

'Sir, do you think Cull's involved in this?'

'Sergeant, the Murder is *always* involved.' Remington regretted saying it even as the words left his lips. His vendetta against the Rev and the Murder were so well known in the city that he was generally regarded with the disdainful pity one usually reserves for the worst kinds of conspiracy nuts.

Vixx, though, nodded back with a look of grim determination

on her face. 'Okay, Sir. So, what do we do now?'

'I'm open to suggestions.'

Vixx tugged at a feather with her beak and tapped the floor with her talons. 'Sir… I…' She trailed off.

'Out with it, Sergeant.'

'It's just… everything… in the city and here… the Murder, Take Back Eden, the chimaera bodies. Is it all connected?'

Remington sucked cool air in through his teeth and cocked his head. 'Great minds, Sergeant. So, what's our next step?'

Vixx bounced on her talons. 'Permission to set up a new investigation wall, Sir? We need to see everything properly. I feel like we're missing something.'

'Get on it.' Remington said, and the young bird, in a flurry of feathers and energy, flustered out of the tent.

Remington stayed and looked into the tunnel. Its dark throat beckoned him in. Something about the snug earth, its smells, and internal rhythms tugged at him. How often had he felt as though a black hole was opening beneath him? How often had he wished for the ground to swallow him up, give him a place to hide in, to shelter from the world, its demands and miseries? He imagined slipping into its embrace, tendrils creaking from deep below wrapping around him and pulling him down.

Remington was so absorbed in his own thoughts he didn't hear the tent flap open, and he didn't sense the creature that crept silently behind him on delicately clawed feet. A frosty breeze slid into the tent and touched the badger's nose, making him twitch. As he did so, the faint drift of the animal's aroma slipped into his nostrils. But it was too late. The creature had leapt onto Remington's back before he could spin around, and in a flash it had clambered up behind his head. Remington curled his paw into a fist, and was just about to swing it up blindly toward his assailant when-

'Rem! I missed you,' Pixie's high, reedy voice echoed through

the tent. She threw her forelegs around as much of his broad neck as she could and squeezed him tightly.

'I missed you too, Red,' he said as she clambered round to his front and beamed up at him.

Pixie's eyes sparkled with mischief. 'Where have you been?'

'Oh, you know me, Deputy. Always working.'

'Taking down bad guys?'

'You know it.' Remington gently extricated the squirrel from his fur and crouched down. 'Have you been behaving yourself?'

'She's been an angel, Francis,' Head Plunkett said as she stomped into the tent. 'Much better than many of my former students.'

Remington rolled his eyes at Pixie, and she giggled with glee back.

'I saw that,' the old beaver said. 'Now, how's the patient today?'

'She's asleep-' Remington began but as he looked over, he saw Red's mother sitting up in bed smiling at the scene before her.

Pixie jumped up onto Remington's shoulders, her tail flicking with excitement. The badger delivered the young squirrel to her mother's bedding. Pixie duly slipped from Remington's shoulders and into her mother's embrace.

'Miss Carrol not with you?' Remington asked.

'I've been doing the honours, I'm afraid,' said Head Plunkett.

'She's not been in school for ages,' Pixie added as she snuggled into her mother.

Remington cocked his head at his former history teacher. 'Ages?'

'How about we leave these two to it?' Plunkett jerked her head toward the exit.

'So, where-' Remington began once they were clear of the tent, but the unexpected force of a slap from Plunkett stopped him. 'What the?' He raised a paw to his stinging face. 'That's assault on an officer of-'

'Least you bloody deserve, Francis.'

Remington glared back at her, but words wouldn't find their

way out of him.

'I told you she was a good one. A good one, Francis, not one to be messed around with, and not one to play any of your foolish bloody games with.'

'I was trying to protect her.'

'Well, your protection has done a grand job. She's distraught since your little, what shall we call it? Knockback? Dumping? Rejection?' She looked like she might deliver another slap.

Remington raised his paws in submission. 'Did she tell you this?'

'Sent a note,' Plunkett smoothed her fur. 'Poor girl couldn't even come in. Couldn't face the humiliation. Fancy being rejected by… well…' Plunkett looked Remington up and down. 'This.'

'Can I see it? The note, I mean.'

'What are you after, some sort of trophy?'

'Look, I don't know what you've read, or what Daisy's said, but I did not reject her.'

'Typical,' Plunkett shook her head. 'Men, never aware of the damage they're causing, so long as they're happy.'

'Have you seen her since she sent the note?' Remington's gut was starting to flip.

'Well, no, but she requested peace and peace is what she'll have.'

'We'll see about that,' Remington said, and he turned away from her.

'Francis!' she called after him. 'Francis, she will not want to see you.'

Plunkett's words pressed heavy on his shoulders as Remington picked his way through the winding paths of the Burrow. The chilly air bit at the skin beneath his fur, and the trees cast their lengthy skeletal shadows across the ground. The habitat seemed to be holding its tongue, waiting for something to crack the silence. His gut was growling at him. He replayed his last conversation with Daisy over in his mind. He had *tried* to put her off, to convince her to stay away, but as far as he recalled, she had rejected the suggestion.

His track record with women, since his wife, lay somewhere between awkward misunderstanding and absolute zero, so it was entirely possible that Plunkett was right, and he had caused harm where he had not meant to. If so, she could scream in his face, tell him to get stuffed, and that would be fine, at least he would know. But something didn't feel right. If his memory wasn't warning enough, then his swirling gut certainly was.

As he neared Daisy's warren, a strange scent drifted out to meet him. It was metallic with a faint bottom note of decay. The fur on his back became brittle. The damp chill of the frosty air that had settled between the strands of his coat seemed to cling to him. At Daisy's entranceway, he considered calling out, but the smell was stronger. Whatever it was lay inside her home. Remington took a deep breath and moved inside.

The outside light faintly filtered through the tunnel, causing a sickly illumination. The main chamber of Miss Carrol's warren was almost as sparse as it had been on his last visit. Almost, except for a hump in the centre of the floor. Flies buzzed around it. Remington dug his claws into his paw pads and moved closer to the mound. A rag had been thrown across something lumpy. Remington took a tiny sniff of the air. He almost gagged. Remington hesitated, not wanting to find his worst fears confirmed by lifting the rag. Eventually though he reached out and pinched the edge of the fabric between two claws. He took a breath, almost gagged again, and drew back the sheet.

Remington's eyes widened. It was not Miss Carrol. In front of him, eyes closed, in one piece, but lifeless, the gleaming smile of a cut throat leering up, was Brigg. The rat's fur was crusted with blood. Remington shivered. The room suddenly smelled of rain. He crouched beside the poor creature. A pang of guilt rose within him. A scuff sounded from deeper within the warren. Remington sprang up and snarled softly. Whatever had done this, was still here.

# Chapter Thirty-Seven

Remington's fur jangled all over. He wanted to call out for Daisy, but the possibility that whoever had slit Brigg's throat was still here squatted at the forefront of his mind like a venomous toad. He tried to feel for any alien rhythms through his paws pressed into the cold earth, but his own thumping heart was all he could find. He held his breath and listened. There were faint, subtle movements, the worms of the earth, the crackle of tiny creatures, the unending creak of the world as it felt its way onward through the season. But there again, it came: a rustle, from deeper within the warren. It was the careful, quiet movement of something trying to be covert. And if it was trying to be quiet, did that mean it knew Remington was here?

He cocked his head and closed his eyes. This time a thump, almost imperceptible, came from the opening to his right. It was so faint it could have been anything: the inevitable dropping of soil from the carved ceilings, or the tumble of an innocent beetle. Remington drew in a deep breath and willed himself toward the sound. He tried to keep his steps soft, and his imagination calm. He pressed himself against the wall and peered around into the tunnel leading from the main room. The light barely reached, leaving gradients of shadow, nothing more. He crept forward, his ears twitching and his nose sampling the air. The warren was deeper, more intricate than Remington had suspected, and though he tried to reach out into the mysterious labyrinth, he could find no sign of another animal. He considered stopping, turning back, but the image of Brigg's wasting body was enough to draw him on. The inky black of the hollow seemed to swallow him up. His vision began to cloud with dark, mingling shapes. He blinked hard. For a moment he thought he saw something glint, a shimmer across the blue-black void. It was soon blotted out though, a trick of his ageing eyes and the failing light.

He winced as his paw pad scuffed the floor. In the silence, it sounded like the unhinging of a heavy door. He froze, waited, listened for the slightest movement. There was none. He continued, careful to lift his paws. He was painfully aware of the low rustle of his breath, and the thunk of his awkwardly beating heart. A loose dusting of dirt began to fall from the ceiling, accompanied by the distant drumming of rain. Remington, senses primed, heard and felt the waking of worms in the walls all around, beginning their lazy ascent to the surface. Their steady sifting confused Remington's already waning perception. The whole warren was an echo chamber of stimuli.

A ghost of black within the black moved. Remington struggled to distinguish between tricks of non-light and the reality of the space. Then the badger's world exploded into chaos. A blur of motion, a rush of air, and Remington was on his back, breath forced from his lungs. The needle sting of sharp claws dug into his chest, pinning him to the floor. The shape was dark, almost impossible to distinguish from the shadows that swaddled them both. Panic coursed; his vision clouded. He felt the hot breath of the creature on his snout, a musky scent of fur, worm, and sweat.

He kicked himself up, and the two animals rolled, a cascade of growls and snarls. Remington's mind whirled. He tried to get his bearings, to identify the attacker, but a claw raked across his snout and the pain bloomed into blindness. Every move he attempted was countered by the skill of an opponent who knew how to use his weight and strength against him. They were of similar size, but his assailant was quick, and seemed to be able to see much more clearly. It saw Remington's blows coming before he was able to make good contact. The noise of their battle clattered around the tunnels.

Slowly though, with each move, Remington could feel the creature's strength beginning to wane. The badger dug deep, kept struggling to break free, knowing each time he did so, the restraining force of his attacker lessened. Remington, too, was exhausted, but the sense of opportunity allowed his adrenaline to spike, and he continued.

With one forceful burst of strength, Remington twisted, kicked, and flipped the creature off him. He lunged, and pinned it to the ground, claws around its slim neck. He began to squeeze. The creature struggled, and then began to fade. It clawed at his forelegs. It tried to push him away. Eventually it tapped uselessly on the badger.

'Det… Detective…' A feline voice croaked. 'It's… it's me.'

Remington released his grip and fell backwards. 'Cat?'

Cat coughed and rolled onto her side. Remington stared into the darkness. Two golden eyes looked back, their usual shine gone.

'Why did you attack me?' Remington pushed himself to the wall and rested his back against the cool earth.

'I… I thought you were someone else,' she murmured. Her voice was quaking. 'I didn't know it was you.'

Cat shuffled to the opposite wall, blinking slowly, willing her breath to return.

'Quills,' Remington said. 'I could have killed you.'

'Fat chance, old man,' Cat half-smiled back, but the usual sparkle of her voice was missing.

Remington's breaths were heavy as he stared at the vague outline of Cat. She was trembling in the dim tunnel. 'You want to tell me what you're doing here? And if you had anything to do with the body out there, Cat?' Remington softened his voice. 'Or is it Winifred?'

The golden eyes widened. She looked away for a moment. 'How...You found my collar?'

Remington gave a solemn nod. 'See, not that bad a detective. So, is that your handiwork out there?'

Cat hesitated, and the golden eyes glazed over with tears. 'Brigg,' was all she said.

'We've been looking for her for a long time. Was it you?'

Cat shook her head, the golden eyes moving from right to left and back, a trail of light across the dark. 'Brigg and I were...' she trailed off. Tears dropped from her cheeks.

'You were involved in the Heartbreak operation?'

'No, no, I swear.' She hesitated again.

'Cat, please... the truth.'

'Brigg... she and I, we were more than just friends. She found me when I was first here.' Her voice quivered and cracked. 'I had a family...a human one.'

'Hence the collar.'

Cat nodded. 'They left me. I came home one day, and everyone was gone. I waited... I waited for so long the moon came and went over and over again, but they never came back.'

'How did you end up in the Burrow?'

'I was so hungry, eventually I went looking for food, but at other houses humans chased me away. They'd hiss at me, throw things. I walked, and I walked. I slept under hedges, and anywhere I could squeeze into for shelter. Eventually I saw the woodland across one of those huge grey paths that have the fast human carriers on.'

'A road?'

Cat shrugged. 'A big one. I tried to cross and I nearly made it. I got tapped, only just, by one but it sent me a long way. I was hurt and I was so hungry. I managed to drag myself into the edge of the woods, and I fell asleep. Brigg found me. If I'd had the strength, I'd have devoured her right then and there. But she looked after me. She brought me food and helped me with my wound.' She blinked, long and slow. 'She even helped me set up the bar.'

'This is all really touching, Cat, but it doesn't explain where you've been or why your friend is lying out there with a smile across her neck.'

Cat closed her eyes and shuddered. Remington could see she was weeping silently.

'I'm sorry,' he said. 'Please help me get my head around this.'

'Brigg wasn't bad, Detective. She got stuck in a situation she was trying to get out of.'

Remington looked doubtfully through the shadows. 'I'm sorry, Cat, but if you'd seen what was happening in that cave-'

'I promise you it would have been a thousand times worse if she wasn't there. It killed her to be in there, to be part of all of that.'

'Then why did she try to stop us getting to Roadkill?'

Cat shrugged, 'Fear, I guess. She probably thought you were no match for the toad. If she'd helped and you'd lost, what then?'

'When I first came into the bar, it seemed like you two barely knew each other.'

'Brigg insisted on always putting on that little show. She was protecting me. Have you never distanced yourself from people you love to protect them?'

Remington's eyes widened. 'Wait, where's Daisy?'

'I don't know,' Cat shrugged. 'Brigg and I have been hiding out here for quite a few moons, and she hasn't been here. I thought she might be staying with you.'

Remington's stomach growled. 'So, Brigg?' He tilted his head toward the main warren.

'I went out last night to find us some food. I found her like that when I came back.' Tears fell again from her dark cheeks.

'Any idea who did it?'

'Whoever did Roadkill in.'

'You knew?'

'Brigg told me. She knew she'd be fingered for it as soon as you lot finally realised it wasn't suicide. That's why she had to hide. If you guys knew your snouts from your rumps, she'd still be alive.'

'So, who?'

Cat shrugged again. 'It's all I've been thinking about all day.'

'Who was Roadkill making the Heartbreak for?'

'Brigg never told me. Said she didn't want me more involved. All I know is, it was taken into the city.'

'You should probably come with me.'

'Are you arresting me?' Cat's eyes flashed for a moment.

'What? No, but I have somewhere safe. Somewhere nobody... well, only a few people know about.'

'What about Brigg? I can't just leave her here.'

'We might have to in case whoever did it comes back.'

Cat nodded, but her eyes told another story.

'Can you stand?' Remington asked.

'You're really not as tough as you think you are, Detective.'

Remington rolled his eyes and lumbered to his paws.

'Before we go though, there is something in here you need to see.' Cat winced as she stood on her four paws. 'It's about Miss Carrol. It's about Daisy.'

# Chapter Thirty-Eight

Cat led Remington further into Daisy's warren. He followed the vague outline of her. Now and then she would turn back, her eyes yellow beams cutting through the dark. Each step dragged with a sick feeling Remington couldn't shake off. The air was thick and dry. Beyond the clustered shadows, an eerie light seeped through one of the walls up ahead.

'Here,' Cat said, stopping at a wall that seemed crosshatched with the faint green Remington recognised from his own sett. It was the same odd bioluminescence of fungi the old bat had somehow willed into bloom. Cat unveiled her claws and pushed them into the perforated surface. She pulled, and Remington realised it wasn't a wall but a curtain of closely twisted vines. The tendrils resisted and finally gave way. Sickly green light spilled from the chamber within.

'After you,' Cat grimaced as she held the unsettling flora back.

Remington took a deep breath and stepped through. Cat followed and the curtain quickly knotted itself back together behind her.

'Well, that's creepy,' Remington shuddered.

'That's nothing.' Cat gestured deeper into the chamber.

As Remington's eyes adjusted to the sudden change in light, he looked around the chamber.

'Here,' Cat said, offering him a faintly glowing mushroom she'd pulled from the dirt. 'Look.'

Remington raised the makeshift torch, and slowly tilted it across the chamber walls.

'Quills,' he said. 'What is all this?'

'You're the detective. I was hoping you could tell me.'

Almost every part of the chamber was covered in strange carvings: words, symbols, pictures, messages. All were scratched deep into the surface of the warren. Remington stepped closer and his skin turned cold beneath his fur. Nightmarish creatures were etched in horrible, twisted distortions. Amalgamated animals, birds and rodents, mammals and reptiles, bits and pieces of myriad biologies were merged together in disturbing tableaus. Phrases swam between the figures' screaming faces: *The World's End is Our Beginning… From Beneath He Comes… Chaos From Below…* On and on they went, some repeated, some incomplete, some indecipherable. The dancing shadows from the awkward light made them seem to move across the walls.

Cat tugged Remington on the leg and gestured toward a particular spot. 'Look.'

Remington followed her gaze. One phrase, larger than the others, more deeply ingrained in the surface, as though it had been traced and retraced over and over again read: *Eden Will Come Again.*

'Take Back Eden?' Remington whispered.

'Look beneath it.'

Remington lowered the light. There, below the four words was the crudely scratched image of a towering bird, its wings outstretched, looming over the body of a badger, its form awkwardly posed in a mockery of death.

'Do you think this was her?' Cat said. 'Daisy?'

'No… no…' Remington felt dizzy. 'It can't have been.'

'Then where is she?'

Remington slumped to the floor. His chest felt tight, and he struggled to get air into his body. His mind tore through his interactions with Miss Carrol; the school, Cat's, their date.

'Look at it, Detective,' Cat slapped her paw on the wall. 'Who else could have done this?'

Remington's fur bristled. 'For all I know, this was you and your girlfriend out there. You've been here long enough.'

Cat's eyes flashed. 'Whoever did this, must have done *that* to Brigg, and I will find them whether you're willing to open your eyes or not.'

Remington opened his jaw to argue, but then he remembered his last and only visit to this warren. Just as they had been about to enter, Daisy had made some excuse about mess, despite how immaculate the place had been. He cursed himself for being so blind. *Some detective*, he thought. Why had he not been suspicious then? Was he so blinded by a pretty face and the rare sense of connection he'd found? The inky markings of Daisy's face reeled before him, mingling with the shadows in the chamber.

'Okay,' he said. 'Okay, say you're right. It's not just her. Look at this, these pictures. If she's got something to do with the chimaera murders, she can't have done it alone. She's part of something bigger.'

'No shit, Detective,' spat Cat. 'Take Back Eden; it's all right here.'

'It's all connected,' Remington muttered to himself. 'It's all *him*.'

'Who? Roadkill?'

'I knew it.' Remington dug his claws into his paw pads so firmly he cut into them.

'Who?' Cat shook the badger.

'Him.' Remington pointed to the image of the bird.

'You're talking about the Murder? You think they're behind Take Back Eden?'

Remington shook his head. He didn't take his eyes of the carving. 'Just him. The Rev.'

'I thought you put him away.'

'Yeah, so did I,' said Remington. 'But that's the thing about evil. You can try but you can never properly clip its wings.'

'So, we need to tell your mates in the force then. Let's get everything you guys have got and find him.'

Remington shook his head slowly again. 'We can't trust any of them.'

'What? Why?'

'Because they're the ones who set him free.'

Cat placed a paw on Remington's snout and gently turned his head away from the picture. 'What do we do now?'

Remington hesitated. He searched Cat's eyes, looking for a sign, something to mistrust. His gut told him nothing. He trusted her. He didn't know why.

'I've got a safe place.'

Remington watched as Cat said farewell to Brigg. He swallowed back tears as she lay a tender kiss on each of the rat's closed eyes. She placed her head to the lifeless body's and then whispered a promise to get whoever had ended the poor creature's life. She stood, licked her paws, and drew them across her face, smoothing over her tear-streaked fur. She nodded to Remington, and they cautiously left the warren.

The Burrow seemed to be lousy with movement as they made their way to Remington's sett. Every rustle in the underbrush, every distant animal call, felt like a warning. The woodland was a contortion of gloom, and both creatures felt eyes pressing upon them.

'I think we're being watched, Detective,' Cat said, her eyes flicking all around her.

Remington said nothing. He led Cat on a complex route, double-backing, and aiming for the thickest protection of woodland he could. The deeper they trudged into the woods, the more sudden shadows Remington thought he saw, but whenever he turned to face the shifting objects, all he found was the drifting miasma of the seething dark.

'Stop,' Cat said suddenly. She arched her back, her ears flicked.

'What is it?' Remington held his breath.

'Something's overhead, over the canopy.'

They waited, and Cat listened. They peered up into the closely knitted branches and leaves. Eventually, she nodded, and they continued. Both animals kept a close watch on the scattering of sky they could see. Remington said nothing on the occasions he thought he saw a bird drift overhead. It was likely just the movement of a leaf, momentarily obscuring a tiny spot of sky.

When they reached an unavoidable break in the canopy, they waited, and watched. Nothing moved. It was eerie how still the sky was, a blank grey slate, the haze of the aftermath of rain dusting the air.

'Are we safe?' Remington asked Cat.

'I can't see anything,' she said.

'Stay behind me.'

Remington stepped out into the unshielded patch of turf. He paused for a moment and then continued. After a few steps, he gestured for Cat to follow. As he did so, a shadow passed over the clearing and a shattering of wings burst through the silence. Remington turned sharply to see a shape drop toward him. Cat shot out into the clearing thrusting her form into the bird. They landed in a chaos of limbs and noise.

'Cat, wait,' Remington called.

Cat sprang back, her fur standing stiff. Vixx squawked and fluttered her wings, her eyes rolling wildly in shock.

'Sergeant,' Remington said as he helped her back to her talons. 'What are you playing at, sneaking up on us like that?'

'Sorry, Sir,' she said, still flapping her wings, and twitching her head back forth. 'I've been looking for you all day.'

'Stand down, Cat,' Remington said. Cat was still primed to pounce, her jaw pulled back into a threatening leer.

'Sergeant, I've been laying low. There's a lot to fill you in on.'

Vixx and Cat were staring at each other.

'Seriously, we've got enough actual enemies to worry about.' Remington drew a paw down his snout. 'Pack it in will you.'

Cat's fur settled, and her puffed up tail slowly drooped.

'We can trust her?' Vixx asked.

'Can we trust you?' Cat added.

'I'm not sure I can trust either of you, but beggars can't be choosers,' Remington said. 'Now, please put your murder mitts away, and follow me.'

Vixx tugged at her feathers with her beak and sighed. Cat licked at her shoulder and did the same.

'Oh, Sir,' Vixx squawked. 'I nearly forgot.' She jumped into the air and cast her eyes around the clearing floor.

'What's her problem?' Cat said, looking at Remington.

'I had a package for you.' Vixx was frantically hopping and searching. 'She knocked it out of my grasp.'

'Butter talons,' Cat muttered.

Remington gave her a look, and she raised a paw apologetically.

'Here.' Vixx swung an awkwardly bound package to Remington.

He caught it with two paws. 'What is this?'

'Don't know, Sir. It arrived at the station this morning.'

Remington turned the parcel over and sniffed it. There was something metallic beneath the papery scent of the wrapping. On one side was scratched: *R.P. For Luck*. He shook it gently. Something shifted in his stomach. Carefully, Remington unwrapped the offering. Cat and Vixx drew closer. It was tightly bound and seemed to take an age to unpeel.

'We should get to shelter,' Cat said, eyeing the sky.

Remington nodded and continued to unwrap. Eventually the contents were freed, and a single object fell to the floor.

'On my...' Vixx said.

Remington gathered the item up. It was small, chocolate brown, coated in fur, matted with blood. A single, severed rabbit's foot.

'What is that?' Cat leaned closer.

Remington gasped as he turned the orphaned limb in his paws. A white band encircled its wrist.

'It's Lennox,' he said.

'What?' Cat gawped at Remington.

'Sergeant,' the badger clutched the item. 'Who delivered this?'

'I... I... I don't know, Sir.' Vixx was blinking in disbelief, the lenses of her eyes shifting in and out. 'It arrived before I got there.'

'Cat, can you smell anyone on this.'

Cat was already running her nose along the discarded packaging. 'There's nothing, Detective. It's completely clean.'

'Sir,' Vixx urged. 'We need to get somewhere safe.'

Remington nodded. His mind was a cascade of images and apologies, his entire history with Lennox looped in his mind.

His stomach churned with a mixture of fury, sorrow, and guilt for the anger he had felt toward her so recently.

'Detective,' Cat shook him. 'She's right. We need to move.'

Remington said nothing, only nodded and cradled Lennox's severed limb to his chest. He trudged onward, a ghost in his own body.

Remington was so dazed as he autopiloted back to the sett he didn't stop to check the surroundings. He didn't push his paws into the earth to sense for movement or other animals. He walked, he walked, he walked, and Cat and Vixx followed silently. He moved blindly into the sett, his heart a dull metronome pulsing a steady thump of anger and sorrow in his ears.

'Rem,' Doc called as the three entered the inner chamber. If Remington heard him, he didn't say. The old bat's eyes beamed out from the corner. Doc, the bat, Vixx, and Cat surveyed each other, eyes moving from one to another to Remington.

'Remmy?' Doc repeated.

Remington slowly unclenched his paw and showed Doc what he was holding.

'Oh, quills, Rem.' Doc reached for the foot, but Remington snatched it back. 'It's okay, Rem. Come on. Let me see. Let me see.'

Remington released his grip, and Doc took the limb. He ran his nose over it.

'It's Lennox's,' he said.

Remington nodded and stared at the useless artefact.

A shuffling sound came from one of the adjoining tunnels. Cat spun round and sniffed the air. Vixx turned sharply. Remington slowly took his eyes from Lennox's foot. He glanced toward the opening. A dark shape moved forward, hulking, stooping to fit into the space. It stepped into the main chamber and seemed to unfurl, filling the gap, blotting out the hole. It rustled its feathers and clicked its long black beak. Remington's stomach seemed to fall from within him. The beak had a crack in its side, giving the appearance of a vicious fang. Its eyes were like tar as it shook its shoulders and loomed over Remington. There, in his familial home, his ancestral sett, stood the Rev.

# Chapter Thirty-Nine

Remington ground his claws into the dry, gritty surface of the sett. His lip curled into a snarl. If he'd paused for a breath, he might have stopped to consider whether or not this was another dream. So often had the Rev visited his sleep, twisting dream into nightmare. Had he paused for a moment to think, he might have wondered why the Rev was here in his family's old home, or how he had discovered it in the first place. But Remington did not pause. His claws had ground into the earth, and his legs braced, his muscles taught and primed. Before the Rev could make a move, or speak, Remington had flung himself toward the enormous bird, the claws of his forepaws flashing in the eerie glow of the bioluminescent fungi.

The Rev hardly seemed to move, but somehow with a shift of those onyx angel wings, he sidestepped the oncoming badger, sending Remington sprawling into the gaping mouth of the tunnel. The badger flipped himself back around and locked his rage-filled eyes with the unfathomable matte black voids of the raven. Remington attacked again. The Rev clapped his wings together in a shield. Remington hammered into them, and the Rev skidded back, dragging his talons into the floor. The Rev lowered his wings and stared down at Remington. The other animals looked on, stunned for a moment by the spectacle before them. The chamber itself seemed to hold its breath as the two creatures began to circle each other.

Remington made his move, this time feinting with a fist and ducking under a defensive swipe of the wing. He drove his shoulder into the bird's midriff and heard air expel from the beak above him. Remington leapt up, slamming an uppercut into the Rev's beak. Startled, the raven staggered backward and retaliated with a horizontal slice of his huge left wing. It caught Remington on the side of the head with a force the badger didn't expect. He gritted his teeth and planted his paws. The two stared at one another again.

Cat lowered her head toward her paws, crouching as if to pounce. Vixx stopped her. 'Wait,' she hissed.

The Rev's eyes flicked to the feline for barely the ghost of a breath. It was enough. Remington closed the distance and struck again. The Rev reacted with an uncanny grace that defied his mass. The ebony feathers rustled and flashed. Every blow Remington tried to land was matched by the Rev's wing or talon. Despite the preternatural speed of the bird parrying each of the badger's attacks, Remington, through his boiling anger, sensed a reluctance in the Rev's actions. Still, Remington fought on, intoxicated by revenge and anger. Repeatedly, the Rev was able to push the badger away, but Remington surged forward again, his claws glinting in the sickly light. The Rev's sinister grace allowed him to evade most of the strikes, but now and then Remington would find a way through the hulking corvus' dexterity. On the battle raged, a bedlam of snarls and wingbeats thrumming around the chamber.

With each passing ebb of his strength, Remington's resolve grew. He wasn't the simpering creature who had cowered in the Rev's shadow in his nightmares. His wife's drenched body jumped into his mind one moment, replaced by the young mouse's limp form the next. Cat shoved Vixx away and leapt toward the Rev. Without looking, he opened his wing and slapped at her, forcing her into the ceiling of the chamber. She landed, spreadeagled and winded. Remington seized on the opening. He darted close, delivering a series of jabs to the raven's chest, making him stagger backwards, his feathers ruffled, his composure faltering.

Whatever shackles had been holding the Rev back seemed

to slip away. With a single explosive motion, he unleashed a devastating counter. Both wings unfurled and then clattered together with a deafening crack on Remington's flanks. The Rev then kicked out with one talon and sent Remington tumbling through the air. He crashed against the chamber wall, the impact jarring his whole body. Despite the pain, Remington refused to yield. He dragged himself back up and charged, claws first, at the Rev's shadowy plumage. He tore at the bird, and strips of feather fell like ink-stained confetti. The Rev let out a caw of pain and jabbed at the badger's face with his beak. Blood spilled from above Remington's eye, rolling down and blurring his vision. Remington swung wildly at his foe, but the Rev kicked out again, toppling the badger. The Rev loomed over Remington and snaked a talon around his neck, squeezing with a grip that could crush bone.

Remington clawed and gasped. His vision swam as the world began to darken around him. Vixx jumped at the Rev, swotting at him with her wings. Doc and Cat both scaled the raven's back and heaved, trying to pull him away. Remington thought he saw the old bat's serrated wing flash across his vision too. The Rev shook violently, shuddering his great frame from side to side. The other creatures were flung from him to the edges of the chamber.

'Enough of this,' the Rev hissed, his voice a ghostly whisper. With a final squeeze, he relinquished his grip and stepped back. Remington spluttered and attempted to push himself upright. Doc came to his side and urged him to stay back.

'Enough,' the Rev repeated. 'I'm not who… I'm not what you think I am.'

Remington sat, bloody and battered against the chamber wall. His eye, blurry with blood, stayed fixed on the Rev, whose torn feathers bore a sticky trail of their own. Cat, Vixx, Doc, and the aged bat tended to their own wounds. The silence was unbearable.

It was Vixx who spoke first. 'Alright big bird, talk,' she said.

'Why are you here?'

The Rev's obsidian stare shifted between each of the animals. 'Because we need each other.'

'After everything you've done?' Doc said over his shoulder as he dabbed at the wound above Remington's eye. Remington said nothing.

'I'm not what you think I am,' the Rev said again. 'I haven't done what you think.'

Doc scuttled forward. The Rev stepped back. The mole took something from the chamber floor and tossed it to the raven. 'So, you had nothing to do with this?'

The Rev lifted Lennox's foot to his tar black eyes. 'No… no… not her.' The Rev's voice cracked as he spoke. His frame shuddered. Again, Remington said nothing.

'Talk, crow,' Vixx commanded. She was digging her talons into the dirt.

'Where did you get this?' The Rev was still studying the foot.

'We thought it was a gift from you,' Cat said, protracting her claws which glinted green in the glow.

The Rev shook his head. 'Not me. It was Cull.' He hesitated and clicked his beak. 'It was never supposed to go this far.' He clutched the rabbit foot in his talon, swallowing it in the black of his powerful digits. 'I didn't know. It was all Cull.'

'Hey,' Vixx snapped her own talons. 'You need to start making sense, now. What was never supposed to go this far?'

'I didn't know,' the Rev said again. 'I didn't k-'

'Didn't know what?' Remington interrupted finally, his voice low and bitter. 'That your sick little games would lead to this?'

The Rev looked up at Remington, his beak open. 'I tried to stop it. I've always been trying to stop this. But Cull…' he trailed off.

'You're saying Cull did this to Lennox?' Doc stepped toward the Rev and pulled the raven's talon open. The mole took the severed limb and brought it back to where Remington sat.

'I'm saying everything, all of it, it's him.'

'You're talking about the chimaera murders?' Doc asked. He handed the orphaned piece of Lennox to Remington.

'Not just those,' the Rev shook his head. 'I was trying to keep him under control.'

'Bang up job,' Remington said.

The Rev shot the badger a look. 'I was doing fine until you screwed everything.'

Remington sprung to his four paws and snarled.

'Wait… wait… come on,' Doc urged as he pushed Remington to back down. 'Seriously, you want to speed this up? How did you get out of your cage?'

'Lennox let him out,' Remington said, his eyes still fixed on the Rev's.

'That can't be right.' Doc wheeled around and blinked his tiny eyes at the badger.

'It is.' The Rev sighed heavily. 'But I didn't know about this, I swear. We were working out a plan to stop him, for me to take back control, and then she went dark.'

'Why would she let you out?' Doc slumped against the wall. 'Why would she want you in control?'

'There's more going on beneath your paws than any of you know, and there always has been.' The Rev squatted, sinking toward the floor, his wings relaxing around him like a black shawl.

'You know each other? You and Lennox.' Doc scratched at his head.

'We were chosen.' The Rev gazed into the green emanating from a luminous mushroom by Remington's side. 'Back when the enclosure acts were introduced, when all this started. We were selected to be two of the faces of the new structure.'

'By who?' Cat retracted her claws.

'Them,' the Rev said. 'The Three. It was all just a big experiment to try to add some control into our chaotic world. A way to stem the violence and the lack of civility. Apparently, civilisation has been tried before, over and over, but it never worked because there are always elements who resist the laws, the structure, the endless rules.'

'So, this whole prince of darkness thing is just an act?' Vixx asked.

'Well,' a glint danced across the Rev's eyes. 'They chose me for a reason, but, in a sense. They modelled the idea on the human world, decided we needed to make things clearer, more obvious, give people lines in the sand.'

'Lines in the sand?' Doc looked from the Rev to Remington. 'You knew about this?'

Remington shook his head. 'Just that Lennox let this monster out.'

'Whenever they've tried to add a sense of control and structure to our world, things always get out of claw, turn nasty,' the Rev continued. 'It's like it's not in our nature to be contained. Some animals always yearn to be wild. Having a single police force to keep everyone in line doesn't work.'

'And that's where you come in?' Vixx muttered.

The Rev shrugged. 'Turns out you need control from both sides. They needed someone to be whiter than white, to head up the Met, and then someone for her to go up against: A symbol of fear, someone who can let the more criminal-minded have their fun, but ultimately keep everything within certain limits.'

'The whole system's a lie?' Doc's voice was high and jittery.

'No, not a lie, just a bit more controlled than you might think. We need balance. Lennox and I play our parts to keep order as best we can. But, since I was caged up thanks to Platypus here, there's been no one to maintain that order.'

'Was it you?' Remington said, his voice almost a whisper.

'Was what me?' The Rev looked back at the badger.

'My wife, was it you? Or one of your people you do such a good job of keeping in order?'

'That wasn't us, Remington,' The Rev said. 'I helped Lennox look into it at the time. I promise you, that was just an accident. A tragedy, and I'm sorry it happened, but it wasn't us.'

Remington exhaled slowly, his shaking breath escaping into the sett.

Doc squeezed Remington's shoulder. 'What does Cull want?'

'Chaos,' the Rev said. 'He wants everything to return to how it was.'

'Take Back Eden?' Cat asked.

The Rev nodded. 'He didn't set them up or anything. There's always some group that springs up. The urge for us to return to the wild, to get rid of the laws and structures, all the dividing lines and control, it's natural.'

'He's using them,' Doc nodded.

'Yes, they're a ready-made army of vulnerable souls looking for a cause.'

'And the murders?'

'They were a message, the first stone dropped into the pond to break our lovely still little illusion of tranquillity. They got folks scared, made them start questioning how safe they really were. Not to mention it gave Cull the chance to act on his *urges*.'

'The mouse?' Remington whispered.

'Aye, the poor helpless thing,' the Rev clicked his beak. 'We came to blows over that. It was then I realised he needed to be contained, but-'

'What about the badger?' Remington asked. 'That was aimed at me.'

The Rev nodded. 'He couldn't help himself. As soon as you got involved it became like a game to him.'

'So, what now?' Doc asked, his nose wheeling almost as intensely as his mind.

'Now, we need to work out how to stop him.'

# Chapter Forty

How many times had Remington thought of the strange black eyes of the Rev? How often had he thought about dragging a claw across the matte surface, somewhere between dried volcanic rock and pitch? How many times had he thought about puncturing the surface to watch the dark evil beneath plume and spill out into the world? Now, with the Rev barely a few paces away, those same eyes were within reach, but Remington's urge to destroy them had drained away like water through soil. If Remington felt anything, it was pity, almost empathy, but too many years of anger were built up to allow that just yet.

'You cared for each other?' Remington said at last. He heard a collective exhalation from the sett's inhabitants as his words finally broke the tension.

The Rev slid his gaze to the badger.

'You and Lennox, you cared for each other?' Remington reiterated.

'Probably not in the way you mean,' the Rev said in a slow deep brogue that resonated through the chamber. 'But there was respect, and dare I say that respect became something akin to friendship.'

'Friends…' Remington whispered to himself.

'The roles we had to play were deeply lonely ones, Platypus. I suppose we were the only ones who really understood.'

'She could have told me.'

'She almost did.' The raven circled his head, stretching his powerful neck. 'More than once, but what would you have done?'

'Nothing…just tried to help-'

'The honourable badger and his crusades?' the Rev interrupted. 'You find out someone's trying to control the populace, that the big bad gangster is part of the ruse, and you'd just keep that to yourself, would you?'

'He's got you there, Remmy,' said Doc.

An awkward quiet fell upon the chamber again. Remington sensed the bat's confusion through some gentle images which he tried to reciprocate.

'Shall we tell them what we found?' Cat asked eventually.

Remington looked blankly at her. *Miss Carrol*, she mouthed.

'What about Miss Carrol?' Vixx chimed in with a pointed chirp.

Remington bit his lip and eyed the Rev.

'You don't have to trust me,' the large corvus said. 'But, if we're going to stop Cull, I need to know everything you know.'

'Fine,' Remington sighed. 'But this works both ways. You first.'

'Very well,' the Rev rumbled. 'What would you like to know?'

'What exactly are we trying to stop Cull from doing?'

'I can't be sure-'

'Great start,' Cat hissed, but Vixx shook her talon sharply at her.

'But I suspect,' he continued. 'He'll target the most obvious symbol of order he can.'

'The Met?' Doc asked. 'You think he means to finish the job.'

'Makes sense,' said Vixx. 'Without the Met, folk won't know what or if any rules still apply. It will be lawless.'

'Anarchy,' said Doc.

'Chaos,' added Remington as he locked eyes with the Rev.

The raven nodded. 'Precisely.'

'Chaos from below?' Cat said as she picked at her teeth with a claw.

The creatures turned to look at her.

'Tell them,' she said. 'Tell them what we found.'

Remington explained what he and Cat had discovered in Miss Carrol's warren: the strange messages, the disturbing chimaera images, the deeply etched picture of the badger and the dark bird, and finally the lifeless body of Brigg. Cat dropped her face into her forelegs as Remington described the scene.

'You think Daisy's part of this?' Vixx asked.

'We can't-' Remington began.

'Yes,' Cat blurted, keeping her face buried.

'All we know is that it looks like Cull has at least one ally in the Burrow.' Remington scratched at the wound over his eye.

'Chaos from below,' the Rev murmured. 'And we've no idea of this Carrol's whereabouts now?'

'Last sighting was days ago,' Remington conceded.

'It does track,' the raven said. 'If Cull is preparing something, he'd call everyone he trusts back.'

'You're sure?' Doc asked.

'It's what I'd do.' The Rev shrugged, and the feathers of his broad wings shook before settling down into a sleek black cloak.

'So, what now?' Vixx stepped forward into the centre of the chamber.

'Chaos from below,' the Rev muttered to himself again.

'Still think the Met's the likeliest target?' Doc asked.

'Maximum impact, and he already knows they can pull it off,' the raven nodded.

'Whatever he's planning, we can't do anything about it from up here anyway,' Remington said. 'We need to get back to the city.'

'Agreed,' said Vixx. 'Why don't I accompany the Rev by air while the rest of you sneak onto a transport-'

'The skies are too dangerous, young one,' the Rev said. 'Cull has the full Murder onside, and his influence has been growing with each new moon.'

'Then, what?' Vixx clawed at the earth with a talon.

'We go together.' Remington stretched his limbs. 'Tonight.'

'I'm coming with…' Cat raised her head from her forelegs.

Remington hesitated. He considered dissuading the feline from joining them, but he could see in her formidable eyes that there would be little point. 'Consider yourself deputised,' he said.

Vixx looped above in meticulous cycles as the odd group made their careful journey across the Burrow. Doc led the way with the Rev just behind. Remington insisted he take the rear of the procession, mostly so that he could keep the hulking figure of the Rev in his eyeline. Cat and the old bat completed their number. Remington had tried to communicate to the bat that he should stay in the sett and recuperate until he was fully recovered, but the bat drew images of bat colonies and caves in the badger's mind. The leather winged rodent may not have been in anything close to fighting shape, but another ally was another ally, and none of them knew what awaited them in the city.

Now and then Vixx signalled with a high trill and the group would dive into the undergrowth. Each time, Remington stuck fast to the Rev. On the third occasion, when the Rev found himself beak to snout with Remington hunched together in a heartknot of bracken, the raven spoke.

'Perhaps you'd like to buy me dinner first, Detective.'

Remington bristled. 'You might not be as evil as you've been painted but you're no saint,' he whispered. 'What about all the Heartbreak, and Roadkill. Cull might have taken over, but Roadkill was working for you to start with, wasn't he?'

'I'll never be a saint, Platypus, and of course part of my remit was narcotics production.'

Remington snorted.

'You're not that naïve,' the raven continued. 'Creatures will always find ways to ruin themselves. At least when I was running things, it was contained and controlled. There was never enough to get out of hand, not like it is now.'

Vixx trilled once again, and the Rev pulled himself out of the bracken. He turned and held out a talon. Remington ignored the proffered limb and pulled himself clear. This time, however, he resumed his march at the raven's side.

'You must have noticed, Detective,' the Rev said quietly.

'What?'

'How much worse things had become in the city.'

'Yes, as it happens, we all noticed, but that was happening long before we stuck you in a cage.'

'You're right,' the Rev whispered and lowered his head. 'Cull's influence was already spreading.'

'And who put him in that position in the first place?'

Doc turned and glared at Remington. The badger raised a paw in apology, and they continued in silence. Remington dropped to the back of the group again. It looked to Remington as though the Rev's shoulders had slumped a little. His usual broad formidable frame, while still intimidating, seemed a little softer around its black edges.

Vixx whistled a thin high undulation of notes. This was the signal that they were almost at the boarding point. The group slunk into a thicket by the side of the steep cutting. Remington watched as the Rev sidled toward Cat who lay licking her paws. Now and then the moon would reflect from her eyes, turning them blank and ghostly.

'I am sorry about your friend,' the Rev whispered to her, and stroked the side of her face with a talon. Cat said nothing but blinked slowly up at the bird. The Rev continued down the line and finally settled next to Remington.

'You're right,' the Rev said. 'About Cull. Of course, you're right.' He sighed, and a long deep whistle escaped from his beak into the night. 'I thought I knew what I was doing. There's always some young spark who comes along with just the wrong mix of enthusiasm, talent, and a gift for the darker side of things.'

'Takes one to know one, I suppose.'

The Rev cawed out a laugh. It was the first time Remington

had heard the raven laugh, and it sent a strange chill skittering through his blood. 'Quite, quite. I suppose I was lucky. They found me and gave me a purpose, something to direct all that energy toward. In a way, that's what I tried to do with Cull, but he was just so ruthless.'

'And when you realised that, why didn't you do something about it?'

'I suppose I thought I could control him, keep him just about on the edge of things. I didn't realise he'd been turning people against me, getting them all ready for his big coup. In the end, he didn't need it of course. Thanks to you.'

'I'm so sick-'

'I'm not blaming you, badger. Just bad timing is all. I tried to show him how the balance could work, the art of it, the give and take. Tried to show him mercy has a place in our world. I had him earmarked as my successor, but…' The bird trailed off as the vibrations of a distant train began to thrum through the bank on which they sat.

'He didn't quite have the savvy?'

'Far from it, Platypus. If anything, Cull was too intelligent.'

Remington cocked his head. 'Takes intelligence to be a psychopath, does it?'

'You'd be surprised. But think about it. Cull sees what we have going as the Murder, the big evil empire, and he's sees what we're up against.' The Rev gave Remington a once over. 'And he starts to question, why are we always holding back? Why are we so concerned about the Met and their rules? Why don't we just take what we want?'

'And you couldn't think of a single answer to those questions?'

'Not one that assuaged Cull's growing frustration and sense of entitlement.'

'Then you should have stopped him sooner. Ousted him from the Murder or turned him over to us.'

'Would that the world were that simp-'

'Enough!' Remington snapped. The other animals turned to look at them. 'You could have ended all this as soon as you realised what he was, and what was happening. Whatever he's done, whatever he's about to do, is on you.' Remington pointed a claw at the Rev's face. 'All of their blood, Lennox's blood, is on you.'

The cutting began to shake with the vibrations of the train as it rolled around the corner and juddered past them, slowing in a wave of noise and movement. Eventually, the long metal snake of the train stopped completely, the front of it far from view. Vixx signalled and dropped, spinning in the air, her wings flashing in the moonlight, a bright star falling from the night sky. The animals followed her position and hurried down the embankment toward the rear container carriages. Vixx hurtled toward the steel roof of one, closer and closer she came. Remington kept one eye on her as he slipped and slid toward the tracks. Finally, just as she looked as though she had underestimated her velocity, Vixx spread her wings and lifted back into the sky. She hung there for a moment and then gently floated down to the container.

'Here, your near corner,' she whistled at them and, sure enough, in the rear corner of the container, the door was twisted with rust revealing a hole just big enough for the animals to squeeze through. Cat and the Rev helped Doc and the bat up, before Cat pounced through dextrously. The Rev offered his talon to Remington.

'You first,' Remington said. The Rev did as he was bid, and Remington, struggling, hauled himself up and into the carriage. Finally, Vixx slipped in, and the creatures hunkered down in a corner of cold steel as the giant metal monster shuddered back to life and began to thunder loudly toward the city.

# Chapter Forty-One

The moon flashed a blinking grey over the animals through a gap in the ceiling of the weathered old container. For the beginning of the journey, each passenger remained silent, locked deep within their own thoughts and solitude. Each illuminating streak of moonlight revealed that all were keeping a close watch on the Rev. Even shorn of the mystique of his own myth, he cut a striking figure up close. His long black feathers glittered through the darkness, and the lift and fall of his broad breast looked like the swaying hull of the boats Remington had often seen moored along the great river that cleaved its way through the city.

The bat shifted awkwardly next to Remington, and the badger saw images of machinery and falling trees. He patted the creature gently, and tried to send images of landing, of arrival, to signify that the journey would be completed soon. The bat replied with visions of harsh weather turning calm. The strange old thing closed its eyes and leant back against the container wall, its head bouncing along with the vibrations. Remington let out a sigh and tried to find a comfortable position. The truth was, these human contraptions made him uneasy, and not just because of the unforgiving materials with which they were made, all hard metal, and jagged angles. Their nature, their speed, and the iron veins that they ran along, slicing through the countryside; there was a violence to them that he felt complicit in, merely by riding along in them.

'Ask you a question?' Cat said over the grumble of the train.

Her golden eyes were glowing toward the Rev.

'Ask away,' he replied. His own eyes, despite their matte finish, were clearly defined in the gloom, darker than shadow.

'What's with the *the*?'

'I'm not sure I follow.'

'The name,' Cat said. 'What's with the Rev? Why not just Rev?'

'Oh, ha,' the Rev cawed the spike of a laugh. Remington noticed Vixx and Doc flinch. 'One of the three's idea. It sounded like a title rather than a name, and it just sort of stuck, I suppose.'

'But what does the Rev mean?' Cat pushed further. 'Reverend, Revenant?'

'I imagine that's part of the allure of the name. Everyone can pick their own meaning, and nobody can be certain which one it is, which one I am.' The raven looked up to the crack in the container and let a soft whistle slip from his beak. 'And tell me, my dear thing, how many names have you collected? One for each life perhaps?'

The corner of Cat's mouth twitched, and she almost smiled, but caught it just in time.

'We have some time before this thing gets us into the city,' Remington said. 'I suggest everyone try to get some rest while you can. I'll wake you when we're nearly there.'

'You should sleep too, Sir,' said Vixx. 'I don't mind taking a shift on watch.'

'I've rested more than long enough too,' the Rev added. The rumble of his deep voice seeming to merge with the juddering of the train.

'I'll be fine, Sergeant.' Remington pushed himself upright against the container wall and stared at the Rev. 'You hunker down.'

The rest of the animals found comfort as best they could while, in the flashing moonlight, a badger and a raven locked eyes.

The rhythmic clamour of the train shifted in tone, the tempo rising as the Burrow fell in its wake like a haze of memories.

Eventually the tone seemed to plateau into a single lilting song that buoyed the creatures and allowed them to slip into uneasy slumbers. Remington felt his own eyelids become heavy, but he fought the urge to close them. He kept his gaze on the Rev, and the Rev continued to gaze back. The raven seemed unaffected by the lilting sway of the train. The moonlight persisted its flicker through the container's ragged roof and now and then ethereal patterns were cast along the walls, a strange silver and shadow dance, a transient mural. Beyond the steel walls, the vast silhouette of the city emerged over the rolling countryside. Remington twitched his nostrils and drew in the air. It had grown denser and was laden with the heavy scents of humanity and industry, a dizzy blend of exhaust, metal, soap, and sweat. He also started to hear the faint flicker of electrical resonance. He curled his paws into fists and wondered if they might ever again feel the tickle of pawsentia, the infinite history and information of the earth.

'Best wake them up then, Platypus,' the Rev said.

The train's rhythms shifted again as it crossed the city boundary and was swallowed up by the jagged buildings piercing the night sky, the false light as it blotted the stars, and the indistinct chatter of city traffic and life. Remington thought he had missed the symphony of the metropolis, but as he heard the volume rise beyond the steel at his back, it all seemed too insistent, too loud, too unnatural. It was jarring and busy, like an orchestra with too many players, each just a single note off each others' score. The animals stirred and stretched.

'So, our target's the Met?' Doc said, whirling his nose in the air.

'We're still agreed it's the most likely target?' Remington asked, looking at the Rev.

'As I said,' the raven replied, stretching out the abyss of his wings. 'It is what I would do.'

'What else would you do?' Remington tilted his head. 'What

do you think we can expect when we get free of the transport?'

'Resistance,' the Rev said as he balled up a talon and slammed it to the container floor. 'Cull will be ready for us, and we will be watched from every rooftop, and every curbside.' The Rev swivelled his head in a long slow arc around the container, meeting each creature's eyes as he did so. 'Be prepared for us to fight our way there.'

'Spare us the prince of darkness crap, will you.' Remington rolled his eyes and peered through the gap of the container as it rumbled slowly to a standstill. 'Right, the raven and I will go first. Once we're clear of the track, follow, but keep your distance. If we are walking into an ambush, leave us to it, and get to the Met-'

'But, Sir,' Vixx objected.

'No arguments. Our priority is stopping Cull. If they attack us, that might give you the distraction you need to get there.'

Vixx nodded.

Doc stepped forward and gave Remington a squeeze on the shoulder. 'Be safe, Remmy.'

Remington placed his forehead to the mole's for a moment and then turned to the Rev. 'Right then, after you,' he said.

The raven looked over the small group of animals and nodded slowly. In a single stride, he was at the container's opening. Before Remington could say anything else, the Rev had ducked down and leapt silently from the metal edge. He spread his great dark wings and glided to the wall beyond the tracks. He turned and looked at Remington. The badger snorted and clambered down from the container. He landed awkwardly and trotted across the tracks toward the waiting bird.

'Do you hear that?' the Rev asked as Remington came to his side.

'What?' Remington twitched his ears.

'What do you hear, Platypus?'

'I hear traffic, and electric…'

'And..?'

'I hear the frequencies…'

'Do you hear animals?'

Remington flicked his ears and tilted his head. Beyond the industrial orchestration of the city, he heard nothing. 'I don't,' he said.

'No, nor I,' the Rev said and drummed his talon on the loose stones by the side of the train track.

'So?'

'Nobody is waiting for us.'

'I suppose that's something.'

'Yes,' the Rev said, his voice vague and distant. 'It is something.'

'You're sure nobody's waiting to ambush us?' Remington nudged the raven.

'Not here at least. I can't pick up a whiff of danger anywhere.' The Rev raised his long beak in the air and juddered his head back and forth. 'But I do scent corvus.'

'In my experience, crow and danger are the same odour.'

'We are safe to proceed, Platypus.'

Remington looked doubtfully at the bird, but eventually sighed and gestured for the rest of the group to follow. They obliged, carefully extricating themselves from the train and hurrying toward the waiting pair.

'Something's not right, Remmy,' said Doc. 'It's like a ghost town.'

Remington nodded. 'That's what we were saying.'

'What do we do now?' Cat asked, her golden eyes glinting through the shadows.

'This whole thing reeks but the plan's the same. We'll still head on in front,' Remington said, gesturing to the Rev. 'We'll keep to the shadows, and the hedgerows. When we move, you wait. Give us as much space as you can without losing sight of us. Once we're at the station, if we still haven't met with any of our friend here's buddies, we'll regroup.'

The creatures nodded.

The Rev took a few strides forward and stopped. He raised his beak again and flicked his head as though shaking off drops of rain.

'What is it?' Remington asked.

'It's the corvus,' the raven whispered. 'It's coming from ground level, and close, but the scent is too thin, and despair clings to it.'

'Perhaps we should find a different exit?' Doc suggested.

'Too many humans elsewhere,' the Rev said almost to himself. 'We'll keep to the usual route.'

'The one everyone, including Cull, knows about?' Cat hissed.

'There is no danger,' the Rev insisted. 'Not here anyway.'

The rest of the animals looked to Remington.

'Well, we can't stay here too long,' he sighed. 'We're conspicuous enough as it is.'

'You're the boss, Remmy.' Doc jerked his head toward the dark wall that lined the tracks, and the Rev led the group onward.

The moonlight glinted off the metal rails providing a silver strip of light for their passage. The Rev stopped now and then, raising his black beak before pressing on. As they met the edge of the track wall, Remington raised his paw signalling for them to wait. He crept ahead of the Rev and looked out over the wall to a small copse awkwardly huddled over an expanse of broken earth and weeds.

'That's our exit,' he said. 'Sense any danger yet?'

'Just the blending of crow and despair,' the Rev said.

'You first.'

The Rev raised himself up and puffed out his chest. Remington heard Cat draw a deep breath over her teeth. The raven stepped out toward the copse. The badger followed a few paces behind. The rest of the group waited and watched. Underneath the sulphur tang of industrial fumes, Remington caught the scent that the Rev had noted. He was right, it was undeniably crow, but it seemed to be swaddled in something, as if soaked in vinegar. Under the twisted trunk of the farthest tree a shape moved, dark and awkward. The Rev cawed and leapt into the air, spreading his wings and gliding toward it. Remington broke into a run.

'No... no... no...' the Rev was muttering as he nudged at the shape.

As Remington drew closer, he tried to peer around the large bird to see what it was that had agitated him so.

'Why would he...How could he?' The Rev was skittering anxiously. Remington had never seen the creature like this, devoid of his usual insouciance.

A low mournful caw came from the bundle at the Rev's talons. Remington moved alongside the raven.

'Quills!' he said.

Two broken crows lay tangled in the weeds. One was dead. The other would soon follow, its eyes quivering, beak gulping uselessly at the air. Blood, black in the moonlight, pooled beneath both of them.

'Cull?' the Rev asked, his voice flat and low.

The pathetic creature blinked back, long and slow.

The Rev placed his head to the suffering bird's and whispered, 'I am sorry I failed you.'

The creature closed its eyes and continued to moan its mournful caw.

The Rev gripped the dying crow's skull, his talons wrapping tight. A shriek tore from his beak - Remington flinched - then the snap of bone, swift and merciful.

Remington said nothing. He looked at the raven and raised a paw to its glistening black shoulder. He paused before making contact though and withdrew the limb, letting it fall to his side.

'They're a message from Cull,' the Rev said. 'He clipped their wings and left them here for dead.'

'He knew you'd come this way.'

The Rev nodded. 'Anyone loyal to me has probably met a

similar fate.'

'We're walking into an ambush.'

'Most likely, but I'm still going to kill him.'

# Chapter Forty-Two

The dead crows were covered over with leaves and loose soil.

Cat's golden eyes flashed intensely. 'We'll make sure they get a proper funeral,' she said, laying a paw upon the raven's cloaking wing.

'As will your friend,' the Rev replied and covered her paw with a talon.

Vixx clawed at the ground and combed her feathers with her beak. 'We need to get to the Met,' she muttered.

'The sergeant's right,' Doc urged. 'We've got to go.'

The Rev pulled himself up to his tallest frame and spat a short, sharp note into the air. 'Keep your senses keen. We'll be watched.'

The journey to the station was an uneasy one. Not because of distance, obstacle, or interference, in fact, the city seemed strangely devoid of animal activity. Remington had expected to find their passage surveilled by a thousand glittering crow eyes, extensions of Cull's panoptic reach. The rooftops were clear though, and the dark night sky, a slab of starless navy blue over the electric radiance of the city, was still and vacant. Each of the animals peered hard into the shadowy alleyways and passages, the slipways and runs of the labyrinthine concrete warren, expecting to find something, some evidence that they were being watched. Other than the distant grumble of deep night traffic, and the occasional thrum of human revelry, the city was dead.

Remington's mind was intruded upon now and then by an image

from the bat who kept pace with them, pinging out inflections periodically. The images were hazy and soft, like a filter had been placed over them, but the feelings that accompanied them, Remington understood well. The bat was anxious, confused by the quiet of the city and the absence of animal life. The bat wasn't the only one whose anxiety spilled over into the urban night. Doc had started emitting a quiet squeaking sound as he nervously fingered the air with his nose. Cat's ears were pinned back flat to her head, and Vixx had begun absentmindedly clicking her beak. Remington noticed his own breath was fast and shallow; short misty clouds popped from his nostrils in the chill air. He tried to attune to one of Lennox's electrical frequencies, but there was nothing, just the cold tone of dead air.

At length the odd group of creatures had meandered for long enough through the vacant corridors of stone, brick, steel, and glass that they arrived at the corner of the broad hedgerow that marked the Met station entrance. They kept low and clung to the shadow of the shallow verge opposite. The entrance was as lifeless and empty as the rest of the city had seemed. Remington sniffed the air, tried to reach out to sense anything that might be abroad, but he found nothing beyond the vague final after drift of burning, still clinging to the air from the attack that had so nearly ended Doc's life.

'Anyone getting anything?' he asked.

The rest of the animals shook their heads.

'It's all ghost,' the Rev said. 'There's a great cloud of animal here, but it's historic. It's like the air's been cleaned somehow.'

'It's your call, Remmy,' Doc said.

'I'll go first,' the Rev moved forward.

'No.' Remington gripped the bird's shoulder. 'Everyone, stay behind me, and keep your senses primed.'

Remington stepped out from the comparative shelter of the verge. The Met entryway loomed. Beyond the stark maw of its opening lay the peculiarly uniform warren that had been his second home, his true home, for so many years. The bustle and business of its former glory now reduced to a cold and rhythmless thing. The badger shook out his limbs, bared his teeth, snorted heavily, and strode toward the lip of the entrance. At any moment he expected the sky to explode with the deathly cawing of crows, the dark cavern of the entrance to begin slithering with the evil intent of the grass snake he'd met in the ghylls, for Cull himself to step from the shadows and open Remington's belly with one of his silver-tipped talons. The entranceway, like the sky, like the hedgerow, like the stale air, remained still. The other animals watched with held breath as the badger disappeared into the darkness.

'Well,' said Doc. 'Together then?'

'Aye,' said the Rev. 'Together.'

The other animals followed the badger into the entrance. They too met no resistance.

The carefully hewn tunnels that slunk beyond the hedgerow were much as Remington remembered. Only the trailing burrow to the right was sealed by collapsed earth.

'Quills!' said Rem. 'How much Heartbreak did they use to bring this down?'

'Barely a fieldmouse's worth,' Doc answered. His face was mournful as he looked over the ruin of what was once the passageway to his lab.

'Imagine what they could do with the piles you lot brought back from the Burrow,' Cat said, sucking air over her teeth.

'Can anyone smell it?' Remington asked. 'If they're planning on bringing the whole place down, it would have to be spread out all along the tunnels, wouldn't it?'

'If there's enough, they could bury it deep and light it from a distance,' the Rev said. He was having to stoop to fit his frame into the corridor. 'The whole place could be a crater in a flash.'

'Then we need to hurry.' Remington scratched at his face.

'Doc, Cat, seriously, those noses of yours picking up anything?'

Cat raised her black nose in the air and breathed in. 'There's too many different things, but they're all distant.'

'Me too,' said Doc. 'I am getting Heartbreak, but not much.'

The group pushed forward into the dark run, each step tentative and burdened with apprehension. Remington's gut churned more fervently with each pace. The only sounds were their own shallow breaths and the echo of their footsteps through the empty shadows.

Cat stopped suddenly. 'Wait, mole, you getting that?' She was twitching her ears.

Doc wheeled his nose in an arc and tilted his head. 'Yes, yes, it's faint. Animals.'

'Crows?' Remington asked.

'No, rabbit, badger.' Doc scuttled ahead of Remington. 'Can you hear that?'

The Rev turned his head slowly. 'It's muffled, but yes, I hear it. Someone's in pain.'

Remington listened hard but couldn't quite catch anything over the roaring of his blood in his ears. 'Where?'

Doc shifted from one side of the tunnel to the other. 'Above us, I think.'

'The holding cages?' Remington asked.

'Must be…' Before Doc could finish, Remington had broken into a run, dashing toward the opening that sloped up toward the higher floor.

The rest followed.

Remington charged through the station, passing the etchings of the three and the slogans outlining the various purposes of the Met. He knew the warren better than the pathways of his own sett, and the other creatures struggled to keep pace. Doc would have called for him to slow, to be careful and mindful of what might await them in the dark corners of the maze, but it was all he could do to scuttle along in the intense badger's wake. As they made the turning to the corridor which contained the entrance to the holding cages, he managed to cough out a 'wait,' and Remington skidded to a stop. The doorway was blocked by a large rough stone.

'I can hear them,' Remington whispered.

'But can you smell that?' Doc raised his nose.

The badger sniffed. 'Heartbreak.'

'It's a small amount, but I smell it too,' Doc said.

'Yeah,' added Cat. 'I smell a trap.'

They hesitated and listened. Sure enough there was a muffled sound, like pained crying coming from beyond the rock.

'Trap or not, we need to get in there,' Remington said. He gripped at the stone and tried to pull it away from the doorway. It barely shifted.

The Rev stepped forward and pushed his broad shoulder to the surface of the object. 'Together,' he said.

Remington nodded. Cat, Doc, the old bat, and Vixx found purchase on the stone too. Doc counted to three and they heaved together. With an immense scraping sound, the rock slowly gave way. As soon as there was gap enough, Remington slipped through into the room.

In the chamber, cages hung awkwardly from the ceiling. All were vacant except for the three central ones. Remington pulled at the bars of each of them in turn.

'Help me,' he shouted.

In the leftmost cage, Nick lay bound, gagged, unconscious, his body curled into a question mark. In the right cage was Lennox, her mouth covered, her eyes closed, a poorly bound bandage dripped with blood over her missing foot. In the central cage was Daisy. She was trying to shout through her own moss gag.

'We can't break the bars, Rem,' Doc said as he scuttled from one cage to another.

Remington, in panic, flung himself from one cage to another, not knowing who to attempt feebly to assist first.

'Get the gag off her,' the Rev said gesturing to Daisy, the only conscious prisoner.

Daisy shuffled backwards in the cage so Remington could reach the knot at the back of her head. As he fumbled awkwardly, his claws refusing to respond to his panicking commands, there was a scuff and a hiss from beyond the partially open entrance.

'Get down,' Doc called, and a loud crack shook the space. Dirt fell all around them, and they turned to see the doorway seal with earth and stone.

'Everyone okay?' Remington coughed as the chamber settled.

The choking animals brushed themselves off and nodded. Cat scrabbled at the wall where the entrance had been. 'We're trapped.'

'Someone sealed us in,' Doc added.

Nick started to stir, groaning through his bindings. Remington set back to untying Daisy's gag. Eventually it fell away and she moaned loudly, choking down heavy draughts of the dusty air.

'Daisy, are you okay?' Remington asked, reaching through the bars of the cage and stroking her face.

She tried to speak but choked again.

'It's okay,' Remington said. 'I've got you.'

She shook her head, wheezing as she did so. Eventually she was able to sputter out something intelligible:

'Vixx,' she said. 'It was Vixx.'

Remington stumbled back from the cage. 'Vixx?' he whispered. 'Where is she?'

The other animals looked around the chamber. The bird was nowhere to be seen.

# Chapter Forty-Three

'She's gone,' said Doc. 'She trapped us.'

Cat continued to scrape in vain at the densely packed wall where the doorway had been. 'How?'

'Must've blown the Heartbreak we smelled out there,' Rem said as he continued to stroke Daisy's face through the bars. 'This whole thing was a set up.'

Nick moaned again and attempted to push himself upright. His legs failed him, and he slumped back down.

'Hey, it's okay, mate,' Remington said as he hurried to the other badger's cage. 'Take it easy.'

The larger badger nodded and tried to gather his breath. Remington was already reaching through the bars of Lennox's cage, testing for a pulse, for the shallow breaths of the unconscious chocolate furred rabbit. The bandage around her missing foot was soaked with dark blood and the precious fluid dripped from the cage. 'We need to stop this bleeding. Lennox,' he called into her ear. 'Stay with us, Len.'

'Vixx attacked me in my warren,' Daisy said. 'I thought she'd come to give me a message from you, Rem. She's been working with Cull the whole time.'

'Vixx killed Brigg,' Cat whispered to herself, and then continued to scratch more fervently than before.

'Was this him or her?' Rem asked, working with Doc to apply pressure to the wound.

'Both of them.' Daisy rubbed at her throat. Talon scratches showed through her fur in deep gashes. 'They already had her caged up, but they made me listen while they took her foot. Vixx held her down while Cull used those vile things he puts on the ends of his-'

She was cut off by the sudden sound of Remington's balled up paw slamming into the side of the Rev's face. The bird, caught off guard, fell backwards clattering into one of the vacant cages. Remington stood over him as he stared up in shock.

'You must have known,' the badger said. 'All this time, Vixx has been connected to the Murder. You must have known.'

'I knew nothing of this,' the raven hissed back. 'If she's been working for Cull then he's been wise enough to keep it far from my eyes.'

'Horse shit,' Remington barked. 'Enough of this nice guy crap. You've been leading us here all this time.'

The Rev wiped spittle and blood from his beak and pushed himself upright. 'I could have sliced your neck open a hundred times on our way here if I'd wished to. Why would I want to be trapped in here with you, Platypus?'

Remington glared at the Rev, torn between delivering another blow, and accepting that the bird had a point.

'Remmy, a hand, please.' Doc was attempting to redress Lennox's drenched bandages.

Remington let out a snort and left the raven where he was. 'What can we do, Doc?'

'We need to get her out of here, she's already lost too much blood.'

'Rem, there's no time,' Nick said through sharp short breaths. 'Cull, he's got the Heartbreak underground.'

'We know,' said Cat still digging at the wall, barely making a divot in the surface. 'That's why we have to get out of here before this place disappears.'

Nick shook his head. 'No, no, it's not here.' He coughed and gripped his ribs. 'He's got it in the ghost station.'

'The what?' the Rev asked, finally back on his talons.

'In the underground,' Nick said. 'We used it as a safe place for the down and outs, and people hiding out from your lot. Cull's taken the Heartbreak and plans to blow it all up.'

'Quills,' said Doc. 'It's directly under the river. Hundreds of animals will be killed.'

'Not just animals,' added the Rev.

'He's got half the Met down there, not to mention anyone still loyal to our old pal big bird.' Nick pulled at the cage door. 'You've got to get us out of here.'

'I don't get it,' Cat said. 'Where are all of *his* people? The streets were empty.'

'They're down there too,' said Daisy. 'He was raving about some grand assembly.'

'Why?' Doc asked.

'Maximum death and chaos,' the Rev whispered.

'He's going full end of days,' Remington said.

The raven nodded. 'Take Back Eden indeed.'

'All well and good guys, but we need to get out of here, now.' Cat let her forelegs fall to her sides. Her claws were ragged.

'First, we need to get these cages open,' Remington said.

'There's no time for that,' Nick objected. 'You can come back for us later. You need to stop Cull.'

Remington pulled at the superintendent's cage door. 'Lennox might not have that kind of time, Nick. There must be something-'

There was a loud click, and they turned to see the Rev withdrawing his talon from the lock on Miss Carrol's cage door. 'Voila,' he said as he pulled the door open. Remington sidestepped to allow the bird access to Lennox's cage.

He watched in reluctant admiration as the Rev easily unhooked the lock mechanism. 'You could have escaped anytime you wanted when we had you caged up,' he said.

'Aye, but who wouldn't enjoy the famous Met hospitality, eh?'

Remington helped Daisy from her cage as the Rev unlocked

Nick's. Daisy hopped up into Lennox's and began to apply pressure to her wound.

The Rev suddenly opened his wings and leapt to the ceiling of the chamber. He pecked at the surface above him and then swept elegantly to the wall and tried the same there, before floating back to the ground.

'It's no good,' he said. 'None of us can dig through this. It's too tightly beaten with stones. It would take even you weeks to get through it, Platypus.'

'There must be something,' Remington said, running his paws along the walls. 'Doc, any ideas?'

Doc was scratching at the corners of the chamber and raising his nose in the air. 'Sorry, Remmy. I can't see anything.'

'Shh,' hissed Cat. 'Can you hear that?'

The Rev inclined his head. 'Friend of yours?' he asked.

Remington listened. At first, he heard nothing.

'There,' Cat said.

Remington tilted his ears. Faint, but insistent, a voice was coming from beyond the fallen entrance.

'Who is that?' Cat called out.

The voice that returned was too quiet to discern properly, but Remington recognised it all the same.

'Oscar,' he called back. 'Speak up lad, and can you get us out of here?'

'Sir?' the young ferret returned. 'What's going on? I just saw Vixx heading out of the station.'

'We'll fill you in, son, but is there anything you can do from that side? We need to get out of here now.'

'I need to get you out of there, now,' Oscar shouted. 'Cull's got the rest of the officers in the underground. He's taken the Heartbreak down there.'

Remington rolled his eyes and huffed. 'Ozzy, can you see anything that might be able to help us?'

Cat pushed her ear to the wall. 'I can hear him moving

around,' she said.

'There's some Heartbreak packed into the tunnel ceiling,' Oscar called. 'Maybe if I just use a little, if I can set it off. It might dislodge some of this.'

'Quills,' said Doc. 'He could bring the whole place down on us.'

'Ozzy,' Remington shouted. 'Try something else.'

'Just setting it up now, Sir,' the ferret replied.

'Oscar, do not use the Heartbreak,' Remington tried again.

'Yes, Sir,' Oscar hollered back. 'Just a little bit of Heartbreak. Now if I can just get some friction from a couple of these rocks.'

'Oscar, no,' Doc squeaked.

They heard a faint hiss. The Rev jumped in front of them and opened his wings. He shoved them all back with one push and crouched down. A crack shuddered through the air. Dirt crumbled from the ceiling. Dust once again plumed up into the chamber.

'Was I glad to see you,' Oscar said as he pulled at the small opening that had appeared in the wall. Remington shoved the Rev aside and started to claw at the gap too. Cat and Doc joined in. As the dust settled, Remington could finally see the gaunt face of the ferret. They gripped paws through the space.

'Look out, Sir,' Oscar shouted and pulled his lithe body through the gap into the chamber. He jumped toward the Rev and lashed out with a paw. The Rev raised his wing and stifled the blow. Oscar continued to attack, but the raven blinked down at him.

Remington pulled the ferret away. 'It's okay, thanks Ozzy,' he said. 'He's with us, for now.'

Oscar looked incredulous for a second, but then shook his head, and gripped Remington's arm. 'Sir, we have to get to the underground. It's Cull, it's always been Cull.'

Remington nodded at the excitable ferret. 'We know,' he said. 'And Vixx.'

'Cull's got the sergeant?' Oscar's eyes were wild.

'We'll fill you in on the way.' Remington turned to the cages.

Daisy was combing Lennox's ears while pressing hard on the bandaged space where her foot had been. Nick dragged himself from the cage and landed with a wince.

'You're in no shape-' Remington began but Nick cut him off.

'I'm still in better shape than you.' The larger badger gritted his teeth. 'That's my home he's trying to destroy.'

Remington nodded. He slipped to the cage that contained the two rabbits who meant so much to him. He kissed Daisy on the cheek. She gripped his neck and kissed him back. Lennox's blood smeared onto Remington's fur. He stroked Lennox's head.

'I've still got a bone to pick with you,' he said. 'So don't even think about dying.'

'Well, if we're all in accord,' the Rev said. 'Shall we?'

# Chapter Forty-Four

*The badger leads*
*from a facsimile of human structure*
*in a hollow in the fractured earth.*
*He leads one of cunning, claw, and fang,*
*one of the night, of haunt and leather wing,*
*one of intellect, led by the nose,*
*one like he with muscular pose,*
*one of anxiety grown to hob from a kit,*
*and one whose shadow still haunts his spirit.*
*He leads…*

The group moved swiftly through the Met tunnels and out into the moon's eye. Again, Remington expected resistance, the sudden emergence of Cull's minions (of which Vixx was one, though this still fought against Remington's powers of reconciliation) from the rooftops and sewer grates. No such resistance emerged though. The tarmac streets seemed picked bare, only the usual flotsam of deep night detritus moved, flapping and shifting in the wind. Even the distant human voices were sparse now, life receding into sleep. Still, the night chimneys breathed; the perpetual drift of steam and smoke lifted like an unturning tide.

Shadows seemed to flicker behind half toppled bins and mounds of rubbish, the hiss and whirr of electrical fields soundtracked the animals' passage, a song of great stone and glass. Remington listened hard, tried to feel for something through his paws, but the concrete was too dense. All he could discern from the tonal frequencies that buzzed around them was a vague shadowpulse, nothing mappable, nothing to hook onto. Despite the vacant streets, Remington kept them secluded as best as he could, clinging to hedgerows, or the shadow of curbside when there was no shelter to find. From the Met, toward the underground, they traced a granite chill.

'I can't believe Vixx had something to do with this,' Oscar whispered at Remington's back. 'Her work ethic put mine to shame.'

'Is that a high bar, Ozzy?' Remington said without turning around.

'That hurts, Sir. I'm sorry, I should have seen it.'

'Don't do that to yourself. I spent more time with her than any of you and I barely suspected a thing.' Remington stopped and turned around. 'She was on duty the night Roadkill…you know. Come to think of it, she led me into the coils of a snake too.' He shook his heavy head. 'I dread to think what else.' He put his paw on the ferret's skinny shoulder. 'Point is, this is on me if it's on anyone, but we can still stop her…stop them.'

Oscar nodded, and they continued.

'What happened down here anyway, Ozzy?' Remington asked over his shoulder as they paused at the edge of a verge, stopping for a late-night taxi to rumble past spilling dirty smoke in its wake. 'And how did you manage not to get caught?'

'It was that last transport back, boss,' the ferret twitched as he spoke. 'I had to stay out of sight because I wasn't supposed to be up there, remember.'

'I recall,' the badger said and then moved out from the verge gesturing for the rest to follow.

'Half the force was already in on it.'

'Half?' Doc yelped.

'Seemed like it, Sir. I managed to slip into a crate full of apples. It was a pretty good journey actually, although I gave myself a bit of a tummy upset-'

'Oscar,' Rem barked. 'Get to the point.'

'Right... yeah... so anyway, as we rolled in to the drop off, I heard some scuffling and yelps. I peeked out and it looked like most of the police were laying out the rest.'

'Laying them out?' Cat said.

'Yeah, choked em, bashed em. And then they bound 'em up and dragged them off. Obviously, I kept in my apples until I was sure it was safe, and then I slunk out. I've been hiding out since trying to keep an eye out and see what they were up to. Looks like Cull's gonna do something with all the Heartbreak we retrieved down in-'

'Thanks Oscar,' Remington interrupted. 'You did the right thing. I don't suppose you've got any idea what he's waiting for though, do you?'

'Sir?'

'Cull, if he's planning on lighting up the underground and bringing the river down on anyone inside, what's he waiting for.'

'I think he was waiting until they got all of the Heartbreak down there,' Oscar said. 'They've been going in shifts for the past few nights but not during the day. I suppose so as not to get caught. The last of it left the Met a little before you arrived.'

'So, he's ready then?' the Rev said. 'He could set it off any time.'

'I guess so,' said Oscar, 'but everyone's still down there.'

'Who's everyone?' Doc asked.

'Well, everyone. All the officers, the ones doing the bashing and the ones that got bashed, but the Murder, the Take Back Eden lot, they've all gone down there too and none of them have come back up. Not that I've seen.'

Remington stopped and looked at the Rev. 'Penny for your thoughts,' he said. 'What's his game? He wouldn't take out his entire following, would he? How crazy is he?'

'Maximum chaos, I suppose,' said the Rev. 'But no, seems unlikely. He's deranged but he's not stupid.' The Rev combed at his wing while he thought.

'Think,' Remington demanded. 'If this was your plan, what

would you do?'

A glint passed through the Rev's eye. 'I suppose if I were planning something huge, I'd like an audience. If I had everyone down there on that grand stage, I'd prepare a speech for the ages.'

'Yeah, I've heard your work,' Remington muttered.

'I'd want everyone to witness and acknowledge my power,' the Rev continued. He grew more animated as he spoke. 'There's no point doing something on this scale if there aren't witnesses to make the memory of it, the legend of it, grow.'

'So, you don't think he's planning on killing everyone?' Doc asked.

'It wouldn't track.'

'So, what would?' Remington was becoming impatient.

'He's going to set everything up, probably has my loyalists, and your officers chained up down there, and anyone he found who's not sold on the Take Back Eden doctrine too. He's going to announce himself as a new messiah, give the speech to end all speeches…' The Rev trailed off.

'And then?' Remington gripped the Rev's wing.

'And then, he'll lead his followers out from the darkness while some poor chosen acolyte sets off the Heartbreak.'

'Quills,' said Rem. 'All those animals lost for nothing.'

'Not just animals,' said Nick.

'This time of night, I doubt there'll be many humans around,' Remington said.

'The ghost station's no longer used by them, but the track still is now and then,' Nick insisted. 'What if he's waiting for one of their transports to come through?'

'Maximum chaos,' the Rev repeated.

'We need to get down there now,' Remington said, and hurried out into the uncovered street.

'Wait,' Cat called as they all set off after the badger. 'Shouldn't we think up a plan?'

'We don't know what's waiting for us,' Remington shouted back. 'So, what's the point in a plan?'

At the mouth of the underground, Remington asked Cat to look first. The great beams of her eyes cleaved the darkness far better than any of the other creatures' could.

'It looks clear,' she said. 'But wait here. Give me two seconds to have a proper look.'

'Be careful,' Remington urged as the feline slipped down the steps and disappeared into the shadows.

The underground was a mystery to Remington. Whenever he tried to think about it, how it was created and conceived, it made his head spin. He'd seen the ingenuity and instinct of incredible creatures create the most intricate warrens and burrows, labyrinths that sung of spectacular engineering prowess. This human equivalent was different though, a gabling of negative space and sprawl, a fragmented paradox underneath the cratered ground and hulking river. It was like an imagined reconstruction of a subterranean habitat that seemed to serve little practical purpose other than to hurry humans along, like they didn't have enough pace and speed in their lives. It had also become a haven for fossorial animals displaced by the ever-increasing spread of concrete and electromagnetics that the humans brought with them. Some fled to the green spaces they could find, but that was more difficult since the enclosure acts, with most of them being under the guiding paw and rules of the Met. For the animals that opted out, there were less and less opportunities for safety. The underground, this odd echoscript of shadow beneath the cityscape, was a ready-made ditch away from the quilted track, a place for anyone who wished to hide from the rules, and from the eczema of humanity.

Cat slipped from the shadows, her golden eyes appearing first, twin moons in the dark. 'It's clear,' she said. 'But I can hear them. I can hear all of them.'

# Chapter Forty-Five

Even if Remington hadn't known how to navigate his way to the ghost station, he wouldn't have had any difficulty finding his way there. The din of assembled animals, so many species all muttering and communicating in their different ways, was clear once they were down in the underground network; the sound carried through on the stagnant subterranean air. They moved quickly and quietly, each wondering what they would find and what they would do when they found it. The haphazard ground of stone and dirt that lined the tracks was awkward under paw and talon, but none breathed a complaint when they slipped as the loose grit gave way beneath them.

Remington listened hard, but the orchestra of mixed voices was impossible to interpret properly. He also felt as though he could hear the phantom hulks that used to hum and rumble along these isolated dour edges as they echoed back across time. Truth was, he never much liked visiting Nick down here. Something about the composition of shadows and fractal silhouettes in this immaculately hewn warren felt unnatural. It held an epoch's worth of ghosts. The air turned to dust on his tongue.

As they swept closer to the growing noise, Remington saw shapes on both sides of the tracks, humps of shadow. He stopped.

'Cat,' he whispered. 'What are those?'

The feline slipped beside him and aimed her golden eyes into the gloom. 'They're animals, I think,' she said.

Remington stepped forward steadily. 'Be ready, everyone.'

As he closed the distance between himself and the first shape, he realised Cat was right. A figure was hunched awkwardly against the wall along the track. Another, like a mirror, was stationed opposite, and through the shadow along the track he could see more, equally spaced as sentinels standing guard over the lone path toward the ghost station. There was no way to avoid them, or to sneak up unnoticed, so Remington broke into a run toward the first of them. If they couldn't avoid them, the fight would have to start now.

Just as the figure was close enough to see properly, he skidded to a stop sending loose stone scattering down the tunnel. He stared open-jawed at the figure.

Doc scurried to his side. 'Quills,' was all the mole could say.

It was one of the Met officers. A weasel that Remington had only known in passing, or at least, it was some of him. The eyes were open, lifeless, staring into the dead blackness of the tunnel. Its tongue hung limply from its jaw, and at the poor creature's neck a thread was jaggedly stitched through the fur. Beneath the neck, a different creature's remains comprised the weasel's body. It was the body of a crow.

Cat stared. Her ears flattened. 'That sick fucker.'

Oscar scampered down the tracks a little way, criss-crossing over the rails. He hurried back. 'They're all like this,' he said. 'All the way down the track. Crows and officers stitched together.'

An image of bats and crows merging in the sky like a vast dark ocean sprung into Remington's mind. He turned and looked at the old bat. His eyes looked worn and tired, his frail body ready to drop.

'Perhaps you should stay here,' Remington said, placing a paw on the old creature's good wing.

It looked back at Remington, and the image in his mind shifted to one of bats overwhelming the crows. The mixed ocean became a swarm of leathery wings. He felt a swathe of rage boil up inside him. He nodded to the bat and turned back toward the epicentre of the noise.

'We will end this, Badger,' the Rev said. The cold tone of his voice seemed to fill the tunnel.

After the first few bodies, Remington stopped looking at them and hurried forward, keeping his eyes on the gathering gloom ahead. With each familiar turn into the twisting underground, more lifeless chimaera revealed themselves. Cull and Vixx had been busy, their wild unnatural creations seeming to unveil endlessly through the shadows. Just as they hit the final stretch before the ghost station, the sound of voices ceased. Remington slowed. The other animals followed suit.

'They've all gone quiet,' Oscar said.

'Perhaps we're too late,' Nick added.

'No.' Remington tilted his ears toward the station up ahead. 'He hasn't blown the Heartbreak yet.'

'If that's even his plan,' Cat pointed out, her claws protracting and retracting.

'It is,' said the raven.

'Because it's what you'd do?' she asked.

'Like I said, I was chosen for a reason.' The Rev continued forward, and Remington picked up his pace to stay at the head of the group.

'Let's cross to the other side,' Remington said. 'When we turn the corner into the station, it'll put us against the far wall. We might be able to stay hidden for a time while we see what we're dealing with.'

Saying nothing, the animals duly followed Remington as he navigated the steel veins of the track and tried his best to cling to the darkest of the shadows offered by the tunnel. As they turned the corner, they could see the platform of the old ghost station. Figures stood stoically on its surface. In front of the platform, a huge mass of creatures was gathered. None of them noticed the interlopers as they perched at the back of the chamber, too intently was their gaze fixed upon the platform in front of them.

Remington slunk behind a mound of stone and peered into the space ahead, waiting for his eyes to adjust. The other animals found similar shelter and did the same. As the scene began to take shape, Remington was able to discern figures that he recognised. On the platform, a line of familiar Met officers stood. Among their number were the marten and otter who had chaperoned Nick and he back from Cat's to the station hut in the Burrow. Between each officer stood a crow, their dark silvering eyes staring at the tracks below them. At the platform's foot, closely gathered over the tracks, was a collection of animals, the volume and diversity of which Remington had never seen before. The silence was stifling. At the back of the platform, behind the crows and officers, the entire wall of the ghost station glittered with a black sticky substance. Heartbreak had been plastered across the brickwork from the platform surface upward. The dark mass seemed to seethe as it caught the shadow, and Remington saw that it spidered over the ceiling too.

In addition to the Heartbreak, and the miasma of odours from the mix of animals, another smell, tart and metallic, caught at the back of Remington's nose. He looked across to Doc, pointed to his nose and mouthed, *what is that?* Doc wheeled his nose around the tunnel and slipped silently to Remington.

'It's oil,' he whispered. 'It's what men use to make all their machines move.'

Before he could reply, a growing murmur moved like a wave through the crowd. Cull strode out across the platform and stood on a small mound of Heartbreak at its centre. A trail of dark liquid ran from the small mound to the back of the platform and the rest of the Heartbreak.

Cull looked over the whispering crowd and placed a single silver-tipped talon to his beak. The crowd fell silent in an instant. He puffed out his black chest, his plumage ruffling in the stilted chill of the station. He shrieked a single caw that bounced around the cold chamber like a thousand Culls were all shrieking at once. He raised the talon again and in one quick motion snapped two of his silver tips together. A spark shot from them into the chamber. The crowd duly responded with shocked chirps and whistles.

'Sisters, brothers, crawlers, brawlers, thieves, and all between,' he began. 'We are here because time could not tell us, but it is high time that we told time.' He cawed again, and the crowd responded with a hubbub of excitement and anticipation. 'Too long have we languished at the bottom of a food chain that we did not deign to agree to. Too long have we taken the scraps from the table of men, and animals that wish to be men. Too long have we accepted the lies of an establishment who refuse to accept our nature and would rather we chain ourselves to the plans and structures of civility. Are we not born free? Are we not born to a world that is ripe to sustain us? Are we not born with the knowledge that we are part of this great unplanned ecology?' He cawed again and clicked his talons, letting another spark loose into the chamber. The throng responded with various sounds of agreement and enthusiasm. 'It is time that we take our world back from those that would thread us bare. They have ruffled us and stuffed us, they have ringed our necks, and clipped our wings, drawn our blood to feed their iron veins. They have picked our world dry, decimated it with their towers and machines and then left them all to rot, their poisons still running wild and free into the soil, while our wild and free days have been torn from us. Our soil is sulphur-sick, our trees too few, too decayed to make house. Will you accept this? Will you go willingly, quiet, with skulls full of regret, while they use their shovels to bury you? Or will you sing as your ancestors did? Will you join me as I sing like the ancients and claw back at those who tell us we must cower and rot in the ruin of a world that is rightfully ours?'

The crowd grew louder as Cull raised his voice and gathered momentum. Someone called out *Take Back Eden*, another *From Below We Rise*.

'Silence,' Cull hissed and clipped another spark from his

glittering digits. The crowd acquiesced immediately. 'My dear, dear brothers and sisters. You are right. We must rise, and we must indeed take it all back, and we will. But first, I have some friends you will want to meet.' He cawed again, and from the darkness of the platform side, a string of bound animals were pushed. Remington recognised some as officers of the Met, and others whom he may have seen in passing, civilians. All were held and pushed forward by a crow or another officer. Vixx stepped up beside Cull. Remington heard Cat hiss under her breath.

'My friends,' Cull continued. 'It is not just the humans against whom we must toil. We must strike back against those of our own who have lied to us, kept us down with their philosophies and explanations that tell us we can all prosper if we follow their rules. They are the rules and lies scraped from the beliefs of man and they do not serve us. They serve themselves. Is that not right, sister?'

He turned to Vixx. She opened her beak and cawed like a crow. 'He speaks true,' she began. 'I have long worked in their system, to see the lies for myself. They sell us a lie of safety and civility, but who among you feels safe? It is a system of corruption designed merely to keep us under their paw, to keep us down, to keep us in line. They told us that their way was the antidote to chaos, that no longer would we need to scrape and hide, that we could live in harmonious accord.' She looked over the faces staring up at her. 'And what harmonious accord have you felt? What peace have you known?'

'We need to get these animals out of here,' Remington whispered to Doc.

'But how?' the mole answered. 'If Cull spots us, he'll set that pile off and then the whole place will come down. We'll be drowned if the tunnel collapse doesn't kill us first.'

'We need a distraction.' Remington thought hard about what they might do, who they might turn to but every move he thought of reached the same outcome: Cull igniting the

Heartbreak and sealing all of their fates.

'It is our time, time to make the world anew.' Vixx cawed again, and Cull stroked her head with his wing.

'Thank you, sister,' he said. 'Shortly we will hear the distant thunder of one of man's toys as it comes this way. Our brave, brave sister here,' he said, still touching Vixx's head. 'She has agreed to be our first prophet. On my word, we will leave these tunnels as one, and our brave sister will ignite our black gold. She, and these savages,' he turned and spat at some of the prisoners on the platform. 'They will be a worthy sacrifice to a new age. They and the humans will be destroyed as we bring the fury of nature down upon their heads. And we,' he said as he opened his wingspan in a welcoming gesture. 'We will ascend to the streets into a new world, a world that knows we will no longer be eternal prey and playthings. We will ascend into our own world, a world we can make in whatever image we please.'

'Detective,' the Rev whispered behind Remington. 'We must act.'

Remington bristled at the sound of the raven's voice, and the feel of his hot breath on his fur. He knew the Rev was right, but he had no idea what to do.

'Do you feel that?' Doc said.

Beneath Remington's paws, the badger could feel the distant, insistent rumble of a train.

'We're out of time,' Remington whispered.

# Chapter Forty-Six

'We have to act,' Cat said and began to move from behind cover.

Remington pulled her back. 'Wait.'

Before she could object, the Rev put his wing on her shoulder. 'The detective is right.' He whispered. 'Cull does not care enough about these creatures to wait until they are free from harm. If he thinks his plan is under threat, he will blow the tunnel immediately and end us all.'

'But that's insane,' Cat said. 'He'll take out all of his followers too.'

'Trust me, feline,' the Rev said. 'Don't underestimate him. He'd rather kill everyone than be stopped.'

'Then what do we do?' Cat's golden eyes were large and wild.

'We need a distraction, and we need to get everyone out of here.' Remington looked from one to another of the group, hoping in vain for someone to suggest a solution. His eyes fell on the bat. He tried with all the imaginative powers he could summon to communicate with the tired old creature, but his mind was crazy with too many thoughts: the lives of the creatures in the ghost station, the oblivious humans who were coming closer, of Lennox bleeding in her cage with Daisy. The only emotion his heart seemed capable of was despair. The bat closed its eyes. Remington saw bats, and crows again. He saw foxes, and rats, toads, and other animals. He sighed heavily. He was sure the poor old rodent wanted to help, but it just didn't seem to understand. The images grew more intense and numerous; a wave of emotion swept over Remington, but it was too much. He reached out to shake the bat, to make him stop. The bat shot out its small skeletal foot and gripped Remington's wrist. It squeezed hard, digging into the badger's flesh. Remington tried to shake himself free, but the bat clung fast.

A churning, thrumming sound began to ebb through the tunnel. It was faint at first but grew in increments. The creatures in front of the platform heard and felt it too, vibrations welling through the underground coming closer.

'It's the train,' breathed Cat. 'It's nearly here.'

Louder the sound grew, a roaring, of strange pitches swirling together in unison. It swelled as it approached them.

'That's not a train,' said Doc.

'What's happening?' Cull called from his platform.

Around the edges of the chamber and along the track, faint hints of green light started to leak out, dispelling the shadows and letting a sickly glow ebb around the edges of the ghost station. Remington turned back to the bat. Its eyes were tightly closed, and its grip still pressed into the flesh of his wrist. The sound grew louder, and panic started to thrum through the gathered crowd.

'It's creatures,' said Doc. 'It's him, isn't it?' He pointed to the bat, amazement across his squinting face.

Remington nodded and looked to the far end of the ghost station. From the shadows, shrieking, cackling, screeching voices were coming, all calling out at once. Suddenly the chamber exploded with a cloud of bats as they swarmed into the ghost station. Beneath them, rats in astonishing numbers, eyes half-blind and wild, swept forward as they pushed like a wave into the tunnel. The other animals cried out in panic and horror.

'Wait,' Cull called to them. 'Stand fast.' But it was too late. Panic spreads through animals much as it does through humans, and the instinct to flee overtook each of them. Flee they did. The wave of black bats swirled and pushed, as the rats became a carpet of squealing movement below them. Soon the ghost station was truly ghost, save for those stood fast on the platform, either bound or free.

'I know you're there,' Cull cawed out into the settling dust of the chamber. 'Rev,' he spat. 'I know it's you. Show yourself, you pathetic charlatan.'

The Rev drew himself up to his full height and stepped out into the hazy green of the ghost station. 'You've been hard at work in my absence,' he said.

'You think you've achieved anything? I'll still fulfil my plan.' He snapped his talons, sending another spark into the air. 'As per usual, your efforts amount to nothing. Clever tricks but ultimately, impotent.'

'Not my tricks, my lad,' the Rev said.

The bat opened its eyes and fell to the floor, breathing hard. Doc grabbed him. Remington stepped out to the side of the Rev.

'What the fuck is he doing here?' Cull hissed at Vixx.

'I needed him to see what we'd done,' Vixx said. 'You said I'd get my chance.'

'Not at the expense of this,' he spat. 'This was more important than your petty vengeance, you stupid child.'

'Sergeant,' Remington called out as he stepped toward them over the tracks. 'What vengeance? What did I do?'

'You see,' Cull said and slapped his wing across Vixx's beak. 'They don't even know the damage they do in name of this law of theirs. You jeopardised everything, and for what?'

'I needed to show him what we'd done before I gave myself up for the cause, brother,' Vixx protested. 'I needed him to see, and I needed him to see what we'd done to his partner.'

'I've seen what you did to Lennox,' Remington said. He and the Rev were taking slow strides toward the platform. 'I saw what you did to Daisy, but she's safe. Whatever I've done, whatever you've done, we can sort it out.'

'Daisy?' Vixx cawed in a harsh laugh. 'You really have no idea, do you?'

'I don't, so tell me.'

'Any closer and I will bury us all right now,' Cull said and clicked another spark into the green air which was beginning to slowly fade back to shadow.

The Rev and Remington stopped. They were directly between the iron rails of the track.

'Tell me,' Remington said again.

The vibrations through the ground were growing more intense as the civilian transport clattered its way closer to the ghost station.

Cull tilted his head, listening or feeling for the vibrations of the oncoming train. He shrugged. 'I think you've got enough time, if you must, sister.'

'You really don't remember what you and your partner, Lennox, did?' Vixx had tears filling her eyes.

'I really don't,' Remington said.

'You don't remember an arrest you made of a single bird who was just trying to hunt, just trying to feed his family?'

'If it was me and Lennox, it must have been many seasons ago. We were only plodding together at the beginning.'

'And how little the lives of those you ruin mean to you,' Vixx said almost in a whisper.

With the green light now almost entirely extinguished, the chamber was back to its former gloom. Remington sensed movement on either side, closer than the oncoming train. Nick and Cat were creeping around the far sides of the tracks toward the platform. Cull twitched his head, and the Rev cawed, drawing his attention back.

'Whatever we did, it was to protect,' Remington insisted softly. 'If we caused you pain then I am so sorry, Vixx, but whatever you went through, isn't worth this. Isn't worth joining him.'

'Him?' Vixx spat, her expression one of fury. 'He's the only one who protected me, who cared for me, when I was starving and lost.'

'For what purpose though, young one?' the Rev asked. 'Not for love or selfless care, but because he spotted an opportunity, a chance to make use of you.'

'That's not true,' Vixx said. 'I'm part of something now, something important. We're going to change the world.'

'And you won't be there to see it,' said the Rev. 'Why must it be you who sacrifices your life and not he?'

'I am going to change the world,' Vixx insisted.

'I'm sorry, Sergeant,' said Remington. 'But you won't. Nothing will change. It never does when folks try to change it this way. Come back to us, Vixx. Let's change the world together, the right way.'

'Right?' Vixx cawed again. 'The righteous detective, what do you know about what's right?'

'I know that this isn't it.' Remington pointed at Cull.

'It matters not,' said Cull as he raised a talon to the side of his head. 'I think our train's coming.' The crow stepped down from the small mound of Heartbreak. He raised two silvery points in front of him.

The ground began to shake more aggressively as the train neared. The vibrations shook Remington's body and skull.

'I guess there's no time like the present, eh?' Cull laughed and snapped his talons together, sending a spark onto the small mound of Heartbreak that Vixx was perched on top of. The eyes of the bound creatures still stuck upon the platform were wide and wild. Cull's followers, crows and officers alike held them firm, unmoved by Cull's actions. Remington and the Rev lurched forward across the track, but they were too far from the platform.

The broad frame of Nick suddenly appeared from the left of the platform. He barrelled toward the centre, knocking bound creatures and Cull's goons aside as he charged. He leapt into the air, shoving Vixx from the ignited mound of Heartbreak and landing stomach first upon it.

Remington let out a silent scream. The Rev, airborne, swept toward Cull, talons outstretched. A sickening crack filled the chamber and the walls shook, as the Heartbreak exploded under Nick's ample body. Beneath the badger, beneath the detonated Heartbreak, a crack opened and spread out along the width of the platform. Blood followed it, spilling from Nick and filling the freshly opened wound in the concrete.

The Rev and Cull were a cloud of black feathers and talons. Cull's blades sliced through the air and the Rev's wings, but the Rev battled on, his power and rage numbing him to Cull's attacks. Cat shot through the mess toward Vixx and pinned her down, shrieking and hissing as she pummelled the bewildered bird. The crows and officers under Cull's command looked on, stunned and frozen. Remington hauled himself onto the platform to Nick's side. He attempted to roll him over but as he lifted, parts of the badger began to spill out onto the platform. Remington instead gripped the lifeless face of his friend and placed his forehead to Nick's.

The fighting continued either side of Remington as he wept and held Nick's face. The train grew closer and louder. The weakened platform shook and crumbled, the crack spreading with the increasing vibrations. As it thundered nearer, stone began to drop from the chamber ceiling. One landed at Remington's side and shattered, a piece sparking off and slamming into his neck. Blood oozed from the wound and Remington shook himself back to his senses.

'This place is going to collapse,' Remington breathed. He turned to see Cat still raining blows down onto Vixx's face. The bird was already unconscious and bloody. To the right, the Rev and Cull were locked in combat in the air. It was impossible to work out who had the upper hand. He pulled himself up and gripped Cat by the scruff of her neck. He pulled her back still swinging wildly and hissing.

'Enough, Cat,' he said. 'That's enough.'

Cat struggled for a moment, but she gradually slowed and let her paws drop, her rage soon replaced with tears.

Just as Remington was about to consider interfering in the Rev and Cull's battle, Oscar jumped to the wall and sprung off, aiming a kick at Cull's head. He connected with a clean blow. While not sufficient to bring the crow down, it was the opening the Rev needed, and he soon had the narrower bird by the neck, his talon squeezing tightly.

'Do something,' Cull commanded his supposed followers. Two of them stepped forward, but the Rev shot them a look and they stopped, powerless in the infinite abyss of his stare.

'Yes,' the Rev said. 'Why don't you do something?'

They looked to each other and then began to untie the bound creatures that they had been guarding. The creatures panted and coughed as they drank in the dusty air.

'Guess you really did prove me right in the end,' Cull wheezed as he struggled in the raven's grasp. 'Some fucking leader you turned out to be.'

Another rock broke loose from the ceiling as the vibrations from the rapidly approaching train intensified.

'We need to get off this platform before that train comes or we might end up buried,' Remington said. He picked up Vixx and heaved her onto his shoulders.

'It's still going to flood?' Oscar said in a panic.

'No, no.' Remington shook his head and looked around the chamber. 'This warren's built thick enough, but it doesn't mean we can't end up flattened by the parts that do crumble.'

'Agreed,' said the Rev, and just as he was about to tighten his grip to choke Cull into unconsciousness, the platform shook with the force of the train. The crow slipped a talon free and dragged it down the Rev's face.

The raven cried out and loosened his grip just enough for Cull to kick himself free and jump back to the corner of the platform.

'Best laid plans, eh?' Cull grinned and raised his talons toward the spread of Heartbreak across the wall.

The train blasted round the corner and into the ghost station, a rush of speed, sound and colour. The platform seemed to cry out as the crack opened further, stones shook from the ceiling and a rain of dust dropped upon them all. There was a ferocious clatter, and the platform was strewn with rock. The train was gone in moments, careening on into the dark. The creatures coughed and shook their fur and feathers. In the corner where Cull had stood was a mound of heavy stone and brick. The Rev tried to pull at the pile, but the boulders were too heavy.

Vixx still hung unconscious from Remington's shoulders.

'Everyone okay?' Remington called out into the slowly clearing chamber.

The animals on the platform replied with affirmative noises.

'Still alive over here,' shouted Doc from the other side of the tracks.

'Hey,' Cat said touching the Rev's wing. 'Come on, he's gone.'

'I need to be sure,' said the Rev.

Another hunk of brick dropped onto the mound that had buried Cull.

'We need to get out of here,' Cat said.

The Rev nodded reluctantly and the animals, together, made their way back out of the tunnels, toward the underground entrance where the light of the early morning was just beginning to filter through the grey city sky.

# Chapter Forty-Seven

The following days were characterised by a general sense of transition and quiet across the animal elements of the city's inhabitants. Once free from Cull's influence, most of those who had been in reverie to him went into hiding, laying low in what shelter they could find in the metropolis and its bordering edgelands. Vixx was taken into custody and officers loyal and fallen were welcomed back to work. Reconstruction of the Met station commenced and soon the suspicious glares, and wide berths that the animals who'd found themselves on opposing sides gave each other, decreased and softened into the old reluctant camaraderie that accompanies most work.

The Rev began reasserting his influence over the city corvus, but, despite his admittedly formidable presence, something of the magic that had once ensured his dominance, had slipped away. It was difficult to maintain an aura of ultimate darkness when the light had so publicly been allowed to shine through. Still, after the terror that Cull had wrought, most towed the line and were glad to have the raven back. The Rev was anxious, though, as such clear cracks in the armour would always serve as an irresistible target to anyone with a thirst for power, and such thirsts were not lacking among the Murder or their allies.

Remington's instinct told him to retreat somewhere dark and deep, to hide away from the burning glare of the spotlights that now sought him out. There was talk of awards, and all manner of plaudits for the detective who narrowly diverted the disaster that could have irrevocably altered the animal world. All of these things Remington was able to avoid, but two rabbits precluded his ability to hide away for too long, or too deeply. Daisy stayed a while in the city, and made him talk about Nick, their old adventures and what had brought them together in the great neon labyrinth they had both called home. At first, he resisted, but little by little he found himself speaking with tear-filled eyes and a broad smile. Daisy told stories of her own and even convinced Remington to accept an offer of dinner with Doc and his wife, Barbara, who was Remington thought, far too joyful to be able to entertain Remington with a plus one.

Lennox's improvement could be measured largely against her growing agitation at being stuck convalescing. Remington spent most of his time at her side helping to stoke her anger. The more riled up she got, the more like her old self she seemed. He vowed to get revenge on her for her secrets, and she vowed to be back to bossing him around as soon as she was able. Doc was working hard on a prototype prosthetic limb, although Remington did offer her an old squeaky wheel he'd found in the general human detritus cast aside his dwelling.

By the end of the first week, invites were sent out across the city for a great animal assembly at Squall's Bar. Any who wished to attend would be assured safety. It was to be a moment of community within a fractured populace that was in dire need of togetherness. Fabulous refreshments and entertainments were promised as a chance to pay tribute to those who had lost their lives in the preceding seasons.

'We are absolutely not going,' Remington insisted, but the look he received from Daisy made it painfully clear that he was mistaken about that.

They heard the revelry from Squall's a street away.

'Quills,' muttered Remington. 'They'll be attracting humans with that racket.'

'Detective,' Daisy rolled her eyes at him. 'Tonight, you will leave your frown on the street.' She nuzzled his cheek. 'Are we clear?'

'Yes, Ma'am,' he sighed.

'Are we clear?' she repeated.

Remington plastered a smile across his face. 'Yes, Ma'am.'

'Better,' she said. 'Now, age before beauty.'

Remington trapped down the steps and was swallowed by the din from within. The place was heaving with creatures in various states of delirium. Added to their joyful chatter and shouting was a blaring wall of noise coming from deeper within the sanctuary.

Remington paused. 'It's not too late to turn around, you know,' he said over his shoulder.

'Keep moving, Mr.' Daisy nudged him forward. She needn't have bothered though, as they had just been spotted by a pair of golden eyes from behind the bar.

'Aha, look who decided to show up,' Cat called out with a grin. She was pouring drinks next to Squall.

'Make space for the detective, if you please,' Squall hollered, and a corridor appeared in the throng of creatures.

Remington accepted repeated pats on his back and hide as he pushed through, embarrassed.

'Welcome back, love,' Squall said and stroked the badger's face with her magpie wing.

'I see you're just letting any old reprobate work here now then?' Remington said and nodded to Cat.

'Hey now,' a familiar voice said. Red's mother, Anne, popped her head out from behind Cat.

'Present company excluded, of course,' Remington squeezed the paw that she offered over the bar.

'What are you doing down here?' he asked. Her face was fuller than when he had last seen her, and her red fur glowed like fire.

'Couldn't miss this now, could we?' she said. 'Besides, Cat said Squall could do with a hand.'

'Red's here?' Daisy asked.

Anne pointed to the far end of the bar. Daisy and Remington both looked over, craning their necks to see beyond the creatures filling the space. At the end of the room, on a makeshift stage made from stacked pallets, Fingle and Glen were hammering away on their homemade instruments. They had quite the dancefloor going already, and right at the centre jumping excitedly up and down was Red, a huge smile on her bright little face.

Remington felt his cheek twitch, and he swallowed back a tear. 'Right,' he said slapping the bar with an open paw. 'What does a guy have to do get some service in this place?'

Squall filled a line of tumblers with something fermented and potent. They each took one.

'To Nick,' Remington said.

'To Brigg,' Cat offered.

'To all of them,' Daisy added.

'Every last one of them,' Squall said, and they each knocked the liquid back, slamming the drained tumblers down.

A chill breeze swept into the bar, and a hush fell upon the crowd as they turned to the door. Even Fingle and Glen stopped abruptly. The Rev stood before them all, his mighty frame barely fitting into the room.

'How does he do that?' Remington asked. 'Everybody barely noticed when I walked in.'

'Like you'd want to be that noticeable,' Daisy said and squeezed his leg.

'As you were,' the Rev commanded, and sure enough, the volume rose again. Soon Fingle and Glen were back to banging out their unique soundtrack.

'Wasn't sure you'd come, Platypus,' the Rev said as he joined Remington at the bar.

'I didn't have much of a choice,' he replied and winked at Daisy.

They toasted again, and once or twice more. They toasted until numbers became vague and the music sounded good.

Remington, as a rule, did not dance, but at some point, he found himself on the dancefloor with Red, and then with Anne, and then with Cat, then Squall, then Daisy. And then there were more toasts, but as the night drew on, and the volume inside grew, Remington found himself hearing less and less. He looked around and imagined Nick there, and how much he would have loved it. Shortly after, he found the drinks no longer tasted as sweet on his tongue.

*Speech! Speech!* Remington heard the word being shouted before he realised it was being directed at him. He held up his paws, and looked over at the Rev.

'Speeches are more your area, I think,' Remington said.

The Rev gave something close to a smile to the badger and nodded in understanding. He raised a wing and silenced the bar.

'Ladies, Gentlemen, esteemed members of our community…' the raven began. What else he said Remington wouldn't remember, but he would never forget the looks on the rapt faces of those in the bar who clung to his every word. Remington stretched his limbs and squeezed Daisy's paw. She kissed him, stroked his face, and mouthed, *It's okay*. He pulled her close, and then, while the rest of the bar were gazing toward the enigmatic raven, Remington slipped quietly like smoke out of the bar and into the night city.

As he walked, half-knowing where he would end up, he thought for a moment he heard the moon whisper to him, a half-song just out of reach somewhere between reason and feeling. His claws ticked on the concrete as he slunk down the familiar pathways toward the great river. How often had he stared at the heaving sway of the water since he arrived in the city all those seasons ago? He had gazed into it, its reflected fractal lights, and wondered if there was a secret meaning in its wet coils, an elusive puzzle that might one day reveal its secrets. But all the river had unsealed for him was a nightmare he was unable to wake from.

He reached the bank and settled in the damp soil, watching

the corrugated moon ripple on its surface. He wanted to count each of his blessings and toss them into the water like skipping stones, but he sighed and lowered his snout, allowing a wave of sorrow to sweep over him. How long he stayed there, he couldn't be sure, reminiscing, and wondering, then reminiscing again.

A swell of images moved through his mind: the multitudes of life in all their scale and form, winding, slithering, growing, living, dying, hoping, needing, wanting. He could see it and feel it. Remington felt it all.

'What would you think about all this?' Remington whispered and closed his eyes.

'First sign of madness, isn't it?'

Remington jolted and looked round. Lennox was hopping awkwardly down the bank. A strange metallic shape glinted in the moonlight where her foot had once been.

'Doc's work?' Remington asked.

Lennox proudly displayed the prototype like a new shoe. 'Like it?' she said. 'I think it's rather fetching.'

'Suits you.'

Lennox settled beside Remington and looked out over the water. 'Daisy said you left the party early.'

'It's still going on?'

'I'm not sure that one's ever going to stop,' Lennox laughed. 'Thought I'd find you here.'

'I'm nothing if not predictable, I suppose.'

'Not the first word I'd choose, but still. You okay?' She leaned in and touched her shoulder to Remington's.

'I'm quite the hero, apparently.'

'You are, Rem.'

Remington huffed. 'How's the rebuild going?'

'We're getting there, I think. There's a lot to sort out. Still need to work out what to do with Vixx.'

Remington nodded. 'She said it was our fault.'

'Remember that old bird of prey who was terrorizing the